THE WATER BEAR

BY GROUCHO JONES

DEDICATION

Thanks to Lindsay Keelan, Nick Asher and Rob Graham.
Thanks to the Bibbulmun people of the Noongar country
of south-western Australia, custodians of the beautiful
land this code was written on.
For my son, Nick.

TABLE OF CONTENTS

This race
And this world
This feeling
And this girl
This revolver
This fire
This I'll hold it up higher, higher, high.

Brian Eno – This

PRELUDE

2068

In the shadow of Lhotse, on Fluxor, in the Orion Molecular Cloud, the primal forests burned. Years of unrelenting heat had turned the once-lush canopy to fuel, and fire now leapt from crown to crown, in diaphanous folds, consuming everything in its path.

In a high mountain glade, cut from stands of sassafras and Huon pine, where the mosses and ferns had been stripped away to reveal the black earth beneath, a young girl rocked on her heels, and began to feel real fear, as she watched the embers fly in the valley below, starting new fires faster than a Pursang girl could run.

The girl understood the bioscience of fire perfectly well. Each year the wildfires burned the vast eucalyptus forests that girdled the world, regenerating them, but these high montane rainforests, once lost, were gone forever, so the people made their defenses.

The forest occupied a mile-high tooth of rock, with its head in the clouds above, where the mountain continued its long march to heaven alone. It was called Atwusk'niges, in the old song, which meant mother sky. Into its tortuous couloirs, the Pursang had made firebreaks, and cut trails deep into its living heart. To preserve the forest, we must first destroy it, her father has said, as they slashed and burned.

Higher, in the limpid airlessness of low orbit, the vast triangularity of Fluxor Station loomed like a massif in space, busied by the complexly polyhedral warships of the Horu fleet. By day, from the forest below, these ships had a strange, translucent appearance, like floating cities of the dead. The girl watched an incoming tender deploy its geometry drive, and a sphere of space unfolded into an impossible shape, and another city-sized rock began its descent to the surface.

It disappeared in flames over the horizon.

She hoped the Horu wouldn't target *her* this day.

When it finally came, the fire flew up the rock with a sibilant roar, fueled by volatile organic aerosols already in the air. It was on the girl in a flash, then gone, leaving dozens of spot fires to fight.

She marveled at the *suddenness* of it, slow then *fast*.

There was no time to lose. Their primary defense was a dam cut into the highest ledge of the forest. This had been filled by truckloads of snow thrown down from the mountain above, a vertical drop of a thousand meters or more. More than one worker had made the same long fall, when scree gave way beneath their scrabbling wheels, and they tumbled into the abyss. Beneath the dam ran a network of microprocessor-controlled flow junctions, and below them a network of fireproof pipes, and below those, the people with their hoses and tools.

The main killer of humans in a forest fire is radiant heat. The girl was well-enough protected by a long-sleeved shirt, and goggles, and a wide-brimmed hat, when she remembered to wear it. She jammed it on, and struggled with her hose towards the flames.

There was a hoary debate, among old Pursang firefighters, about the best way to use water to fight a fire. At an early stage in a fire's development it was generally said that the water should be used to directly douse the flames. Later, when the fire came in sheets, some believed the water should be sprayed in the air at the trees to remove the greatest amount of heat from the system. She was in the air mist camp, because that was what her father said, and he, a Pursang holy warrior, who had journeyed between the stars, knew *everything*.

It was filthy work. Her hose had to be worked through dense and prickly underbrush, once lush but now bone-dry, that crackled and stung through her clothes.

But it must be done.

Ash and dust filled the sweltering air.

She was hungry, and tired.

She was finally at rest, perched on the lip of a narrow arête, exhausted, but exhilarated by the day's extraordinary events, and was unfolding her afternoon's food from a waxed paper bag, when the next great gout of fire flew up from below, at impossible speed, and engulfed her in flames.

The heat was unbearable, but she was alive.

Her whole world *slowed.*

She knew she had two options: go in or go down. Down was generally the right move in a high mountain fire, since it leads below the suffocating pall of smoke that rises from the flames, but that would mean a twenty-meter drop or more to the level below. The alternative was to burrow into the rock face, which was riddled with fissures and cracks. She had no time to think. She ran towards the first gap she could see. This meant a ten-meter sprint through swirling flames. As though in a dream, she saw other Pursang make similar binary choices around her.

Time slowed again, and she was *fast.*

She found a crack, but it proved to be an unlucky choice: A shallow notch, with the bone-dry undergrowth inside it already smoldering, ready to burn. She scrambled in and up, for just a few meters, until she reached a dead end.

And gamely turned to meet her fate.

When a strong hand reached down and pulled her to safety.

BOOK ONE

1 ∞ A LIGHTSHIP TO ALDEBARAN

2075

The human historian Ophelia Box rode a lightship to Aldebaran, and so became the first of her kind to travel between the stars.

The lightship was all she could hope for, and more, although the journey to reach it was less convincing. She had boarded a civilian space shuttle at Kennedy Center, amidst the rusting gantries of the old American space program, after only a few hours' tuition.

Everything seemed both horribly over- and under-engineered. Rust was everywhere. Rust and graffiti.

Like the set of a film that was never completed.

You're payload, they said, grinning. *Hold on tight and enjoy the ride.*

She held on very tight indeed.

The solid rocket boosters separating after two minutes had terrified her. First it felt like she'd stopped accelerating, and then a bright orange flash. She was sure the engines had failed, and they were at the start of a long fall to Earth, fifty kilometers below.

The calm demeanor of the pilots, and the mission controller's slow Texas drawl, brought her back to her senses.

She was no astronaut, that was for sure.

Inside the shuttle was *old*. It looked like a ham radio set had been strewn round inside an American school bus. The array of blue screens below the letterbox windscreen was quaintly futuristic, like experimental satnav installed in a 1950s American car.

Her watch had more processing power.

Under acceleration it boomed and shook like all its surfaces were made of tinfoil, while she was pushed down towards unconsciousness by an invisible hand. It was what it was: a mothballed machine, called back into service, like an old trooper drafted for a new kind of war.

But it got her there.

Box had watched the first lightships arrive, twenty years before, as a skinny wee bairn, sweating in the warm night air outside her home on the wrong side of Aberdeen, when they filled the sky with their majestic aurorae. *Aurora Galactinus* the BBC called it. The promise of hope for a future. There were rapturous street parties, with techno doing rambunctious battle with the Proclaimers.

That was before the troubles, when the 6, Wu and Po were still being fêted as the saviors of humanity.

Box still thought they were.

That they saved us was indisputable.

It was what came after that alienated so many.

Paris, the abiding city of resistance. *Libertê, êgalitê, humanitê.* She liked that slogan. It was the rallying call of the Parisian intellectuals. *Finis les sondes!* She liked that much less. Out with the probes! That was the cry of the mob. Probes was trash talk for the otherworldly Wu. *Finis les sondes! Tuons les démons!* She could still hear the ululating howl, like wild animals in the streets. Thankfully the mob had no idea who she was.

Une collaboratrice.

There were riots the day she closed her rooms at the University. Effigies were burned. People were dragged from their cars and beaten on suspicion. The 6 defused it in their usual way. The violent few found themselves repositioned, *sans* Molotov and AK-47, to their homes, or less convenient places. There would have been a few disgruntled would-be insurgents traveling home on the Channel tube that night, costumed for anarchy, jeered by the England football supporters.

The peaceable majority were left to protest unhindered.

It was a lesson in effortless power.

Now she was strapped in an American shuttle, approaching an alien starship, bound for Aldebaran.

You don't say that every day.

The lightship was small, compared with the original leviathans that had first delivered the climate factories now in geostationary orbit. It consisted of two unattached discs, about a hundred meters across, about a hundred meters apart. One of the discs was covered in circuitry. Lines of multicolored light crawled over its surface like random ideas, precursors of what was to come. Box mused that you could see it thinking. It was in that disc that the mathematical problem of the ship's spatial relocation was solved. The second disc was covered by vivid fractal designs. Up close, these resolved to ever-smaller fractals, Box guessed down to the molecular level. Maybe they went on forever. You could rely on the Wu to be thorough.

Her fellow shuttle passengers were mundane by comparison with the exquisite starship. In repose, they looked like any other humans. They looked like civil servants, which she guessed they probably were.

They had *luggage*. This detail fascinated her. Ordinary suitcases, strapped down with webbing in the shuttle's cargo bay. One of them had a multi-pocketed backpack, made by a popular American sportswear manufacturer. Its sunburnt and bushy-bearded owner saw her looking, and bared his white teeth.

Is he going to eat me?

She smiled neutrally back, and reminded herself to lose the comedy shtick, in case some of it came out her mouth. She didn't want to be exposed as a rube, away from home for the first time.

Or worse, a *racist*.

The real problem was that Sixes looked like any other human until they moved. Then they displayed an insectile suddenness that didn't quite scan as Earth-normal.

Finis les sondes.

This 6 didn't have that insectile quality. He smiled and introduced himself. He was called Ito, he said, and he was the amanuensis of her employer, the Regular of Threnody.

10

He used that word, *amanuensis*.

His secretary? she asked.

He was a compactly athletic man, in his mid-thirties by Earthly appearance. He looked like he could climb a mountain, or just had. Maybe his adventure backpack had been put to good use.

More like a journalist, he said in an easy mid-Atlantic drawl. *I observe and interpret events.*

Oh, she said. *Like a spy?*

He laughed. *Something like that,* he said.

She cursed herself as a fool. Of course, this healthy-looking outdoorsman was something to do with her mission. Probably someone important.

He smiled again and showed her how to propel her soft bags in the weightless conditions.

She'd first met Alois Buss, her new employer, a week before, in the Bistro Bofinger, an elegantly faded brasserie on the *Rue de la Bastille*.

"You have a French name," she began, idiotically.

"You couldn't possibly pronounce my real one," he replied with a Gallic shrug.

He was larger than life, almost two meters tall, and theatrically charming to go with it. In his crumpled brown suit, and unfashionable spectacles, and his courtly manner, he was quintessentially Parisian. All he needed was a pack of Gauloises to complete the ensemble.

He had that insectile tic going on.

He told her he was the Regular of Threnody, which he said was a minor functionary role, like being the ambassador of a small principality.

"Like the Mayor of Vaduz," he said, rolling his eyes disconcertingly, before fixing them on her. "But *remoter.*"

He said, "I'm aware of your work."

11

She experienced a *frisson* of concern. She was researching the Po, the secretive military third of the alien troika. Was this the thought police? Was she about to be warned off?

He said he could arrange access, if she wanted. He had a project, if she was interested, as a working historian, in his personal employ.

Offworld.

"It could be hazardous," he said.

She was never any good at factoring risk.

"I accept," she said.

Now she was falling headlong towards a translucent surface, like a ceiling made of soft crystal, on which a crowd of people were gathered to meet the new arrivals. An invisible hand reached out and turned her, so her feet touched first. She landed halfway gracefully. For the first time since leaving Earth's gravity, her vestibular system pointed down.

Some of her fellow travelers were greeted warmly. Ito was hugged fiercely by a teenage girl, who leaped with balletic grace from local gravity to catch him in mid-air as he debarked.

So, they have family.

Good.

What was she expecting? Endless lines of birthing pods, stretching towards an apocalyptic horizon? She cursed herself for having read too much sci-fi.

O brave new world, that has such people in it.

Her bags landed softly beside her.

"Welcome to Pnyx."

This from an androgynous person, a Wu.

Ze was like all hir kind: eldritch and fair, with a slightly oversized head, like an elf, or a beautiful child.

"Please follow," ze said. "I'm Charh. Ship will assist you."

Ze beckoned Box towards a vertiginous space. She didn't consciously choose to follow, being frightened of heights, but a pulse in her back gave her no choice. Inside the disc was like inside a geode. Crystals crossed the open space like spearheads thrust through the side of the ship. The outer skin, which she knew to be covered with fractal designs, was transparent. Overhead, the battered American shuttle spun in graceful lockstep with the disc. It looked rather magnificent. Off to one side spun a more modern design: a Chinese x-wing lifter. A hundred meters below her feet, across an intervening gap, she could see the pulsing circuitry of the drive disk, rehearsing its *Aurora Galactinus*. Below that, the Earth shone like a jewel in space, and beyond it the stars, her destination.

Sixes floated in the open space, and gathered on convenient surfaces. This ship was crowded. And it was *busy*.

No one paid her any attention.

She followed Charh, without trying to.

This was like cycling on trainer wheels.

Like flying.

This *was* flying.

Her stateroom was the size of her entire *Rue Pigalle* apartment, embedded within a crystal encrustation in the disc's outer rim, with a startling view of the Earth. Box spent her first hour admiring it, still wired with adrenaline, unable to let go. There was gravity, to her relief, and a glow that seemed to emanate from nowhere. After a long, restive comedown, during which she tried to make sense of the day's events, there was a chime, and she reached out with her mind to open the door.

The compulsory alien brainware had its uses.

Standing there was the teenager who'd hugged Ito.

"May I come in?" she asked.

Box beckoned her in.

"I'm Kitou," she said.

"Ophelia. But please call me Box."

"I'm instructed to call you Dr Box."

"That'll work."

"You have fiery red hair," said the girl, after a few seconds of industrial-grade staring, for more seconds, and more industrially, than would have been proper for strangers on Earth.

"That's a rare mutation," she said brightly. "I'm told you're a fierce warrior."

"I'm a kickboxer," admitted Box.

"The Scottish champion."

"A Scottish atomweight champion. I'm only wee."

The girl beamed in reply. She was exceptionally attractive, with white-blonde dreadlocks that hinted at bioengineering. Box had never seen dreads so *healthy.*

"How old are you?" asked Box.

"Sixteen."

"Earth years?"

"It's all the same," said the girl. "In the adaptive language."

"Can you explain that, please?"

"Our wetware mediates our speech. I hear what you mean."

"Wetware being this alien neurocomputer in my head?"

The girl nodded.

"Like some kind of universal translator?"

"More than that," said the girl. "It works at the fundamental level of language. Your Broca area interacts with mine."

"Broca area. That's impressive."

The girl laughed. "I come from an advanced alien civilization."

Box had to laugh too.

The girl stood up.

"We're about the same size, Dr Box. *Atomweights*. Can we fight now?"

A few minutes later, they were warming up in a gymnasium, that the ship had conjured up on Kitou's request, to Box's visualized design. It was like her first gym in Glasgow. There were canvas mats, a battered Muay Thai bag, and a full-sized ring. It even smelt right.

Box showed Kitou how to use the kickboxing head gear, mouth guard and gloves. The girl was a quick study, and startlingly athletic. Box had fought Olympians who were slower. Soon they were sparring. Box soon struggled to keep up.

"You're fitter than me," she said, breathing hard. "Let's slow down and I'll teach you to kick."

The girl nodded. "There's no kicking in my art. I'm eager to learn it."

Kitou proved equally adept at that, and after a few tries delivered a roundhouse kick that shivered the bag in its stirrups, and would have knocked an Earthly opponent flat had it connected.

"Okay," said Box. "You're definitely an alien."

The girl laughed.

"Now show me yours," said Box.

The boxing equipment disappeared and was replaced by a soft, crystalline floor.

"My fighting art is called Po," said the girl. "Just as my people are called Po. The first form of our art is called the Geometry Game."

Kitou stood in front of her, relaxed.

"The point of this game is to move to an irresistible position. It is based on Fibonacci spirals. The Earth art it resembles most is Aikido."

The girl took a step to the side and spun, and before Box could begin to process what had happened, Kitou was behind her, breathing lightly on her neck.

"From here I could kill you, and there's nothing you can do about it."

Box grimaced.

How can we war against that?

"Teach me that trick."

Half an hour later, with the help of her wetware drawing rosy patterns in the floor, Box was dancing Fibonacci spirals. She learned that Po consisted of interconnected moves, like a board game, but liquid and dynamic. Moves were related to moves, like pieces to squares. Fibonacci spirals were countered by opposing Fibonacci spirals, always with the objective of outthinking your opponent.

"This is excellent," she said.

"Your long-term training goal," said Kitou, "is to be able to do this instinctively, without wetware."

"You remember all this?" she asked.

"Repetition trains the animal brain. Over time, it becomes programmed."

"You mean you practice a lot?"

Kitou nodded. "Five hours a day, since I was nine."

"You guys must be tasty in bar fights."

"It has been known."

16

The next three days were spent by the lightship transitioning to its departure location, with the sumptuous disc of Earth slowly receding, and the silvery orb of Luna looming shockingly close, then falling behind. Box spent her time exploring the ship. Nothing seemed to be off limits. Her solicitous guide, who seemed to be the ship's only crew, was only a thought process away.

When Box asked why they were moving so far before leaving, Charh said that it was to be considerate neighbors. "The light of my drive is as bright as a star," ze said. "Better shone from a few light seconds away, with your moon in between."

The internal fit and finish of the ship was superb, like a boutique hotel, and it was produced on demand. After Kitou showed her how, Box magicked up a pair of red Dali sofa lips, and fresh flowers, and a bookcase piled with books, for her stateroom. These began as grids of light, that interacted complexly, until the finished objects appeared, like in a wireframe simulation.

She picked up a Gutenberg Bible. It was perfect. This was better than a post-scarcity society, she mused. Here you could have *anything*.

How can we war against that?

There was something puzzlingly non-Euclidian about the interior geometry of the ship. The geode was simple enough, although it sometimes seemed larger than it should, but the edges of the disc were askew, with corridors that curved farther than they should. Box estimated that the space enclosed by her corridor could hold only two of her rooms, and yet there were five stateroom doors.

When asked about this, Charh shrugged.

"Pnyx's topology is mysterious," ze said.

Charh showed her the drive disk. They reached it through an irising door in the base of the habitat disc. Once inside the door, there was no space between the discs, although a hundred meters of separation was clearly visible through the skin on each side. The drive consisted of thousands of primary-colored geometric solids, floating in the cylindrical space, with lines of energy arcing between them.

"This system works by recalculating the positional attribute of all of the fundamental particles within its domain," explained Charh. "Location in physical space is a variable, just one of many possible solutions of the quantum wavefunction. Pnyx remembers where we wish to be, and then we are there."

She felt humbled – awestruck - by the power of a machine that could think its way between the stars. It crackled and hummed like God's server farm. She imagined the quantum foam, flowing like blood in its veins.

There are more things in heaven and earth, Horatio,

Than are dreamt of in your philosophy.

"Pnyx is the most advanced technology," said Charh, discerning her mood. "Given to us by a civilization called the Xap, who it is said can move through n-dimensional spacetime using only their natural minds."

Box had no reason to doubt it. Any of it. She felt her ingrained cynicism draining away. Why would a society that can do such things, lie to us?

We're primitives, worshiping effigies of cargo planes.

We don't matter at all.

Charh showed Box hir personal space, which consisted of a contoured bed, and a model of the ship, like a cherished family heirloom, and soft crystal walls covered with celestial maps, with long arcs showing their path through the heavens.

Charh sat on the bed, and smiled, and seemed perfectly happy with hir life.

As well you might be, thought Box.

She tried not to cry.

On the third day, Box was invited to join Alois Buss, her employer and sponsor, and his travelling companions, to observe lightfall, and celebrate their departure from Earth space. With Buss was Ito, now clean-shaven, but still sunburnt, and a skittish Kitou, who seemed unsure of who she was showing off to who.

Buss had brought champagne.

"Dr Ophelia Box, meet Ito Nadolo," said Buss with a flourish, popping a cork. "And Kitou Gorgonza. My court magician, and his lovely assistant."

"We've met," said Box.

"You really caught the sun," she said to Ito.

He stared back at her, then laughed.

"Utah," he said cryptically.

The shipboard sixes seemed to have all lost their insectile expressions. Perhaps she was getting used to it. Perhaps it was an affectation, for Earthly consumption. The Po, by contrast, based on a sample of two, had an otherworldly quality, as though they were only occasionally tuned in to their local surroundings.

She found it rather delightful.

Buss was dressed in his best Parisian costume, an oyster-grey suit with a lemon *boutonniere*.

"Still playing the Frenchman, Alois?" she said with a smile. Buss bowed, clicking his elegant heels. Ito was wearing a military-style uniform in plain black, elegantly cut. Pinned to his lapels were two carbon starbursts. Kitou was barefoot, in emerald-green silk pajamas. The crowd gathered around them was dressed in a dazzling array of styles. Box watched a woman in a gown of floating hoops float past.

An unseen band played Earthly bossa nova.

Box felt like a frump in her shapeless coveralls.

Kitou must have seen her slight embarrassment, and took her aside, and then to her cabin, which was a fraction the size of Box's stateroom, where she produced a small velvet package, from which sprang a baroque judo suit, calendared with curlicues of caramel and cream.

"It's beautiful," said Box.

"It's yours," said Kitou. "Please take it."

"I couldn't."

"Please. I'll feel pleasure each time I see you in it."

The luxurious suit was made from fibrous, opalescent cloth, softly yielding to the touch, as light as spider silk.

"Where did you get it?"

"On Earth."

"You've been to Earth?"

"I went with Ito to London, to see a strange man."

"Plenty of those in London," said Box with a wry smile.

"This one seemed to know you."

"Me?"

"He said, take care of the Scottish woman."

"Really? What was his name?"

"I can't say."

"Secrets?"

Kitou nodded.

"He said something else. A message for you. I parsed it as friendly. He said to tell you you're a feisty wee shite. I hope you aren't offended."

Box just laughed.

"Do you know who he is?"

"I might."

From a hundred meters, the Pnyx's *Aurora Galactinus* was nothing like the delicate lightshow visible from Earth. It began with swells and pools and gobbets of color, welling up through the drive disc's circuitry, like a stormy sea of artist's paint. The colors became a vortex, which flowed around the habitat disc, until they were enclosed in a whirlpool of light. Inside the disc, floating balls of static energy appeared, and people's hair stood on end. Kitou, girlishly delighted, played with the balls on her fingertips. Box, a flute of French champagne in her hand, looked on in astonishment.

The ship was quiet as a church. This was clearly a cherished event, even for jaded space travelers. Then the colors *exploded*, and drifted away, leaving only the inky blackness of space, and new stars.

And a deep orange sun.

Aldebaran.

Between the ship and the star were a red planet, and a lustrous white cube. Box knew from her assigned reading that Aldebaran was 44 times the size of the Sun, and 425 times as luminous, so the skin of the Pnyx was not nearly as transparent as it seemed. She knew that the red planet was the gas giant Aldebaran B, and that she was the first of her people to directly observe it.

21

She shivered, with the enormity of the idea.

How can I even think about this?

She christened it Ophelia.

"Behold the Aldebaran Orbiter," said Alois Buss with his signature flourish, encompassing the translucent cube, like a magician conjuring a rabbit. "The main travel hub in this busy region of space."

As if to punctuate his words, another *Aurora Galactinus* flowered in the space between the Pnyx and the red planet, and where was empty space, now floated a second lightship.

The party was soon back in full swing. Kitou danced an energetic Salsa with a brown-skinned boy of her own age, leading all the way, and doing so in great style, their deft feet skipping over the inky backdrop of space. Box was starting to discern more types of human here. Her initial assumption that they were all Sixes might be misguided.

She asked the ship about this.

[The "thousand worlds" is a metaphor,] said the Pnyx in her wetware. [There are about five thousand worlds in this local civilization, give or take a few hundred in various states of transition.

[Of those, about five hundred are of the cultural alignment called the 6, and those include many ethnicities, some you might not immediately recognize as human.]

[How many here are Sixes?] she asked.

[Most of them are, because Earth is a 6 world.]

[We'll see about that.]

Ito asked her to dance, and he proved to be as skillful as Kitou. Dancing across the emptiness of space, with the red planet beneath her, at first proved too much for Box, and she was forced to ask the ship to show her a personal dancefloor instead. Then she lost herself in the smoky rhythms of the music, and asked for the heavens to be restored. Later, during a slower Puerto Rican number, with the cosmos spread out beneath her feet, she asked Ito, "What are you going to call us?"

"Call who?"

"Earth's people."

"Sixes."

"You know that won't fly."

He nodded.

"In your space fiction, you're called Earthlings."

Box made a face.

"Can I be a Po?"

He laughed.

"You mean, you honestly want to be a Po?"

"Yes. It's a serious question. Are you a closed society or an open one?"

"We are inclusive. Our custom is that anyone who can breed with us can be a Po by marriage."

"Can I breed with you?"

"Is that a request, or a technical enquiry?"

Box snorted.

"It's a technical question."

"No, we're incompatible."

"What, we're different species?"

"No one uses that meaning of speciation."

"I can't be a Po?"

"Sadly not.

"You could be a Lo," he said, after they'd finished dancing, and were sharing an Aldebaran-themed alcoholic drink, with gobbets of sweet orange, and foaming white cubes, floating in a bitter smoky liquid.

"Who are they?"

"Our symbiont culture."

"What do they do?"

"They fly our ships, and fight beside us in battle. They're our brothers and sisters."

"Are they like you?"

Ito laughed. "They're... different."

After a turn spent dancing with Kitou's young partner, who proved to be a divine dancer, and a turn with Kitou, who allowed Box to lead, she reclaimed Ito.

"Ito," she said. "One last thing."

"Yes?"

"Please, don't treat me like a fool."

He said, "I won't."

The Orbiter grew, until a side of it filled her horizons, a gleaming white plain, tens of kilometers across. Their companion lightship grew with it, until it occupied most of the space between them and the Orbiter. It was an open-ended cylindrical design, massively larger than the Pnyx.

"A military design," said Buss, joining Box near the Pnyx's exit vestibule.

"The Wu have warships?"

"Everyone has warships," said Buss with a shrug. He pointed out the circuitry exposed in the otherwise hollow cylinder, crawling with strange energies.

"Their drive is their weapon," he said.

She shuddered.

In the final moments before debarking, as the Pnyx slid into an irising void in the Orbiter's side, and her fellow travelers milled around the exit, she sought out Charh.

"Dr Box," said the Wu.

"Charh, thank you and ship. This has been a beautiful experience."

"Thank you, Ophelia. It was a great honor, carrying the first of your people through space."

"Charh?"

"Yes?"

"Is ship your lover?"

Charh looked at her and smiled.

"Of course, isn't he the most beautiful lover?"

"He's the most beautiful thing I've seen."

Charh inclined hir head.

"Dr Box?"

"Yes, Charh?"

"We Wu, we see things."

"Yes?"

"Be careful."

Ah.

"Remember us here. When the time comes, we'll remember you."

She looked back into the cathedral space, now empty of travelers, with its crystal buttresses, and the Orbiter's docking machinery visible through its transparent skin.

"I will," she said.

And then she crossed over.

2 ∞ THE WATER BEAR

2075

[Welcome to Aldebaran,] chimed a voice in her head.

[Who are you?] she asked.

[The City of Praxis.]

She felt *heavy*.

She opened her eyes.

"No floating here," complained Alois Buss, pulling his wheeled luggage towards her. Then he looked up, and Box followed his gaze. Suspended over them was an upended city, a ceiling of spires, a thousand Manhattans. Towers hung like stalactites, ending a kilometer above their heads. The air between Box and the towers was swarming with traffic, from small flying taxis like trishaws, to heavy industrial lifters.

She could hardly take it in. It was like looking into a kaleidoscope.

It appeared to be dawn. The lights in the nearest towers started to flicker and fade, and the sky, or what passed for a sky, at the far periphery of the bewildering space, became powdery blue.

She could hear city sounds.

Engines, horns, snatches of music.

She could see clouds, drifting between the towers.

Rain started to fall, heavy drops, splashing in the oily grime beneath her feet. It occurred to her that she was in an airport. She saw hoses and pipes connected by scuttling machines to waiting orifices, presumably leading down to the Pnyx.

A spaceport, not an airport.

A distinctly cool breeze lifted her hair.

Time to get off the tarmac.

She followed Alois to what resembled an arrivals lounge, with impersonal rubber seating, and snaking baggage conveyors, where they waited for the others to arrive.

"This is all very utilitarian," she said.

"Transit is industry," said Buss with a shrug.

The lounge enclosed a bank of cylindrical elevators, that Box was dreading to use, in case they whisked her into the abyss above. She cursed her fear of heights. Some space traveler she was. The destination list for each car was displayed in her head, a spatter of visual noise. Travelers bustled around, collecting their bags and leaving.

She was jetlagged.

Spacelagged.

She had so much to learn.

Ito and Kitou arrived in a car that whispered up from below. They were wearing plain coveralls, cinched at the waist with utility belts, complete with realistic tools. Kitou had grease smeared on her cheeks, although on her it looked like warpaint. The car was opaque, for which Box was profoundly grateful. It had scuffed metal grates, and a general air of being used to haul cargo. Travelers milling in the lounge ignored it. She wondered if they even saw it. The door hissed shut, and her feet briefly left the metal floor.

"What just happened?" she asked.

Ito conjured up a holographic display. It showed a web of corridors beneath the Orbiter's skin, where objects flowed like blood through arteries and veins. Sleek cars harried fast trains, amid a swarm of darting elevator cars. Slower-moving industrial vehicles parted the traffic like rocks in a stream.

It was chaos, yet nothing collided.

"This transportation system is called the capillary network," Ito explained. "This appliance is essentially a space vehicle."

Their car was shown as a pulsing white lozenge, accelerating along a Bézier-curved tube, into the chaos beneath. All Box felt was an occasional tremor. They joined the traffic flow, and jinked and dipped towards an empty part of the map.

"How are we moving?" she whispered.

"Gravity drive," said Ito.

The car chimed and slowed.

"Our stop," he said.

The city's voice in her head said, [Restricted].

The door slid open, to reveal a different type of industrial mayhem. Machines hurtled past with a dissonant roar, like fistfuls of knives, accelerating and decelerating, narrowly missing each other. There were hisses and outpourings of gas, as tubes were connected and disconnected by robotic arms.

It was like the spaceport, speeded up a hundred times.

"The city's autonomic defense systems," said Ito.

They were the only humans here.

"Stay close," he said.

Box fell in line, with Ito first and Kitou in the rear, and Buss and her still hauling their civilian cases. The muffled thump of rolling wheels echoed off hard carbon surfaces.

Ito carried his backpack. Kitou had nothing.

"Where are your things?" Box asked her.

"I have none," she said.

"Where's your green silk number?"

"I'm wearing it," she said.

They reached an irising door, at the end of a train-sized conduit, where a young man stood waiting. He had starbursts on his lapels, like she'd seen Ito wear. He seemed to be watching something on his interior cinema. As they approached, he glanced in Box's direction. She felt a thrill pass through her. A head-up display appeared in her virtual space. It showed information about her surroundings. Information about the Orbiter: where it was in space, where they were inside it. Information about her bodily functions, and those of her companions.

Too much information. She felt faint.

"Water Bear," said the young man, nodding to Ito.

"With Dr Ophelia Box," he added formally.

The door flowed open.

Before them was a spacecraft.

Box guessed it was a spacecraft. It could be a submarine. It was about fifty meters long, painted a black so liquid that it seemed to drain light from its surroundings. There was a segmented leg at each corner, knees held high like a spider.

It bristled with antennae, and obscure protrusions.

It looked purposeful, and ugly.

Ito said, "My ship, the Water Bear."

Waiting for them inside the ship were two extraordinary humans. The man's blue-black skin was minutely tattooed, like Maori *ta moko.* His hair was ornately beaded. The woman was equally striking. Straight as a blade, her head clean-shaved, with powdery nebulae in place of the elaborate ink, she looked like a weapon.

As on the Pnyx, there were fierce hugs all around, and tears from the women. If crew unity was a thing, Box observed, this group had a good thing going.

Ito turned around.

"Dr Ophelia Box, please meet Brin and Pax. Pax Lo, the hairy one here, is the master of my ship. Brin Lot, like Kitou and I, is a soldier.

"Alois, you all know.

"Team, Dr Box is our mission specialist."

They wasted no time departing.

[Dr Box,] said a contralto voice in her head.

[Let me guess, the Water Bear?]

[That is correct. Please allow me to assist you.]

[Go for it, sister.]

[This ship has what you might call a warp drive. We bend space to form a local bubble of spacetime. We move that bubble in space by projecting a gravity wave.]

[Like surfing?]

[Very good.]

[I've seen the movie.]

31

[We have no local gravity here. It will be free fall all the way.]

Box groaned.

[However, I can help you with your feelings of nausea. In fact, I can cure you of vertigo completely.]

[Seriously?]

[It will be helpful in your travels.]

[Do it.]

[Do you prefer neutrality, or pleasure?]

[Pleasure, always.]

Another thrill passed through her.

[You now have the upgrade.]

[Thank you. You don't know how much that means to me.]

[I do.]

[Another thing.]

[Yes?]

[How do I turn off this damned head-up display? I really don't need to know when Alois Buss takes a piss.]

The console effect disappeared from her interior vision.

[Can you teach me how to control that?]

She felt another thrill.

[You now have the upgrade.]

[Ship, we're going to get along just fine.]

[We are. Now please strap in and enjoy the ride.]

The control room of the Water Bear was like a carbon womb, with three rows of acceleration chairs, arrayed in a lattice, on heavy industrial gimbals. Only millimeters separated the curved braces of the lattice from the spherical walls. It looked like it was designed for violent motion. Box was put in the middle row, in the center. Brin, Buss and Kitou were in the back row of three. Then the walls disappeared, and she was shown an uninterrupted view of the surrounding hangar deck, where hundreds of tubes and lines were retracting.

Kitou strapped her tight, all business now.

The city's voice said [vacuum].

And then [thank you for visiting].

Box had never liked rollercoasters. It wasn't just the sickening feeling of weightlessness, which welled up from the pit of her stomach and filled her with a bone-jarring emptiness. It was a rat's nest of primal horrors.

The fear of heights.

The fear of being cast into the abyss.

All that now changed. When the ship fell out of the Orbiter, into the gravity well of the gas-giant planet, and the lattice of seats swiveled smoothly to anticipate a change of direction, she whooped with exhilaration.

"Engaging gravity drive," said the ship, delivering its lines like a Hollywood starlet playing Chuck Yeager. There were a few moments of intense acceleration, and they were falling in a new direction.

Box laughed out loud.

So, this is what I've been missing out on.

Except that she was falling through the ecliptic of Aldebaran, with some kind of black-ops space soldiers, not riding on a Blackpool rollercoaster with children.

"Engaging warp drive," said the ship.

She laughed again.

She felt the others grinning at her.

"Alright," she said. "That was embarrassing."

"Not so," rumbled Pax. "We whoop too."

"Frost," said the ship.

"That means we can all relax," said Kitou, grinning and unbuckling.

"Downtime," said Brin.

And so it proved to be, for the next nine days, while they bent space to Threnody.

There was something about the soft hum of the ship at warp speed that Box found intensely pleasing. That, and the rhythms of shipboard life, and the easy companionship of the crew, who ate, slept, trained, and talked, all in about equal measure. For Box, the child of militant separatists, who had learned to fear the staunch English squaddies stationed throughout the Northern Highlands, these thoughtful and articulate soldiers proved to be excellent company.

As was the ship herself. In the quiet hours before dawn, when Box was the only one still awake, they spoke at length.

"Can't you sleep, Dr Box?"

"I like not to sleep, Water Bear. The wee hours are my most productive."

"You will need to sleep if you wish to repair."

"I know," she admitted.

"I can help you with that."

She considered it.

"Nah, I think I'll keep this one."

"As you wish."

"Ship, may I ask you some questions?"

"Yes."

"Tell me about your propulsion systems."

"I use a gravity drive to move through local space."

"How does that work?"

"Do you want the physics?"

"I do, but I also want to hear you explain it."

She felt a mild tingle.

"You now have the physics."

"As easy as that? I can take it home and patent it?"

"I'm not going to stop you."

"Heh."

"It works by projecting a gravity well. We fall towards that point, as does everything around us."

"Not so good in crowded shipping lanes?"

"It's a high-performance system, designed for combat use. Simple and effective. The hardware is the size of your hand."

"How high-performance?"

"1035 Earth gravities maximum acceleration."

"Bloody hell. At which point we're all jam?"

"You feel no external forces, Dr Box. As long as we're travelling in a straight line, you're simply falling."

"What was that strong acceleration after we left the Orbiter?"

"That was me converting angular momentum, so we were pointing in the right direction. I must carefully regulate that to keep my humans alive."

"Else, jam?"

"More like a jelly."

Box heard someone rising, then skipping noises in a gym, then someone punching a speedbag.

"I also produce gravity waves, for my warp drive."

"How does that work?"

Ship thought for a moment.

"I can't tell you."

"Why not?"

"Your people will be given access to that level of technology when it's safe to do so."

"When will that be?"

"When you stop killing each other."

"Ah."

Box asked about weapons.

"I carry none."

"Not even a wee phaser?"

"No."

"Why ever not?"

"My purpose is to protect my crew, not to destroy things. I would be a dangerous machine if I could kill from a distance. There's no reason for society to take that risk."

"They don't trust you?"

"It's not about trust. It's about the separation of powers. A sentient killing machine must be psychotic. We try not to build too many of them."

"How can you defend people without using weapons?"

"I have more adaptable resources."

"Such as?"

"I can think."

"Ship, I like you already."

The ship's gym was of the conventional kind, with fixed appliances, and better training machines than Box was used to. One of the machines was a hand-to-hand fighter. Box watched as Kitou taught it kickboxing moves. It moved much faster than a human.

Kitou said a Po master of the third form could defeat it. Box couldn't see how. It struck with a whirring flicker of pads.

The gym had gravity.

"Ship will make a gravity source when requested," Kitou explained. "Our training requires it. But the Water Bear is a combat design. No feet-down spaces here."

They were joined by Brin, who was a few years older than Kitou, and polite, but aloof. Box put it down to a soldier's natural reticence. Box watched them play the Geometry Game. Kitou was faster than Brin, but Brin was better. A more skillful, superior athlete. When Kitou seemed about to make a winning move, Brin shouldered her aside.

She moved like a soldier.

Box demonstrated the basics of kickboxing with Kitou, then Brin proceeded to beat Kitou at kickboxing. Box saw there was a method in her bullying. Brin was an excellent teacher. Box watched how she played to Kitou's weaknesses, patiently teasing them out, working on them, diligently repeating, improving, then doing it again. They trained for hours at a level of intensity that Box couldn't hope to match.

Instead she fought against the machine.

All she got was cuts and bruises for her troubles.

"That's how they all are at first," said Kitou.

They were alone in the Water Bear's communal space, a comfortable suede-lined cocoon. Box was teaching Kitou the basics of Kundalini yoga, adapted for zero gravity. The others were sleeping. The ship was quiet except for their voices, and the distant whisper of life systems.

"The Lo are intense," Kitou explained. "You're new in her space. Just give it some time.

"Also," she said, "Brin only loves women."

"Well," said Box. "There's nothing wrong with that."

"And you're a woman."

"Ah."

"It's a Lo thing."

"Pax?"

"He only loves men."

"Now that's interesting. How do Lo mate?"

"Carefully.

"What about you, Dr Box? What is your sexual orientation?"

"Strictly milk 'n two sugars, honey."

"What does that mean? A common beverage?"

"Heterosexual. And you?"

"I only love boys."

"Safe choice."

As well as her historian's record of the journey, Box kept a personal diary: a bulging paper volume from Casenove's, a stationer on the *Rue Pigalle*, just three boulangeries from her Paris apartment.

Pax gay, she wrote. *What does a girl have to do to get laid around here?*

Alois is charming, she wrote. *But a complete fraud. In a sense, that's reassuring. He hasn't explained my role yet. I don't suspect him of duplicity, only a love of drama. I have no great problem with it. The process by which a story unfolds can be as revealing as the story itself.*

I worry for Kitou. Such a sweet, talented girl. What happens when she must kill? How is this different to any child soldier? What's her story?

Po, a fascinating martial art. Do they really dance spirals in combat?

Do I trust these people? It seems I already do. I'm behaving like an embedded reporter.

Where's my vaunted objectivity?

We shall see.

"I want to learn Po," she announced the following morning.

"You can't," said Brin.

"Why not?"

"Pax already has two students."

"What about Ito?"

"That isn't the role of a First."

"What about you?"

"I'm not a Po master."

"You teach Kitou."

"I train Kitou. Pax is her teacher."

"Train me."

"We could *show* her," said Kitou.

"And what would Pax say about that?"

"Pax will say he trusts your judgement."

The two younger women stared at each other.

"Show her," said Kitou, standing and crossing her arms.

"Don't play dominance games with me, child," said Brin.

"I'm not your child," said Kitou.

Brin arched her eyebrows, then relented. Box understood that Brin had intended this outcome, with Kitou her tacit accomplice.

Like two willful children.

"Dr Box, observe," said Brin. "One move. It's called the clever dog."

"I like it already," said Box.

Brin and Kitou took up a starting position, angled toward each other, hip-to-hip, relaxed.

"All Po begins here," said Brin, "within striking distance, although few moves start with a strike, since Po is a game of the head, not the hand. The point of this move is to move your opponent. It has merit in the real world, and so is usually the first one taught."

Brin stepped forward, muscling Kitou backwards with her hip. Then she stepped forward again, rotating through ninety degrees, forcing Kitou to turn along with her, pushing her backwards again.

"An unskilled opponent can be pushed to the wall in this way," she said. "The essence of the move is to roll through their center of balance with your center of gravity. The timing is everything. A small woman can push back a large man."

"The Earth art this resembles most is Sumo," said Kitou, brightly.

"An underrated art," said Box.

"A weaker opponent may strike out with their fists, but striking from a position of being continuously pushed off balance is hopeless. A better response is to try to withdraw and strike from a distance."

Kitou danced back, but Brin followed her, bullying forward, still hip-to-hip.

"Thus, it becomes like a dance. The unskilled opponent cannot retreat fast enough. I am always in their face. This is how dogs fight, Dr Box. Chest to chest, the stronger dog raining down blows on its weaker opponent.

"But how does a clever dog fight?"

Brin bullied forward again, but this time Kitou spun with the grain, and was instantly behind her. Even at walking pace, Kitou's rotational acceleration was astonishing.

It was like watching a snake strike.

"From there she bites me in the neck, if she's a dog. Being a skillful human, she instead uses a fast hand blade to the glossopharyngeal or vagus nerves, or to the dorsal motor nucleus at the top of my neck.

"But it isn't my day to die."

40

The two young women turned and nodded to each other.

"Now you."

Box's personal space was almost the exact opposite of her stateroom on the Pnyx: a soft corpuscular nest, that could be gently spun to provide the impression of gravity. It was cosseting, and for once in her life, she had no trouble sleeping. The others' nests were the same, set in a ring of nine identically shaped pods around the ship's middle. Kitou's had a bonsai aspen tree, with miniscule golden leaves, which she said she'd grown from a sliver of wood. Pax's and Brin's had images and sounds of the sea. Ito's was a surprising thicket of words, a collection of holograms of poems and scraps of language he'd collected.

Box said,

"An old silent pond...
A frog jumps into the pond,
splash! Silence again."

Ito looked up from a book, to where Box was floating outside his slowly turning cocoon.

"Haiku?"

"Matsuo Basho," she said.

She chose her moment, and settled beside him.

"*Splash*," she said. "Am I okay here?"

"Of course."

"You're a gracious man, Ito Nadolo."

"Thank you, Dr Box."

"I mean it."

"I know."

"Can I ask you some questions?"

"Go ahead."

"What do you do for sex around here?"

"Here on the Water Bear?"

41

"Yes. It must be hard, locked up with two beautiful women."

"*Three* beautiful women, Dr Box, counting you, and one of them a child."

She blushed.

"I didn't mean to suggest... but, you're all so... attractive."

"Even Alois?"

"Even Alois, in his way."

"Post-evolutionary societies tend to select for physical attractiveness."

"Post-evolutionary?"

"Evolutionary pressure has become the same as social pressure in our society, and we've been at it for a long time. People select partners with heritable qualities they admire."

"Like wit and intelligence?"

"And beauty."

"What about places where bucktoothed gingers are considered attractive?"

"Then there will be more, as you say, bucktoothed gingers. But to answer your question, we do nothing together, sexually. This ship is a family. Instead we have virtual worlds, that we can each visit separately."

"Sex sims?"

"Yes, as real as you desire. Do you want me to show you?"

She blushed again.

"No, I'll ask the Water Bear.

"I guess Brin and Pax's sexual orientation helps?" she ventured.

"To a certain degree."

"I mean, I suppose it means no one's available."

"Except you?"

She felt suddenly naked.

"What, I can't make a pass at you?"

He laughed. "You may do as you like. But while we're on this mission, on my ship, I'd politely decline."

"Then you and Pax had both better watch out, when we're finished."

"Am I forewarned?"

It was her turn to laugh.

"Yes, please consider it official."

Brin and Kitou invited her to a virtuality, but it had nothing to do with sex. It was a training simulation, set on a domed monolith, looming over a cloudy infinity. A fitful wind drifted thin wisps of snow across a stone circle. Even now, with her vertigo gone, all her senses tingled.

Pax was waiting there.

"Dr Box," he said. "Your mission with us here isn't a combat mission."

"Thank goodness for that."

"But, as they say, shit happens. Since you're already a martial artist of repute, then if you'll consent, we'd like to teach you a skill. You may think of it as a life skill, that you can take away and use elsewhere. One day, it might save your life, or ours."

"Okay."

"But please be aware, the lesson's a harsh one. It will test your emotions."

"In what way?"

"We'll show you how to deal with fear."

"Does it involve fighting you?"

"It may. We have to see what frightens you."

"You don't frighten me."

He nodded.

"Dr Box, are you a brave person?"

43

She thought about that. "No," she said, selecting honesty. "I'm reckless."

"Interesting. Also candid. What do you mean?"

She shrugged. "I'll take on any halfway plausible challenge. It's compulsive."

"What would you say, if I said that was courageous?"

"I'd say you're talking horseshit, mister."

"Courage is the willingness to put yourself in harm's way. The rest is technique. I can improve your technique."

"How?"

"What frightens you most, Dr Box?"

"Sharks with lasers?"

He waited.

"You want a serious answer?"

"Yes."

"Everything, Pax. I'm frightened of everything. I'm feisty, but weak."

"And yet you *will* fight," said Pax.

She shrugged.

"How we acquire fear is important," Pax was saying. "Cognitive fear is rational. Fear you can see is fear you can use. Do you fear pain?"

"Are you serious?"

"Yes."

"Less than most, I suppose."

"Good. This lesson may involve pain, but not injury. We're in a virtuality, as you can see."

"But injury, here?" she said, eyeing the fall to a virtual infinity.

"Maybe."

"Can I think about it?"

"By all means."

What choice did she have, after all she'd just said?

"Alright," she said, "let's do this."

Pax nodded, which seemed to be the go-to Po mannerism. The girls looked on impassively.

This is what we do, they seemed to be saying.

"In past times," said Pax, "when humans fought routinely in disorganized close combat, they became seasoned fighters, or they died. The first time they fought, some froze, and of those, some were killed. With each passing fight, they became harder to kill. By about the tenth such mêlée, those that were left sought only to do damage. They'd become soldiers.

"Three synergetic processes were in play: the least able and the least willing were the first to die; the more able became more willing over time; and the most willing became the most able, by surviving the longest in battle.

"Some people never freeze. We consider this to be evidence of psychopathy, or an overstimulated fight response combined with insufficient empathy. We try not to invite such people to join us."

"Are you inviting me?"

"It means we value you enough to wish to trust you."

"Ah."

"I'm not going to train away your flight response. That would be foolish, although I could do it. I'm going to help you prevent it taking control."

She was starting to feel nervous. This was some preamble.

"Nor am I going to plumb your worst terrors. Cover you in spiders. Plunge you into a fire. That would be an assault. This is more subtle than that.

"Ten contests," he said.

The Water Bear's hand-to-hand training apparatus appeared. Instead of being fixed to a ceiling, it descended from a floating torus. Instead of soft pads, it had a convincing facsimile of elbows and fists.

"This machine is set to a level below yours," said Pax. "Fight it."

She squared up, and started to spar. As Pax had promised, it was set to a level below her, but when it snuck past her defenses, it stung like a bare-knuckle boxer.

"*Ow.* Motherfucker."

Pax nodded.

"I said it would hurt. Now *fight.*"

She squared up again, and it knocked her off balance. The domed convexity of the rock caught her, and she fell into the abyss, where she was caught by an invisible membrane, that sagged and swayed like an old-fashioned circus net.

"Fuck!"

The net spasmed, and she was thrown back into the ring, in an ungainly tangle of limbs.

"Sometimes," said Pax. "We fear the wrong things. Do we continue?"

She nodded. This lesson made sense. Fight what's there, not the pain it might cause. It wasn't even real pain. All this was happening in her sensorium. Now she fought sensibly, knowing it would hurt, riding the punches.

Pax called a halt.

"Very good," he said. "It's like fighting a man with a knife. There is no man; there is no knife. There's only a line, and a point.

"Now for a human opponent."

The training machine was replaced by a soldier, dressed in a gambeson tunic. He was filthy, and stank:

the ripe aroma of feces. He was shifting his weight from side to side, staring in her eyes, getting her measure.

She knew straight away that this wasn't a victim. In Pax's taxonomy, this was a survivor.

Or worse, a predator.

She felt a flutter of anxiety. This shit just got real.

"Is he better than me?"

"Find out."

She stepped forward, and he was straight through her defenses, poking his fingers into her eyes, blinding her, until he had hold of her ear, and flung her out of the ring. She lay in the net, in the fetal position, cradling her injuries.

It had taken maybe ten seconds.

She found herself back in the ring, her wounds healed.

"That's enough," she said.

"No," said Pax. "We continue."

"What?"

"I'm instructing you to continue."

"I don't respect your authority, mister."

Pax shrugged, and waited.

What was going on here? Feeling in turns nauseous and angry, she decided to find out.

"Alright," she said.

Pax held up his hands.

"Before you resume, Dr Box. Why did you lose? Because you're afraid: You fear to risk everything, against this violent, unhinged man, for fear he might hurt you, and so you risk nothing.

"This can never be a winning strategy.

"Be like the wolf, Dr Box, protecting her children."

It took five rounds, but in the fifth, after more painful injuries than she'd suffered in a lifetime of martial arts competition, something *shivered* inside her. Her world didn't change. It went deeper than that, like a ripple, on the surface of a still lake.

She won, easily. With a flurry of Muay Thai combinations, as good as she'd ever produced, she backed the berserker up to the edge; then stepped behind him, and helped him off the mountain.

She was furious, and exalted.

"Fuck you," she said, as he fell through the clouds.

Well, she wrote in her diary that evening.

Now **that** *was a bracing experience.*

On the tenth day, they reached Threnody. They'd come nine light-years from Aldebaran, to add to the sixty-five already travelled from Earth. When Box looked back at Sol, which she hoped to do soon from the surface, the light will have left at the start of her millennium. In the last few moments before their arrival, she cornered Alois Buss, by allowing Brin to strap him in, like a hapless opponent in Po.

"Alois, you owe me a briefing," she said.

Buss tried to shrug, but failed. Brin grinned at his predicament.

"I'll take that as a yes."

"Yes," he said.

"Kitou, please strap Dr Box in *now*," said the ship.

Box felt herself being pulled back in her seat by a gravity pulse. Kitou snapped her harness closed, then strapped herself in. After a sustained burst of lateral acceleration, during which the gimbals swung through a hundred degrees, they fell back into realspace, and below them was their destination.

Where Earth is a blue-white jewel in space, Threnody was all the vibrant colors of an Appalachian autumn. What shocked her most was its tonal complexity. It was like a world made of living coral. The polar ice caps were white gold, as were the clouds that marched across the face of tangerine seas. As they approached, a great river system caught the light of the system's yellow dwarf star, and for an instant, a whole autumnal continent was limned with golden fire.

"A cinnabar-rich world," said Alois Buss, by way of explanation.

"I'm speechless," said Box.

Buss smiled, then grinned at her.

"It is beautiful, yes?"

"Beyond words."

"My home."

Ⅎ ∞ THRENODY

2075

"You want me to *what* to the surface?"
"It's what we do," said Pax.
"No," said Box.
"It's really quite easy," said Buss.
"Fuck off, both of you."

She was aware of her companions, but only as voices. She was floating in space; not physically, but in an immersive simulation. The ship conjured a viewport. She saw a snow-capped mountain range, towering over a striated desert. The peaks looked like metal, burnished bronze-gold in the sunshine. A dot moved over the landscape, sliding towards the mountains. Under increasing magnification, which conveyed an impression of scale, the dot became a cone, then a conical structure, with spiraling ramparts, like an Italian hill town, or a fairy-tale castle. Tracking the town [a number in her sensorium said twenty-five kilometers, and closing,] was a storm, its bruised anvil head towering over the landscape. Lightning flickered in its depths, and crawled over the top of it.

This floating castle, she guessed, was their destination.

"If we're fast," said a voice from one side. "We can beat that weather system."

The idea of jumping from space didn't terrify Box in the same way as it would've before the Water Bear messed with her neurology. There was no longer a primal fear of the abyss, just a rational rejection of the impossible.

"No fucking way," she said.

Brin and Kitou held her close as they edged towards the circular portal. Box could already see the haze of the upper atmosphere in her peripheral vision. They'd squeezed her into a skin-tight black jumpsuit, which had morphed out of nothing, then extruded a face-shaped mask, like uncanny scuba.

At least she was in shape. Alois looked ridiculous.

"Remember, all you have do is to step out," said Ito. "Your suit will do the rest."

Box pulled back instinctively. Falling through space in a carbon titanium spacecraft was one thing. Falling in a spandex catsuit was something else altogether.

"Trust me," said Kitou.

Objects in planetary orbit burn up on entering an atmosphere because of their angular momentum. Orbital speed is typically measured in thousands of meters per second. That velocity must be washed off by friction. The Water Bear, with its gravity drive, could simply hover over any point on the surface.

That meant they could jump.

After that it was a matter of falling.

If the view through the ship's shared sensorium had been impressive, the reality of being immersed in it was overwhelming. The stars were like jewels, scattered on black velvet. She felt like she could reach out and take them. The vacuum had texture. The planet had the hyperreal appearance of an animation.

She started to retreat into the safety of her imagination, before a neurological helper gentled her back to full attention.

They *fell*.

At fifty thousand meters, they were accelerating through near vacuum. After thirty-five seconds, they went supersonic. At ten thousand meters, they experienced mild buffeting, as if the air had developed washboard corrugations. Brin and Kitou let go, and her suit grew vestigial winglets.

Now she was *flying*. Overhead, the sky went from black to mauve to a piercing blue. The suit began to let air into her mask, jolting her fully awake. It smelt just like real air, from Earth.

At five thousand meters, the winglets spread out to become a circular wing, and she felt a pillowy whoof of deceleration. Her companions sailed around her like helicopter seeds. Kitou grinned and gave her the universal thumbs-up of approval. It occurred to Box that she'd led a sheltered childhood.

If only her father could see her now.

They glided for several minutes, the suit making steeply banked turns that wiped away the last of her vertical momentum. The city loomed up below, suddener than she expected. With no help from her, her wingsuit blossomed, and she settled on gossamer wings in an empty piazza.

Her facemask retracted.

She took a breath of cold, clean air.

Took one step, and fell over.

Mission specialist Box.

Who would have thought it?

The two younger women were smiling down at her. Only Alois Buss looked concerned.

"The suit gave up on me," she said, groggily.

"Sensory overload," said Ito.

"My head is still buzzing."

"It isn't your head."

She scrambled to her feet. There were no people in this city. Instead, there was the hum of a trillion wings. Every surface was covered with insects. What Box had thought were painted rooftops were layers of glimmering exoskeletons, colored to match the flagstones and tiles. The piazza was a vast, crawling, heaving mass of insect life, which had somehow parted to provide a safe landing zone.

Ito said, "You have nothing to fear."

"Pigment-bearing cells," said Alois. "Combined with Rayleigh scattering."

"Chameleons," she said, wanting to reach out and touch them. She had no fear of insects. This was completely astounding.

"Listen," said Buss.

Their hum was like a song, of inexpressible sadness.

"Once they tune in, they'll speak to you."

"Are they intelligent?"

"Singly, not so much. But the colony is unknowably more intelligent than we are."

"Why are they here?"

"We built this place for them."

"Incredible."

The storm announced itself with a rattle of thunder, followed by an alien coda, like firecrackers exploding. The hair on her neck stood on end.

"Time to be inside," said Ito.

He pointed at the anvil cloud, that rose like a bruise in the near distance. Lightning flashed in its center, then crawled along its extremities, more delicately and for longer than lightning would on Earth. It looked more like a physics experiment than natural weather. An icy gust of wind blew across the piazza, lifting the wings of the insects. Ito led them to a door, then up a spiral stair. Box followed, then the others. She saw that there were no metal fittings or fasteners. What looked like timber and brick was honeycomb composite. She picked up a flake of masonry and dropped it. It drifted like a feather.

"Like Disneyland," she said.

She watched the others access the cultural reference. Buss nodded.

"The Fa:ing are fascinated by humans."

"Fa:ing?"

"This species."

"Alois, I've just realized."

"Yes?"

"These are *aliens*."

He laughed and said, "Unquestionably."

They entered a control room, in the top of a forest of spires, overlooking the piazza. The city was still rising. On its lee side, a wall of carroty granite slid past a low stone balustrade. She could feel a slow rocking motion, like a ship in a long swell, or a tall building swaying in the wind.

The room was how she'd imagined the bridge of a spaceship would be, with contoured chairs and holodisplays, and expansively curved, photochromic window walls.

She felt her ears pop.

What keeps this place afloat? she wondered.

[The Fa:ing do. Their wings provide lift.]

[Is that you, Water Bear?]

[None other.]

[How's the forecast?]

[Hang on, and enjoy the ride.]

[Brace,] rumbled Pax in their heads.

The city swung through forty-five degrees then back again. Sheets of snow and hail marched across the piazza, mixed with curtains of rain. In the control room, remote from the storm, holographic screens flickered into life. The only sound was the faraway thrum of weather on polycarbonate. Her fellow travelers seemed completely relaxed. Box decided she should relax too. She pointed out the nearby roofs, where sheets of Fa:ing were being peeled off by the wind.

"They'll find their way home," said Alois.

"Won't we lose lift?"

"No," said Ito. "The real drive comes from beneath."

"Why are we still climbing?"

"To outrun that," he said. He conjured a viewport, and magnified a toroidal wall of inky-black cloud, writhing in the crimson heart of the storm.

"What's that? A tornado?"

"Similar."

"Is it dangerous?"

"Not to us. We can gravitate away."

"To the Fa:ing?"

"Yes, these storms are a menace to them."

"Is that why we're here?"

"It's why we hurried down, yes."

"What are we going to do?"

"Wait..."

She felt weightless, even though she was still standing.

"A petatonne gravity source, positioned directly above us," said Alois.

The city gathered speed, as though a huge weight had been lifted from it, until they burst through into brilliant sunshine. Then they were sailing through clear air, between snow-capped cinnabar giants. Alois Buss had climbed into an oversized captain's chair, and was studying a holodisplay of the storm.

"Do you see how it's pursuing us?" he said.

He was right. Tendrils of the storm were rising in the clear air behind them.

"How can that be?" she asked.

"It's a psychic event."

"It's not real?"

"No, it's certainly real. But it has a psychic component."

"See that notch up there?" said Ito. He pointed out a narrow gap between the highest mountains. "That's safety."

She stared at the notch, and down at the storm, and saw it'd be a close-run thing. The city was rocking again, as the uncanny vortex snapped at its lower extremities. Slowly, then with increasing speed, the city started to spin.

Still they climbed.

Darkness rose up and engulfed them.

Then, in the last moment, the city threaded itself through the high mountain pass, thanks to some adroit twisting by whoever was steering, and they were falling down the other side, fast enough for Box to feel unsteady, followed by clouds of insects that had been blown clear.

Below was a forest, stretching into the boundless distance, and the gathering night.

"What would've happened if we weren't here?"

"There wouldn't have been a storm."

Ito and Box were watching the young women fight. It was dark, and they were in the piazza, gathered round a fire, made in a ceramic brazier. Fa:ing insects flew around them in the darkness. Kitou and Brin were in a state of high excitement. Blood flew. Suddenly, with a haymaker blow out of nowhere, Kitou broke Brin's nose, with a sickening crunch.

Box blinked as the girls conferred, then carried on.

"Aren't you going to stop that?"

Ito gave her his quizzical stare.

"No."

She sighed.

"What do you mean, no storm?"

"It was a psychic event."

"So, it really was an hallucination?"

"No, but the eye helix was."

"So, when Alois said it was following us?"

"It was."

The girls gave up, and approached Ito. Brin was bleeding profusely.

"Ito?" asked Kitou.

"Up you go and get that fixed," he said to Brin.

Brin nodded.

"And don't tell Pax what caused it," he called after her.

"Kitou, learn some control."

Kitou nodded. Ito motioned her to sit down.

"Dr Box, there are incredible mysteries here. Tonight, you may experience some of them. But remember, there's nothing to be afraid of.

"Except perhaps children with unintelligent fists.

"Tomorrow, we'll explain as best we can."

He touched Kitou's shoulder.

"Now you, up to the ship and apologize."

Box watched as Kitou's training gear morphed into a skinsuit, and extruded a facemask. In just a few seconds, the girl was sucked up into the night.

"You people don't muck about."

Ito grinned.

"No, we don't."

Box did experience an uncanny event that night.

The city spoke to her. It emerged from the hum, like a binaural beat.

Ophelia.

Ophelia Box.

Alois had installed her in a comfortable room, overlooking the piazza. Soft downlights bathed the room in a gauzy light, reflected off a honey-colored floor, that she knew wasn't real timber. Her bed was a riot of flowery iron, that she knew wasn't metal, covered in pillows and duvets of billowy cotton, that just might be cotton. She could see the last embers of their dying fire, glowing in the brazier in the piazza below.

At first, she thought she was dreaming.

Ophelia Box, it said.

Open your mind.

She sat bolt upright in her bed. She'd been dreaming. Her sheets were a sweaty tangle.

Ophelia Box.

Open your mind.

[Are you getting this?] she asked the ship.

[Loud and clear.]

[It knows my name.]

[It does this all the time.]

[Does what?]

[Says your name.]

The following day, over breakfast, an ebullient Alois Buss explained that she hadn't been dreaming at all.

"But you will be," he said.

They were gathered in a dining hall, with trefoil windows that looked over the forest below. The breeze of their passing filled the hall with scents of damp earth and pine resins.

Box was nursing strong coffee, and a bad attitude. She didn't like the way this was heading.

"Here's the thing," Buss said, "The absolute crux of it. The city knows you. You, personally. It's been saying your name for years. Since before you were born."

The girls had reappeared, and were eating. Box had always been bemused by how much elite athletes could eat, and these young soldiers were no exception. Ito was taking his turn to cook, and was making real food, in pans, over electrical appliances. Some of it had near Earth analogues. She could see convincing eggs, and large meaty mushrooms.

There was fresh bread, and crumbly, artisanal sausages.

One of those, and coffee, were her breakfast.

Alois only drank coffee.

Box said, "Alois, that's ridiculous."

Buss shrugged.

"And yet, here we are."

"There must be hundreds of people with my name."

"It's an unusual name."

"Come on, Alois."

He nodded.

"Maybe thousands. It's a large galaxy. But only one with your Hopf number. Ship, if you please?"

A viewport opened in their shared sensorium, the size and dusty appearance of a university mathematics blackboard. It loomed over the breakfast table. Alois produced a virtual chalk and wrote on it:

20589586480370709106240436361869795218463828640166256164965072397199487287276338731859267908616747870179353454570050768156391968572352509817711989490279405697080854177626612002936345304273785723738584883282227347739602422898483269363848030702037751672930139389261170209487702777689810515634324727774394389543552553500377705268252536182762431651890806953162228402192462666679279444021216332900174400520589586480370709106240436361869795218463828640166256164965072397199487287276338731859267908616747870179353454570050768156391968572352509817711989490279405697080854177626612002936345304273785723738584883282227347739602422898483269363848030702037751672930139389261170209487702777689810515634324727774394389543552553500377705268252536182762431651890806953162228402192462666679279444021216332900174400520589586480370709106240436361869795218463828640166256164965072397199487287276338731859267908616747870179353454570050768156391968572352509817711989490279405697080854177626612002936345304273785723738584.88328222734773960242289848326936384803070203775167293013938926117020948770277768981051563432472777439438954355255350037770526825253618276243165189080695316222840219246266667927944402121633290017440052.

"Very impressive, Alois. Do you do children's parties?"

"Dr Box, this is your Hopf number. It's a coordinate in four dimensional spacetime. Give or take a few seconds, or several meters, it's the time and place of your birth.

"Specifically, the Henderson Maternity Unit of the Caithness General Hospital, in Bankhead Road, Wick, on Earth, at 4:16 p.m. on September 30, 2049."

He wrote all that on the board.

The girls had stopped eating, and were watching Box expectantly. Ito wore an enigmatic expression.

"Alois, where did you get that?"

"Good question."

After breakfast, on a grassy prow, overlooking the forest below, a swarm of Fa:ing waited expectantly. Buss wheeled out his treasure: a battered Scottish golf buggy, with a small selection of clubs. He grinned, and threw a ball in the air. A swirl of Fa:ing followed and caught it.

"We call the Fa:ing 'insects'," he said. "But they're not *Insecta*."

The Fa:ing dropped the ball at his feet.

"Insects have distributed brains. Fa:ing individuals have mammalian brains. An interesting case of convergent evolution." He teed up and hit the ball, a curling fade that only went thirty meters. He groaned. A flurry of Fa:ing followed and caught it.

The forest slid serenely below.

"Brin?"

A squadron of Fa:ing flew into the middle distance.

"Observe their behavior," said Buss. "They know just how far Brin can hit it."

Brin teed up and easily hit the ball two hundred meters. The Fa:ing followed, matched trajectories, and caught it. A shimmering, hand-sized individual deposited the ball by Brin's feet.

"In analytical-deductive terms, they're about as intelligent as dogs are. In spatial terms, about as clever as we are.

"Ito, please?"

Ito repeated Brin's easy stroke, almost meter for meter. The swirling Fa:ing swarm chased and caught it.

They were *enjoying* this.

"Dr Box, would you like a turn?"

Box picked out a ball. The Fa:ing seemed unsure. They appeared to confer, a swirling conversation of fluttering wings, until they split in two groups. One group flew a hundred meters. The remainder stayed close.

"They talk with their wings." she said.

"Very good! They converse by sound, using a phonetic language, like we do. And we can talk back to them in the same way, as individuals. The Water Bear is especially fluent."

Box hit the ball, a shank. The closer group of Fa:ing caught it, and swarmed it into the sky, before dropping it at her feet.

"I was never a golfer," she said, biting her lip.

"Better than me," said Buss.

"Now, here's the thing," he continued. "The Fa:ing are a colony mind. One mind, consisting of about a trillion individuals. There are Fa:ing here so small you can't see them. The *colony* thinks in numbers. Beautiful, perfect mathematics. The *neurons* – these individuals – propagate the underlying signals using sounds. That hum you hear, it's the hive *thinking*. That's not the same as its *thoughts*."

Box thought about that. "What does that mean? I mean, what does it mean when it hums my name?"

Brin cleared her throat.

"Brin is our mathematician," said Buss.

"Dr Box," nodded Brin. "Are you familiar with steganography?"

"Messages hidden in text?"

"Yes. The words we hear in the colony hum are like finding language encoded in an encephalogram readout.

The hum is packed with that type of information. Literally packed. We only hear a subset addressed to us. There's much, much more we don't hear."

"It's a profoundly different way of performing the act of thinking," said Buss. "Signals encoded within signals, as though real textual meaning emerges from the tones of a choir, or a symphony, or the sound of a loved one's footsteps in a crowd."

Kitou took a ball.

"Watch this," said Buss with a grin.

The Fa:ing became more animated, zooming and chittering before all spiraling off into the far distance. Kitou unwound, and with no obvious effort, hit the ball four hundred meters.

"Golly," said Box.

That night, Box took a bottle of Alois's scotch whisky, and sought out Brin. She found her perched on a balustrade, listening to the sounds of the forest below.

"You can't hear it by day," said Brin. "We're too far up, but by night, listen."

Box heard a faraway crashing.

"A big beast," said Brin.

Box showed her the Lagavulin bottle.

"Brin, tell me something about yourself."

"What's to say? I'm a soldier."

"Then tell me something about the Po."

The younger woman smiled, and her face lit up in a way that Box hadn't seen before.

"We come from Polota," she said.

"The Po, Lo and Ta?"

"That's right. The Ta administer our world. They're traders and merchants. The Lo are seafarers. You see this makeup I wear? It's the Eye nebula, in the constellation of the Navigator. It points true north on Polota. The natural-born Po, like Ito, are a warrior cult from antiquity. Today, the Po military are the elite soldiers of the thousand worlds."

"So, are you a Po or a Lo?"

"Both. I'm a natural-born Lo, and I fight with the Po. I'm a Po soldier. We're a *Hand* of the Po. A special forces unit. We're an elite of the elite."

"We?"

"Ito, Pax, Kitou, me and now you. And the ship of course. We're the Hand of the Water Bear."

"Alois?"

"Alois is a 6."

"Aren't I a 6 too?"

"Of course not, Dr Box, you're our mission specialist."

Box felt a thrill of pleasure at that.

"Ito's your First?"

"Yes."

"And Pax is your Navigator."

"Yes."

"Who ranks higher?"

"They're equal."

"What rank are you?"

"A soldier."

"What rank is Kitou?"

"A novice."

"When does she become a soldier?"

"That depends. There are protocols. Excellence in the field. Approval by her peers. A trial by combat."

"How's she doing?"

"Perfectly. She'll be a great Spirit."

"What's a Spirit?"

"An exceptional leader. Ito will be a great Spirit."

"What about Pax?"

"Pax is already a Lo Navigator, one of the most respected roles in thousand worlds society."

"And you?"

"What about me?"

"Will you be a great Spirit?"

"No, I aim to be a science officer."

"Mathematics?"

"No, an exobiologist."

"Will you study the Fa:ing?"

"And the rest. We've barely scratched the surface of the cosmos, Dr Box. I want to go and see it, in a Po expeditionary mission."

"How do you get to do that?"

"Five years of study, at the university in Praxis."

"Can't you just download the knowledge?"

"I could, but what would be the point of that? My development as a person will benefit from the experience of learning."

"Nicely put."

The crashing in the forest became louder, as though they were descending closer to the beasts there. It soon became clear they were. Soon, the highest treetops were visible around the piazza.

The city, giving them a present.

The following morning, Box felt sordid from having drunk nearly a third of a bottle of Alois's whisky. Brin seemed unaffected, and was making breakfast. Buss was in his most expansive mood, and excused her for taking it. While the Po soldiers were eating, he unfolded his blackboard again. This one covered almost half of one wall. It was covered in mathematics. He swiped his hand to one side, and the blackboard was replaced by a similar blackboard, similarly covered with symbols and numbers.

He did it again, and again.

"I could do this for years," he said. "Each board holds about a megabyte of data. There are millions of boards. He swiped his hand again, and there, in glowing text, was the string he'd chalked up the previous day.

Box's Hopf number.

"So, Dr Box, to your question. Where did we get your personal information? We got it here. This is the Fa:ing number."

"What is it?"

"It's the thoughts of the hive."

"How did you get this?"

"By analyzing their synaptic processes: their binaural hum. The same way the colony talks to you."

"You interpreted its brainwaves?"

"Yes."

"Alois, that's horseshit. You can find any string in a sufficiently large set of data."

"Of course, that's usually true," said Buss. "There's a chance we're producing a self-fulfilling prophecy out of noise. That's the nature of strings. The difference is the mathematics is real. It's much harder to find random strings in a formula."

Box scowled, but could see no immediate flaw in his arguments.

She shook her head in annoyance.

"Alois, that's where I *start* to have problems."

"I thought you might."

"I'm not here as an historian, am I?"

"Not strictly, no."

"Did you invade Earth because of me?"

"No," said Ito and Buss together.

"But because of… this?"

"Dr Box," said Buss. "We saved Earth because it's a piece in a game that we don't understand. You were in the act of sacrificing that piece, by random obtuseness, for the sake of your politics. We couldn't allow that to happen."

"Dr Box," said Ito. "We brought you here because the Fa:ing asked for you."

Kitou was sitting cross-legged on Box's bed, in the Padmasana lotus position Box had shown her, when Box returned sweating from a conditioning run.

"Do you know I have a brother?" asked Kitou.

Box sat down beside her.

"No, what's his name?" she asked.

"Totoro."

Box rose and looked out the window. It was a wet day, streaming and grey, but nothing like the storm that announced their arrival. It was a pleasing, melancholy kind of rain. Ordinary water pattered on the windowpane.

Box was dripping wet, but she'd ceased to notice.

"I once had a brother," she said.

"You did?"

"Yes, but he died."

"Oh, Dr Box."

"That's okay. I was only small. Tell me about yours."

Kitou nodded. "My brother's a soldier," she said, "a good one, like I am, but fiercer than me. He's fighting for the Free Pursang, in the war against the Horu."

"Is he safe?"

"Yes."

"You're sure of that."

Kitou nodded.

"I know it."

Alois led her into the bowels of the city, to the industrial base, where the service zones were. "The Pursang? A remarkable people. You know they're originals?"

"Originals?"

"First humans. Not a product of the diaspora."

"One of your thousand worlds?"

"No, non-aligned."

"Who are the *Free* Pursang?"

"Well, that depends which side of the fence you sit on. Some excoriate them as a terrorist group. An asymmetric insurgency. Or else they're freedom fighters."

"What side of the fence are you on?"

"Again, that depends. The Pursang have just cause. Ten years ago, a race called the Horu laid waste to their world. Not only laid waste, but made a show of it. An infamous genocide, and a provocation, with us the provokees. We choose not to be provoked. We leave it to the Pursang. For now, they're our terrorists."

"A proxy war?"

"Well..."

"But?"

"The best course of action would be to leave the Horu alone. Let them get away with their genocide."

"Won't they just do it again?"

"Why would they, if the intention was to provoke us?"

"Then why are you fighting?"

"We're not. The Pursang are fighting, and to stop them would be unjust."

"So you let them fight a proxy war you don't want to be in?"

"Yes."

"Do they attack civilians?"

"They try not to kill civilians."

"Then they're not really terrorists."

"Good luck with that line of argument."

"How are they doing?"

"The Pursang are clinical. Their plan appears to be to slice the Horu up, a supply line at a time, so some larger predator can destroy them later."

"And if you're that predator?"

"Then, I suspect, the larger trap is sprung, and we learn the real extent of it."

"Alois, I need to learn about your politics."

"You do."

"And Kitou?"

"Kitou's a Pursang."

"I thought she was a Po."

"She's a Po now. Ito saved her from a fire."

"What happened?"

"Ito and Pax were soldiers on the Water Bear. In an act of conspicuous valor, Ito, Pax and their First, Idira Law, jumped down to the surface of Fluxor, hundreds of times, bringing out people."

"Why didn't the Water Bear lift them all at once? With one of those petatonne gravity sources?"

"Horu suppressor fields. That was the nature of the siege. The Po broke through it by launching themselves at the planet, daring the Horu to interfere. The Po soldiers jumped down to the planet with no sure means of return, challenging the Horu to trap them there."

"Did they?"

"Ito and Pax are still here."

"Brinkmanship."

"I call it game theory. The Horu weren't ready to make war with the Po. If they were, the Po needed to know about it."

"Are they ready now? To make war?"

"We hope not."

They were passing through an empty residential district, past deserted parks and along empty boulevards.

"This used to be teeming with people," sighed Buss.

"What happened?"

"Bad dreams."

They reached a heavy-industrial zone. The number of Fa:ing individuals around them increased exponentially. They stopped outside a hatch, which Buss reached out to unlock.

"Dr Box, don't be alarmed by what you see here."

He opened the hatch. There was a sulfurous glow. Layers of Fa:ing crawled over a house-sized container: the source of the ghastly light. To one side, Box saw a spent waste storage pool. Her inner display lit up like a Christmas tree.

Having grown up in a country scattered with the hulks of abandoned nuclear facilities, she knew exactly what this was.

"Alois, is that an unshielded fission reactor?"

"Yes. But you're immune. Nanomachines in your travel shots."

"Alois, I'm not happy with this."

"I understand."

Ito turned to look at them. He was sitting, relaxed, on a bench, gazing into the poisonous light.

"Ah, Dr Box, you've discovered our guilty secret."

"This is weird."

Buss bustled her onto a catwalk, cantilevered over open space, into clean air, out of sight of the reactor. The

71

forest flew by, only meters below. Thousands of Fa:ing, some twice the size of humans, were clinging to the city's ventral surfaces, changing position to minutely vector the thrust. The polyphonic thrum was deafening.

Buss beckoned her inside, where they could talk.

"Lifting bodies," he said.

"The city's propulsion system?"

"Yes. The Fa:ing convert energy from the unshielded gamma radiation into thrust for the city, by consuming it and beating their wings. More poetically, they convert gamma rays into mathematics."

Box glanced at Ito.

"It's hypnotic," Buss said. "And addictive. We all experience it. We don't let the girls down here, although they once mounted an effective reconnaissance raid."

Box shivered. "Take me upstairs," she said.

That night, Box had a dream.

She was riding over a ruined battlefield, on a pale horse. The horse had its tail in the air, and was picking its way between steaming human remains, heaped ribcages and spines, that looked freshly dead, but with no flesh on them.

They'd been broiled clean.

Her armor was bone. Voluptuously carved, translucent bone, like mother-of-pearl. There were bone beads in her braided red hair. On her shield was a red right hand.

Across the battlefield was Kitou. She was on foot, also picking her way between the steaming remains, wearing her Po training gear. Her right hand was red, dripping with what Box understood was alien blood.

Behind the sky was the Enemy. He had modern beam weapons, powering up with a distant whine. Spaceships. A circling fleet. A galaxy, in flames.

She wanted to cry out, to warn Kitou of the terrible risk, but she couldn't. Instead she looked up, and saw herself, looking down.

She said, *Ophelia.*

She woke, with a whimper.

Box asked Ito about what she'd seen in the base of the city.

"Everyone gets it," he said. "Visions. Strange addictions. It drove the researchers away. We think deliberately."

"Why?"

"Clearing the decks."

"Except for you people?"

He nodded.

"Have you had the dream yet?" he asked.

"A field made of bones?"

"Yes, we were anxious to see what you looked like."

"You've had the same dream?"

"Everyone has who spends time here."

"His red right hand."

"The device on the shield?"

"It's a poetic symbol, in Earth literature, for the vengeful hand of God.

'Should intermitted vengeance arm again
His red right hand to plague us?'

"What it means is, how can a benign God allow so much suffering? The answer is, we don't understand his ways."

73

"Or he's not benign," said Ito.

Box nodded.

"Also in the basement is a spacetime anomaly," he said. "Created by the Fa:ing processor. We call it the Fa:ing rip. One theory is, when the end-time war begins, the Fa:ing will leave through it."

"End-time war?"

Ito shrugged. "It's a theory."

"And if they leave?"

"We follow."

That night, in the piazza, Brin showed Box a new move. "This is called the wind shadow," she said. "It's about exteroception."

Box watched the two young women shadow each other's movements, back to back, without looking. It was an uncanny skill. At the sound of Brin's voice, Kitou launched a taekwondo back kick Box had taught her, which Brin allowed to pass by the side of her head.

Ito joined them in the piazza.

"What's this?" he said.

"We're training Dr Box," said Kitou.

"For what?"

"To be a Po fighter," said Brin.

Ito raised an eyebrow.

"And how is that enterprise going?"

Box's training gear was slick with sweat. She was out of breath, and nursing a livid bruise on her arm.

"She has ability," said Brin.

"Praise," said Ito.

Brin nodded.

"Does master Pax know about this?"

"He will," said Kitou.

Ito nodded acknowledgement.

"Keep at it."

The following morning, Buss unfolded his blackboard again, while Kitou fussed over breakfast. The hall filled with the aroma of scorched milk. With a sigh, Brin rose to help her.

"Who are the Fa:ing?" Buss scrawled on his board.

"Ito?"

"They come from the future," said Ito.

"Wait," said Box, arching her eyebrows. "Time travel? Is that a thing here?"

"It is," said Buss. "I know, because I also come from the future."

Box stared.

"Alois speaks truly," said Ito.

"Okay," said Box. "You have my attention."

"How far in the future?" wrote Alois.

"Anyone?" he asked.

"The math suggests $10\text{\textasciicircum}10\text{\textasciicircum}3$ years," said Brin.

"But?"

"But it could be $10\text{\textasciicircum}10\text{\textasciicircum}10\text{\textasciicircum}56$ years, depending on how you read the Fa:ing algorithms."

"Wait," said Box. "I'm no mathmo, but that's a big number."

Brin nodded. "A very big number. $10\text{\textasciicircum}10\text{\textasciicircum}3$ years is about the time to heat death, when the universe can no longer sustain processes that increase entropy. $10\text{\textasciicircum}10\text{\textasciicircum}10\text{\textasciicircum}56$ is such a large number that there aren't enough photons in the universe for Alois to write it here."

"Why those numbers?" asked Box.

Brin nodded. "We can hypothesize," she said. "$10\text{\textasciicircum}10\text{\textasciicircum}10\text{\textasciicircum}56$ is about the time required for all the elementary particles to cycle through all their possible states, which is the longest time required for a quantum-tunneled big bang to produce a new universe identical to our own. In a sense, the most time possible."

Box paused to take that in, then shook her head in annoyance.

"You're seriously telling me the Fa:ing come from the end of time?"

"Maybe. It's one of the possibilities."

"Why are they here?" Buss wrote with a signature flourish.

"Kitou?"

"To change our past," said Kitou.

"Very good," said Alois. "To change *our* past. *Their* future. The Fa:ing individuals experience time like we do. The Fa:ing *consciousness* appears to experience it backwards.

"Dr Box, yours isn't the only Hopf number in the Fa:ing corpus." He conjured up a green-white planet, floating above the breakfast table. "Fluxor," he said. "Before the genocide. A beautiful world. Not unlike Earth, but wetter and cooler."

The view zoomed out, until Fluxor became a pulsing green point at the edge of a starfield, that spanned an arm of the milky way galaxy. An orange point appeared, with a curved line between them. A glyph said [1,527 light-years].

"Threnody.

"I first began to study the Fa:ing in your year 2135, seventy years from now, as a young computational linguist, when Threnody was a thriving scientific adventure. In my timeline, the thousand worlds are at war with the Horu. A shooting war, but manageable. Then, someone fires a doomsday device."

"That sounds bad," said Box.

"A sphere of annihilation, spreading at lightspeed across the galaxy. So yes, bad. An enduring hypothesis of experimental physics is that one day, supercolliders will inadvertently destroy the universe. A myth. It can't happen. Unfortunately, weapons manufacturers stepped into the breach, so it has."

"Shit."

"Indeed. Hopefully someone can stop it."

"Stop it from what, exactly?"

"From destroying *everything*, Dr Box. Our civilization, to start with. Then everything else, in a slowly expanding bubble of annihilation. Or maybe not so slow. We don't know. Space can move faster than light. Hence the need for secrecy. There are species that would destroy us instantly, if they knew."

"You really don't know how it ends?"

"No, the Fa:ing carried me away before I could find out."

"Carried you where?"

"Here, ninety years ago."

"Alois, you're older than you look."

He shrugged. "My people practice germline ageing modification. I appear as old as I wish to be."

Outside, the forest flowed by, like Autumn being carried past on a stream. The air in the hall was heady with the aroma of pinecones and resins. Box checked the lines on her hands, to see if she was dreaming.

"That's quite a story," she ventured.

"It gets better," said Alois.

Kitou and Brin had joined them beneath the blackboard, food now forgotten. "I already told you the story of Ito and Pax at Fluxor," he said. "The point is, why were they there? Consider this your briefing, Dr Box. What was the Water Bear doing at Fluxor? Why was Ito present at the precise place and time to save Kitou from the fire?

"The answer is Kitou's Hopf number."

"The place of her birth?"

"No," said Alois. "Her death."

"Ito saved her?"

"Yes."

"And changed the past?"

"You have it."

"Our mission," said Ito, "is to prevent an historical genocide. We can think through the wider implications later. We're peacekeepers, Dr Box, working with dangerous knowledge, in secret."

"The question," said Alois Buss, "is are you with us? We're not the conquerors you may have once thought we were. You already know that. Nor are we railroading you, or your people, into anything. We're trying to save another world, and perhaps everything else, with the help of these strange creatures from the end of time, who have asked for you personally.

"Now we've found you.

"What do you say? Will you help us?"

The physics weapon began as a package of ice: a comet's nucleus, in the system's Oort cloud, a light-year from its F-type main-sequence star. It was accelerated to near-lightspeed using a bootstrap drive, in which a gravity source is projected ahead of the object. The gravitational field was a mere 10 m/s^2, or just slightly more than one Earth-normal gravity. Time did the rest. It fell for twenty-nine million seconds, which is slightly less than an Earth year. Then it went dark: just a comet, among millions.

The five Horu ships unfolded space at equidistant points in an ellipsoid around the system's ecliptic. The nearest was 599 light-seconds from Threnody. Seeing this, the Po warship floating above the planet's surface launched a flurry of messages.

Her Navigator, instantly awake, brought her military systems online.

In the city below, her crew also woke.

Box was jolted by a burst of adrenaline. She stumbled naked from her bed. There were people in her room. Her skinsuit found her. Its facemask extruded, sealing her panicked objections. She was bustled out and up the spiral stair. In the control room, Alois was clipping himself into the oversized captain's chair. Holographic displays were flickering into life. A plexiglass window popped out, and fluttered onto the piazza.

Seconds had passed.

Alois was talking calmly to Pax.

"Ah, Dr Box. Good to see you're dressed. We're getting ready to leave."

"What the hell is happening?"

"Visitors."

"Who?"

Alois manipulated a display. A ghostly flower, floating in space. Then five ghostly ships, scattered around the ecliptic plane.

"Horu," said Kitou.

"More than we've seen in one place since Fluxor," said Alois.

"Are we safe?"

"For now," he said. "They're at a safe distance. Ten light minutes away."

By the time it passed the nearest Horu ship, the ten-tonne comet nucleus had accumulated $.5mv^2$ ˜ 420,500,000,000 GJ ˜ 100,000 Mt of potential energy, or more than the deployed nuclear arsenal of all the nations on Earth, ever. As it passed through the perimeter ring, its bootstrap drive restarted, this time at full power, creating pressures unknown outside the center of collapsed stars. The ball of snow and ice fell into the drive, to form a sphere of degenerate matter, indistinguishable from the crust of a neutron star.

The drive had become the weapon.

Alois was explaining their situation.

"Threnody's best defense was always its secrecy."

"Was," said Box.

"So it appears. There's nothing we can do about five Horu warships. It might as well be five thousand."

"What about the Fa:ing?"

"There's nothing we can personally do for them now."

"What about the cavalry? That big Wu warship we saw."

"A half-hour away."

"Ten light-minutes vs. half an hour?"

"That's the equation."

"It's a shitty equation."

"Yes."

"Where's Ito?"

"In the basement."

"Why? Someone go get him."

"It's as the Fa:ing have requested."

The Water Bear's sensing apparatus used the same physics as Wu lightship drives. Beefy quantum computers reimagined the origin of incoming gravity waves. The weapon's bootstrap drive was acquired instantly upon restarting. The first Pax knew of it, was when he began to lose consciousness. At over a thousand Earth gravities, even the smallest change of direction manifests as violent lateral acceleration.

[Sorry, boss.]

Ungh.

On the planet, Alois Buss said, "Merde."

[On my way,] said the ship in their heads.

"What's happening?" asked Box.

"Planet killer," said Alois.

"Out we go," said Brin a few moments later.

Box felt herself falling towards the piazza. She'd been thrown bodily from the tower. Overhead, the decelerating Water Bear announced itself with a shuddering boom. It looked like a moth, spiraling into a dish. Box felt herself pulled towards the Po warship.

She awoke in the ship's control room, for just a few seconds. She was strapped in her usual chair.

She passed out again.

She had a dream.

She dreamed she was looking into the eyes of a striking, flaxen-haired woman. "I was worried you were catatonic," the woman was saying.

"Who are you?" asked Box.

The woman stepped back. Box saw Pax, Brin and Kitou, studying a holographic image of the Threnody system.

"I'm the Water Bear," she said. "This is my gamespace. A military virtuality. I've slowed things down, so we can think."

"You look familiar," said Box.

"A cultural reference, especially for you."

81

"Kara Thrace? You really have got to be kidding."

"Dr Box," rumbled Pax.

"I have no idea what's happening," said Box.

"Don't worry," said Pax. "We're the soldiers here. This is our time. Later, you can say how we went."

"A kinetic weapon has been fired," Pax said to everyone. "The planet is lost."

A communal groan.

"Ito has made his way to the basement, as planned. Alois is still in the Threnody control room, not as planned. What happened?"

"Alois accidentally locked himself in a chair," said Brin.

"Can I please go get him?" asked Kitou.

"No," said the ship.

"Solutions?" asked Pax.

"Extract his brain," said the ship.

"How?" asked Pax.

"I can recover it though a ceiling fan."

"What, intact?" asked Box.

"No," said the ship.

"When?" asked Pax.

"Sooner better," said the ship.

"But he's alive," said Box, aghast.

"Do it," said Pax.

Seen from the planet's surface, the weapon arrived unannounced. Not only was it travelling at near lightspeed, but it was only a few centimeters across. It passed through the atmosphere in a fraction of second, and ten cubic kilometers of ocean and crust disappeared in a flash.

The Fa:ing disappeared.

Ito was in the basement, ready to be extracted.

And then he wasn't.

In the Water Bear, concentration.

"Final recommendations?" asked Pax.

"We go as originally planned," said the ship.

"Dr Box?"

"Me? You're asking me? Go Pax, go."

He nodded.

"Take us in, please."

Bodily, they were strapped in the control room lattice. In the Water Bear's gamespace, they watched as the ship performed high-g maneuvers, inside the base of the city, moving towards the unshielded reactor, towards the Fa:ing rip, which now seemed half the size of the universe. Now that the Fa:ing lifting bodies were gone, the city belonged to gravity. The planet awaited its prize. Ten seconds after impact, the crimson forest raised a gnarled hand to receive it.

As a wall of fire rose over the horizon.

"Go," said Pax.

The Water Bear accelerated.

4 ∞ BY Λ MILKY-WHITE SEΛ

2056

On Xerxes, in the Pleiades, in the region of space called the Smear, the city of Avalon basked under an emerald sky, beside a milky-white sea. Once a fortress, then a frontier spaceport, now a trading hub, bunting fluttered from its brutalist gun emplacements.

In a rough dockside bar, crowded with spacers and whores, the cryptologist Felix Revelstoke weighed the delicate game of risk to be played by helping the three foreign women. He watched as a troupe of bioengineered transvestites sought to gain the attentions of a visiting krëw of Magellanic Navigators. The tranvies worked hard, but the Magellanics had eyes only for themselves.

The thousand worlds were characterized by their genetic naturalism. They were a civilization on a biological mission. Here, in the Smear, by contrast, anything was possible. One of the tranvies gave Revelstoke a lascivious wink. He smiled politely in reply.

In the same dockside bar, on a crowded dancefloor, Kitou Gorgonza was being pawed by three outsize youths, while Brin Lot looked on disinterestedly. The young men's older, harder companions, bristling with radical piercings and body enhancements, also looked on, too hungrily for Ophelia Box's liking.

"That's not a fair contest," said Brin.

Brin was wedged into a corner, nursing a drink.

"Aren't you going to help her?" asked Box.

Brin shook her head.

Box knew this bar well. In Aberdeen, high on ecstasy, evading the clumsy advances of roughnecks and squaddies. In Marseilles, where the gangsters cut smiles into the faces of their enemies with cutthroat razors. In Punta Arenas, when Antarctica was first opened for mining exploration.

A frontier slaphouse.

Kitou became bored with the youths trying to lay hands on her, and rejoined her friends, leaving the young men searching comically.

"Foreign men are strange," she said.

"It's not strange," said Box. "They're displaying."

"They want to copulate?"

Box nodded.

"How do they think behaving like fools will impress me?"

"Thinking doesn't come into it."

The youths had surrounded another woman, and were pushing her from one to the other. Pushes became shoves, then slaps, and the woman was pressed to a wall.

"Put an end to that," said Brin. Kitou rose and walked towards the group.

Box rose to follow, but Brin held her wrist.

"Observe the Po art in combat mode."

Kitou seemed to move at walking pace, but when she struck it was a blur. It was like liquid violence. None of them got near her. They were in more danger of striking themselves.

One by one, the youths went down.

No one seemed to realize there was a fight on.

Kitou was sauntering back to their table. The young men's older companions were piling onto the dancefloor, looking for payback.

One was striding towards them.

"That was provocative," said Brin, "leaving the older ones standing."

"I was being deceptive," said Kitou.

Brin nodded, and got to her feet, and with a snarl, marched towards the advancing man, and folded him in two with a vicious side kick to the solar plexus.

"The Lo art does include kicking," said Kitou.

"Well, that should get someone's attention," said Box.

Revelstoke did realize there was a fight on. After all, as a secret policeman, and a relatively senior one, with turf to defend, it was his job to be observant.

The *how* of it was interesting.

The *who* was unlikely.

He finished his drink, and departed.

[Well done team,] said Pax from the Water Bear.
[I think we have him.]

87

They were thrown from the bar.

"For fighting the wrong assholes," said Box.

They sat down on an upturned pallet. A passing law enforcement prowler slowed, then let them be. A handsome young man came out of the bar, and gave them the address of a religious congregation.

A sharp tang of salt air, and diesel, swirled around them.

Gulls cawed in the distance.

Brin was bleeding from a lacerated eyebrow.

From somewhere, came the sizzle and heady aroma of sausages. Box thought, this is the best time of my life. It can't get any better than this.

They burst out laughing.

They found a room in a dockside hotel, overlooking a doglegged lane, leading down to the harbor. By comparison with spaceflight, it was a ramshackle palace. A neon sign flashed sporadically outside their window.

"Otel," it said.

Box asked the ship to disable her Broca transfer. Now it flashed gibberish.

They were woken at dawn by lively commerce beneath their open window. The lane had become a market. While Box lay in bed, Kitou morphed her discarded party clothes into loose training gear and set out running. Box dragged herself from bed, and watched Kitou disappear toward the harbor.

She noticed that Kitou was followed.

With her Broca transfer still off, Box listened to a dozen languages. The prevailing argot sounded like Mediterranean Arabic, a beautifully liquid language.

She smelt the heady aroma of the stalls. Clean air, fresh produce, hot food, and an undertone of rotting garbage.

Brin rose, scowled, and seeing that Box's translator was off, began to make the Avalon equivalent of strong coffee.

Kitou ran down to the harbor, then along a wide corniche, beside a tumbling sea. Finding her stride, she surged onto a steep hill, which climbed towards a beam-weapon emplacement, and accelerated.

Running was pure pleasure. Her simple shoes slapped lightly on the salt-encrusted concrete. Soon her pursuers were left far behind, as plain as day on the steep ocean road. She relented, almost letting them catch her.

At the top, she waited, breathing.

There were two young men and a woman. One of the panting men said, "We're the police."

Kitou said, "I know."

The second man said, "Are you really a Po soldier?"

Kitou wrinkled her nose. "Not really.

"But my friends are," she said.

They companionably enjoyed the view, like any young runners would, at the top of a challenging climb. Avalon was a beautiful city, by its milky-white sea, with its military towers painted every color.

"Can we run with you tomorrow?" asked the young woman, politely.

"Yes, of course."

"Well," said the first young man.

"I guess we'll be off," said the second.

Kitou nodded.

After her police escorts jogged self-consciously down the hill, Pax said, from above, [Good job]. Kitou, knowing she was observed, gave him a virtual thumbs-up of approval.

Then she set off at a fast lope, back to the hotel, for breakfast.

They spent the day buying local clothes, and food for the room, and cheap souvenirs. The local currency was paper and coins, and Pax had given them pocketsful each, with instructions to spend it.

Garner attention, he said.

In the early afternoon, they found themselves in a larger market. This was what Box would call a souk, or bazaar. The street food and local attire gave way to consumer electronics, entertainments, and in one section, weapons. For the Po, these were of little value. They regarded them with professional curiosity.

"Why," asked Brin, "would any sane person buy a weapon?"

"To defend themselves?" asked Box.

"Nonsense. It only puts them in danger."

Kitou only seemed to partially understand the concept of property. She spent all her money on gifts for the others, then happily asked for more. By the mid-afternoon, they were local celebrities. Box steered Kitou away from a sex shop, not to protect her, but for fear of the number of things she might buy there. They were enjoying a meal of sticky rice, served up with raisins and pine nuts, and the ubiquitous local sausage, when Pax broadcast in their sensoria.

[You're about to be arrested.]

The Water Bear chimed in.

[Dr Box, please follow my instructions. Brin is about to rise and pay for your meal. At the same time, you rise and follow the pulsing red line, at normal walking pace.]

A red line appeared in the floor, leading from the café. Box did as she was instructed.

[Our main goal here is to not get you shot. There are three local heavies. They may or may not be professional law enforcement. They could perceive you as a threat, and might over-respond.]

The red line snaked behind some market stalls. She followed it. She heard crashing behind her. The pulsing line then passed through a laundry, and snaked towards a tall, professorial man, who was standing by a wall, speaking into a throat mic.

[At the same time as keeping you safe, we wish to make a point. I want you to approach that man, and put your hands in the air.]

She saw Brin and Kitou doing the same, from opposite directions. They would finish up on three sides of him.

[If this goes wrong, I'll lift you straight out of there. If anyone shoots, I'll lift the bullets in flight. You're completely safe, Dr Box.]

Box was intrigued. This was real cloak and dagger stuff. She did as she was told, and raised her hands in the air.

The man stiffened, and said, "I have you surrounded."

Brin raised one eyebrow.

The three local heavies crashed into the open space behind them, brandishing snub-nosed weapons. One shouted, "Hands in the air."

Another one bellowed, "Drop your weapons."

The third, who had brightly colored clothing strewn around him, just crouched and pointed his handgun.

Brin said, "We surrender."

The man sighed, and motioned his men to holster their weapons. They did so with military precision.

Not amateurs, then.

"I'm Revelstoke," the man said.

"We know," said Brin.

"Will you come peacefully?"

"As you wish."

The gunmen escorted them to a nondescript building, with Revelstoke following at a respectable distance. Inside, they were regarded with frank curiosity. Kitou waved at a young woman. They were taken to a dusty, academic's rooms. Open books of mathematics and criminology climbed over each other. Revelstoke appeared, and motioned them to sit.

"What do you want?" he said.

"We're a Hand of the Po," said Brin.

"If that were true, I'd never have seen you."

"We gave you cause to see us."

"So you say."

"We deployed the barfight signal."

He sighed. For a double agent, a special ops team was like an anxiety dream. They'd have their own, stifling agenda. Worst of all was a Hand, if that's what they were. They'd burn all the oxygen in his room, in sips and then gulps, then leave, never to be seen, never having been there.

"What do you want?"

"We need backup, with utmost secrecy."

"Secret from my own people?"

"Yes."

"I suppose you can justify that?"

"Our mission is to prevent a major war."

"Who are you?"

"We're the Hand of the Water Bear."

He shook his head. "No, you're not. I've sequenced your DNA."

"We're from the future."

He sat with his chin in his hand.

"You appear to be serious," he said, after Brin told him the parts of their story he needed to hear. "Can your ship send me a cryptographically signed message, confirming all that?"

Brin nodded. "You now have it."

He stood and paced the room, too rangy for it, constrained by the walls. "You know," he said. "The simplest course for me is to inform my superiors."

"But you won't."

"No, I suppose not."

"We need money," said Brin. "And medical services."

"You have wounded?"

"A man dead."

"You want him... what, resurrected?"

"Yes."

"You know that's illegal."

"This is the Smear."

He laughed, an agreeable laugh, thought Box, for a secret policeman. She watched the chemistry of feelings play over his face, as he considered his options.

Who are you, officer Revelstoke?

Not a poker player.

Or a good one.

"Let me think about it," he said. "In the meantime, keep a low profile. In particular tell this one to run slower."

He shook his head.

"I suppose this is what I get paid for."

The following day, Box watched Kitou weave her way through the market, this time with her escorts beside her. The friendly waves of the market traders were less in evidence. Box didn't like that there should be police waiting for Kitou. It implied the industrial heft of a Soviet-style surveillance operation.

All for three innocent strangers.

Box read her political backgrounder. Avalon had all the hallmarks of a benign kleptocracy. There were no political freedoms here, but the people were prosperous and happy.

Happy is cheap.

And prosperous is relative.

The real money flowed through Avalon Station, 35,000 km above. This was owned by the Avalonia Cpy, a private corporation, and presumably Revelstoke's political masters. Her historian's nose told her that profitable sinecures like Revelstoke's were bought and sold here, so as well as being a Captain of the Security Police, Revelstoke was likely a petit oligarch himself.

A recipe for corruption.

Are you corrupt, officer Revelstoke?

She suspected the company didn't much care, provided he was plausibly competent.

But what did she know? She was extrapolating, from similar places on Earth. She was a stranger. She resolved to try to suspend judgement.

For a while, at least.

Half an hour later, Kitou called.

[Can you come to me?] she asked.

Brin was doing her own exercise routine. Chin-ups and crunches. More in a session than Box had done in a lifetime.

[Yes, why?] Brin replied.

[Mr. Revelstoke wishes to visit the Water Bear.]

Box followed Brin down the crooked street to the harbor front. It was a wet morning, and the slippery concrete splashed under their feet. A brisk wind blew white spume over the corniche. It felt delightful to be out in the weather. Thirty minutes later, breathing hard, they crested the brow of a long hill, that floated above the tops of the low clouds, to reveal a glorious sunrise.

Kitou was sitting cross-legged, talking animatedly with Revelstoke.

"Ah, here they are," he said with a smile. He seemed a far more relaxed secret policeman than yesterday.

"Alright, let's talk," he said.

It was a beautiful day in heaven, with the fresh wind in their faces, looking out over a billowing cloudscape. She felt a thrill of endorphins.

A prowler descended.

"Our ride," said Revelstoke.

They climbed into the pilotless machine, which surged into the emerald sky. They rose like an express lift, until the horizon curved to an arc, and the stars became pinpricks of light.

The ship spoke in their sensorium.

[I have you, Avalon prowler.]

They assembled in the gymnasium, which the Water Bear had repurposed as a meeting area. The training machines had folded flat in the walls. The practice ring had become a soft crystal table. The ship had even made gravity, for Revelstoke to pace in.

"I've found you your money," he said. "But you have to go get it."

Pax nodded. "You mean steal it?"

"Yes," said Revelstoke.

No surprises there, thought Box. She knew from Earth history that military units on covert missions often had to misappropriate resources.

Steal clothing from washing lines.

Rob the occasional gas station.

"Steal what?" asked Pax.

"For a ship refit and a full-body resurrection, plus ten years of covert ops, about 250 kg of gold."

"Why gold?"

"Because I know where there is some."

"Where?"

"It's an unusual strategy."

"Just tell us."

"Steal your own money."

"From where?"

"From the central bank on Praxis."

"Explain."

"One," he said, counting off his fingers. "There's no victim. After all, we *are* the good guys."

"Yes," said Pax.

"Two, you have insider knowledge.

"Three, no one will ever suspect what has happened. I promise you, as a policeman, the idea that this group travelled from the future to steal its own money will never emerge as a law enforcement theory.

"Finally, you have the Water Bear's private key. You can prove her identity. It's the perfect crime."

"But," said Pax. "The Civics."

"Yes," said Revelstoke.

"Who are they?" asked Box.

"The AIs that govern our society," said Pax.

"Like the City of Praxis?"

"No, Praxis is a person. The Civics are a widespread, composite intelligence."

"They'll work out straight away," said Revelstoke, "what's happening."

Box said, "How?"

Revelstoke shrugged. "Because they can."

"What Mr. Revelstoke means," said Pax, "is that knowing what they know, no matter how improbable, we're the most likely explanation. The question is, will they permit us to do it?"

Revelstoke said, "I think they will."

Box said, "Why?"

"Game theory," said Revelstoke. "Dr Box, why did you start operations here in a state of imperfect secrecy, starting fights and spending money on trinkets?"

Box shrugged. "We spent information," she said. "To buy options."

Revelstoke nodded. "Exactly. The Civics work on similar principles, but on a much larger scale. They occupy saddle points. They keep those positions open, for as long as possible. When they intervene, they make the least intervention possible, until they have complete information, then they act decisively."

"Like the art of Po," said Brin.

"So, we're an option?"

"Yes," said Revelstoke. "A wavefunction that needn't be collapsed."

"Why don't we just talk to them?"

"No one talks to the Civics."

"This system works?"

"It has for ten thousand years."

"Then go for it."

"So," said Revelstoke. "Let's plan a robbery."

"One more thing," said Box.

"Yes?" asked Pax and Revelstoke, in unison. Brin stifled a laugh.

"How much is 250 kg of gold?"

"It depends on what you mean by 'much'," said Pax. "It's a weight we can carry."

"I mean, what's it worth?"

"Its monetary value?" said Revelstoke. "What can it buy? A ship refit costs about 25 kg. A human resurrection slightly less."

"Then steal all of it," she said.

"Explain," said Pax.

"Don't mess about with 250 kg. Forget what you can personally carry. That's amateurish. How much is actually there?"

In addition to his role as Navigator, Pax was the ship's financial controller. In fifteen years he could withdraw this money legally.

"About a hundred times that," he said.

"Steal it all. Most military operations fail because of logistics. Why take the risk of running out of cash? Trust me. Make up a number. Double it."

"She's right," said Revelstoke.

"Agreed," said Pax.

"How do we steal 25 tonnes of gold?" asked Brin.

"Deceptively," said the Water Bear.

Kitou reappeared, carrying a weighty grey cylinder, the size of a hatbox. She laid it on the slab. Beads of moisture slid along its surface.

"What's this?" asked Revelstoke, although his expression suggested he knew.

"This is Alois Buss," said Pax.

"Our friend," said Kitou.

"Amen that," said Brin and Pax.

"Well," said Revelstoke. "How dead is he?"

"Not too seriously," said the Water Bear. "His neural structures are repairable. When he wakes, he'll be the same individual."

"How did it happen?"

"I extracted his brain through the control room ceiling of the city of Threnody, before it was destroyed by a physics weapon."

"How?"

"Shaped gravity pulse."

Revelstoke winced. "He was alive at the time?"

"Conscious."

"That's not good."

"Tell us about it," said Box.

"There'll be psychological trauma."

"Undoubtedly," said the ship. "He was still sensing when I got him here."

Box shut that idea out of her mind.

"Why didn't his wetware sedate him?" asked Revelstoke.

"There was separation," said the ship.

"We'll have to erase those memories," said Revelstoke.

"Of course."

"But..."

"I understand," said Pax. "There may be irreparable damage. Do what you can. Cost, we all agree, is no issue. Bring him back to us."

"We were responsible for poor Alois," said Kitou.

"We *are* responsible for him," said Brin.

"Amen that," said Pax.

5 ∞ ANDROFORM ALOIS

2056

The Water Bear slid into its dock, like a wasp invading a chrysalis. Box felt a swell of pride when she heard a worker whisper *Po warship* to another. This was *her* wasp. She had to admit it had a certain fuck-you beauty.

If Praxis was a thousand Manhattans, Avalon Station was all the worlds factories, as though the glowing entrails of a gas refinery had been strung along fifty kilometers of space. The hundreds of unmatching pieces were held together by a thread: a magnetic train that went from end to end in a minute. Pax said the string formation was intended to reduce its attack surface, since a string is harder to hit than a cube or a plate. To Box's eyes it looked happenstance, like a bristling industrial town, with life growing out of every crevice, or a rave party gone haywire. She found it intoxicating.

Pax Humana. That was the name the Avalonia gave to the centuries of peace, since the Tung had stopped trying to destroy Avalon Station, and instead chose to live there. Of course it wasn't called that at all. *Pax Humana* was how her wetware replayed it to her. She guessed it came from a far older language then Latin.

How long had the Tung been here? According to her wetware, six hundred years.

Since before Michelangelo's David.

Since Copernicus.

Now they were everywhere, wispy cartilaginous obscurities, air breathers, with the ability to turn corners using spat silk, and thus move much faster than humans in weightless conditions.

In another time and place, they'd be nightmare creatures.

Box was wearing their silk now, a confection of adaptive pashminas, just enough of it to be decent, perfect for the sweltering humidity. With a thought, she could whip them all into her hair and be naked, and no one on Avalon Station would notice. Sometimes she did, for the experience.

Kitou and Brin had cautiously surveyed the local bacchanalia, and assigned themselves to protection duty, and took turns outside Alois Buss's surgical suite.

Looking fly in police uniforms, thought Box.

The suite was in a mildly disreputable part of the Station, between gun shops and discothèques. The guns were more serious here than on the surface. They looked like military hardware. She got the sense that nothing couldn't be bought or sold in this place, with the right budget.

Alois was in the clonal phase of his treatment. The suite had extracted a single nucleus from his brain tissue, and implanted it in a donor egg, taken at random from Box, Brin or Kitou. One of them would become his biological mother. Gestation would take three days. Maturation, in which he became a viable human again, would take months.

The surgical suite was called Cloethe, and she was a citizen of Avalon Station: a cyborg of Tung manufacture, with a human personality. Box found her delightful.

Cloethe explained that restoring Alois's exact wiring was the objective.

"Not a problem, surgically," she said, "but culturally significant. Thousand worlds custom requires that a person has neurological continuity, or else they're a copy."

"So this brain?"

"Yes. This brain plus its personality."

"Why's that a thing?"

"Without continuity, the original is considered to have died, with all the moral, legal and emotional loss that entails."

"It's important to Alois?"

"Quite likely."

"I don't understand. What does continuity even mean? What about sleep? Is that continuous? What about coma?"

"It is. The key difference is tissue. Living brain tissue. Frozen is fine."

"You do a lot of this work?"

"It's my purpose."

"How does it feel, to have a purpose?"

"My prime directive is to desire it."

"A complicated answer."

"I'm a complicated person."

"How difficult is Alois's surgery?"

"Your ship did a very good job under the circumstances, but I have to consider every neuron. It will take me a month, of carefully sequenced surgery and recovery, to restore the same person."

"When will he be awake?"

"I plan to briefly revive him tomorrow."

"Tomorrow? Really?"

"Yes, and I need you all to be there. His friends. It's vital."

"We'll be there," she said.

"Alois?"

"Ship? Where am I?"

"You were in an accident."

They were all together in the visiting room of the surgical suite, which resembled a mortuary, with drawers where Box imagined the bodies were kept. Box felt cheated. For 25 kg of gold, she'd expected equipment. A Swiss rejuv clinic would've handled this more theatrically.

"Big accident?"

"Yes."

Alois's brain was nowhere to be seen. She tried not to imagine its condition.

A soup, becoming a stew.

"Ship," said the brain through a speaker, "I can't see or feel anything. Are the others alright?"

"Yes," said the ship. She was physically present, wearing her androform body, which mirrored her gamespace persona.

"What's my prognosis?" asked Alois.

"Optimal," said the ship.

"How long?"

"Alois," interrupted Pax.

"Pax, my good friend. How are you?"

"I'm well," he said. "I'm here with the team."

"How is Threnody?"

"What do you remember?"

"I remember going to bed."

"Threnody is gone."

"Gone?"

"Details later."

"The Fa:ing?"

"Safe, as far as we know. Escaped through their wormhole."

"Down the rabbit hole."

"Yes."

Alois sighed, despite having nothing to sigh through. It was a forlorn burst of white noise.

"All those years," he said.

"Validated, Alois."

"Yes, I suppose that's true. And me?"

"Growing a new body."

"Am I a backup?"

"No, we got your physical brain. You're real."

"Well, thank goodness for that."

"Now you should rest."

Box spent her days on the planet, haunting the souk and the coffee shops. Avalon was starting its high summer, and the city was steaming. She'd taken to wearing the local dishdasha, in place of her adaptive skinsuit, or her Tung scarves, which would've got her arrested. There was monsoonal rain, heavy and warm, then baking hot cobbles and concrete, so hot they hissed in the sunshine.

Box loved this place. She could live here forever. She learnt the rhythms of the market. Every day, before dawn, the ships would arrive in the harbor. They were real ships, wind powered ocean vessels, sailing over the water from places unknown. They'd unload in the docks. Some of it would go to the markets. Some would disappear on lorries, bound for places unknown.

Why did this happen?

Why was this city here?

Revelstoke provided answers.

Far from being kleptocrats, he said, the Avalon Cpy had saved their world, and its economy, from the ravages of Smear economics. "Spacers need a place to invest in," he said. "Agreeable and properly managed. This is that place. It's good business."

"A place where the trains run on time," said Box.

"There are no trains here," said Revelstoke.

They were relaxed on a beach. The tumbling waves were like carbonated milk crashing. The sand was made of seashells, miniscule crabs and bivalves, so silky-soft it was like talcum powder.

[Biogenic silica,] said her wetware.

She'd decided that Revelstoke was attractive, in a craggy, Sherlock Holmes kind of way.

"And besides," he said. "The oligarchs are real people. They don't want their home to become a sordid little appendix to a spaceport."

"So, they get filthy rich," she said.

"Of course," said Revelstoke. "Why not?"

"It's unequal."

"Why should anything be equal?"

"There's no freedom here."

"Political freedom is the illusion of freedom."

"Says the secret policeman."

"Dr Box, the Po are the secret police."

"Humph, maybe so."

The skin of the Water Bear came away like a veil, to reveal the workings beneath. First it was swarming with Tung; then she was naked.

She was *dense*.

[Half of me is battery,] she said, [and half is processor. My humans live in the other half.] She was only half joking.

Her chassis was a billet of titanium, into which cavities had been drilled, to accept interchangeable parts. Those parts were being replaced. Box was with Pax, looking down from a gantry. Kitou was playing the Geometry Game, deep inside the gutted chassis, with a half-dozen Tung workers. For once, she was hopelessly outclassed.

"Nine years?" asked Box.

Pax nodded. It would take them nine years to reach Fluxor, at the Water Bear's cruising warp speed, although they planned to make a few stops along the way. Her crew would sleep, in stasis.

"It's like time travel," she said.

"Yes," said Pax. "It is a form of time travel."

"Did it take you nine years, the last time you went there?"

"The defense of the planet?" asked Pax. "No, we were given a ride."

"On a lightship?"

"No, the Xap carried us there."

"A Tung in a bar told me the Xap are a myth, an invention of the Thousand worlds Civics."

Pax laughed. Like all the sound he produced, it was a bassline. "Yes, that's one theory. Like all negatives, easily disproved."

"You've seen a Xap?"

"I have."

"What are they like?"

"They're the most interesting beings."

"Tell me more."

Pax shook his head. "Your turn will come."

She laughed. "You tease."

He laughed back. "The process by which a story unfolds can be as revealing as the story itself."

"Did I say that?"

"Among other things."

"Did I really make a pass at you?"

Pax and she had spent a night on the surface below, in the Otel room. She remembered strong liquor, and fumbling.

"You did," he said. "I was a perfect gentleman."

"A perfect gentleman would've performed as I requested."

"For that, you'll have to wait till after the mission."

Revelstoke invited them into his home, which was in the decommissioned weapons blister of a gun emplacement. The Po soldiers were interested in this. Personal weapons were easily dismissed, but there was no arguing with a house-sized hydrogen maser.

He'd brought platters of Avalonian street food, with murmured apologies for not having made it himself. There were soft, nutty rolls, and vine leaves baked around chewy cephalopods, and sweetmeats, and bone-dry, fizzing white wine, and the ubiquitous sausages.

"Why would the Po send a mathematician to this forsaken place?" he asked, when the food was all eaten. His apartment overlooked the central bazaar. Box could see the café where they'd been arrested, and the hill where Kitou had outrun her pursuers.

"I'm not even a Po," he said.

"To count all the money?" she asked.

"Very droll. You trusted me with your secrets. I'll trust you with mine. I was sent here to solve an urgent cryptology problem."

Alois Buss looked up at that. He was present in his ambulatory body: a metal skeleton, which Box found uncannier than any alien. Alois had spent most of the meal, pushing a single pastry disconsolately around his plate.

Revelstoke conjured up two beings in a holodisplay. One was an opulently beautiful woman, the other a humanoid reptilian.

"These are Thesps," he said.

[I'm not aware of that species,] said Alois.

"It isn't a species," said Revelstoke. "It's a performance artform."

"They have a disease," he said. "A cryptographic virus, called the Thespian disease, and it's killing them."

The party precincts of Avalon Station were the most dissolute places Box could imagine. The nakedness was just the start of it. There was willful abandon. They could be in wartime Berlin, or Imperial Rome, except that parts were in freefall, and parts were in gravity. Night fell like a switch. Unlike Praxis, which floated at the confluence of gravity waves, Avalon Station was in a geostationary orbit. One moment

Xerxes' star was filling the Station with blazing light, then it was hidden behind the planet. Adjacent to the party zones was the theater district. This was where the Thesps were to be found.

Box was thrilled to be out with her friends. They dressed for the event. Alois's skeleton was entwined with black ribbons, and Kitou had found it a top hat to wear. Kitou had reprised her emerald pajamas from the Pnyx. Box wore her baroque judo suit. They'd chosen a play, whose cultural nuances escaped her, despite the best efforts of her wetware to translate it. It seemed to consist of three people, in a room, talking elliptically about nothing.

One was a ghost. The other two were partygoers.

Or all three of them were ghosts.

Like Japanese cinema, she decided.

Her companions seemed equally baffled.

Revelstoke took them backstage. This meant going into the street, then through a nondescript door, into a hidden part of the Station.

"This precinct is called Backstage," he explained. "It's a shared service area."

Here there was gravity. Box's heels clacked dully on dull metal.

Box could see the players from their show, disrobing.

Bacchanalia, on the cusp of beginning.

Backstage was gloomily lit, and full of dramatic shadows. Revelstoke clicked his fingers, and a streetlight ambled towards them.

Box giggled. This was fun.

Revelstoke explained that this was the oldest part of the Station, which had originally been an orbital brothel, out of reach of the laws of the city. The rest of Avalon

Station had grown from the embryo of the bordello, to become first a dormitory, then a factory, then part of a planetary defense system, and now this.

He took them to a rundown house, that appeared to survive by leaning on the houses beside it, where he knocked on a door, which was opened by a reptile. He was a beautiful being, almost two meters tall. Box knew he was a he, by his astonishing genitalia.

"Flex," said Revelstoke. "These are the covert operatives I talked about. They've been working on a problem like yours."

Box sensed Revelstoke was pleading. There was a backstory here.

The reptilian sighed, and let them in.

Flex's partner was called Salmonella Dysonsphere, and she was a shadow of her former beauty. Where she'd been a big woman, now she was emaciated. She reminded Box of a famine victim, in a society where there was no scarcity.

Flex proved to be a demonstratively tender person. He took his lover's hand, and wept openly.

[Flex is a Span,] said the ship in Box's sensorium.

[Hey, Water Bear. What are we doing here?]

[I don't know,] said the ship.

The dying woman lay in an unmade bed, in a clothes-strewn room, and she was barely conscious. She was murmuring, incessantly, with feverish energy. Her boudoir resembled a proscenium stage, with chairs around the bed for an audience, and sliding theater flats behind. Tonight, the room was set as a forest, with shafts of sunlight falling through majestic trees. Box could see it'd been set that way to give the poor woman some peace.

"Alois," said Revelstoke. "This is mainly for you." He projected symbols in their heads: page after page of abstruse mathematics.

They reminded Box of the blackboards from Threnody. They had a *shape* that even she could recognize.

The skeleton clacked. [Where did this come from?] it asked.

"From an autopsy," said Revelstoke.

[Yes,] said Buss. [It's like the Fa:ing number.]

"It *is* the Fa:ing number," said Revelstoke. "Or I think so. But seen from a different angle."

[Yes,] said Buss. [I see what you mean. Its simpler. Like a weaponized version.]

"What can you do?" asked the Span. His voice was pitched as low as his testicles suggested.

Buss said, [Let me think.]

[Why Avalon?] asked Buss, after they left the woman and her partner to their suffering.

[And why the Thesps, of all people?]

"Good questions," said Revelstoke. "I don't know the answers. That's why I'm here. So far, I've failed. So, you see, our tasks are somehow related."

They were returning through the backstreets of Backstage, followed by their streetlight, casting looming shadows in the encroaching darkness. Box felt like a thief, stealing glimpses of shows, seen through half-exposed theater sets.

Just a few meters away, though meter-thick steel walls, the party was only beginning. Here, behind the scenes, it was quiet.

All they could hear was the sounds of their voices, and the clack of their heels on the roadway.

The skeleton clacked again.

[Why didn't I know about this?

[Why didn't the thousand worlds tell me?

[Let me get back into a human body, with my real brain,] he said. [And then I'll see what I can do. We might have already solved this problem. How long does she have?]

"Salmonella? A few days."

[Merde. Then there's no chance to save her.]

"Why?"

[I'm months from a full recovery.]

The Water Bear said, [Alois?]

[Yes?]

[You remember I have a full backup of you?]

"This is exceedingly strange," said Alois, holding up a hand in front of him. The Water Bear had installed a copy of Alois Buss's full consciousness in her androform body, which was a military cyborg, with ship-level wetware.

[This raises complex legal issues,] she explained. [A restored copy is a person, and it has rights. You have rights. We can't just turn you off now.]

The new Alois smiled. "Astonishing," he said.

[It's a very good body,] said the ship. [Ready for combat. Please don't break it.]

"I was referring to your brain."

[It has ship wetware.]

"You're like this, all the time?"

"Better."

Buss laughed. "My goodness. Now I have ship envy."

Brin and Kitou grinned. They loved this development. Since his sacrifice, and his brave way of dealing with it, Alois Buss had gone from being a mildly eccentric passenger, to their hero. If he hadn't been before, then he was a part of the Hand of the Water Bear now.

Pax arched one eyebrow.

"So," he said. "The disease?"

"In 2135," said androform Alois, "with the help of sixty more years of crypto research, we'd begun to understand that the Fa:ing number wasn't a problem at all, but an attempt at an answer. It's a question the Fa:ing have been working on asking for centillions of years. Essentially, it's trying to infer our universe from its ending conditions, working backwards in time. A task of immense computational difficulty, since in theory a whole universe is needed to model its own state.

"But it's done very well. It's found you, Dr Box, which seems to be a milestone.

"It's also sentient, although we already knew that, but not in the way we'd imagined.

"Consider this. The Fa:ing number sees time backwards. Your Hopf number, Dr Box, is no longer in it, because it's in their future. To them, we're the time traveling aliens. Us bringing you to Threnody allowed them to find you. You're not part of the answer. You're part of the question."

"I have no idea what you're talking about," said Box.

Alois nodded. "Understandably.

"But

that's beside the point. We don't have to *understand* the Fa:ing number to know how to use it. We've been harvesting its symbols for decades. Felix, does the Thespian disease begin with bad dreams?"

"Yes," said Revelstoke.

"Can you describe them?"

"Not from experience."

"But?"

"Like nothing."

"Like our end-time war?"

"I had made that connection."

"Those are our dreams too," said Kitou.

"Followed by... a fugue state?" asked Buss.

"Yes," said Revelstoke. "Dissociative fugue, then psychosis, and death."

"Those are symptoms of the Fa:ing number in its terminal phase," said Alois. "Think of it as crowdsourcing neurons. The computation uses up all the brain's processing capacity. First, sleep suffers. Then mental disturbance. Neurosis. Dementia. Finally, death as the lizard brain is consumed by the task.

"Left unattended, the Fa:ing number would kill people, just like the Thespian disease is."

"How do we stop it?" asked Revelstoke.

"Simple," said Buss. "By surgery.

"It's just a few cells, in the occipital and parietal lobes of the brain. An organ. We literally call it the Antenna."

"We?" asked Box.

Androform Alois nodded.

"Have you had this operation, Alois?" she asked.

"I have, and I'll probably have it again."

"Do you know how to perform it?"

"No, but I bet Cloethe does."

Later, when Revelstoke had gone to find Cloethe, Box took Alois to one side.

"Why the Thesps?" she asked. "Why performers? Do you have any ideas?"

"I'd have to reach for hypotheticals."

"Please."

"The virus is conscious. It seeks to succeed. The most successful virus is the one that infects the most hosts, not the one that kills the most victims."

"So the Thesps are infectious?"

"Not in the terminal phase. But they once were, or the disease wouldn't spread. I think the mode of transmission is ideas. The same ideas, repeated over and over."

"You mean they've been infecting their audiences?"

"That'd be an elegant virus."

"How long has this been happening?"

"Diseases have phases. Revelstoke's been here two years. That's just the terminal phase. Quite a lot longer. Years. Maybe decades."

"That's a lot of audiences."

"Yes."

"Where do they come from? Who comes here?"

"Everyone, eventually."

"Why is it killing the Thesps?"

"Why does any successful pathogen destroy its host?"

"Because it's already served its purpose?"

"A terrifying idea."

Cloethe made house calls. She arrived outside the Dysonsphere brownstone, wearing a birdlike androform woman, with an acoustic scalpel engineered into one hand.

"Is that all you need?" asked Box.

"Ample," she said.

Inside Salmonella's boudoir, which now resembled a nautical scene, with seafarers waving cutlasses at sea monsters, the surgeon waved her scalpel at the dying actor. Dysonsphere's eyes flicked open, then fluttered shut, and she sank into a calm sleep.

"There," said Cloethe.

"She's cured?" asked Flex.

"Yes," the surgeon said briskly. "When she wakes, give her something nourishing to drink. Then love, plenty of love. She was lost, now she's home. She needs to know that."

A printout emerged from her breast pocket.

"Get this script filled, and visit me. This is for her nutrition.

"You people," she said to the Po team. "If you'd only told me about this earlier, I could've saved others."

"We didn't know," said Revelstoke.

"Why didn't you?"

"We are where we are," rumbled Pax.

"Leave out the homilies, young homo sapiens," she said. "Do you know what your species' problem is? Too much secrecy."

"I'm sorry," said Revelstoke. "Our investigations should've converged before this."

"You're supposed to be the great strategists. Space help us if that's true. It took two heads being banged together by randomness to make this connection. It took Alois's head to be turned to soup. How do you explain that? Do you know how angry this makes me? How can you hope to solve the actual problem, if you don't talk?"

"What actual problem is that?" asked Pax.

"The end-time war?"

"How do you know about that?"

"How do you think I know, master Navigator? Because I rewired every goddamn synapse in Alois Buss's space-forsaken brain."

"Then we must swear you to silence."

"Or what?"

Box said, "Cloethe, please."

The doctor scowled. "I'm outraged, Ophelia."

"You have every right to be."

"Humans," she said.

"I know."

"All those poor Thesps."

"I know."

"Do we have to worry about Cloethe?" asked Pax.

"No," said Revelstoke. "Leave her to me. She only has the best interests of her people in mind."

"A dangerous mindset," said Pax.

"Thumbscrews?" asked Box.

Revelstoke scowled.

"How are we going for money?" asked Pax.

"We have none."

"How are you paying for this?"

"Credit, and favors."

"Your credit?"

"Yes, and my favors."

"Then it's time to get going," said Pax.

"Yes," said Revelstoke. "It is. Your refurbished chariot awaits you."

"Alois?"

"Please take the androform copy. It's already asked my permission. I don't want it around here. Merge the real one later."

"Alright," said Pax. "Then let's do it."

The Water Bear was whole again. To Box's eye, she looked unchanged, but now she was configured to cross 3,000 light-years of space, to Fluxor and back, with a detour to Praxis. This was her long configuration.

In the last few hours before departing, Box visited Cloethe.

"Dr Box," said the surgical suite.

"Cloethe, thank you for healing Alois. You healed me too. All of us."

"Thank you, Ophelia. This is what I do. Sometimes, it's more than what I do. This is one of those times."

"I'm sorry about the Antenna."

"I know, it isn't your fault. It isn't the fault of any of you. It's the way humans operate. The apotheosis of the individual. It's your strength, and your weakness."

"Take care of Alois," said Box.

"Has anyone said, take care of yourself?"

"Heh, I've heard it before."

"You have a good heart, Ophelia Box."

"You think so?"

"I know it."

6 ∞ RISK

2056

The car hummed powerfully from lane to lane, pressing her down in her seat. Curtains of rain fell through forests of glimmering towers. Fast trains flowed like quicksilver between island conurbations. Each turn opened a new vista. It was like all her adolescent dreams of an advanced, spacefaring civilization.

Five hundred million souls, in a cube.

Praxis.

It was Box's first look at the orbital city, after her brief glimpse, six weeks before. If she narrowed her eyes, it looked like lambent forests of glass. Pax said the appearance of floaty architectural disconnectedness was an illusion.

"This is a stiff structure, as befits a starship," he said.

"This place can move?" she asked.

"Far across the galaxy, if need be. In a serious emergency, this spacecraft could reach Andromeda, in a series of hyperluminal jumps."

"The art of running away?"

"An excellent strategy, for a city."

They'd entered through the docks that speckled one side of the cube. These vast industrial works made Avalon seem like a roadside garage. Box watched a ship being repaired: a teardrop-shaped lozenge, the size of a mountain.

"A municipal project," said Pax, "built here by the local community of spacers."

"Where does it go to?"

"It's a deep space exploration vessel. It goes where it likes."

The Water Bear had reached into her bag of disguises, and become a small tramp freighter, battered and tough, with gases venting from welds.

"Good luck," she'd said, before departing.

Now they were on their own.

[Ophelia Box?] said a voice in her head.

[Praxis?]

[No, this is the Aldebaran Orbiter, the vehicle that carries Praxis through space. Praxis has chosen to be unaware of you.]

[Did we do something wrong?]

[No, you're on a covert operation.]

[But you can see us.]

[I lack the city's talent for self-deception.]

[Zing.]

[I'm pleased you have a sense of humor.]

[I'm glad you do too.]

[Welcome to Aldebaran. Call me if you need me. Remember, I'm a ship.]

[You mean you kick ass?]

[I can.]

Their safe house was an apartment, set high in a dormitory zone of the city. Alois and Pax confirmed it was perfectly ordinary, as a safe house should be. It backed onto rice paddies, which Box could see were the terraced rooftops of adjacent buildings. If she looked through the gap between the buildings, she could see Aldebaran spaceport, kilometers below.

Back where she'd started from.

Kitou threw herself on a couch, like an Earthly teenager would, and powered up a wall-sized entertainment system. The room filled with thumping music, like a mix between grindcore and Icelandic trance. Onscreen, performers bowed and banged and plucked at their instruments, while a crowd waved its hands in the air.

"Churn," said Kitou, brightly.

"I like it," said Box.

Androform Alois was doing just fine, in his dual role as the passenger and occasional captain of the Water Bear's cyborg remote. Today he was the captain. You could tell by his beatific expression. He sat beside Kitou, and smiled at the music.

Box asked him the reason for his good mood.

"It's because I'm a new person," he said. "Without this mission, I'd never have existed."

[Alois is an ideal houseguest,] said the Water Bear, from her listening post, five thousand kilometers away.

122

"That's easy for you to say," said her remote.

"As long as he doesn't move in," said Box.

[I can always make another androform body,] said the Water Bear.

Alois ignored them, and smiled.

For three days they wargamed their mission, testing assumptions, rehearsing the angles.

"We're here to commit a serious crime," said Pax. "Let's waste no time on the ethics of that. Sometimes, we work in strange places. This is such an occasion.

"Given time, we could do it in secret. No one would know we were here. No one would know the money was gone. But we don't have the time, so we need some support."

"I propose to make contact with the local crime syndicates," he said. "These will have already been penetrated by Po intelligence, although I don't know the details. I'll find out. We have signals."

"More bar fights?" asked Box.

"No," said Pax. This is a more complicated society. A particular commercial transaction will occur."

"I intend to sell you as a slave," he explained.

"What?"

Pax and Box were sitting relaxed in an open-air brasserie, in a park below their apartment, among happy families, with laughing children running through. The last of the afternoon rain was being deflected by shadesails. A freshness filled the air. The aroma of flowers and grass, and delicious food being cooked.

Pax summoned a waitress, about Kitou's age.

"Hi," she said.

"Hello," said Pax. "What's your name?"

"Sophie," she smiled.

"Why are you here, Sophie?"

"Why am I working?"

"Yes."

Her smile increased by a few thousand watts. "I'm saving for my grand tour," she said. "Would you like to order?"

"Yes," said Box. "We're ravenous."

"What was that about?" Box asked, when Sophie left with their orders.

"I want to introduce our economics.

"We live in what you might call a post-scarcity society. The state provides what people need, but not all they want. That's a deliberate choice. Effortless societies are unstable. They select for decadent behaviors. As pleasant as that might be for a while, it's no way to run a civilization.

"So, we encourage people to contribute. Sophie is contributing. In return, she receives money."

"Which she can spend on her tour," said Box.

"Exactly," said Pax. "And with it a sense of accomplishment. No one gave her that tour. She earned it. Anyone can look in the history of her money, and see it."

"I like it," said Box.

"Thus, as well as being a post-scarcity society, we're also a quasi-capitalist, socialist, utopian one."

"You saucy devils."

"We must also deal with other societies. Thus we have trade, diplomacy, and war, usually in combinations of two. That means our currency has an extrinsic value."

"So... you have crime?"

"Yes. We have organized crime, and a black market for all kinds of goods."

Evening was gathering, and with it a powerful sense of expectancy. Box could feel it in the air, like electricity. Cities were cities, and this was the mother of cities. Lanterns lit up among the trees. Partygoers were gathering on the cantilevered boulevards. A happy clattering spilled out of the kitchen. Sophie returned with their meal, and the particulars of her travel itinerary, to show them.

"The Magellanic Clouds?" asked Pax. "That's an expedition, not a tour."

"It's a grand tour," said the girl.

Box recommended a hotel, in Avalon. "It's nothing flash," she said. "But it overlooks a perfect street market, and the people there are lovely."

"You've been to the *Smear*?" asked the girl, wide-eyed.

At that point, Box might've exploded with pleasure.

"My friend is from Earth," said Pax.

"You're shittin' me?"

"No, no shit," said Pax.

"You made her day," said Box, later, after Sophie left with their empty dishes.

"The gratuity will make her day," said Pax.

"We aren't law enforcement," said Pax, "We probably break more laws than we uphold. But there is a crime we take a direct interest in: slavery."

The paddy field was larger, and wilder than she'd thought from above. During the growing season it'd be flooded. Now it was lush. Box heard tiny animals rustling near her feet. She'd taken the liberty of entwining her hand in his.

"Why?"

"Because it falls in the gaps between societies."

"Where you people operate?"

"Yes, we're uniquely placed to police it, so we make it our business. It's also an assault on those least able to protect themselves. Praxis is a center of human trafficking."

"Seriously?"

"Yes, in part because we help make it so. We cultivate the conditions for certain crimes to exist here."

"A honey trap?"

"Not quite, no. A market intervention."

Box frowned. "But Pax," she said. "for that to work, there has to be actual honey. People must be sold. You end up policing a trade that only exists because of your intervention."

Pax nodded. "We understand the complexities, yet we grasp the calculation."

"You mean you buy and sell people."

"We do. What choice is there? To condemn a larger number to the same fate by our inaction would be immoral."

She shook her head.

"There's no such thing as a moral dilemma," he said. "Only a lack of moral clarity.

She sighed.

"I know there'll be a Po agent," he continued. "At or near the top of the slave trade here. I need that person's help. Specifically, I want a dark way out of the city, so we can escape, once the robbery is complete. A coded signal will be deployed, like the barfight signal on Avalon. I'll offer to sell a human woman – you - after betting a perfect number of Praxic cryptos on Bolo. 8,126, which signifies the utmost secrecy."

"What's a perfect number?"

"In mathematics, a positive integer that is equal to the sum of its proper divisors."

"You learn something new every day. And Bolo?"

"A bloodsport."

"Can it possibly get worse?"

"It can, and it does. I'll be betting on Black Bolo, an illegal death sport."

"Seriously?"

"Yes."

They boarded a train, that rose from a vertical platform, slowly at first, then with increasing speed, until they were spearing into the heart of the city.

"Now this is cool," said Box.

Polyhedral towers gave way to onion domes, then slippery lozenges, then neogothic follies, like a flickering architectural slideshow.

"Fashion," said Pax, following her startled glances. "Changing over the centuries."

She'd decided she liked Praxis almost as much as Avalon. It wasn't as exotic, or as strikingly alien. It was like any great city on Earth, until a vista opened, and the cityscape marched to infinity. Then, it was magnificent.

After just a few minutes, they reached their destination. A dripping-wet metal plain shone dully overhead, like nothing else she'd seen here. It was pitted and rough, like she imagined an asteroid might be. It was like the emerald city had a pig-iron core, and they were about to climb into its belly.

"Warning," said a voice. "Please disembark now. You've reached the Deregulated Zone."

They stepped onto an escalator. For a few dizzying moments, Box wondered if the Orbiter was messing with her wetware, replaying her cultural references.

She came to her senses.

This place was real.

The air above the metal plain was warmer than the city below, and steamy, so that water beaded on every surface. And crowded. People of every size, shape and ethnicity; every imaginable body modification. Not just humans. Chimeric beings wore bristles and fur. Aliens, like on Avalon Station. Music spilled out from bars and floating soundsystems.

Instead of buildings were machines: huge turbines that must've once delivered services to the city below, and were now infested with people. It was as though life here had adapted to survive in the spaces between.

And information. Everywhere, neon, or neon-equivalents. Holograms. Interference patterns in the air. Steam from vents that shimmered to conjure up advertisements. Drones buzzing in her ear. Subliminal displays, neutralized by her wetware.

Box was fascinated. "This was how I imagined space would be," she said.

"The original Orbiter," said Pax. "With all its imperfections. Ten thousand years ago, all human space was like this, so in a sense you're right. This is how space was."

"Why are people... so much poorer here?"

"They're not," said Pax. "The style is a choice. The Praxis DRZ is among the wealthiest places in the human galaxy."

They found a basement bar, smoke-filled and as crowded as the street outside, built in the bearings of an outsize electric motor. People of every gender looked on disinterestedly as they found a table near the middle of the floor. A pulsing arrow said, **Sex**. A half-dressed couple copulated in a corner.

She noted abstractly that here she was again, doing Po business, in another slaphouse.

"Now," said Pax. "This is where it becomes interesting. Don't look, but do you see those two men over there?"

Box looked in her wetware, which opened a window on her peripheral vision.

"The goons with the Soviet haircuts?"

"Yes, they've been following us."

"Is that normal?"

"No, but I permitted it to happen."

"They're the police?"

"Yes, and we're going to make a run for it."

"Why?"

"Trust me."

She nodded, remembering Revelstoke and his three knuckleheads.

"First, some instructions. If we get separated, trust the Orbiter, completely. If you're arrested, go quietly. Say nothing. We'll come and get you."

"I can't believe I'm doing this."

Why was she so nervous? Did she trust Pax? Of course. He was the most capable person imaginable.

It was the lack of the Water Bear. No amount of human competence could make up for an omnipresent warship with gravity drives.

"Trust me," said Pax.

She nodded.

"Remember the market in Avalon. The worst that can happen is you spend a few hours in a cell. The real powers here are all on your side. You'll be fine."

"Okay."

"Dr Box, relax."

"I am relaxed," she lied.

"I need to give you some wetware," he said. "Look straight in my eyes."

She felt a slight shiver. Now she was two people. She was Ophelia Box, and she was also a woman called Pris, from the Trappist-1 confederacy.

"My god, I have a *backstory.*"

She was here to sold, as a consensual slave.

For six months.

Six months.

A timeshare agreement. Someone gets part of her life. She gets part of the money.

Not enough of the money.

"It's called a wirewall," said Pax. "Military spec. It will stand up to the most intrusive scanning. All you have to do is get in character."

Pax was called Ray, and he was a small-time crook, and a part-time human trafficker.

A despicable piece of shit.

"You see?"

She nodded.

"Otherwise, stay close and follow my lead.

"Okay, let's start. I want you to stand up when I do, and have a good look at those two police officers. Don't stare, but I want them to know you see them."

"Why, *Ray?*"

"To put them off balance. Law enforcement works best in managed encounters, where they can fall back on their systems. A regular person would avoid eye contact. You eyeballing them takes us outside the soft part of the bell curve. By displaying unpredictability, we gain an advantage."

She snorted derision.

Since when did Ray know anything?

"Let's go."

Ray stood up. Pris turned around and gave the cops the evil eye. They - or men like them - were why she was here. They glanced away, then turned and stared right back at her. She got up and followed her owner. Ray moved expertly. He got the bulk of the bar between him and the goons, then turned into an open doorway. Pris followed, and Ray locked the door behind them. They sprinted headlong down an unlit alleyway. There was a crash, and then the goons reappeared, fifty meters behind them. Pris wasn't sure who she hated the most, Ray or the cops.

The cops, she decided.

Better the devil you know, eh?

They ducked into a smaller alleyway, then down a rickety letterbox of stairs. The goons clattered past overhead.

A door slid open in a wall.

"In," said Ray.

They were in a freight elevator.

With a surge of conventional power, the car ascended.

"You can come out of character now."

Box giggled with nervous energy. She hadn't outrun the *gendarmerie* like that since Marseilles, a decade before.

"How did you know to do all that?" she asked.

"The Orbiter helped me."

"Where now?"

"To Core."

Core was a ragged sphere of cargo nets, strung inside an iron-nickel cube. Between the nets and the walls of the cube were rows of stadium seats. There were a dozen people there, scattered in the seats. Box watched a man light powdery drugs in a pipe, and suck on it greedily, before passing it on.

"What is this place?"

"The belly of the beast, where the Praxis asteroid was first hollowed out, fifteen thousand years ago. Each face of the arena has its own version of down. Inside the netting is zero-gravity, curving towards gravity at the edges."

"Is that where your death sport is played?"

"Yes. When they play Black Bolo here, the net is removed. It isn't just the players who die. Tonight, there's what you'd call an illegal rave."

"Oh, are we going to that?"

"No, we're waiting for someone to come and take my bet."

"Shame," she said.

"Get back in character, please."

She was Pris again.

The man who came for Ray's money looked like any Trappist-1 accountant, a slicked-back cunt in an expensive suit. Pris hated him instantly. She figured the suit's suit was worth twice what she was. Bodies like hers were what paid for it.

Ray got in line and waited. Pris was surprised by his meekness, his subservience in the face of a higher criminal authority. No trash talk was exchanged. He simply handed over a package. Hard Praxic rubles, and with it a business proposal.

Offering *her*.

The street accountant moved on to his next easy mark. Ray grabbed her, not unkindly by the arm, and led her down a broad stairway, and out of the arena, into the street, and into a bar, called the Arse, as far as she could tell. As a non-citizen, her rudimentary wetware was comically poor at translation.

She didn't give a fuck. It was a bar.

Ray wasn't so bad, she decided. She was starting to miss him already. Her new owner could be anyone.

It was only for six months.

If she lived that long.

She was on her third drink, a fiery local rocket fuel called unpronounceable, and just starting to feel sexy, when the boss man arrived, all gold teeth and a practiced, piratical grin.

She knew him.

No, not as Pris. As Box.

This was a man from her real past, on Earth.

[In character,] warned Pax in her head.

The man was in a cocaine-colored limousine, the biggest car Pris had ever seen, although that wasn't saying much, with her just a pleasure model from the boondocks.

The car rose into the night.

"Ant de Large," she said.

Ophelia Box had first met Anthony de Largentaye in Brixton, in 2069, six years ago. He was a clubbing impresario, a well-known fixer, a man famous for being famous. She was a girl about town, just over from Paris.

She'd been his posh totty; except she was never posh.

Except it wasn't six years ago.

It was in his future.

"Do I know you?" he asked.

"Oh, fuck," she said.

"Do know this man?" asked Pax.

"Not here," warned Ant. "The walls really do have ears."

The limousine surged down narrow streets, descending through a labyrinth of diagonal subways, until they stopped outside a nightclub. It was uncannily like Brixton, 2069. There was even a queue of bright-eyed partygoers, craning their necks to see who emerged from the car.

The neon sign said *Leopardskin Moon*.

Ant's office was suspended over a crowded dancefloor: a transparent cube, with a transparent desk, powdery with party drugs. Praxis-does-London, down to the lasers strobing over the writhing bodies of the dancers below. Pounding dance music – it could've been churn – made it impossible to talk in the room.

Ant waved his hand, and the music faded away.

"Do you two know each other?" said Pax.

"Never seen her before," said Ant.

"Yeah, I know him," said Box.

"Then," said Pax, "you're from his future."

"What d'you mean," said Ant, "from my future?"

Pax transferred the details of their mission, using de Largentaye's public key, just received from the Water Bear, so only the real Ant de Large could read it.

The first shimmy in a cryptography twostep.

"Can your ship send me a signed and encrypted message, confirming all that?" said Ant.

Pax nodded. Then, Ant said, "Okay, I'll get whatever you need."

"Easy as that?" asked Box.

"You want hard?"

"My part in this is done," said Pax. "Ant, you know how to reach me. I'll rejoin my crew."

"What about me?" asked Box.

"My backstory requires that you stay here a while."

"How long?"

"A few hours."

"Seriously?"

"Brin will come and act as your buyer."

134

"Yeah, I'll look forward to it."

Pax exchanged a brief look with the other man.

"Pax, did you know about this?" she asked.

"Emphatically not."

"Why 'Anthony de Largentaye'?" she asked, after Pax had left the building.

"It's an alias I use."

"On Earth?"

He shrugged, an uncomfortable gesture. She could sense the cogs of their story meshing in his head.

"You're really a Po spy?" she asked.

"Lo, actually."

"What's your real name?"

"You know I can't tell you that."

"You really don't know me?"

He shook his head, no less uncomfortably.

She crossed to a wall of his office. Through the glass the dancefloor heaved. She pressed a hand against the wall, and felt the syncopated beat. Yes, it was churn. She wished she was down there.

"I slept with you, Ant."

"Yeah, I figured that out."

"So now you go and fuck me in London? Is that how it works?"

"I honestly don't know how it works."

She pressed her head against the glass. Now, more than for years, she really wanted some ecstasy.

"What would you do with a real Ray and Pris?"

"Pris would be quietly saved, if we can possibly swing it that way. She might have some adventures, but she'd get through them okay."

"And Ray?"

"If Ray brings his business to me, we might bankroll him. Let him rise through the ranks. It depends."

"Where's the payback in that?"

Ant shrugged. "In the wild world, babe, it's never about payback. There's just less-bad choices. My job is to help people."

Less bad choices. Maybe this mission wasn't as straightforward as she'd thought it'd be.

It was bright night in the scintillating avenues of the city. The rain had departed, leaving the skyways like glass. The car hummed as it swooped through the traffic. Box and Brin were wearing business suits. Kitou was dressed in casual streetwear. They were here to play victims. The Water Bear had infected their wetware with a plausibly virulent virus.

"Military grade malware," said the ship. "Enough to absolutely terrify them."

The ship's remote was back in command of her androform self. Pax and the ship were dressed in exaggerated military finery. Pax's uniform was Po black, festooned with medals and braids. On his lapels were his carbon-black starbursts. The ship's uniform was pristine white.

The ship admitted the uniforms were overwrought.

"Sometimes it pays to exaggerate," she said. "Although some Po might like them." With her cropped blonde hair and cyborg's physique, she looked imperious.

"They're going to think the Water Bear is the battleship Potemkin," said Box.

The ship laughed. "Should I have a dueling scar?" she asked.

Box said, "Don't overdo it."

She could barely believe she was riding into action with her friends, in this astonishing place. For a moment, as she watched the lights and mist flash by the car windows, she was overcome with emotion.

She started to cry.

It wasn't for sorrow. She didn't know what it was. A perverse kind of melancholy. Maybe it was for joy. Where has this been, all my life?

Kitou, sensing her mood, leaned up close. Brin took her hand.

Mission specialist Box.

This was fantastic.

The plan was straightforward. They'd go into the bank and ask for the money. Since a basic information check would instantly reveal that Pax didn't exist, they would take the city offline, by declaring a malware infection.

Po ships had the power to do this.

Po ships were considered incorruptible.

The Civics would then have to choose. They might've already chosen. This plan hinged on their tacit acceptance. A saddle point. Without it, they had better be fast. They estimated they had a window of about five minutes, from when the infection was first reported, until an intervening authority could override the local law enforcement systems and launch a pursuit.

Five minutes was two sigmas, which included about 95 percent of the data.

So, they might have to be faster.

The bank at Praxis was *the* bank, Pax said. "We only have one bank in our society, and this is its office."

The half-mile-high atrium was clearly meant to impress. What wasn't made of polished stone, was made of unobtanium. Box took up her assigned position, in the exact geometric center of the public space.

This was a clue for the Civics.

Trust us, it said. We're nerdlingers.

[Remember,] said the Water Bear actual, now just fifty kilometers away. [Just fall down. I'll take care of the rest.]

Pax and the androform ship approached a human assistant.

"I want to make a withdrawal," said the ship.

The woman smiled.

"How much will you need today?"

Information was exchanged. The assistant smiled again.

"My, that's a large amount. The largest I've seen. Can I please take a moment?"

"Of course," said the ship.

The assistant looked in her internal cinema. Her eyes widened.

"You're a Po warship," she said.

"Yes. What's your name?"

"Gemma Geminorum."

"A pretty name."

"Thanks."

"Gemma, whatever happens, you'll be taken care of. Do you understand?"

"No."

"Good. Now, the money."

"How would you like it transferred?"

"By ejection."

The woman frowned.

"You mean, like actual gold into space?"

Ship nodded.

"Don't worry, I'll pick it up."

"I'll... I'll need a counter-authority."

Ship motioned at Pax.

"My Navigator."

The woman's eyes widened.

"A Lo Navigator. Wow."

Then she said, "Oh, we have a problem."

"What kind of problem?"

"Oh, a cyberattack."

Kitou, Box and Brin fell to the floor, writhing.

"Is it happening now?" asked Pax.

"That's what it says in my sensorium."

[Initiating security lockdown,] said the Water Bear actual. [We are now the ranking civil authority.]

"We're taking command," said the ship.

"Oh," said the assistant.

"Please eject our gold now."

The woman hesitated for a moment, frowning.

Then, "Ejecting."

Pax and the ship turned on their heels. Security staff surrounded the three writhing women.

"We'll take care of this," said Pax.

In the taxi, four minutes later, Pax said, "That was neatly done."

Box said, "That was fucking terrific."

"You may all whoop," said Pax.

They laughed uproariously.

The Water Bear said, "Does Earth idiom include, don't count your chickens?"

"My wetware translated it," said Box.

"Tick, tock," said the ship.

High above the city streets, balanced on a windowsill, the Watcher watched. Behind him, a family enjoyed their evening meal.

They weren't aware of him. He wasn't watching them.

He had no physical manifestation, although that partly depended on what spatial dimensions you were listening in. He existed as transient noise in the processors of countless individual computers.

What to make of these bold imposters?

He sprang lightly to the roof of their car, as it passed a half-kilometer below, his trajectory a passing physics problem.

He listened.

The Po warship was real. Both the android remote, and the real ship in space. Unlikely, but real. Perfect originals of a real Po warship and its remote. The Lo Navigator was in his physics class in the Academy on Polota, a hundred light-years away. The Lo woman was recently born.

The wild-haired child was a Pursang.

Military lore:

What do you get if you cross a Po with a Pursang?

The redhaired woman was an Earth native.

The Earth native.

He initiated a network transaction. For a moment, the entire system veered dangerously close to hyper-intelligence. After a few picoseconds, or enough processor time to control a large industrial city for a day, he had a solution.

He knew before he asked, what the answer would be.

He assigned it a truth function.

He decided.

The city of Praxis was less susceptible to gaming than they'd hoped for. Certainly, it could be deceived, but once deceived, its responses were reflexive.

Its autonomic defenses included three deep-space Interdictors. These were what the Water Bear would call psychotic machines, designed to patrol the big empty, far from vulnerable humans. Cuckoo attacks were in their decision matrix. They launched at upwards of a million gravities.

This was how conflict was handled in the wild, outside the boundaries of civil society.

By psychopaths.

"Is this car space rated?" asked Pax.

"No," said the ship. She'd attached an optical cable from her waist to the taxi's control panel, and the car was now fully under her control.

"No matter," said Pax: they would only be minutes.

The car wound through the city's intricate under-spaces, pressing its passengers into their seats as it made short radius turns, heading towards the exterior. Box saw the spaceport flash by. She felt a pang of memory.

The bowels of the city were full of machines. Capacitors, the size of mountains. Strange energies arced between monumental coils. These were the engines that powered the city now: the great, great grandchildren of the DRZ turbines.

There were cities within cities. Inexplicably, they passed by housing complexes. Who would live down here, in the interstices?

The more Box saw, the more interesting it became.

141

She saw a street market, in the slipway of a dam. The dam was the size of the Three Gorges Dam, and the market was like a car boot sale, except with gargantuan lorries.

What kind of strange, black market deal was going down there?

Worlds, without end.

Then, they were in the interplanetary vacuum.

The car held its atmosphere passably well. Box felt the air sucked out of her ears as its bodyshell expanded, then settled. Outside the Orbiter's induction grid, the car lacked drive. They were ballistic. Momentum carried them free.

Then the Water Bear actual spoke in their sensoria.

[I have you, Praxis taxi.]

The bank vault came next, tumbling through space, already in the grip of the ship's gravity drive. One tonne of gold is a cube of about 37.23 cm. 25 tonnes is the size of a domestic refrigerator. The ship reeled it in, a miniscule mass. A second later, two Interdictors appeared. They had some difficulty locating the Water Bear, but the car and the vault were instantly acquired. There was a brief tug-of-war, then the vault accelerated towards the Orbiter, as though on the end of a ten-kilometer bungee.

Box watched these events unfold from the car, unable to make any sense of them.

The Water Bear jinked several times, at a rate that made her crewmembers wince. The Interdictors followed, unable to be shaken. They were ugly machines, all spikes and knives bunched in a fist.

They powered up beam weapons.

The Water Bear responded with a suppressor field.

[**STOP**,] was broadcast on every channel.

[I can escape,] said the ship actual.

[Go,] said Pax.

It was a brutal calculus. With or without the gold, with or without her crew, the ship could still finish the mission.

Her humans were expendable. They'd either be killed, or arrested. Either outcome was acceptable.

The ship disappeared, in a ripple of warp.

Then, inexplicably, the Interdictors stood down.

Their weapons still primed, they melted away, into the darkness.

7 ∞ EQUITY

2056

Box regained consciousness, in a hospital room, with a soft breeze tugging at gauzy curtains through an opened window. The sky through the window was powdery blue. In the distance were towers, leaning crazily in on each other. She could see gardens, and folds where the gardens met at ninety degrees. She could hear children, laughing. A man in a suit was beside her. "Dr Box," he said.

"Where am I?" she asked.

"Acadia, a corner of the Orbiter."

"Who are you?"

"I'm Praxis."

"Where are my friends?"

"They're safe. Your androform ship will come in a short while. First, I have to ask you some questions."

"Do I have rights?" she asked.

"What do you mean?"

"Can I call my lawyer?"

"Dr Box, you're the victim of a crime."

The Water Bear appeared, five minutes later, as Praxis had promised. She seemed in vivid good health, unlike Box, who felt like stretched-out cellophane.

"What happened?" she asked.

"You nearly died," said the ship. "The city was locked as tight as a drum. It took them almost four hours to collect us from the vacuum."

"These bruises?"

"I had to shut parts of you down."

"The others?"

"All safe, but it was a near thing."

"The ship?"

"Gone to finish her mission."

"How are we alive?"

"This androform body can metabolize fat to produce breathable oxygen."

"You're not fat."

"Not now," said the Water Bear.

"Why are we still here?"

"You mean, why did the killing machines spare us? Someone pulling some strings, I suppose. A shame it took so long for the puppets to move."

"What now?" asked Box.

The bank vault was empty.

Box was riding in the Water Bear's sensorium, seeing what the Water Bear saw, experiencing her sensations. It felt good, after the recovering wreck of her body.

"I'm sorry," said the urbane city avatar. "It looks like somebody stole all your money."

"All of it?" asked Pax.

They were in a deep sub-basement of the bank, in the plane where the city kissed space. Box could see raw vacuum through membranes in the Orbiter's skin. She recoiled at the thought of it.

In front of them was a wardrobe-sized container, made from vanadium steel [the ship's wetware told her] with a twisted-open door.

The ship got the loot, she thought.

Then she remembered: the ship winking out of existence. Gone to finish her mission. Without them. Without the gold.

Now the bank vault was open.

Was that a good or a bad thing?

Even in the ship's androform brain, she only seemed to have half her senses.

She didn't care.

I'm happily anesthetized, she concluded.

"Military malware," said the city. "Memories lost. Everyone terribly confused."

"Fancy that," said the Water Bear.

[Why is it broken?] asked Box.

"It struck the Orbiter with considerable force. How do you want to handle this?"

"This is Po business," said Pax. "Do nothing."

Praxis nodded. "One thing though," he said. "A clue." The city messaged a text string to their sensoria. A sequence of decimals appeared.

[A Hopf number,] said Box, gazing out through the ship's eyes.

Now she knew how *much* the ship saw.

Maybe she had ship envy too.

"Yes," said Praxis.

[Mine?] asked Box.

"No," said the city, not missing a beat. "Not that one. It's the spacetime address of the bank actual, several days from now. It was encoded in the crystalline structure of the vault. That's extraordinarily sensitive information. We've checked. No other vaults have that feature."

[What's a bank actual?] she asked.

[Samppo,] said Alois, from somewhere beside her.

"Why was it there?" asked Pax.

"I don't know," said Praxis. "But you may want to go find out."

"We have no ship."

"I can help you with that."

The Bat was a quarter the size of the Water Bear. A battered towing vessel, ugly as a warthog, with oversized engines, and bristling with surveillance gear. Its pilot was a small AI, about twice as smart as a bat, from which it was evolved.

The Water Bear declared herself satisfied.

"This is a *good* ship," she said.

"And I have some good news," said Praxis.

"Yes?" asked Pax.

"Your missing crewmember is safe."

"What? Ito? How do you know?" asked Pax amid the rising clamor.

"I can't say."

"What can you say?"

"That he doesn't exist. Now. Except as a young novice, on Polota. But the version you lost, the grown one, he's safe."

[You're talking in riddles,] said Box.

"You'll work it out."

"City?" said Pax.

"Yes?"

"Thank you."

"It's been a pleasure, Navigator. Just please don't come back for, shall we say, twenty more years?"

Progress inside the Bat's warp bubble wasn't as serene as the Water Bear's. The smaller ship's machines smelt of hot metal and lubricants, and made chuntering mechanical noises. Box thought it was just fine. Her mind was still recovering from her body's ordeal. After the bone-chilling emptiness of space, the thumping made her feel solid.

"We're the Hand of the Bat," said Kitou, delighted.

"Pax is the Bat," said Brin.

"Silence," rumbled Pax. "All of you."

With news of Ito, came a blissful sense of release. Box saw that a weight had been lifted from all of them. Kitou and Brin were like different people. There was no longer the fear that they should be searching for him instead of pursuing their mission. Wherever Ito was, and what he was doing now, were anyone's guess, but he could take care of himself.

Brin and Kitou taught her the Po of small spaces.

"This move is called the brainless monkey," said Brin.

The girls assumed the Po starting position, floating within striking range, and then started hitting each other. There was nothing artful about it: it was a barrage of punches and blocks. They turned off the lights, and continued the fight by the lights of the instrument panels.

"The Earth art this resembles most is Wing Chun," said Kitou, panting.

Box said, "Don't be ridiculous."

They found handholds in the ship's machinery, and swung from them. As they hurtled past, they threw punches and kicks at each other.

Thankfully, few landed.

"This move is about survival against a chaotic opponent," said Brin, breathing heavily. "We fight to exhaustion. The nature of the attack is incidental. We use it to unwire reflexes."

Box saw that while the striking was deranged, the blocking was a variation on Fibonacci spirals.

Maybe it was like Wing Chun.

The two girls stopped, exhausted.

"Now you," said Brin.

Pax asked what happened to her face.

"Moving equipment starts without warning," she recited.

"Well, this ship has a medibay. Please have it seen to."

In the small hours before dawn, when Box was the only one left awake, she talked with the androform Water Bear.

"What's it like, being two of you?"

"It has the potential to become distressful."

"In what way?"

"According to our customs, a divided person, over time, becomes two different people."

"Like Alois?"

"Yes."

"I can see how that might be distressing."

"It's like your transporter dilemma."

"What do you mean?"

"When you make a copy of a person, for beaming them down in your space dramas, is it the same person?"

149

"Oh, that old chestnut. I never thought so. My dinner party opinion is that a copy's a copy."

"So, what becomes of the original?"

"That never gets shown on TV. I suppose they're quietly disintegrated."

"Thankfully, we lack transporter technology."

"But I've seen it."

"Where?"

"On Earth. The 6 transport political agitators."

"That's a sleight of hand."

"What?"

"They move people using gravity drives, then edit your perceptions."

"You're shitting me?"

"No."

"That's awful."

"Do you prefer the alternative?"

She talked at length with Pax. They were in the Bat's snug common room. There was no luxury here, but it was a comfortable space for several people. Pax stayed up, consenting to be interviewed.

"Thank you," said Box.

Pax nodded.

"I mean, really thank you. For everything."

"You're most welcome," he said.

"You're a wonderful leader."

"I'm not quite Ito."

"No, you're not. But Ito's not quite Pax."

He smiled at that.

"I remember the lesson you taught me." she said.

"In the mountain sim?"

"Yes. I'm starting to get it now."

"We planted a seed," he said.

"You know Pax, those questions...

"What am I scared of."

"Ah yes."

"It's true. I'm brave. I know I'm brave. I'm the one who runs towards the fire. But when the real pressure's on, I fold like a house made of sticks."

"And you know this?"

"Yeah, but I can't seem to help it."

"Then accept it. That's how your flight response intervenes."

"You said you could train it out of me."

"But I won't."

"Why?"

"Because it's there for a purpose."

"What purpose?"

"Dr Box – Ophelia - you're not a soldier. I don't have the luxury of walking away from a problem that scares me, but you do. I have a lifetime of training. You don't. Bravery combined with obstinacy will only get you killed."

"So what, I run away?"

"Yes, you run away."

"I'm allowed?"

"Yes."

She sighed, and then nodded.

"What did Praxis mean about Ito?" she asked.

"He means Ito's not in this universe."

"How can that be?"

"Maybe it means he'll arrive later."

"Tell me," she said. "Who's this Samppo character?"

"A complicated person."

"How so?"

"Samppo's the bank."

"He owns it?"

151

"No, he is it. I'll try to explain. Have you heard of hyper-intelligence syndrome?"

Box shook her head.

"There's a theory that intelligent machines can transcend our baseline reality, and pass into a higher plane of being. As well as being the front end of a supercomputer, Samppo's a religious figure: the head of a cult, called the Cult of the Bicameral Mind."

"Your financial system is run by a cult?"

"Yes. And our central bank exists permanently on the edge of madness."

"This works for you?"

"Yes."

The Cult of the Bicameral Mind was an accumulation of industrial garbage. On the largest piece of garbage was depicted a human skeleton, with a cleaved skull, an axe, and outsize male genitalia. The genitals were partly obscured by an accretion of more recent garbage.

A voice said, "Who the fuck are you?"

"We're a special operations unit of the Po," said the Bat. "Please welcome us on board."

"Fuck."

A second voice said, "It's the Feds."

Beam weapons swiveled to face them. Box saw them in her head-up display: Spidery things, behind layers of refuse.

"How can we dodge those?" she asked.

"I'll know they're powering up before they do," said the Water Bear.

"What then?"

"The Bat will disassemble them in a shaped gravity pulse."

"He can do that?"

"Oh yes."

"Put the weapons down," said the Bat.

"Or what?"

Pax broadcast, "This is Navigator Pax Lo. We're here at your request."

"We didn't request no one," barked a new voice.

"We come on business," said Pax.

"This display of firepower is a ritual game," said the Water Bear. "The precursor to a negotiation. Out here in the big empty, where force equals law, it's expected. They're showing us the size of their weapons."

"Like baboons," observed Box.

"Two armed parties can do business," said Pax. "These oddballs appear to be armed about as well as a heavy warship."

"Not afraid of little old us then."

"On the contrary."

Kitou, Brin and Box crossed over in the usual way, by jumping. Box was getting used to it. The Bat propelled them across the gap along three unpredictable courses.

Deep space, far from any world, was a strange, lonely place.

She shivered.

Kitou and Brin landed at the edge of a filmy membrane, in a relaxed military crouch. Box landed slightly less elegantly, but still on her feet, just behind them. Their skinsuits relaxed, until they were in combat versions of their Po uniform coveralls.

"What the fuck is this?"

A youth in a filthy monk's habit was gabbling into an old-fashioned radio microphone.

"Space vixens!"

"You won't need that," said Brin.

"Broca transfer?"

"Yes."

The young man put the microphone down.

"You Po have all the gadgets. Now please, tell me about your ship. I've never seen a Po tugboat before!"

The monk turned out to be an engaging conversationalist. He pulled off his habit, to reveal a cleaner one underneath. While he was busy with that, he sheepishly apologized for the previous profanities. "We have a brand to protect," he said.

"How many of you are there out here?" asked Brin.

"Sixty, not including Samppo and the Engine."

"What do you do?" asked Kitou.

"We're a hedge fund," he said.

"Or a bank.

"It depends on your theory of money."

"I see you've met my boy," said Samppo, grinning impishly. He was an old man, in rude good health, with a shock of white hair.

"He's your son?" asked Kitou.

"We're all sons here, young woman. Macro's a clone, as am I. We've been happily cloning ourselves for thousands of years. When I expire, Macro will become Samppo. There'll be a party, and we'll get back to our models."

Samppo wasn't remotely as Box expected. Happy and avuncular, like everyone's favorite uncle, he twinkled.

"You're all men?" she asked.

"Trust me," he said. "It's safer that way."

The interior of the scow was like an exclusive gentlemen's club: smoked glass and waxy carbon fiber.

Box felt intimidated. She smelt power and money. Old money. Maybe the oldest money of all.

"How do you like our island of warmth," he said, "in the great sea of nothing?"

They were sitting in a cross between a board room and the control room on Threnody. Long curving windows looked out across what appeared to be a trading floor.

Samppo got to the point.

"Dr Box," he said. "Why are you here?"

"Me?"

Samppo looked around. "Is there more than one of you here?"

She gathered her thoughts. She was at her worst, sparring with privileged men.

"What happened in Praxis?" she asked.

"You were going to steal my money."

"That was our money."

"Money belongs to the bank."

"Bullshit."

He smiled, and raised his hand.

"I've been a poor host," he said. He opened a drinks cabinet, with a door that reminded Box of the bank vault on Praxis, and produced five heavy glasses.

"Macro," he called.

"Look, Dr Box, we're in a post-scarcity society here. You know what that means. You people can have all the things you want, but money is mine, unless I choose to give it to you."

Macro arrived with a bottle of spirits. Samppo motioned him to sit, and poured five equal measures.

"The woman you were so kind to on Praxis," he said. "My employee."

"Gemma," said Brin.

"Yes. Why was she there?"

"To make money," said Box, remembering the girl, Sophie and her grand tour.

"Wrong. Money's a game, a means of abstracting value. You can't gargle money. Cash is only a position. She'd be just as comfortable, lounging at home, drinking strong liquor, consuming."

"She wants more," said Brin.

"Yes, but she doesn't want money. Who the fuck wants money? You can't hold it close in the long night of the soul. You can't do anything useful with it, except buy things. She wants what it buys. That's true. But more to the point, she wants to be *busy*. She wants to be a productive member of her society."

He motioned them to consume. Kitou gagged, but made a decent fist of it.

"Also, she finds it interesting. The same reason you do your jobs. It fills up her life with distraction and puzzle. Last week she met a Po warship and its Lo Navigator. It was the greatest event of her life. There was a robbery, and somehow, now she's the hero. Soon she'll get to meet me. It'll tickle her silly.

"But money... money only matters to *me*."

Box shook her head.

"Dr Box, take my advice. You need to lighten up, stop seeing shibboleths. It'll give you conniptions. Now, let's see what you need."

"You're going to help us?"

"Yes."

"We can have our gold?" asked Kitou.

"How about we leave that for the real Water Bear?"

"What, then?" asked Box.

"Central bank credit is no use where you're headed, so how about some fungible assets to carry?"

"Fungible?" asked Brin.

"Precious metals, stones and memory cores. Things you can spend."

"You'll give those to us?" asked Box.

"As long as you promise not to spend it locally."

"We get to own them?"

"Whoever has them, owns them. That's what fungible means."

"Can we spend it on Avalon?" asked Brin.

"Perfect. They're always trying to rob me. Sell them some inflation."

"What about our ship?" asked Box.

"That souped-up little spy boat, the Bat?"

"No, the Water Bear. It's on its way to Fluxor."

"Then follow it."

"The Bat doesn't have the range," said Brin. "It would take a century of bending space at maximum economy."

"What do you need?"

"A lightship."

"I can't help you with that. But I know someone who can."

"Where are they?"

"Earth."

"Welcome to the Cult," said Macro, leading the three Po women on a tour of the Station. In Macro, Kitou had met her match for boundless energy. She followed gamely behind, inspecting everything he showed them. "This is the crypto trading floor," he said. A group of preoccupied teenagers looked up from wall-sized holographic displays, harrumphed, and returned to their work.

"Are you really all clones?" asked Kitou.

"Yes, and all men."

"Why?"

"We're not a normal society; we're a religious order."

"Who do you worship?" asked Brin.

"The Finance Engine."

"But you're all physically different," said Brin. "Some are dark, some fair. You have light brown skin and almond eyes, with epicanthic folds."

"Yes, we introduce ethnic diversity at the zygotal stage."

"Why?"

"Fifty identical clones would be boring."

"What do you do for sex?"

"Nothing."

Macro claimed a strongroom to store their fungibles in. The room was pure white, as pristine as a laboratory cleanroom. Box asked why it was empty.

"We don't keep any valuables here," said Macro.

"Not even a wee float?" asked Box.

"No," he said. "We only do numbers here. Otherwise some trigger-happy desperado might come and blow us to bits, just to harvest the atoms."

"Could that happen?"

"No," he admitted. "We have a lightship drive, and a powerful computer to steer it with. We'd win any fight by a hundred parsecs."

The first piece of bounty to arrive was a fire opal, the size of a hen's egg. "That's for the resurrection of your colleague on Avalon," said Macro. The next was a milky green cube, veined with circuitry.

"What's that?" asked Kitou.

"The most valuable object you're ever likely to see," said Macro. "An unprogrammed mainframe AI."

"What's it for?"

"To pay for your ship's refit. It's worth more than the shipyard that did it."

"Why are you giving them that?" asked Box.

"Oh, we need a shipyard."

These riches were followed by boxes of thumbnail-sized silicon slivers, and trays of small diamonds. "Every gemstone is unique," he explained. "But we try to source gems whose signature has never been recorded. Memory cores are the hardest. We make our own for this kind of covert application."

"You do this kind of thing often?" asked Brin.

"More than you might think."

He took them to see the Finance Engine. It consisted of a room, about ten times the size of their strongroom, containing only a blue haze. Embroidered throughout the haze, hardly visible at first, Box could see wisps of circuitry: ghostly logic gates and eerie registers, stretching to a luminous infinity.

"Where is he?" asked Kitou.

"What you see here is a model, like the pictures of animals painted on cave walls. A synecdoche. It's here to help us experience him. Would you like to say hello?"

Kitou nodded.

"Is it safe?" asked Brin.

"Yes," said Box. "I thought Samppo was needed to interpret."

"I'm learning," said Macro. "But yes, it's perfectly safe. All that Cult propaganda is only for show. The Engine's delightful company."

"I'd like to meet him," said Kitou.

"He is quite mad," said Macro.

"Well, in that case let's certainly do it," said Box

Then they were *elsewhere*.

Box gasped. "Oh, it's Paris."

They were standing in the rain, in the *Rue de la Bastille*, outside the Brasserie Bofinger, where Box had first met Alois, six weeks before. The headlights of cars were reflected in the glistening pavement. Box couldn't shake the feeling that they were in Paris. It was more than correct: it was perfect. Under the cupola of the restaurant's grand dining room, a pajama-clad man was hunched over a honky-tonk piano, playing boogie-woogie like his life depended on it. He struck the keys with such gusto that the piano inched slowly forward, until he was forced to hook his leg around the leg of his stool to pursue it.

"He's playing Jelly Roll Morton," said Box.

The man looked up, and beckoned them inside.

"Paris!" he shouted, tossing his head back with pleasure. "*La Ville-Lumière*. The city of lights! *Fluctuat nec mergitur*. Tossed by the waves but never sunk."

Box was instantly charmed. There was something in all this rigmarole that was a personal compliment to her.

"Paris is my home," she explained to the others. "This restaurant, I almost live in this place."

"It's wonderful," said Kitou. "I like Earth."

"This is Earth?" asked Brin.

"Oh yes," said Box.

They found themselves at a table piled high with oysters, mussels and snails, beneath a glorious *art nouveau* chandelier. The world was filled with people and noise. White-aproned waiters balanced platters of food on their arms. The room filled with the heady aroma of Choucroute.

Box sighed with pleasure. Kitou gazed with concern at the lobsters.

"Hey, Mr. M," said Macro.

160

"Macro, tuck in my boy!" said the man, who was inexplicably not only playing the piano, but was also at their table. He attacked the shells with the same gusto as he'd attacked the piano. Slowly, the table inched back.

"Is this food?" asked Kitou.

"It certainly is," said Brin, filling her plate.

"These are the people I told you about," said Macro.

"I know they are I know I know I know they are. Look what they've sent me! Can I work with this? Can I work with these raw materials? What d'you say, Macro? What d'you think?"

"I think they're perfect," said Macro.

"Perfect? Perfect? A perfect expression! A perfect number of soldiers. Tuck in, young soldiers! You can't build perfect muscles without perfect mussels. Put some skin on those bones. Ha-ha!"

He leaned back and stared. "I haven't seen you in a while," he said to Kitou.

"I've never been here before sir," she replied.

"Never been where? Never been here? Here? Where are we where are we where are we, here? Oh yes, your brother is coming. And you!"

He turned to stare at Brin. "The soldier the soldier the rock in the storm; the defender at the gates. Tell me, young soldier, what *is* mathematics?"

"What do you mean?" asked Brin.

"Oh, I know you know you know you know the *answer*. Did we find it or did we invent it? It's important to me. Is it invented or discovered? I must know. I have to know have to know I have to know now."

"I believe it's discovered."

"You know what I think, d'you know what I think? I think mathematics is *God*.

161

"And you, Dr Ophelia Box! Oh yes. The one we've all been waiting for. What have we got here? All three at once? Is this all three of you here? The soldier the scholar the child. Dr Box, I have something for you."

"For me?"

He made to reach under the table, then sprung back and grinned.

"Yes, oh yes, I owe you some *information. Les fruits de la mer.* A porpoise for your visit. Something you can take away and eat later.

"Go to Earth, Dr Box. See Yokohama Slim."

"That's it?"

"Trust me, it's enough."

"I know Yokohama Slim," said Kitou.

"You do, you do you do you do! Look at that!"

Outside, a shaft of sunlight split the *Rue de la Bastille.*

"I get tired," he said. "Macro, what, yes, got to stop talking, got to stop, got to stop, it's a problem isn't it? Is it a problem? Do you think so? Perhaps I should, perhaps I should stretch my legs, should I stretch my legs?"

"I think so," smiled Macro.

"I will," he said.

They found themselves back in the street. Inside the brasserie, the computer played boogie-woogie as if his life depended on it, a mischievous smile on his face.

The clouds closed ranks again, and a soft rain started to fall. Box, for a moment, shaking her head, thought the golden light from inside the brasserie was like the light shining from heaven.

"This is your religion?" asked Brin.

"Yes," said Macro.

"I approve."

Box and Brin teased Kitou.

"You do see she's smitten?" asked Box.

"Really?" asked Brin.

"He's lovely," said Kitou. "Clever, kind and not too beautiful. Beautiful people live in a warp bubble."

"Kitou," said Box. "You're stunningly beautiful."

"No, I'm not," she said. "I have a bird's nest on my head."

"Ask Macro about that."

"Oh, he loves me."

"And why do you think that is?"

"Because of my spirit."

"There is that."

Box interviewed Samppo.

"Do you mind if I record this?" she asked.

"No," said. "If you win, we can suffer being famous for a few milliseconds."

"May I ask, who are you?"

"I'm the bank. This human being you're addressing now was promoted into the role. His wetware speaks to the mainframe computer called Samppo, and Samppo speaks to the Engine."

"So, you're not really Samppo?"

"I'm a complex, evolved person. Are you the cells in your body? Once, I was a physical human like you."

"What was your original name?"

"Oh, that'd be telling."

"What do you do?"

"I'm a central banker. I'm *the* central banker. I'm also a hedge fund manager. And a religious leader. The Cult of the Bicameral Mind."

"What is the Finance Engine?"

"A god."

"You believe that?"

"Any sufficiently advanced being is indistinguishable from a deity."

"That isn't an answer."

"That wasn't a question."

"Why do you do what you do?"

"You mean, why does a god condescend to help run a bank? Because it's interesting."

"I mean why do *you* do what you do?"

"Me personally? The human? Dr Box, I'm not a private citizen. I'm a branch of government. I do what's required of me."

"Which is?"

"I manage the value of money, for the benefit of our society. Our economy runs hot. People want to live productive lives. We overproduce. I manage that by taking it out of the system."

"You steal it?"

"Don't be ridiculous."

"How?"

"Typically, in the form of complex derivatives."

"What do you do with it then?"

"A lot of it is just bank credit. We make it disappear. We try to spend the real money outside our economy. Some of it goes on the Thousand worlds military. Some of it is to honor political commitments. The Xap rely on us to defend one of their frontiers. We finance that. We provide aid, philanthropically, and in return for astropolitical favors. If there's a disaster, on a sufficiently large scale, our society is often a first responder."

"So, you're the good guys?"

"We like to think so."

"Everyone keeps claiming that for themselves."

"Maybe because it's true. We're a benevolent society."

"Why did you stop us stealing our gold?"

"Partly because I wanted to meet you in person. To see your faces. Talk it over. Maybe find a better solution. But holding up the bank was good. I like your cojones."

"Why was the bank vault empty?"

"Oh, there's people I'd like to think you got away with it."

"You're framing us?"

"For a crime you intended to commit."

"Do you know what's happening, Samppo?"

He thought about that. "No. Maybe the Finance Engine does, but me? No. I can only make inferences."

"Why are you helping us now?"

"The great randomizer is war. I fear it exponentially."

"How far would you go to prevent one?"

"I'd give up a great deal, but not to the point of abandoning our values. What's the point in sacrificing what you set out to preserve?"

"What'll you do now?"

"About the drums of war? Nothing. The Po are the operational wing of the executive. You're the covert wing of the Po. I depend on you people for doing things."

"Us people?"

"You're a Po soldier, Dr Box."

"Why me, Samppo?"

"You mean, why you, personally, of all people? Why are you here?"

"Yes, does anyone know why?"

"Maybe the Xap know."

"When will I get to meet them?"

"Soon."

Piece by piece, their fungibles arrived. Sapphires and emeralds. Hypercrystals used in warp drives. Memory cores. Objects Box didn't recognize. Fabulous riches. Some of it arrived in small, cylindrical lightships, about the size of a person. These flitted in and out of existence around the Cult, with their lambent *Aurorae Galactini* playing over the layers of refuse.

One shipment arrived in a ship made of shadows: Magellanics. This one, Macro wouldn't show them.

"It's a surprise," he said.

"There's enough wealth there to fund a new world," said Samppo.

"Or a small war?" asked Box.

"If need be," said Brin.

Pax monitored proceedings from a thousand kilometers away, declining any social invitation to visit. "We have our systems," he said. "I can best protect you from here."

Instead, Kitou took Macro to the Bat, a long fall through space in their respective spacesuits, Kitou's unreflective black nano, Macro's like a deep-sea diving suit. Box watched them drift away, hand-in-hand, into the big empty.

Again, she shivered.

It was lonely out there.

Kitou returned with Alois, still steering the Water Bear's androform body, who promptly disappeared to talk business.

"I'm staying," he said, after he and Samppo finished.

"What will you do?" asked Box.

"Samppo has kindly offered me the use of a virtuality."

166

"What for?"

"Oh, some enquiries."

"Permanently?"

"Oh no. Please come and get me, when you get my original back."

"You'll merge?" asked Brin.

"If he'll have me," said Alois.

Everyone seemed to agree that this was for the best. Kitou and Brin reluctantly agreed. Box felt bereft. The Water Bear's remote wanted her systems free for the mission.

"What kind of virtuality?" asked Box.

"A simulation of Threnody," said Buss. "I'll continue my research. I have work I want to do on the Fa:ing number, with the help of the computers here."

"What kind of work?"

"I have ideas, based on what I saw Backstage. I want to try to talk with it, instead of trying to understand it. A more heuristic approach."

"Talk, using mathematics?" asked Brin.

Buss nodded.

"I want to ask it what it thinks it's doing."

"The Finance Engine told me mathematics is God," said Brin.

"Then perhaps I'll be speaking with god," said Alois.

After seven days, with their treasure secure in the Bat, they prepared to leave. The war chest was smaller than Box had expected, hardly larger than a suitcase.

"It's been good having you," said Samppo. "We don't get many women here, much less three archetypes."

"What do you mean?" asked Box.

"It should be obvious by now. You, the scholar. Brin, the soldier. Kitou, the child. Beings of mythos. Who can oppose you?"

"I hope you're right."

"As do we all."

Box looked out across the space they were about to cross. It was lonely, out here in the big empty. The stars were so few. If there was a demon who lived in the sky, it lived here, in the nothing.

Kitou was heartbroken. As they were leaving, on the airside of the filmy membrane, on the edge of the scow, Macro gave her his package.

"It's for your ship," he said.

"And for you.

"Remember us here."

2056

Box awoke to an argument. She, Brin and Pax had slept through the journey to Earth. Kitou was left in command.

"This is unacceptable," said Pax.

Kitou was hanging her head in contrition.

"What's happening?" asked Box.

"Kitou used the Cult device to contact Macro," said Brin.

"What's wrong with that?" asked Box.

"Everything."

The device was a milky green sphere, the size of a grapefruit. It reminded Box of the mainframe core she'd seen at the bank. Brin said it might be a sex toy. Kitou rolled her eyes at that.

Pax said to Kitou, "Explain."

Kitou said, "I was experimenting."

"I have no problem with that. Details?"

"I asked the Bat. He suggested an input. I tried it. It opened a channel."

"To the Cult?"

"Yes."

"The interesting thing," said the Water Bear, "is that this happened inside a warp bubble. That's new physics."

"What happened then?" asked Pax.

"I asked for Macro."

"First mistake," said Pax. "And then?"

"I called him again, after."

Pax sighed. "How did the Cult react to all this?"

"They were unsurprised."

"You should have told the Water Bear, and woken me."

"Yes."

"Consequences."

Kitou looked up. She didn't care about consequences. She was already experiencing the consequences.

"See me in the practice area," said Pax. "In five minutes."

"What's going on?" asked Box. Kitou seemed relieved.

"Pax will teach her a lesson" said Brin.

"He's going to hurt her?"

"Probably."

There was no great skill in the fight. They had their wetware off, in the Bat's erratic local gravity, and there was skin in the game. Pax advanced, and Kitou danced away. Pax advanced again. He tried to ease into his Po routines, where he had the advantage, but Kitou avoided him.

Then Pax caught her off guard, and slapped her hard on the side of the head, drawing blood.

Box winced.

Kitou shook her head, and returned to the Po starting position. This routine continued, until Pax launched a fluid combination of punches, and caught her again, flat on the same side of the head.

She sprawled on the floor.

"Stay down," whispered Brin.

Kitou rose to her feet, to the starting position.

Pax nodded, and went directly after her, launching a second flurry of punches, and caught her again, this time with a flat fist to the shoulder, and she went down, hard.

There was an unpleasant pop.

"Stay down," he said.

Kitou shook her head, and rose unsteadily to her feet. Pax moved in to finish her, but she anticipated him. With blistering speed, she spun inside his defenses, and landed a full-powered elbow, directly in his ribcage.

"That's going to hurt," said Brin.

Kitou danced away, and Pax couldn't catch her. She sprang forward again, while he was advancing, and landed a perfect Muay Thai combination, to the same part of his ribcage. There was a meaty crunch.

"And that," said Brin.

It was finished a few moments later. Pax simply ignored her defenses, marched in, and delivered a clinical punch to the point of her chin, knocking her unconscious.

He looked down at her, and frowned.

"Brin," he said.

"Yes, Navigator?"

"Take her to the medibay. Bring her to me when she's able."

Brin nodded.

Box watched Kitou stirring on the medibay. She couldn't begin to untangle her feelings. Anger. Disgust. Reluctant admiration. Nauseous rage. A mother's pain for her injured child.

An ultrasound machine began a bone knitting operation.

"Will she have scars?"

"Only if she wants them," said Brin.

"You seem remarkably sanguine about this."

Brin seemed surprised. "What do you expect?"

"What do you think, Water Bear?"

"I approve."

"How can you?"

"A sharp punishment is superior to a long humiliation. Now the air is clear. Kitou won't forget this lesson. Nor will Pax."

"I don't get you people."

"You can't," said Brin, gently. "You're a normally socialized human. We're soldiers. We wager our lives. We must absolutely trust each other."

"How is this different to a training injury?" asked the Water Bear.

"They're not deliberate."

She stormed out of the medibay, as furiously as she could in zero-gravity, and cannoned into Pax, who looked puzzled.

"What was that all about?" she demanded.

He raised his hands placatingly.

"Don't give me that horseshit, Pax. You're a grown man. She's a child. You could've killed her."

Pax winced. "I could not have killed her."

She stormed away.

Later, Brin and the Water Bear followed a serene Kitou into the communal space. Box sensed the presence of strong analgesics in Kitou's demeanor.

Pax nodded. "You fought like the wind," he said.

He took a pouch from his pocket.

"Ito was saving this, but it's time."

He gave Kitou two carbon-black starbursts.

"You understand your responsibilities?"

She nodded.

"Then excuse me, young soldier, while I have my injuries seen to."

He pushed himself gingerly towards the medibay.

Later, Box watched as the Water Bear installed Kitou's combat wetware.

"Will it hurt?" asked the Bat.

"More than Pax's blows did," said the Water Bear.

It didn't look painful. Kitou just fell asleep.

"What does it do?" asked Box.

"It's a full military system," said the Water Bear. "Built on a different architecture. It attaches lower in the autonomic nervous system. She'll be better, faster, stronger."

"God help us," said Box.

"Indeed," said the Water Bear.

"Will it affect her personality?"

"Not a bit."

"Poor Kitou," said the Bat.

"Does it really hurt?" asked Box.

"Yes," said the Water Bear.

While Kitou nursed a powerful headache, the others looked down on Earth. It was the same blue-white jewel she'd seen from the Pnyx, twenty years in the future. On the ground, it'd be a different story. The biosphere was in a death spiral. Soon, without intervention, the methane monster in the Arctic would begin to stir, and that would be the end of it.

"There's a young Ophelia Box down there," said the Water Bear.

"It's been a year since my family died," said Box.

"I'm sorry," said Pax.

"If only we'd come a year earlier."

"It may have made no difference," said the Water Bear.

"What do you mean?" she asked.

"There are a few theories of retro-causation: of the future changing the past. One is that time is self-healing. No matter what we do, it returns to its original shape. Another is that when we try to change past events, we become the cause of them."

"You mean we could start the war we're here to prevent?"

"Or cause the atrocity at Fluxor."

"Then why are we even here?"

"Because we were sent," said Pax. "And we're taking the path of least assumptions."

"Hopefully, the universe has no problems with paradox," said the Water Bear.

"That hurts my head," said Box.

"Mine too," said Kitou.

They fell in the usual way, trusting their suits not to trigger a terror alert. More than one Caliphate cruise missile had been intercepted over the skies of southern England.

They drifted over a sprawling metropolis. This was London, in the dog days of the climate wars. Some parts of the city raged in uncontrolled fires. Box could see all of

Bow, up in flames. She saw Ashburton Grove, spotlit for an Arsenal game, surrounded by flashing blue polis.

Half a country away, a twelve-year-old Ophelia Box was learning to sell black-market pharma in the mean streets of Glasgow.

Her skinsuit blossomed, and she settled with gossamer wings on Wimbledon Common.

Her facemask retracted.

She took a breath of fetid air.

London, before the *Aurora Galactinus*.

The parched grass of the Common was tufted and spiny.

"Like Fluxor at the end," said Kitou.

"Okay team," said Box. "Listen to your mission specialist. We've come at a time of great social upheaval. I chose this route because it takes us through four safe areas."

"We could've landed closer," said Brin.

"I know," said Box. "But I wanted to see it."

She'd dressed them in halter tops, loose-fitting combat trousers, and trainers. London's ubiquitous summer streetwear, although this was winter. Since no one in 2056 had wetware, Kitou and Brin had downloaded Box's soft highland burr.

They were three Scottish lassies, walking in London.

They set off to walk the 15 km to Clerkenwell.

At the edge of Wimbledon Village, smiling boom-gate guards waved them into the Glorious Nation of Tooting. One man, a young Rastafarian, asked for Brin's number.

"Are those real countries?" asked Brin.

"It all began as a surreal joke," said Box. "Then the gates were installed."

It was past midnight, and there were street parties spilling out everywhere. Every bar was filled to overflowing. Groups of youths gave them good-natured waves.

"This isn't threatening," said Brin.

"London has a history of this kind of thing," said Box, "of bringing out its best in a crisis."

"I like these people," said Kitou.

"So do I," said Box.

London's streets had always had a bustling, overcrowded feel, now even more so in the new age of *fin-du-temps* parties, when the town centers were continuously filled with revelers. Closed borders hadn't put a brake on the population. Twenty million people now lived here. They stuck to the high ground of the obvious party areas, passing directly along the high streets of Earlsfield and Clapham, avoiding the swampy fens of crack houses and drug deals. Brixton announced itself with a lightshow, spilling over the brutalist Clapham skyline: a wall of sound, and a tremor in the pavement.

"Is that another country?" asked Brin.

"No," said Box. "It's the 24x festival. There's another in Notting Hill. They alternate. When Brixton is banging, Notting Hill is chilling."

"Is Brixton banging?" asked Kitou.

"Oh yes," said Box. "I do think it is."

Brixton had always been Box's London postcode of choice. Partly, because of its eclectic history. Electric Avenue was the first street in London to be lit by electricity. Its tough history resonated with her politics. It was also her fondness for diversity. London had it in abundance, but Brixton was the wellspring. All life was here, as the old bromide went. She was drawn to this time and place, and wasn't about to miss a chance to see it.

And to party, of course.

Kitou chose a shiny plastic party frock with ballet flats. Brin wore a cocktail dress and heels. Box kept her combats and trainers, and wore just a frilly black sports bra on top. The passing revelers who saw their clothes morph, hooted approval.

"We're dangerously sexy," declared Box.

The hulking, concrete church on Brixton Green was garlanded with bunting, like a medieval castle; like the gun emplacements on Avalon. Round the edges of the Green was a funfair, complete with sparking old dodgems and chuntering fairground rides. A calliope wheezed along with the electronic dance music. People of every age, color and gender were dancing. There was even a hayride: a magnificent Percheron, unfazed by the commotion, hauling cartloads of shrieking children around.

The soundtrack was pure twenty-sixties. Balearic trance had made its decadal comeback. The death metal of the forties and fifties had been discarded as a tautology.

"This is great music," said Kitou. "What is it?"

"This is called house music," said Box. "Down the street there is reggae. Over there is drum 'n bass."

"They're all intoxicated," observed Brin.

Box nodded. "Many of them are. 3,4-methylenedioxy-methamphetamine, commonly known as ecstasy, the party drug of choice in this milieu."

It was ironic, thought Box, that at the end of the world, the consumption of alcohol had fallen. The great, poetic drug of depression had been replaced by uppers. It was partly a function of cost. Now that the

178

world had crowdsourced the supply of precursors, pills cost only pennies. Tobacco had disappeared. Party drugs had taken over. In some respects, the population had never been healthier.

On the other hand, there was the teeth-grinding paranoia.

"You're an expert," said Brin.

"I'm an expert *historian*," said Box.

"Can we take some?" asked Kitou.

"No," said Box.

"I want to dance," said Kitou, and for the next few hours they did; three good friends at a festival.

"Pax will be shaking his head," said Kitou.

They all laughed at that.

"Dr Box," said Brin, as they left Brixton town center behind. "Their world is ending, yet these people are having a huge party."

"Yes, and not a creepy bacchanalia, like some other places on Earth. This is a party you can take your family to."

"A positive attitude," said Brin. "I'd do the same, if my world was ending."

"London is wicked," said Kitou.

"It's the best," agreed Box.

Lambeth gave way to the People's Republic of Southwark. This was a quieter place. Most of the crowded tenements were sleeping. Box imagined them full of sleeping children, waiting on an uncertain future. She wished she could reach in and tell them the good news. That they'd be saved. Would it be good news? She hoped so. She hoped they weren't all heading down some other rabbit hole, where death arrives by a different entrance.

179

A sphere of decoherence, or some bug-eyed monster throwing an asteroid.

Instead of by our own hand, by broiling.

After a few kilometers of inner-city housing estates, they gazed over a sandbagged Thames, into the mazy canyons of the financial district. They'd taken a scouting position on Southbank, where soundsystems turned the archways round the bridges into miniature Brixtons, with parties all through the night. Across the river, the City had a darkly post-apocalyptic feel. Out on the river, barges were burning. These were kept going for years, fueled by oil from a tanker grounded on the Thames Barrier.

"We call that the Square Mile," she said, pointing over the river. "It used to be one of Earth's great banking centers."

"Like Praxis?" asked Kitou.

"Not quite like Praxis. More like an old-fashioned market."

"What happened?" asked Kitou.

"Political schism. When Britain brexited from the regional economic union, the City cexited from Great Britain, so they cut off its power supply."

"Is it safe to go there?"

"Yes. If anyone makes trouble, they get zapped with a laser from orbit."

There were no gates to the City in a city, only hundreds of CCTV cameras. The few people they saw hurried past with their heads down.

"We're here at a pivotal moment in Earth history," said Box, as they walked beside the smoked-glass facades of venerable banks and insurance companies. "Europe's become a techno-anarchic freakshow. North

America's a shooting gallery. The start of the complete breakdown of society."

"A system on the edge of chaos," said Brin.

"Yes. And in a year, when the first lightships arrive, everyone will shake their heads, and pretend it never happened."

"So no closure?" asked Brin.

"Not really," said Box.

They crossed into a modish warehouse district, with fashionable shops, hunkering over narrow, crooked streets. Here, there were people: the same festivities as in south London, winding down for the heat of the day. Just a few miles west was Notting Hill and the other 24x festival.

The streetlights sputtered, due to the endemic coal shortages.

"Clerkenwell," said Box. "We're almost there."

A rosy dawn was climbing over the spiky inner-London rooftops. Already, the temperature was rising. They arrived at a small shop, hardly more than a kiosk, in a quiet back street.

The sign said, **Yokohama Slim, Esq. Rare Books**.

The towering man who answered the door was of mixed oriental ethnicity, with long black hair tied back in Kanzashi sticks, dressed in a blue city suit, despite the early hour. Slim claimed to be part Japanese, part Tuniit nomad, part Koryak fisherman. He looked down his long nose at their party frocks.

"Well, it's Ophelia Box and Kitou Gorgonza. And you must be Brin Lot. Please, come in."

He ushered them into his shop, which Box knew so well from her past. Dusty first editions lined the shelves. Books about magick, and philosophy, competing for space with Manga collections.

Slim was the Slim she remembered, a rawboned man in late middle age, immaculately dressed, as always.

"How can you possibly know me, Slim?" asked Box, while he boiled water for tea. "Why are you the same? We don't meet for two years."

"Let's say I have a good memory."

Over bowls of tea, he told them more.

"Ito and I have been working on the Fa:ing problem for some time," he said.

"You mean you *will* be working on it," said Box.

He shrugged. "Time is a knot, Box. Best cut right through it. Pretend I'm the Slim of your era. Now introduce us."

"Okay. Well, everyone, Slim's my best friend. My father. My mentor. My kickboxing coach."

"Saved you from the mean streets of Glasgow," he smiled.

Box laughed. "That's right. Slim found me a home, like a lost kitten. Sent me to Paris. Cured my addictions. Taught me to fight. Slim's an excellent kickboxer."

"No, I'm not. I'm a klutz, a *kuruttsu*, compared to you."

"You should see these two fight."

"Well, they're Po soldiers."

"Slim, why are you here? I'm confused."

"I work for the Po."

"Obviously."

"I also freelance a little."

"For who?"

"This isn't the place. First, to sleep. You know where your room is. I'll sort out the others."

"And after that?"

"Then, under cover of darkness, like good spies, we'll hatch our plans."

Box's room was exactly as she'd left it: a narrow bed, slightly mildewed, tucked high under the eaves, overhanging the street. She felt a strong rush of memory, here in this familiar place. She'd led a hard-enough life, she supposed, although she was mindful of those who'd experienced worse. She was alive. Right here, in this milieu, people were dying in their millions, directly from wars, or of starvation in the forced labor camps of the Med.

For the first time since leaving Earth, she felt safe. Nothing could hurt her here. Not with Slim down below, smoking his rollup cigarettes. The weirdness ebbed away, and for a moment, she was just Ophelia Box, not a bit-player in a game she didn't understand.

She sighed. Whatever was happening here, it wasn't what she signed up for, but what choice did she have?

It wasn't as though she said no.

It wasn't as though she wanted to.

Slim gave the others the bedroom below. All day, they slept. Outside, the swelter settled on the city like a shroud, smothering the streets, as the mercury climbed past 40°C. Later, when the sun was dipping beneath the spiky Clerkenwell roofs, and the first cool air was creeping through the backstreets, they visited a local restaurant, one Box remembered well. She ordered dolmades, acres of mezédhes, and more retsina than was wise.

"This is delicious," said Kitou.

"Oh, to be sixteen again," said Box.

The food *was* delicious, and so was the place, all twisted up with its rival antiquities. Russians and Persians, playing chess. Taxi drivers, arguing in Greek.

Dolmades, duqqa and dumplings. While the girls ate, Slim told them the story of his ancestors.

"My people, the Tuniit giants of *Kalaallit Nunaat*," he said, "travelled east in the age of the ice spirits, tracking walrus and seal."

It was a story Box had heard hundreds of times: a staple of her childhood. Slim had a beautiful voice, and a magnetic way of storytelling. Later, as a young historian, Box would learn that the Tuniit - the Dorset giants - were the fabled first peoples of the Arctic. The origins of their story were shrouded in myth, but Box knew the truth. She'd heard the dogs, howling in the mist; the rattle and thump of runners on ice, in Slim's sonorous baritone voice, too real to be make-believe.

Just hearing it here, made the hairs on her neck stand on end. It was like an electrical circuit, wired directly into her memories.

The girls were full of questions, which Slim answered directly. He told them about survival on the ice - how to stay warm, how to track seal, how to find water - as though he'd been there himself.

"Two thousand years after that," he said, "the Vikings came to the high arctic tundra. They called us the Skræling, and couldn't defeat us in battle. They didn't have to, because although we'd fight, we were a gentle people. In the end, the fierce and clever Inuit drove us from our lands, not by war but by competition for resources, and we disappeared forever."

"But you're here," said Brin.

"Hidden," winked Slim.

"This was how long ago?" asked Box.

"The last diaspora was about the time of Christ."

"You're one of the old ones?" asked Kitou.

"Even older that you," he said.

184

That night, the Bat descended out of a tangerine sky, lit from below by the fires in Bow, like a bat fluttering into the underworld. The four of them climbed onto Slim's rooftop, into the belly of the ship.

"Mr. Slim," said Pax when they were aboard, and the Bat had risen high above the crowded air lanes, and London was spread out below them like a warzone.

Like a patient, etherized upon a table.

Brin had originally offered to lift Slim up, using the Bat's gravity drive.

"It's faster," she said.

"No," said Slim. "Tuniit and gravity drives - not a happy combination."

"Master Pax," said Slim. "Ito has spoken well of you."

"And you. Please meet my ship, the Water Bear."

"We've met," said Slim, to the Water Bear's androform remote.

"It's been a long time, Yokohama Slim," said the ship.

"And the Bat."

"Welcome," said the Bat.

"Where're we going?" asked Pax.

"Not so much where," said Slim, "as when."

Slim asked Kitou to bring him Macro's device. Kitou frowned disconsolately at that.

"It won't bite you," smiled Pax.

"Do you mind?" asked Slim.

"Go ahead," said Pax.

Slim touched its surfaces with his long fingers.

"This is a functioning time travel drive," he said. "You just have to know how to work it." Something flashed inside it. For a moment, Box thought she saw star systems, reflected in its depths.

185

"As you may know," he said, "I serve several masters. Our friend, the bank. Po intelligence, of course. Our alien compatriots, the Xap. Others you don't want to know about.

"This, this is Magellanic. Or at least, the box it comes in is. The tech, not so much."

He touched the object again. It flashed, and again Box had the sensation of a revealed infinity.

"Which I happen to know how to drive."

He touched the object again.

"And we're here," he said. "Or then. We just travelled in time, to 1851. A great many things happened, in 1851. We're going to visit the Great Exhibition.

"Tell me," he said to the Water Bear. "Do you have anything resembling a robot here?"

"This ship has a maintenance drone," she said.

"Can it fight?"

9 ∞ THE SPIRIT MOLECULE

1851

Driving through Victorian London in a horse-drawn carriage was like crack cocaine for a modern historian. It was a crisp autumn day, and the city stank, of sewage from the Thames, and coal smoke from a hundred thousand chimneys.

Their cab was a Clarence, known as a growler, for the noise its tires made on the cobblestoned streets. They rumbled down Piccadilly, jam-packed with carts and steam-powered cars, and saw posters for the Great Exhibition of the Works of Industry of All Nations, at the Crystal Palace, in Hyde Park.

Slim had them dressed in the height of Victorian fashion, with bonnets, gloves and voluminous skirts, and parasols against the watery sunshine. As usual, their clothes were a perimeter defense of nanobots and fields. Slim was wearing conventional fabrics: a raffish but threadbare frock coat and vest, as befits an Inventor. He'd disguised the drone's pincers in red leather boxing gloves, which had been hanging in his 1851 kitchen. This milieu was on the cusp of the Queensbury Rules, and the gloves showed signs of regular use.

They were highland lassies again, in company with their uncle, the Oriental Inventor, and his Fighting Machine, the Mechanical Spider.

The growler dropped them at Hyde Park Corner, by Burton's Ionic Screen, during the fashionable hour, and Slim tipped his top hat at the promenading women, who ignored him, or blushed furiously.

"You always did cut a dashing figure," said Box.

"I astonish them," said Slim. "They can't tell if I'm a gentleman or a savage."

"They desire both," said Brin.

"This place is incredible," said Kitou.

The Spider scuttled behind, waving its gloves like a crab. In 21st century Hyde Park, such a device would've drawn a crowd of delighted teenagers, but these Londoners hardly seemed to notice it.

"They don't recognize it as technology," observed Kitou.

"We exploit that phenomenon," said Brin.

"We're exploiting it now," said Slim. "Four time-travelers, hiding in plain sight, and the best available scandal is my ethnicity."

At 115 million cubic feet, the cast-iron and plate-glass Crystal Palace of the Great Exhibition was one of the great buildings of its time. Its interior volume was divided into halls, and in one of the halls, in a section reserved for the Russian inventions, was a sign:

Box groaned.

"What's wrong?" asked Kitou.

"Nothing," said Box.

The Russian Firing Solutions [*Zakrytoe Aktsionernoe Obschestvo*] stall was only slightly larger than a full-sized boxing ring. In it was a boxing ring, and room around it for standing. Inside the ring were two machines, being fettled by men with oily cloths. Crowded round the ring were excited gentlemen, waving banknotes at bookmakers. This was before the wave of laws against the aristocratic vice of gambling. Constables looked on, interested only in maintaining public order.

Slim waved a fan of pounds in the air.

"I have the next winner," he yelled.

The crowd ignored him. They had eyes only for the two machines already in the ring. One was a kind of horizontal trebuchet. It spun, and an arm swung out, then a second arm appeared, with a ball on the end. Powered by a tightly wound spring, it struck and struck again, with bewildering speed.

A weaponized double pendulum.

It was called the St Austell Slinger.

Its opponent was a more conservative design. Humanoid and bipedal, it lumbered around the ring, thinking before striking. It was called the Matryoshka Doll, and according to the posters pinned to the walls of the stand, it was the Mechanical Fighting Champion of the World.

It was clearly hopeless.

It wasn't even a Matryoshka Doll.

Its owner waved the championship belt in the air.

He caught Slim's eye, and they exchanged a complicit smile.

The fight was over in under a minute. The Doll thought once, and again, then reached through the chaos of the pendulum's arcs and pulled a mechanical pin. The payload jack-knifed into the crowd, where it knocked a gentleman unconscious.

The undefeated Champion had won, again.

It had won by thinking.

Box found that reassuring.

Slim hoisted the Mechanical Spider into the ring, to hoots and groans from the gentlemen. As on the promenade, these bettors didn't recognize its biomechanical actuators as technology. Bets were made on the Doll. The fight began, and the robots circled each other. After a few moments, Kitou and Brin began whispering among themselves.

"The bipedal machine knows Po," said Kitou.

Box recognized some of the moves. There was a clever dog, in which the lumbering robot pushed the nimble drone back, and then the drone spun and pummeled it ineffectually.

The crowd laughed.

"They're colluding," said Brin.

"Yes," whispered Slim. "We like to think of it as putting on a show."

More bets were placed, and the fight became more kinetic. Soon the Spider's speed was outmatched by the Russian machine's greater reach, and it was punched from the ring. The crowd dispersed, and several gentlemen slapped the back of the Russian.

"What just happened?" asked Box.

"We lost," said Slim.

Slim led the women toward the Russian Inventor and his robot. Kitou moved like a blur. Before anyone could react, she had the Russian pinned to the side of the ring, and was whispering to him in a songlike language. Somewhere, Kitou had found a knife, and was turning it against his carotid artery, not gently, arching him back. Brin peeled her loose, and accepted the blade, which Kitou willingly released.

"That's mine," said the Russian. He was a sallow young man, and he was showing them an empty shoulder scabbard, as though being bailed up with his own weapon was an everyday event for him.

Brin pocketed the knife.

"What the fuck was that?" asked Box.

"Pursang," said Slim, "If I'm not mistaken."

"What was she saying?"

"I'm not especially fluent," said Slim. "But, approximately, I kill you later."

Slim took a glaring Kitou by the shoulders.

"Listen, my little stiletto. Your first mistake is that to understand events, we must first talk to the Horu."

"I know that," said Kitou. "It's why he's alive."

"Your second mistake is that the Horu is the machine."

"Yes," boomed the robot.

"Why do you want to kill me?"

The Russian's suite of rooms at the Grosvenor Hotel, on Park Lane, in Mayfair, were the epitome of regency bling: gold-leaf wingback chairs, gold velvet drapes, and a guttering fire. The Russian, who was called Ned Mulligan, broke out whiskey, which he'd just brought from the robot's share of the money, and left to count his day's winnings.

Box was sure she remembered his name, from her high-school history lessons.

"Why do you want to kill me?" asked the robot.

Slim said, "Kitou?"

"I'm a Pursang, from Fluxor."

The robot clanked, then stopped moving. Unlike the Mechanical Spider, it was a reasonable facsimile of Victorian technology.

"Ah," it said after a moment of silence. "Fluxor. That was a crime against all reason." It clanked again. "But hear me out, young Pursang. My people are innocent of that crime. I've already persuaded Ito Nadolo of it."

"This Horu is called Chance," said Slim. "Despite all appearances, he is a human. Chance, these are the ones you have to convince, not Ito."

Chance clanked again. "Then I'll put my case plainly. It's inconceivable that we'd ever attack Fluxor, let alone destroy it so cruelly. We're your friends, in ways you can't begin to imagine.

"But those are just words. To know the truth, you must travel to Horax."

Mulligan returned with a tray of ice, and five crystal tumblers, as though nothing had happened. He had the air of an indomitable fraudster, who believed he could talk his way around anything, and carried himself accordingly.

"Who are you, Mr. Mulligan?" asked Box. "Not Russian, to be sure?"

"I'm a Young Irelander," he said.

Now she remembered. This Ned Mulligan was an infamous murderer.

"You'll be a Fenian then," she said.

"And what would a Fenian be?"

"You fought in the Famine Rebellion."

"That I did, and bravely. How d'you know?"

193

"I know you'll be a murderous traitor."

"And what would you be, a witch?"

She snorted.

"Slim," said the robot. "You should take them to the aspen glade."

"I will," said Slim. "It's our next stop."

"Pursang?" asked the robot.

Kitou raised her chin.

"Please, have an open mind."

She nodded. "I will, if Mr. Slim says so."

"You have my offer of friendship."

"We'll see about that."

"I understand."

Day became night, and while the others lounged around Ned Mulligan's comfortable rooms, waiting for London to sleep, Box interviewed the robot. Mulligan seemed not to mind. She understood that Chance was in charge here, and it was the Irishman who was the chancer.

"Why are you here, Mr. Chance?"

"I'm observing the Xap."

"On Earth?"

"Yes."

"There are Xap here on Earth?"

"Of course, where else would they be?"

Again, Box had a sense of a world beyond her comprehension. Robots on Earth, in 1851. Her, interviewing one, as though he were no more than a mildly exotic Mayfair personage.

She had to admit, she quite liked this austere, clanking robot.

She breathed, and carried on.

"Why are you helping Ned Mulligan?"

194

"For my amusement."

"Why are you here, in 1851?"

"We are when we are, Dr Box. I'm no time traveler. I came here in the traditional way. These are my last few days in the Real. Soon, I ascend."

"Ascend? You mean, you're going to die?"

"No, we Horu are in the process of moving our civilization to another universe. I'm the last living Horu."

"Why?"

"Why am I the last?"

"Why are you moving universes?"

"For cultural reasons, Dr Box. Many perceive the Horu as a death cult. There's truth in that. For many millennia, we've stored our dead in digital necropolises, so they can live on in a better future. We're in the act of crossing over to that future now.

"I'm the last, because someone has to be."

"The anthropic principle?"

"Yes."

"So, about your extinction..."

"Extinction isn't the right word, Dr Box. Evolving is nearer the meaning."

"Is it tied up with Fluxor?"

"Do you mean are we escaping? No. We had nothing to do with events on Fluxor."

"But there are witnesses."

"Who saw our ships. We'll have all gone, by the time it occurs."

"Then get rid of those ships."

"That's impossible."

She decided to change her line of questioning.

"How did you find out about the genocide?"

"Ito Nadolo confronted me."

"How did you feel?"

"Shocked and confused."

"What did you do about it?"

"I told my people."

"Who've gone?"

"Our ships remain. Our necropolises."

"How did you meet Ito?"

"Yokohama Slim brought him here."

Box frowned, and resolved to press Slim about his part in this. Like Ant de Large, he seemed to be stitched into her life from the inside.

That he had saved her was indisputable.

What else had he done?

The Bat was where they'd left it, floating over Slim's bookshop. During the day, it had engaged its adaptive camouflage, so that what was behind it showed through it. In 1851, anyone seeing the boundary distortion would've questioned their eyes, or the thick London fug. A freezing rain had settled on Slim's roof, which made the granite tiles slick. They clambered across it, followed by the Bat's maintenance drone.

Bat actual was bursting to upload the Mechanical Spider's experiences.

"Did I win?" it asked.

"You did better than win," said Slim. "You lost deceptively."

"We got what we wanted," said Slim. "The most important thing." he said. "We now have the Horu as allies."

"How did we achieve that?" asked Pax.

"By the undeniable existence of Kitou. She made quite the impression."

"This Chance is so influential that he can speak for his people?"

"It's not about being influential," said Slim. "He's in a majority of one."

"Can he be trusted?"

"I bet my life on it," said Slim.

The Bat lifted into the air, and turned west.

"So, this aspen forest?" asked Pax.

"Yes," said Slim. "Our next destination."

"Where is it?"

"Utah."

The Bat flew low over a churning sea, buffeted in a turbulent pocket of supercavitating air. Box saw distant smoke from coal-steamers plying the busy North Atlantic routes. This was the start of the great age of maritime steam. The ships would've only heard a rumble of thunder, or from the vantage of their crow's nests, a hazy rooster's tail on the horizon. Box found the control room of the Bat, with its conventional windows, flying low over the rough water, an exhilarating place to be. Unlike the Water Bear, which had the quiet ambience of a luxury train, being in the unfiltered Bat was like being in a low-flying submarine.

Yokohama Slim joined her, and they watched the waves rush past below.

"Why are we flying so low?" she asked.

"I expect for the joy of it. Pax only asked the Bat to take us there. The Bat chose the course."

"Not stealthy?"

"You can't be stealthy forever."

"Slim, what's it with you and gravity drives?"

"Oh, I have a different type of neurocomputer than yours. Gravity messes with it."

He pointed at the Bat's circular wings.

"You see those discs?"

"Yes."

"The Bat moves by exerting a gravitic force on them. We're not *in* a gravity field. It's a handy design for someone like me."

"Did Praxis give us the Bat so we could carry you?"

"I suspect we're all pieces in a game."

"How do we get to be players?"

"The person you're going to see is a player. You should ask her."

Kitou joined them, and then Brin, so they were pressed shoulder to shoulder in the control room. Kitou looked down at their destination.

"Holy mother forest," she said, matter-of-factly.

"Pando," said Yokohama Slim.

Brin, Kitou and Box dropped at dawn, from five thousand meters, onto a misty carpet of fallen leaves, tiny aspen shoots, and gnarled fungus: a clonal colony of quaking aspen trees, considered by some to be the world's oldest living thing.

A place that breathed slow time.

The psychedelic drug Slim gave Box to take was predominantly Dimethyltryptamine, or DMT, a powerful tryptamine.

"Like the Ayahuasca sacrament?" she'd asked.

"Stronger."

A beaker of slippery ooze.

"The spirit molecule," he said.

They sat in a clearing, on a silvery blanket that Brin had unfolded from a streamlined rucksack, and Box drank the drug straight down.

"Buy the ticket, take the ride," she said.

Her friends leaned companionably against her.

The first thing Box saw was that the forest was trembling. It was the leaves. They were trembling in the slight breeze. Tiny drops of water trembled *in* the leaves. Then her senses seemed to flip, and she was alone in the forest glade.

That was *fast.*

She looked at her hand. It seemed solid enough. No sudden disorientation, or nausea.

Then she experienced a hollowed-out sensation. Curiously, the forest was inside her. Synesthesia. She was becoming physically confused.

She started to panic.

The universe dissolved in jagged angularity.

Then the forest *held* her, and she relaxed. It was the most surprising sensation. It was as though the branches, and stems, and leaves, were rotating slowly along their axes, sparkling in the wintry dawn light. Box felt the Earth, turning beneath her, and the stars, wheeling in the heavens.

Sitting cross-legged beside her was a smooth-skinned, nut-brown woman, of unknowable age.

"Who are you?" Box asked. "Are you the forest?"

"No," said the woman. "I just live here."

"Are you a spirit?"

The woman thought about this.

"Maybe I am."

"Slim promised me answers," said Box.

The woman laughed.

"Then answers you'll have. But first, I'll tell you a story."

They took a breath together, and the forest breathed with them.

"A long time ago, on a world like this (you might even say it was this one) a species evolved. They inhabit the trees, like a mind inhabits the brain. You call those people the Xap."

Box looked around. She'd always marveled at the sheer amount of invention in psychedelic trips: the neural processing it implied, and what it implied for the idea of a reality, based on observation.

But this: surely it had to be real.

"Are they our friends?" she heard herself asking.

"They are. A friendship that goes back millions of years, on this world, and others. More than a friendship. A dependency. A symbiosis. We carried each other to the stars."

"And you evolved here on Earth?"

"We did. This is our homeworld, Ophelia Box."

"What about us?"

"Humans came later."

"The diaspora?"

"Yes."

"Where did we evolve?"

"On Fluxor."

"Fluxor's the human homeworld?"

"It is."

"Holy moly. No wonder everyone's so antsy."

The woman sighed. The forest breathed. Box felt the inexpressible sorrow of the mother for her lost child, welling up through the soil.

"Yes," she said, after a while.

After some time, it could've been moments, or it might've been years, Box said, "What do I call you?"

"Call me? I have so many names. Forest? Mother? Pando? Those seem to work."

"Pando?"

The woman smiled.

"Pando, what's happening?"

"A war is coming."

"Yeah, so everyone keeps saying."

"We have a prophecy, Ophelia, that this world age will end in nothing. Not entropy, or heat death, but nothing. I cannot see beyond the destruction of Fluxor."

A rainstorm passed through, trailing soft peals of thunder, drenching the fallen leaves.

"What about the Fa:ing? Aren't they from the future?"

"The Fa:ing are a new mystery to me."

"Have they come to help us?"

"I think so."

"Will you help us?"

"I *am* helping you, Ophelia Box. Go to Fluxor. Find a man called Jaasper Huw. Tell him what I said here. Then go to Horax. Finally, seek your answers in Möbius space."

"Where's that?"

"The Horu will show you."

Box sighed, and the forest sighed with her. A sparkling rain of droplets drifted to the forest floor.

This was a helluva psychedelic.

"Pando, why me?"

"That's a good question. The long answer you must learn for yourself. I'm sorry. The story is its own explanation. The short answer is, you're the key, like I was the key."

"The key to what?"

"Everything."

"That's awfully cryptic."

"The best I can do."

"Does Ito Nadolo know about this?"

"I told Ito his own story."

"How will I know what to do?"

"Trust in your friends."

"Kitou and Brin?"

"And your wise navigator, and your doughty ship. And Yokohama Slim, who is mine as much as anyone's. But the young Pursang girl, she's the way."

"What does that mean?"

"Take the ride, Ophelia."

"Bollocks."

The nut-brown woman laughed, and the trees in the glade trembled with her infinite compassion. Box felt a rush of pure, physical bliss, and the miraculous forest drifted away, on a returning tide of consciousness. Snow dusted the clearing. Where she lay, was a nest of pillowy fungus. She was covered by a silvery space blanket, and was deliciously warm. Brin was preparing to cook, handfuls of meaty mushrooms in a pan, over an open fire.

Darkness was falling.

Wood smoke curled into the canopy.

She felt absolutely wonderful.

Her mouth watered.

"Was I under all day?"

"A week."

"A week? Seriously? You weren't worried?"

"Slim said it was fine."

A bloody Kitou stepped into the glade, with a freshly skinned and gutted deer.

"Aren't we the outdoorsman," said Box.

"I thanked it for its life, as the old ones who live here said to."

"The indigenous people?"

"The Navajo people, of Fish Lake."

"You've seen them?"

"They gave me this gift, for you to eat. I prepared it. Brin, will you cook it for us?"

"Cut some pieces off and throw them in the fire," said Brin.

"We should eat the heart and liver raw," said Kitou.

"All those toxins," said Box.

"We should," said Brin.

And they did, blood streaming down their faces.

The rich, dark meat sizzled and popped in the fire, and the mushrooms sizzled in the gamey juices.

It was the best meal Box had ever eaten.

10 ∞ ATWUSK'NIGES

2065

The Water Bear dropped into realspace near Fluxor. Po warp re-entry points are calculated by an algorithm, based on the structure of elliptic curves over fields, using the curved geometry of local spacetime as data. The secret was in its simplicity. At any time, near any star, there is always a place, where stealthy Po ships can always find each other.

She was intrigued, but not unduly alarmed, to find another ship in her vicinity. It was small - about a quarter her size - and heavily cloaked, although not as heavily as she was. It bristled with surveillance gear.

A Po ship then.

Or a hapless imposter.

She launched a drone, and from a random location, requested a cryptographic handshake, using a one-time pad, which all Po operatives carry in their wetware.

Now they had a channel.

She tried an encrypted message.

[This is the Water Bear.]

[Hello, I'm the Bat.]

[Do I know you?]

[You certainly do,] said a voice she knew. [This is Pax Lo.]

After the tears and congratulations had ebbed away, the Water Bears gratefully merged. To Box, who'd spent two hundred years in stasis, the inside of the Water Bear was exactly as she remembered.

But it should, since only nine years had passed here.

"To business," said Pax.

"Brin, Kitou and Dr Box, I'm assigning you to the Bat."

Box groaned. As much as she loved the little ship, she'd been looking forward to her suede-lined, corpuscular nest.

"Brin, you're in command there."

Brin grinned at that.

"Dr Box," he said. "Please see me in the gym."

"Hit me," said Pax.

"Is this another one of your trials by injury?" she said.

"I know you've been learning Po," said Pax. "Do you want to be my student or not?"

She assumed the Po starting position, and they danced through the moves she knew: the clever dog, the whirligig, the indisputable fist. She felt good, and it showed. Pax switched the Water Bear's gravity off, and they danced the monkey. He allowed her to hit him. He didn't make it easy,

205

but he left openings, and she was good enough to take them.

"Show me the Muay Thai combination punch," he said. "The one you taught Kitou, that she used to break my rib."

She showed him, and he grunted approval.

Then they sparred. He pushed her far past the limits of her past endurance, until she could hardly stand, then he demanded more. For over an hour, they worked. She was heavier than when she'd left Earth, and it was all fast-twitch muscle fiber.

An hour stretched into two.

"You'll do," he said.

She whooped, then remembered herself, and nodded.

"Something else."

"Yes?"

"We like you, Dr Box. I like you. Kitou has you on a pedestal with Ito. I want you to be a permanent member of the away team. A permanent member of this group. Do you understand?"

"I accept."

"Please be aware, we do dangerous work. I won't hesitate to send you into danger."

"I'd insist on it," she said.

Pax nodded, and said, "We all know the risks."

"Yes Pax, we do. Trust me. I'm all in."

While Pax and Box fought on the Water Bear, Brin showed the Bat the mainframe AI core they'd been given to repay Felix Revelstoke's debts. She'd found a better use for it than paying for shipyard repairs.

"I propose to make you smart," she said. "As intelligent as a Po warship."

"As smart as the Water Bear?"

"Maybe not that smart. She's an outlier."

"Will it hurt?"

"Not at all. All it requires is the addition of your personality to this mainframe. We'll ensure continuity, in accordance with our customs. You'll become a citizen. Would it matter if it did hurt?"

"No, I aspire to be like Kitou."

"Aww," said Kitou.

Unknown to anyone but the Water Bear, the Bat was built at the same Debian manufactory as her, by a specialist shipbuilding firm, whose only customer was the thousand worlds security service. Despite the Bat's industrial appearance, it shared the same unitary design as the Water Bear. If anything, it was less compromised.

It would soon be a he, and after that, anything it wanted to be.

The Bat's maintenance drone took the mainframe away, into the ship's interstices, and a few minutes later, the Bat's lights flickered.

"Are you there?" asked Brin.

"I am," said the Bat.

"What's it like?"

"Lordy me, it's interesting."

The triangular massif of Fluxor Station had been cut from a living mountain range, in the far past, on a forgotten world. Its basalt base bore the scars of ancient fusion drives, whose hardware had been unbolted and hauled down to the planet below, to provide raw materials for a new civilization. Its topmost surfaces were forested with giant sequoia and redwood trees. Its atmosphere was contained by a field, which gave the appearance of the forests being open to space.

The Po ships introduced themselves, and were welcomed as friends. The crew of the Hand of the Water Bear dressed in their field uniforms - not the gaudy regalia of the bank job at Praxis, but practical khaki. Pax, Brin and Kitou wore their starbursts on their lapels. Box wore an aspen leaf, for Earth, milled from silvery-white palladium, that the Water Bear had made in her fabrication bay.

The dark-haired Pursang who met them expressed his pleasure, and surprise, to be visited by the Po.

"Is this a secret visit?" he asked.

"No," said Pax. "But our message is crucial."

"Then we'll see you straight away."

The man smiled warmly at Kitou. "Welcome home, young Pursang of the old blood," he said. "Have you been far?"

"Blood of my blood," said Kitou, resting her hand on his arm. "I've been a long way."

"What is this place?" Box asked, staring up at the huge trees, under their energy dome. The cinnamon and turpentine aroma of the giant sequoia wafted all around them.

"This is one of the colony ships the new people came on," said Kitou.

"New people?"

"Do you see how most people here are dark-haired and green-eyed?"

"Unlike you?"

"That's because I'm one of the first people."

"What does that mean?"

"There's a story," said Kitou.

'Tell me it," said Box.

Kitou nodded. "A long time ago," she said, "in a time we call the Dreaming, Fluxor was a snowball

208

world. Once it was green, but a precursor civilization destroyed it with a war, and it froze in a nuclear winter. We Pursang became hunters and fishermen then, and we took what we could from the ice and the sea.

"It came to pass that visitors arrived, and asked if they could transform our planet for their purposes. They'd preserve what we already had, they said, and they'd plant the rest with their seeds. They weren't meaty predators like us, but creatures of pure mind, spirits of the trees, travelling on ships made of light.

"What choice did we have? Although some warned against their enchantments, we were enchanted. Of course we said yes. Their forests spread over the world, and everyone prospered. Over a hundred centuries, we formed an unbreakable bond. Then they left, and some of the people went with them.

"We who chose to stay developed a modern society, which fell into a slow decline, until we became simple hunters and fishermen again. We call that the Longtime, and we don't know how long it lasted. Some say millions of years.

"Then new ships came. They were the colony ships, and they brought news of a galactic civilization, and a war, and ruined worlds. They said they'd brought their forest home.

"They were the new people, and this is their forest."

"How did you react to that?" asked Box.

"Badly at first. The usual clash of colonists and first peoples. We were the hunters, proud and unbending. We didn't like their new ways. They were pious and strange. They perceived us as savages. There were wars. We held our own, but they were more numerous. Victory eluded everyone. But we were all Pursang. Finally, we resolved our differences, and became friends. Now only friendship remains."

"How many of the first people are left?"

"About two percent, by population."

"Why haven't you bred out?" asked Brin.

"We intermarry, but the old blood and the new blood persist, along the female line of descent."

"Meaning you'll have blonde children?"

"Yes."

"What about those original visitors, the alien terraformers. Are any still here?" asked Box.

"Of course, they're everywhere."

Later, Box said to the Water Bear, [I worry about Kitou.]

[In what way?]

[She seems to have caught religion.]

[What's wrong with that?]

[Water Bear, you surprise me. Religion is a metaphysical tic, an irrational response to complexity.]

[Only if it requires the supernatural as an explanation. Kitou's gods are natural beings.]

[You believe they exist?]

[Dr Box, I'm told you spent a week with one.]

[The Pursang worship the Xap?]

[It's more complicated than that.]

[Try me.]

[The Pursang worship the forest, as a philosophical idea. The forest shaped their destiny, the trajectory of their civilization. It manifests the divine. They choose to return the favor. Pando is the living personification of the forest, its representative in the Real.]

[Are you saying there's only one Xap individual?]

210

[That would be a simplification. The Xap extend throughout the galaxy. It would be a mistake to think of Pando as an individual.]

[But she's an aspen forest, on Earth.]

[Maybe.]

[Is the Pando forest that old? Millions of years?]

[Who knows?]

[How did it get into space?]

The Water Bear shrugged, virtually.

[I need to get my head around it.]

[Reality is strange, Dr Box, and the Pursang are a highly sophisticated people. They live in the mystery. You could say they live in grace. Please give them the benefit of your uncertainty. You could find there's something to learn here.]

They descended to the surface in a glider, fitted together from pieces of interlocking wood, like a sailboat. "Its simplicity is an illusion," said Pax as they climbed aboard, and sat shoulder to shoulder in its welcoming seats. When they touched the atmosphere, the aircraft pitched back, and Box watched heat build, a rosy plasma sheen, only centimeters from its leading edge.

"An adaptive field," said Pax. "No moving parts. It knows its way home."

They banked and pitched, and Box heard a whisper, as the air began to transmit sound to the cabin. Centripetal acceleration pushed her back into her seat. The whisper became a roar.

A readout in her sensorium said [1649°C].

"Why is it made of wood?" Box asked.

"For beauty," said Kitou.

"I thought you people worshipped the forest?"

"We do," said Kitou. "We make the most of its gifts."

211

After several minutes spent converting velocity to heat, the craft waggled its delta wings, pitched its nose downwards, and dived.

"Holy moly," said Box, five minutes later. "That was exciting."

"I'm glad you enjoyed it," smiled a blonde Pursang woman, who had put down a trowel to greet them. Her hair hung in braids, and she was beautiful, in the same way Kitou was.

It wasn't just her appearance. It was an unfathomable serenity, and a palpable toughness.

Like a Norse goddess.

They were in a clearing, near a small village, consisting of low houses and domed agricultural buildings. Their shuttle was already soaring away on its energy field. It was late afternoon, and the sun slanted down through a silvery haze. The air had the heady aroma of spring. Bee-like insects bumbled in the long grass. Kitou reached down, and crumbled the soft, loamy soil in her fingers.

"We're looking for Jaasper Huw," said Pax.

"Jaasper? I think you'll find him loading his truck."

The village was strung out like a necklace, between a forest of eucalypt trees, and open fields in which dozens of people were working. There were no obvious agricultural machines.

"Growing season," said a smiling, middle-aged man. Then Kitou was down on her knees, and the man was touching her shoulder.

Pax said, "Sir, it's a great honor."

The man laughed heartily.

"It's Jaasper Huw, or Jaasper to you. There are no formalities here. You must be the Po emissaries I heard talk about. Welcome to Stratego. Welcome to Fluxor. Will you help me fill my vehicle?"

The man's truck was a large, sleek crawler. Its oversized tires were soft, like ruggedized party balloons. The tray was half-filled with hay bales, and boxes and bags of produce.

[What was all that about?] Box asked the Water Bear.

[You're in the presence, Dr Box.] Even the ship seemed impressed.

[Of what?]

[A Pursang holy warrior.]

The combined group of five made short work of the load, Brin and Kitou especially reveling in the honest labor. Jaasper grinned, and motioned the others to let those two finish.

"Young muscles," he said. "I wish I still had those."

"So, sir Navigator," he said to Pax, as they sat in the shade of a lofty gumtree, sharing cold drinks brought by a blushing Pursang boy. "If I may start with you. What brings you to Fluxor?"

"Pando sent us," said Pax.

The man nodded.

"This is Ophelia Box," said Pax.

"I know that name."

"Join the queue," said Box.

"Dr Box has spoken with Pando directly," said Pax. "We have reliable information, circulating outside the usual channels, about an existential threat to your world. Pando said to bring it to you. She named you in person."

Jaasper sighed.

"I half expected this," he said.

"What do we do with it?" asked Pax.

"Well," said Jaasper. "First tell me your story. Then, if need be, at first light, we leave for Jura, to petition the Recorder."

"Who is that?"

"Insofar as we have one, she's our leader."

"How far is Jura?"

"Two days."

The village was called Stratego, or Strategos, depending on whether you were from it or not. The people laid on a festive meal, that stretched into the long twilight, to welcome their visitors. Meat, fish, fruit and drink were laid out on a long trestle. Children ran wild, at the opportunity to stay up past dark, and show off to the strangers. Box found the Strategos [or Strategosi,] instantly likeable. They were variations on Kitou: open, bright, and agreeable.

Strange, atonal music was played by a disordered ensemble, consisting of instruments that seemed to move randomly around the party, with players joining in and dropping out as it passed. Long, stringed instruments and drums were passed from hand to hand, or hustled by delighted children, who made a game of guessing where the music would go next, and thus helped guide its direction.

Box asked Jaasper what it meant to be a holy warrior.

"Oh," he said. "We're mostly old farmers, who dreamt we were soldiers."

"Do you remember I told you," said Brin, "that no natural human could beat a Po master in a fair fight? Well, there's maybe an exception."

Jaasper laughed at that.

"Maybe? Po master," he called out to Pax. "An exhibition? Shall we settle the old question, for once and for all?"

Pax grinned.

The villagers roared approval.

The children made a ring, with clothing, rope and ribbons. Clearly, such contests were a regular part of Strategosi festivities. The two men squared off, and circled, and lunged at each other.

What followed was the finest fighting Box had seen. Jaasper lacked Pax's imperious bearing, and his catlike menace, but he moved like poetry, and he was fast. Neither man hit hard, since there would've been injuries if they'd connected, but they put on a bravura show. It was hard to say who won, or if winning was even an issue. Jaasper was marginally the better fighter, and faster, despite his middle age, but Pax was the superior athlete, and the Po art was far superior to Jaasper's showy mélange of styles. Both were magnificent, and Box wondered how good Jaasper must've been in his youth.

Or what Pax would be like, with his combat wetware switched on.

After ten minutes they laughingly stopped, with both men breathing heavily.

Jaasper looked at Kitou.

"Now you."

Kitou hesitated, then stepped in the ring. There was silence.

"Activate your combat wetware," said Jaasper.

Kitou looked at Pax, who nodded.

Then Jaasper started to sing: a beautiful and haunting melody, of mountains, and forests, and snow in high places. Box realized it was only in her sensorium. No one else could hear it.

Except Kitou, who arched her eyebrows.

Then Jaasper lunged, and this time there was no holding back. He tried to hit her.

Kitou reacted, just in time, and skipped away.

The crowd gasped.

This was a different Jaasper. He pressed the attack, and this continued for the next several minutes, but he couldn't get near her. She was too fast for him. Kitou had no chance to counter. She was fully defensive. It was an instinctive fight for her survival. Box wondered if he meant to hurt her.

Then he held up his hands.

"So, it's true."

He leaned on his knees, and took a series of breaths.

"Master Pax, when we come to Jura, can I borrow this one, for a day or two?"

Pax nodded. "Who am I, to deprive her of her birthright?"

"It's not a right. She'll be tested."

[Will it hurt?] asked the Bat, in their sensoria.

"Bat?" asked Jaasper.

"You two know each other?" asked Box.

"The story entangles," said Pax.

"They do," said Jaasper.

At first light, when the first coral white of day was rising over the fields, and the village was first stirring, Jaasper powered up his truck, checked his load, and drove them into the darkness. At first, he picked an easy route through wide open spaces, between ghostly gum trees, with the looming beams of the truck lighting the way for kilometers ahead. Then they found a switchback trail, and they climbed, and the forest grew closer.

A field had firmed up the truck's balloon tires, and they bounded efficiently along the track, with the suspension soaking up the terrain, providing a surprisingly good ride. They joined a wider trail, and emerged into open hill country. Soon they were powering along a grassy avenue, at speeds over 100 km/h, with the rising sun flashing through the trees.

Jaasper offered Brin the wheel. "I can see you want to," he said. "There's a fairly nonintrusive autopilot. Just push the throttle and steer, as fast as you dare, and the big lug'll go where you say."

Brin took the wheel, and egged on by Kitou, they were soon going faster again. They bounded onto a wide-open ridge that ran straight to the horizon.

"Put your foot down," he said, and [260 km/h,] soon flashed in Box's sensorium.

The truck's cab was an ovoid bubble, clear at the front and opaque at the rear. In the front were two shapely seats, designed for long-distance travel. There were no seat constraints, the ubiquitous Pursang forcefield instead holding the riders in place. Behind was a comfortable living space, with a wide couch and two rearward-facing chairs, and an overhead sleeping compartment. A table appeared from a recess, and over a breakfast of cold meats and cheeses, Jaasper told them his story.

"I was once a bruiser," he said. "A prize fighter, and a good one. I was surprised enough to get the call to be tested, since I was sure I lacked the right character, but I did well enough."

He made a hot drink, like bitter vanilla, and passed cups around, and gave two to the drivers. The slow rocking

217

movement of the truck's ride, over the wide-open terrain, was hardly noticeable.

"I was so good at bruising," he said, "that I was assigned to bodyguard duty, for important people, in rough places, and I became a specialist in that line of work. I became the personal bodyguard of a Pursang officer, called O Roza, who you might have heard of."

"The former commander of the thousand worlds army," said Pax.

"Former, you say? Oh, of course, you come from the future. Well, I rose on Roza's fast-rising tails, and when she decided my apprenticeship was completed, I became an officer, and in time, I was given responsibility for the security apparatus."

"O Roza's security detail?" asked Pax.

"No, the thousand worlds security service."

"You were a spymaster?"

"*The* spymaster. When I came home, I'd amassed enough credits for this," he said, gesturing around the cab. "And several more like it. Now I'm a farmer."

"Are you happy?" asked Box.

"I do like to keep my hand in, with other things."

Night fell while they were still on the ridge. It made for a spectacular sunset. Fluxor's star, smaller and brighter than Earth's, fell through a china-blue sky, then two brilliant moons rose, then Fluxor Station. Boundless blue forests stretched out either side. The darkness seemed to ooze out of the air, quite different to nightfall on Earth.

This is an alien world, she reminded herself. It might look like Earth, but it isn't.

They stopped to set up camp.

"This ridge is called the Igháán," said Jaasper. "The Spine. It runs the length of this continent, south to north. We've come almost a thousand kilometers. Tomorrow we'll climb, then descend into Jura."

He pointed into the sunset, where the Igháán joined a snowy mountain range. "Out there is Lhotse," he said, "and Atwusk'niges."

Kitou looked at him.

"You have family there. Do you want to visit them?"

She shook her head.

"When this is over," she said.

He put his arm companionably around her.

"So be it," he said.

And then, "let's establish a perimeter."

He opened a hatch in the back of the cab, exposing six open tubes, like muzzles. He stepped back, and six cylinders soared up, and landed fifty meters in every direction. Six sets of spidery legs unfolded, and they began to crawl like spiders.

"The nightlife is dangerous here," he said.

Over a meal of hot, spicy soup, and freshly made bread, and excellent Stratego wine, they talked about farming.

"We Pursang believe that farming is a way of being," said Jaasper. "Not just a practical thing. We try to cultivate good people, who can live in harmony with the world they exist in."

"We Lo have similar ideas," said Pax, "about the sea and its gifts."

"How goes it between the Lo and the Po?" asked Jaasper.

"We're seafarers," said Pax. "It's a great honor for any of my people to be chosen to be a Navigator."

"To be the Po's soldier."

219

"We're not the Po's soldiers," said Pax. "We fight beside the Po people as equals. But first, we all must prove our worth, as soldiers."

"Like Brin here?"

"Brin is an excellent soldier," said Pax.

"She's an oak," said Jaasper. "I can see that. But she's hardly the archetype."

"What do you mean?"

"The eternal soldier is driven to war. I perceive that Brin chooses to go there."

"So it goes for us all," said Pax. "We choose to be soldiers."

"And are you soldiers?"

Pax shrugged. "Our mission is to wage peace," he said. "It suits us to be called soldiers."

"What about holy warriors?" asked Box. "Are you soldiers?"

"We're mercenaries, Dr Box. We fight for money."

"In foreign armies?" she asked.

"Yes," said Jaasper. "It provides necessary income for our world. Our only source of exchange, since we export nothing else. However; like Brin we choose."

"A Pursang holy warrior is a great military asset," said Pax. "And also a liability."

Jaasper nodded. "We've been known to change sides."

"Why?" asked Box.

"When our masters fail to be righteous."

"Who would employ you?"

"The righteous."

Jaasper turned to face Pax. "A great war is coming, Navigator. Some say it'll consume us all."

Pax nodded. "It could."

"I hear things about these three women."

"What things?"

"They're already famous, in some circles. Three archetypes, come from the future to save us."

"Samppo said that," said Box.

"I wonder," said Jaasper, "which ones you're supposed to be? We Pursang believe there are twelve; twelve human archetypes, after the twelve first humans."

He rose to tend the fire.

"Did you see that snow-capped mountain range in the north?" he asked. "That's called the Aø, the Curtain Wall. Past Aø is the Aør, the Freezer, which runs straight to the pole. Beneath Aø is Jura, and the twelve stones it's built on.

"Then we'll see," he said with a smile.

"Which ones you are."

As the conversation wound down, and silvery blankets were being laid out in the fast-cooling air, a howl split the night. In her sensorium, Box saw a feline carnivore, inspecting the perimeter field.

"One reason we're good fighters on Fluxor," said Jaasper, "is that we have real things to fight. Those big felines are nearly as smart as we are."

The mottled blue cat, which was about the size of an Earthly puma, stared directly at Box, raised its hackles and snarled.

"And fuck you too," said Brin.

The following day, they climbed into a high mountain pass, with granite sentinels towering on every side, beneath a sky of pure cobalt. Patches of snow lined the trail: first pillows then sheets of it, until they were bouncing over a domed plateau, like the roof of the world, and surfing through deep powder. A truck came the other way, and rows of incandescent diodes flashed hello.

"The Freezer has its own microclimate," said Jaasper. "The work of the Xap, ages ago. The cool air of the north is kept bottled up inside the Curtain Wall, keeping the temperate parts mild."

Ahead, to the north, they could see an endless frozen waste. To their left, to the west, was an ocean.

"Geoengineering?" said Box.

"On geological timescales," said Jaasper.

Then they were descending a wide couloir, down a switchback trail to the sea, and Box was unnerved by the drop. She regretted taking a front-row seat, as the balloon tires scrabbled and bit. Falling through space had become a routine event, but this truck ride was too close to her lived experiences, of buses speeding through high Andes passes, stopping to see where other buses had crashed into the ravines.

It was colder up here, in the door to the Freezer. The blustered ocean below them was milky green. Pack ice flecked the sea to the horizon.

Fresh, Box would call it.

A city appeared in the mist, directly below them.

"We have a Jura in Scotland," said Box.

"What's it like?" asked Jaasper.

"Not like this."

The Archetypes of Jura were pillars of stone, rising out of a wild tidal race. All twelve were built up, and burrowed into, by buildings carved into every surface. The white of the rock was so luminous, and the facades so bright, against the wild sea, that it was like they shone from within.

Jaasper Huw pointed out a worn nub of rock, the last of the twelve, almost lost in the mist. "The Scholar," he said.

[Also known as the moonlit bridge,] said the Water Bear, in Box's sensorium. [The bridge that connects logos and mythos.

[The world,] she said, [and the sea.]

The trail deposited them with disconcerting suddenness onto a sweeping coast road, which became a multilane highway, which dipped under the ground, into a network of tunnels and transportation halls, where they drove beside fast-moving trains. From time to time they burst into clear air between two of the pillars.

There was none of the bombastic futurism of Praxis. Everything connected, simply and without fuss. What was new, was frankly new. What was old was conserved. There was no pretense here. The place was a result of its story.

What a story it must be, thought Box. This city was here before her people climbed down from the trees.

With Jaasper relaxed behind the wheel, they were delivered to their destination, the Land Bank, where robot arms started to unload Jaasper's cargo. He showed them an amenities block, where they could wash away the dust of the road trip. The crew of the Water Bear emerged in their regimental uniforms, while Jaasper was transformed from a farmer, with dirt under his fingernails, into a prosperous businessman.

They set off, to find the government of Fluxor.

[I see you looking,] said Brin, in Box's sensorium, as they made their way through the cafés and shops of the Angel, the main shopping precinct.

Jura was larger and more elaborate than it looked from a distance. Each of the rocks was a town; some of them large enough to get lost in. There could be tens of thousands of people here. The Angel was third from the end, and sunk low in the water, so its energy dome prevented it being drowned by the waves. From street level the size of the seas became apparent. It was like being in a washing machine.

[So what?] said Box. [He's adorable.]

[They all are,] said Brin. [Haven't you noticed? It seems to be a racial characteristic.]

[Races have characteristics?]

[All ethnicities have characteristics.]

They *are* adorable, thought Box. Strangers smiled in the street. Happy children ran up to Jaasper, hoping to be introduced to the Po soldiers. They were especially fascinated by Kitou.

Box spoke to some of them, then parsed her own words.

"I just realized," she remarked. "I'm speaking Pursang."

"Yes," said Jaasper. "You have been since you arrived. We have no wetware."

"But I heard you, in my sensorium."

"Heard what?"

"I heard you singing, while you were fighting with Kitou."

"Really? That's surprising."

"Then you spoke to the Bat."

"He spoke to me."

"What is it with you and the Bat?"

"Oh, we go back a long way."

The office of the Recorder was perched high on the Innocent, the second-to-last of the islands, in an emerald tower, whose scintillating appearance was due to cascading gardens and parks, refracted in its trapezoidal exterior. It was probably the most exposed structure on the islands. Inside, there was a constant pitter-patter of rain in a forest. Rainbow-colored birds screeched as they dived through the vertical spaces. Inside an atrium was a wiry woman, dressed in denim workwear, trapped in a scrum of young people. Jaasper caught her attention, and she politely extricated himself from her interlocutors.

"Sama," said Jaasper.

"Ah, my Po sleuths are here. Welcome. Please. My home is your home, and that sort of thing."

Sama was a distinct political type - to an historian, instantly recognizable. The Aurelian commander-in-chief. A good kind of leader in a crisis. She twinkles like Samppo, thought Box. They could be siblings.

"See me later," she said.

Then she returned to her audience.

"That's more than I usually get," said Jaasper.

The tower's innermost core rose in a disorderly double-helix, occasionally winding around a secondary core, both floating free in the cylindrical void. "This is our seat of government," said Jaasper. "Where the business is done. We also have a Parliament, where gasbags can talk."

"It's called politics," said Box.

"The Regular is elected by our Parliament," said Jaasper, "and Sama has been in the same role for thirty-nine years. In many respects, she *is* the government."

"A benevolent dictator?"

"We believe so."

The elevator consisted of a disc without handrails, that spiraled up through leafy helical tunnels, with the sound of falling water all around them.

"This is thousand worlds technology," said Pax.

"This place was a gift from your people," said Jaasper. "Nine hundred years ago, when we decided to experiment with representative government."

"Has it been a successful experiment?" asked Box.

"We're getting used to it."

"I'll get to the point," said Sama.

They were gathered in a luxuriant ceiling atrium. Grasses, ferns and vines spilled everywhere. There was no hint of pattern or order. Night had fallen, and they had the space to themselves and the creatures who lived there. The space overhead was lit by a moon, refracted and intensified by the Fresnel effect of the building's exterior. The birds were bigger up here, and impressively clawed. They preyed on smaller birds below, and on fauna in the cantilevered gardens. Box watched a crimson-colored raptor disappear into the night with a snake in its beak. Outside, spume from the sea spattered against the lenses.

"I believe you," she said. "We believe you. Consider us warned. What will we do about it? Jaasper?"

"We can probably defend ourselves against a frontal attack," he said. "By calling in favors from friends."

"Probably?"

"We face an unknowable force. The Horu are a myth from antiquity. How many ships do they have? What new technology do they possess? How long is a blade of grass?"

"What *do* we know?"

Jaasper shrugged. "They store their dead in digital necropolii. Their drive is called a geometry drive. It unfolds space in peculiar ways."

Sama snorted. "I can learn all that in an entertainment sim. How do we know it's the Horu?"

"We know it was Horu *ships*," said Pax.

"They deny everything," said Box.

"They would," said Sama.

"I doubt any of this is as it seems," said Pax.

"Someone should go and ask them directly," said Sama.

"Easier said," said Pax. "Horax is a conjecture."

"We can help there," said Jaasper.

"How?"

"Old backdoors. Secret lines of communication. I'm sure I can conjure up a Horu or three."

"Then do it," said Sama.

She held up her hands. "Navigator Lo," she said. "What is your mission?"

"To prevent the genocide at Fluxor."

"And what of the supposed end-time war? Isn't your job also to prevent that?"

"The priorities merge. By preventing one, we act to prevent the other."

She frowned. "You don't know that."

"No," Pax admitted. "We can't. The task is just started. We may have to go deeper."

"How deep? To where your friend is? Ito Nadolo?"

"Perhaps," said Pax. "But Ito can take care of himself."

"So it's Fluxor, and then humanity, then your friend, in that order? No moral dilemma?"

"There are no moral dilemmas," said Pax. "Only a lack of clarity. The needs of the many always outweigh the needs of the few."

"So it's the species first?"

"Of course, but my job is this planet."

"What if it became a binary choice? What if the needs of the many outweighed this place?"

"Then I'd act to preserve our species. I know you would too."

"But how would you make the decisions? I'm not asking for your obedience, Navigator. I'd think less of you if I thought it was on offer. I simply want to know how your mind works."

"I give you my word that I won't sacrifice your world."

"Like it was sacrificed in your timeline."

"I had no say in that."

She nodded. "Then your word I will have. You're mine now, Navigator Pax Lo.

"Meantime, Jaasper Huw, call the thousand worlds, request military assistance. Actual warships, here tomorrow. Call in whatever favors you wish. Threaten them, if need be. In that sequence."

"Will they come?" asked Box.

Sama looked up into the atrium, where the apex predators flew, and then at Box, and she felt like she was being measured by one of the raptors there.

"Now *that's* a good question," she said, before turning her eyes on Pax. "Pax Lo, why *didn't* the thousand worlds come to our aid in your timeline?"

"I don't know," said Pax. "If I knew I'd tell you. But they'll come this time. By being here now, we've collapsed the equation."

Sama turned to leave, then turned to face them again. "Please don't think me harsh," she said. "I have a world to consider. You have my blessings, and our thanks. It goes without saying, but I'll say it. Take whatever you want from us here. Were a small society, but not without resources. We won't forget this."

"May we have Jaasper?" asked Pax. "We're short a fast pair of hands in a corner."

"You may," said Jaasper. "This is obviously more interesting than cabbages. But before we begin, I must borrow young d Atwusk'niges here."

"She's to be tested?" asked Sama.

"Yes, the child eluded me in a fair fight," said Jaasper.

"We grow old," said Sama.

Kitou returned from her testing, two days later, in a haze of contentment. Box and Brin took her to a woodland park, nestled in the labyrinthine halls of the Wizard, the most ornate of the twelve, that twisted like a candlestick into the sea, and as they trained, they asked her about her experience.

"Did you have to fight?" asked Brin.

"No, nothing like that at all."

"Then what?" asked Box and Brin together.

"They measured my character," she said.

"How?" asked Box.

"We talked, and there was a test of courage, which I thankfully passed, although it was hard, and I made a friend."

"What kind of test of courage?" asked Brin.

"I can't say," said Kitou.

"What kind of friend?" asked Box.

Kitou opened her hand, and there was a silvery distortion, and then a dancing point of light. She blew lightly on her palm, and a salt breeze lifted the leaves in the nearby trees.

"He's a sea spirit," she said.

"Does he have a name?" asked Brin.

"No, he's just a newborn. We have to learn his name together."

The pressure for Kitou to visit her family had become unbearable. They'd found out, as they always were going to, that their little girl had come from the future to save them.

"Please, come with me," she said to Box.

"I'm there," said Box.

The journey to Atwusk'niges took nineteen hours. They drove through the night. The holy mountain Lhotse swung into view, long before the forest did, a soaring triangle of rock, rose-gold in the first sunlight.

"Oh, this is too much to bear," said Kitou.

"You know what that is?" asked Box. "That's the fear of happiness."

She nodded. "I'm frightened it will be given to me, and taken away again."

The great rift valley of Fluxor, called Algoma'aa, meaning the valley of the flowers, ran arrow-straight for five thousand kilometers, from the balmy equator to the Freezer, where some Pursang still lived the old life in its sheltered valleys. At Atwusk'niges, the straight line from Lhotse's summit to the valley floor was almost nine kilometers.

"Holy fuck," said Box.

Jaasper laughed. "You could say that."

"Ah, I'm sorry, that was culturally insensitive."

"No," said Kitou. "It is apt."

Atwusk'niges was a high montane rainforest; a mysterious world, shrouded in mist, cascading down a mile-high tooth of rock. The village of Atwusk'niges clung to its roots, a kilometer above the valley floor.

They were looking down on it from across the Algoma'aa valley, where the road from Jura ended.

"How do we get down?" asked Box.

"In the usual way." said Kitou.

"I'll wait for the freight plane," said Jaasper.

Kitou and Box stood on the edge, and jumped.

Kitou at six was a faithful miniature of the sixteen-year-old one. She darted out of the crowd to see her new sister for the first time, wide-eyed with astonishment. Box burst into tears before Kitou did, but it was a close-run thing.

"A beautiful entrance," said a craggy, green-eyed man.

"Oh, father," said Kitou.

Then Kitou was in the middle of a tangle of humans.

"Dr Box," she said after a few minutes of this. "I'd like you to meet my family. This is my mother Vanja, and my father Akito, and my little sister, also called Kitou.

"This is Ophelia Box, my friend."

"Welcome," said Vanja, a woman of rare beauty, with her daughter's warm smile. "Our home is your home, now and for always."

"Two Kitous," said a grinning Akito. "Who would have thought it? Ophelia, please come inside, and we'll make you some tea."

"Our friend Jaasper is coming," said Kitou.

"On the descender?"

"That fat thing?" asked Box, squinting at a glider, banking steeply, like a plump fly beneath the west wall of Lhotse.

"That's the one," said Akito.

231

Kitou was showing Kitou her sea spirit, and was teaching her how to make a fresh sea breeze, when Jaasper appeared at the door.

"Jaasper Huw d Strategos," said Akito.

"You know each other?" asked Box.

"We know *of* each other," said Jaasper. "I'm honored to visit your family, Akito Gorgonza d Atwusk'niges."

"The honor is ours, Jaasper Huw. Please come in. Now for that tea."

Box found Pursang traditional tea to be disgusting. Not only was it rank with animal fat, but this festive version had strong alcohol in it. Vanja smiled at Box's involuntary reaction. "Give the poor woman a sensible drink," she commanded, and the tea was replaced by a cup of the sour vanilla beverage, softened and sweetened with cream.

The men drank the tea, and the older Kitou had a cup, and made a face.

"I'd forgotten that vile stew," she laughed.

They were sitting comfortably in the open living space of the Gorgonza's home, which had the simple construction of all Pursang architecture. Kitou had stopped playing with little Kitou, who was now slouched on her knee. They were both piled up bonelessly against Vanja, a pose Box had seen a hundred times before.

"So, Jaasper Huw," said Vanja, "What brings you to Atwusk'niges?"

Jaasper leaned forward. "Kitou's been tested."

"We can see that," said Vanja.

"Normally we'd counsel a family first."

"Then counsel us now."

"She was chosen by a water spirit."

"Not just any water spirit."

Jaasper nodded. "An undine."

"What does that mean?" asked Box.

"It means she'll fight," said Vanja.

"I already fight," said Kitou.

"Undines kick ass," piped young Kitou.

"Shush," said Vanja.

Akito laughed. "It's true though," he said. "Undine are wild, like the sea itself is."

Part of the Gorgonza home was cut into the Atwusk'niges rock, with a curving glass wall, overlooking the Algoma'aa valley below. Box watched a rain squall come marching along the valley, spread its load of rain, then march away again, leaving a sky like watercolor.

They discussed the defense of Fluxor.

"There'll soon be a thousand worlds battle group stationed here," said Jaasper.

"Stronger than any possible Horu force?" asked Akito.

"Perhaps not. But a deterrent."

"When does it arrive?"

"Imminently."

"Our son would want to be in that," said Vanja.

"Where is he?"

"Fighting the Badoop," said Akito.

"As far as it's possible to be from here, and still be in the human galaxy," said Vanja.

"In our timeline," said Kitou. "Totoro fights with the Free Pursang."

"I pity his enemies," said Akito, with emphasis.

"Totoro kicks ass," piped young Kitou.

"Shush," said Vanja.

"How long till the genocide?" asked Akito.

"Three years," said Jaasper. "In our timeline."

"What if they come sooner, in this one?"

"There's no defense against sooner," said Jaasper. "If the enemy can adapt in the past, there's no time soon enough for us to begin. So, we defend against the attack we know, and beat the underbrush to frighten the snake."

Kitou took Box and her little sister into the high rainforest canopy, a mile overhead, where she'd fought the fire. The Water Bear lifted them up, to the younger Kitou's pure delight. "Normally we climb by muscle alone," said big Kitou. "But the climb to the top takes a day."

It truly was a cloud forest. Scallops and lenses of damp mist hung between the ancient rainforest trees. Trickles and runs and tumbling cascades of pure Lhotse meltwater appeared out of nowhere, only to fade back into misty whiteness a few meters below. Kitou showed them a streaming rock face, carpeted in fungus and moss.

In the rock face was a notch, barely wide enough for a small girl to climb into.

"Here," she said. "Here is where Ito saved me."

She showed them a narrow arête.

"And here is where the fire first bit me."

"High," said little Kitou.

"Yes," said her older sister.

"I can't imagine all this destroyed," said Box.

"All down there was burnt," said big Kitou, pointing out into the valley below. "Burnt trees and dancing flames, for a thousand kilometers. All the world, burning."

"Stratego," said Box. "All the children."

"And Jura," said Kitou. "Sama in her tower."

"Everything, gone."

11 ∞ THE MÖBIUS TRIP

2065

O phelia Box watched an origami bird unfold in space. It hurt her eyes to see it happening.

"That's impressive," said Brin.

[Geometrically impossible,] said the Bat.

Box, Brin and Kitou were strapped in the Bat, watching the event from close quarters. They were the away team for this mission. The Water Bear was a thousand kilometers distant, with Pax and Jaasper Huw aboard, ready for fight, flight, or parley.

Half a system away, three Wu warships guarded Fluxor Station. They were the same cylindrical design as Box had seen at Aldebaran. She was told that to attack, they would remember their target in three different places. Now, it didn't bother her as much.

Now they were *her* warships.

When it finished unfolding, the Horu ship was larger than all the Wu warships combined, and incorporeal, with the ghostly blue-green glow of ocean bioluminescence. Box glanced at Kitou, who watched with rapt attention.

[Horu ship,] broadcast the Water Bear, over a wide range of the electromagnetic spectrum. "We are Po warships, the Water Bear and Bat."

The Water Bear had acquired a good working knowledge of Horu, and was about to try a dialect, when the Horu ship responded.

<<Friends.>>

"How are you getting this?" asked Pax.

[Semantic primitives, directly into my eloquent cortex,] said the Water Bear.

[New technology,] said the Bat.

[Are we friends?] asked the Water Bear.

It seemed to take an age for the strange ship to consider the question. Moments passed. Either it was pretending to think, or relaying messages over a long distance.

Moments stretched into minutes.

<<We are. I understand your politics.>>

[Can we meet?]

<<We are.>>

[In person?]

<<I am in person.>>

[Your crew?]

<<I have none; in any sense you'd recognize. I have a virtuality, where our personalities can manifest individually. Would you like to meet me there?>>

Pax considered this.

They were under instructions to treat this as first contact.

Contact was what they were here for.

"Yes," he said.

<<Follow.>>

An opening unfolded in the ghostly ship. To the team on the Bat, it was like seeing a flower blossom, until it was the size of a mountain, and spread its petals wide, until there was a city-sized hole in its stigma. Through the hole was a space whose volume defied physical explanation. Based on the optics of the sunlight slanting through the opening, it was a flattened sphere, ten thousand kilometers across, and hazy, as though it held an atmosphere. It was many times larger than the Horu ship that contained it.

Inside the mysterious space was a pulsing light.

<<We call this chamber the Manifold,>> said the bird-shaped ship.

<<Follow the light.>>

The Water Bear accelerated, and a few minutes later, so did the Bat, so they fell through the portal together. The interior walls of the Manifold were a fathomless grey, with a slippery, viscous appearance, that seemed to ripple with their passing.

Like the aspen forest in Utah, this place breathed old time. If anything, it seemed incredibly older.

Like death, thought Box.

They fell for hours, to all appearances becalmed inside the world-sized void. Wispy skeins of dust caught long shafts of light, shining from nowhere.

"What is this creepy place?" asked Box. She'd sometimes felt lost in the openness of space. Here she felt like she was nowhere at all.

[You want me to speculate?] asked the Water Bear.

"Please," said Pax.

[A transportation abstraction. This spheroid correlates to physical spacetime in some nontrivial way. I suggest we're going to exit far from where we entered.]

"No shit," said Box.

"Like a wormhole?" asked Brin.

"Not an unreasonable analogy. Perhaps a wormhole in a higher dimension."

"Do we have those?" asked Box.

"In experiments only. Not for transportation purposes."

A second flower unfolded. It followed the same uncanny unfolding as the original flower. Through its portal were stars. They decelerated through it, and were orbiting a dark, turbulent planet. Fire and lightning flickered in the planet's atmosphere. Below them was a smaller, more corporeal version of the bird-shaped ship. It was made of the same pearly, depthless material as the walls of the chamber they'd passed through.

Surrounding the planet were hundreds of similar ships.

[628 ships,] appeared in Box's head-up display.

Box was shaken. Almost a thousand. She'd seen what a handful can do, in the Water Bear's memories of Fluxor.

How can we war against that?

<<I am Flux,>> said the small ship. <<This is my self. You may connect with me.

<<We are the ships of the dead.

<<Welcome to Horax.>>

Box, Brin and Kitou found themselves in the Grosvenor Hotel suite, that they'd visited with Yokohama Slim in 1851. They were accompanied by the Bat, who had puckishly taken the form of a bat.

[Acerodon jubatus, a golden-capped fruit bat,] said the Water Bear, in Box's sensorium.

[Can I be anything I want?] Box asked.

[Within reason,] said the Water Bear. [Some things, like the sound of the rain on a hot summer night, are hard to personify.]

Apart from the Bat, who was suspended from a gasolier, they were seated in green velveteen chairs. The pile of the cloth was worn thin, as though a thousand pairs of hands had rested on them. A coal fire guttered and spat in the grate. Box could sense the gritty darkness outside. It was an astonishingly convincing simulation. Facing them were two people: small, neat, muscular dark-haired men.

If this were a film, Box thought, they'd be vampires.

One resembled the Horu fighting robot.

"Mr. Chance?" she asked.

It was strange to see how the man resembled the robot. It was something about the way he carried himself: in a surprised way, with his head held back at a certain angle.

"Dr Ophelia Box," he said, in a perfectly ordinary voice. "It's good to see you again. With your eponymous ship, who clearly enjoys a good joke."

"Aren't you departed by now, Mr. Chance?"

"Long since, Dr Box. I'm in Möbius space. Hopefully doing well, though I can't say for certain. This is a projection of my original self: a visual-interlocutor; a form of AI, my emissary in the Real."

He turned towards the second man.

"Please meet our host, Mr. Flux."

The man leant forward in his chair. He was about Box's age, but with an old man's rheumy eyes, combined with an intense stare, that put Box in mind of an old man's toothless smile.

Something told her the man was also a machine, and could also be any shape it wanted to be.

So, toothless was perhaps the wrong analogy.

An impression, meant to be given.

"You have so many questions," he said.

It was overly warm in the room. It had exactly the air of a real Victorian sitting room, at the onset of winter: at first stiflingly hot, then cold, through a flue, or a gap in the wainscoting.

"Please explain," said Brin.

"It isn't an easy explanation," he said. "But follow, and I'll show you everything..."

They were on the bridge deck of a spacecraft. The bridge was manned by humans, dressed in military uniforms. They were strapped into acceleration chairs, under a canopy, like an outsized jet fighter, giving a view of the world above them. They were shorter and more muscular than Earth normal, with small, high ears set back on clean-shaved heads, and their faces tattooed with elaborate designs.

"Fluxor?" said Box. Or was it? She saw the line of the Aø, where it crossed the Igháán.

"But also not Fluxor," said Kitou. "The icecaps are smaller, and there's desert."

"Fluxor, two million years ago," said Flux.

"Is this a recording or a simulation?" asked the Bat.

"Neither," said Flux. "And both. We are here. Now watch..."

A scattering of small, hard points of light limned a coast of one of the islands, spreading like an aurora. The humans on the bridge averted their eyes. Some shouted.

One sobbed. A few minutes later, a field of searing pinpricks lit up another part of the world.

"A limited nuclear exchange," said Flux. Two hundred thermonuclear weapons, about a kiloton each."

"The dawn war," said Kitou.

"Watch..."

Hundreds, then thousands of progressively larger explosions erupted in waves on the surface. The watchers looked on in horror, interlopers and bridge crew alike, as nuclear firestorms incinerated cities and forests. Plumes of ash and smoke eructed into the atmosphere, merging into continent-spanning storms. In an hour, the surface was obscured.

Under the clouds, firestorms raged.

"All the atomics deployed," said Flux.

Box looked at Kitou.

"Are you okay, kiddo?"

"I'm not sure. It was so long ago, but these were my people."

"Want my advice?"

"Please."

"Forget the past. There's so much wrong there; it'll drive you insane. Let it go."

"Then what must I do? What's seen can't be unseen."

"The reason history exists is to learn from."

Kitou nodded.

"This is the story of our people," said Flux. "All of us here, including you Dr Box. This is your past you are seeing.

"Now forward five years."

They were on the same bridge, but the crew had visibly aged. All semblance of military formality was gone. Beards were entangled with military insignia and primitive cultural charms. Men and women, all bare-chested. Unsheathed knives were thrust in belts, and by the appearance of scars on the bodies of the crew, sometimes used.

The ship fell into the atmosphere, in a spiraling dive, and after the thunder and fire of re-entry, flew under the roiling clouds, over a shattered, frosty landscape. They circled low over a wretched community. People came out to see, waving their arms in the air, emaciated, dressed in rags, some naked to the cold.

A woman held her swaddled baby in the air.

"Nuclear winter," said Flux. "The ice-albedo effect. As the planet cools, more ice forms, which reflects more solar radiation into space. Fallout, pyrotoxins, ozone depletion. Extinction. We were the Pursang politico-warrior class. We started this war, and we ended it. We escaped in the remaining spacecraft."

"You left these people to die?" asked Box.

"Yes."

"That's despicable."

"Yes, we were despicable."

"You were the precursor race," said Kitou.

"Yes child, we were. And we left your people to die."

"Now forward five hundred years..."

There were no humans left on the bridge. Instead, systems flashed in the dark. They were orbiting a green world, like Fluxor, but less obviously oceanic. Instead of oceans, there were extensive, interconnected river systems.

"Horax," said Flux. "A goldilocks world, near-perfect without terraforming."

"I was born around this time," said Chance.

"Wait," said Box. "Are you saying you're two million years old?"

"In elapsed time."

"Watch..." said Flux.

The planet spun faster. Days became minutes, then moments, then instants. Small clouds of lights, spreading out from river ports, became sprawling megalopolises. The ice caps shrank, and disappeared. Green swathes of wilderness became checkerboard farms, then heavy industry, then an industrial waste, and finally desert. The sky grew grey with pollution, then black with particulate clouds. Vast fires burned as toxic waste then methane in the soil caught fire.

Finally, it resembled the storm-wracked, vaporous world they'd seen in the Real: Horax.

"This was our legacy," said Flux. "In two thousand years, we destroyed a second world, not by war but by greed. The child is correct. We were the precursor race, but also her race. There were two castes of human on Fluxor. We believed ourselves to be the warrior elite, but it was a fantasy. We were a political class. We pursued wars, to stimulate production, to improve the breed, to gain wealth, for our pleasure, until finally we pressed a button too many. Then, given a second chance, on a perfect new world, we destroyed that as well.

"Eventually, we were faced by the truth. The problem was us. Something inside us was broken. We were like a bacteriophage, killing the cells of its host.

Ships like the Flux appeared in orbit around the dead planet.

"Totemic arks," said Flux. "Flowers, spiders, birds. Charms. Symbolic offerings, to unknown gods. We digitized what was left of our people, and set sail for the future."

One of the ships was the Flux. The warship they were in slid in through an iris-shaped port in its side, which was sealed shut behind them. Its systems grew dim, then flickered off.

"Our last, best hope was that our species might someday be saved from itself. That a better, more productive strain of humanity might emerge.

"Little did we know that strain already existed.

"Now, forward two million years..."

A shining disc, ten thousand kilometers across.

A water conveyor, encircling a dark star.

An orbiter, the size of a planet.

A swarm of city-sized habitats, travelling at near lightspeed, halfway to Centaurus A.

A juniper forest, orbiting beneath the blazing glory of the galactic core.

Moon-sized spheres and cubes.

Hollowed-out asteroids.

Natural worlds.

Avalon, a painted fortress, basking by a milk-white sea. Threnody, all the colors of Autumn. Earth, in its jeweled glory.

"Behold, humanity. Nothing special, by the standards of a successful galactic species, but we exist. We passed through the eye of the needle. We're still in the game.

"The Horu abandonment proved to be a beneficial culling event for our species. By accident, we extracted the worst from our gene pool, and left the best to abide, in terrible circumstances, and then to succeed. Not just persist, but excel.

"Not by war, but by a just society.

"How do we feel about that? We feel ashamed, but proud, like absent fathers looking on a lost child from afar. We were abusive, so we took ourselves out of the picture.

"We'd do nothing to hurt this species.

"We'd do anything to defend it.

"But there's a problem, and I fear it's our doing."

Now they were floating disembodied, over a dense knot of circuitry, like a convoluted Möbius strip, curling in on itself with oily precision. It was orbiting a planetoid of similar construction. It reminded Box of a particle accelerator, but turned inside out, with its intimate engineering on the outside.

It was hard to judge size, but Box guessed the planetoid was about the size of Earth's moon, and the device itself was about the size of the Aldebaran orbiter.

"The Möbius machine," said Flux.

"Also known as Rabbithole," said Chance.

"As in down the?" asked Box.

"Yes," said Chance.

There were no stars in this place. Below them was a geometric plane, as though the universe was split in two halves. The only reason Box could see it was her wetware, telling her it was there. The reason there were no stars was that they were under a world-sized umbrella.

Box sensed more stars than she could possibly imagine, above the umbrella.

"I will explain...

"But first, observe..."

A siren wailed in their sensoria, a forlorn sound, like all the world's emergencies were about to begin. Then a voice began to sing: a haunting, eldritch melody.

"The old song," said Kitou.

"Yes," said Flux. "There are vital similarities."

A second voice followed the first, its pitch subtly different, creating a wavering vibration. The melody swelled, and more voices joined, then more, and more, until it was as though every voice in creation was singing.

"A worldsinging," whispered Kitou.

"Yes," said Flux. "It's the Pursang creation myth, replayed. But not by twelve voices."

[Twelve factorial voices,] said the Water Bear.

[You're still here?] asked Box.

[Oh yes, and I'm aware of this experiment, although not of its outcome.]

[What's happening?]

[The Möbius machine is cycling the voices of 479,001,600 artificial beings, into a moment of simultaneity.]

"Ophelia Box," said Flux. "Don't imagine you're here by accident. You, or the soldier, or the child: you're here to witness this; what you see here is testimony.

"Now, everything becomes possible."

Box flipped inside out. There was no other way to describe it. They were falling. No, not falling. They were protons, crossing the primordial cell wall. They were angels, blazing trails of fire through the heavens. Instead of a flat plane, below them was a nebula.

More than a nebula: what they were falling towards was the moment of creation.

Then, silence.

The machine disappeared.

"Behold," said Flux. "The birth of a new universe."

Box found her fingers sunk in the plush of her velveteen chair. Something important had just happened, although she couldn't get her head around it.

"I'm gonna be sick," she said.

"The feeling will pass," said Flux.

"Bat, please make sure she's not vomiting in the Real," said Brin.

"What just happened?" asked Kitou.

[The Horu created a new universe,] said the Water Bear.

"Correct," said Flux.

[And proved some old physics.]

"The memetic theory of everything."

"Memes, as in... ideas?" asked Box, looking up.

[Yes,] said the Water Bear. [The theory of reality as a persistent illusion.]

"A democracy of ideas," said Flux.

"Explain," said Brin.

[May I?] said the Water Bear.

"Yes," said Flux.

The Water Bear's gamespace avatar manifested in one of the velveteen chairs. "In the memetic theory of things," she explained, "also called the illusory interpretation of quantum mechanics, there is no fixed reality, only a wavefunction, the superposition of all possible states. Observers create their own reality by collapsing the wavefunction into a state, but all that changes are the microtubules in the observers' brains. Thus, reality is a synaptic illusion: an hallucination, shared by a sufficiently large number of observers. 12! is a number suggested, to start a new universe."

"Which we proved," said Flux.

"I'll need to see your results," she said.

"You'll have them."

"Which brings us to the big question," said Brin.

"Which is?"

"Do we believe you?"

They found themselves back in the Real, floating in space, in an immersive sim. Around them were hundreds of necropolii: flowers, spiders, birds. Unlike the Flux, who showed glimmers of blue-green bioluminescence within his pearly substrate, they were dark.

"We call this the Boneyard," said Flux.

"What happened?" asked Brin.

"Their humans are in Möbius now. The vessels are empty."

"Abandoned?"

"No, they still have their personalities, but without their humans aboard, they're incapable of true consciousness. They sleep."

"What about you?" said Box. "You're conscious."

"I still carry my people."

"Literally?"

"Not physically. There are no bodies buried here, Dr Box. My humans dream they're a starship."

"Except me," said Chance.

"Yes, Mr. Chance's copy has kindly agreed to be animated.

"Now, please watch..."

A ship came alive, but not with a ghostly light. Its legs started to move. Like a real spider, it began to crawl across space. Box saw a hint of spiny bristles appear on its skin, the hint of shining eyes. A nightmare creature. Then a slug of degenerate matter, moving at relativistic speed, flashed into the side of the spider-shaped ship, and space around it dissolved into featureless white.

They were back in the Grosvenor Hotel suite.

"What just happened?" asked Brin.

"A kiloton kinetic," said the Water Bear.

"Yes," said Flux. "I destroyed her."

"Why?"

"She became possessed. Like others before her. Left in that state, she would've regained her full offensive capability in a few seconds. Now I keep a gun loaded for each Boneyard ship."

"You say 'she'," said Brin.

"Yes, her name was Thea. She deserved better."

"That was a death?"

"Yes, of a two-million-year-old being, and my friend."

"Oh, I'm so sorry," said Box.

"Who was doing the possessing?" asked Brin.

"I wish I knew," said Flux. "I call it the Enemy. But whatever it is, it comes from Möbius space, and it desires to be here, in this universe."

"Through the network links you sent your people to Möbius through?"

"Yes."

"You've severed them?"

"I have, but the connection persists. The physics escapes me. I conclude that some part of each ship is now entangled with Möbius space."

"Then destroy them."

"That would be a genocide. Those ships are my people."

"What about the millions on Fluxor?"

"Who aren't dead yet."

"You believe this Enemy is the source of the Fluxor atrocity?"

"I'm sure of it."

"Evidence?"

"I'll give you full access to my mind."

"A full, forensic scan?"

"Yes."

"Ship?"

"Yes," said the Water Bear. "That'd be conclusive."

"Pax?"

[Return. Let's wargame this.]

The Flux's interior spaces were like the inside of a musical instrument, with organic frets and tubes, and light slanting through mysterious gaps, passing through air that looked dusty, but wasn't.

"This is a spooky place," said Box.

"Because it's full of dead people," said Kitou.

"There is that," said Box.

"My sea spirit senses them."

"This way," said the androform Water Bear.

After a few minutes' walk - more than the exterior dimensions of the Flex would suggest - they reached what appeared to be the Horu warship they'd journeyed through time in. It was exactly as she remembered, with its domed canopy facing an exterior wall, where it'd been sealed in, two million years before.

Box picked up a carved bone ornament, coated in dust.

It was the shape of a bear.

Bone. Where would they have got bone?

She pushed the thought away.

Waiting on the bridge deck of the ancient ship was Chance, in his robot body. One of the acceleration couches had been replaced by an old-fashioned clinical chair, with its headrest at the nexus of a swarm of robotic arms.

Box could imagine it in a dentist's studio, or on the set of a horror movie.

Brin touched the arms. "What are these for?" she asked.

"I will use them to alter your physical brain."

"Actual surgery?"

"Yes. Consensual reality is encoded in your reptilian brain, in regions of the pons and medulla oblongata. I will build a new reptile, by repurposing the neurons there. Then I'll stimulate the occipital and parietal lobes of the cerebral cortex with dopamine, to encourage your belief in the new paradigm."

"What does that mean?" asked Box.

"It means you'll be in a different place," he said.

"When does transition occur?" asked Brin.

"When the subject wakes, typically in a state of religious ecstasy, during the dopamine experience."

"The subject being me."

"Yes."

"If it goes wrong?"

"The subject dies. But it doesn't go wrong. I've done this before."

"On living humans?"

"Yes. Every Horu soul has travelled this way, in a surgically altered, vat-grown body."

"Like zombies," said Box.

"Don't worry," said Chance. "This is mature technology."

"Success rate?"

"Recently, a hundred percent."

"Recently?"

"In the early days, not so much."

"You?"

The robot shrugged, a disarmingly human gesture.

"Do we trust these people?" asked Box.

"I do," said Kitou.

"Explain," said Brin.

"We gain nothing by not trusting Flux now, except maybe our lives. By mistakenly distrusting him, we stand to lose everything. So, we risk our lives."

"Good girl," said Brin.

"Also, I actually trust them," Kitou said. "They're undeniably strange, but people are strange."

"Amen that," said Brin.

"Okay, let's do this," she said.

"How long will it take?" asked Box, as Brin prepared herself, retracting her skinsuit so that it became like a second skin.

"About ten seconds. Brin, please?"

Brin took her place in the clinical chair, with her head inside the robotic swarm, which waved smoothly to fit her head and neck. "How is the surgery performed?" she asked, holding the arms at bay.

"By gravitic impulse, no incisions."

She leaned back.

"Then begin."

She appeared to fall asleep. The arms waved soundlessly around her head, and Box was appalled. A million years of biological programming was being rewired.

Brin's eyes opened, and widened, and she disappeared.

"Fuck," said Box.

"Now me," said Kitou.

"You're aware of the additional risk?" asked Chance.

"Yes."

"What additional risk?" asked Box.

"Kitou isn't wholly human," said Flux.

"Her undine?"

"Yes."

"Why's that a risk?"

"It's a complexity. The undine spirit is the larval stage of the Xap lifecycle. They're in a symbiosis, and will be until the end of Kitou's lifespan."

"We don't talk like that," said Kitou.

"I know, there's a spiritual element, which I respect. But we must speak plainly here."

"What could go wrong?" asked Box.

"The embryonic Xap might reject the new model. We could lose one, or both," said Chance.

"I see you waited until Brin was gone before raising this."

"Dr Box," said Kitou. "We have to learn whether my kind can enter here."

"I want to ask Pax."

"Pax knows," said Kitou.

"Is that true?" she insisted.

"Yes," said Flux. "The child is right. The risk is acceptable, and this is essential, for the sake of our species."

"How risky is it?"

"Twenty-five percent, to lose both of them."

"Twenty-five *percent*? What kind of horseshit odds are those?"

While they argued, Kitou lay back in the chair. "Begin," she said, and the robotic arms waved. Like

Brin, she seemed to fall asleep. Her eyes flicked open, and she disappeared.

"Success," said Chance.

"You're sure?" asked Box.

"I am. Now you. Time is short. The downlink's at risk."

"Ship?"

"Go, Dr Box," said the androform Water Bear.

Box lay in the chair. The arms waved as before, performing their bloodless intrusion. She fell into a trance, not unlike the euphoric state produced by the sacrament she drank in Utah. She saw the same forest. Drops of water trembled on the same aspen leaves.

She sensed Pando, and her love, not a soft and sumptuous thing, but ferocious.

She heard her friends, calling in the darkness. For a moment, that might've been forever, she imagined she was God. Not just a god, but God the creator, giving bloody birth to a new cosmos; she was Amon, rising over the first sea; Dayuni'si, come to Earth to see what was under the water; Krishna, the preserver, returning in the age of pain.

She was the first child, gazing out of a primordial forest.

She saw Kitou, trailing a blaze of fire in the heavens.

She saw Brin, defending the gates with her soul.

She could get lost in this place.

Then she came to her senses.

Her frontal lobes, accepting the newly consensual.

She lay in a green field, under a supersaturated sky. The colors were so rich, they were pulsing. Her friends were smiling down at her.

"Holy fuck," said Box.

"Are you alright?" asked Kitou.

"My head is still buzzing," she said.

"It isn't your head," said Ito.

How did Ito get here?

It emerged from the hum, like a binaural beat.

Ophelia.

Ophelia Box.

Open your mind.

BOOK TWO

A thousand years ago
Ten thousand Chinese marching on the plains
all turned their heads to Heaven at once to see the Moon.
An old man catching fireflies on the porch at night
watched the Herd Boy cross the Milky Way to meet the
Weaving Girl...
How can we war against that?

Allen Ginsberg - Iron Horse

12 ∞ OPHELIA, DOWN THE RABBITHOLE

314

The Red Lady was confused. The Blue warrior, Marius D, looked on impassively. This was only to be expected. Her shieldmaidens were there to help her.

And the prophet, Ito Nadolo.

This was a great day.

The Blue people believed they had sung the world into existence, and three heroes would come to lead them to heaven. The Reanimated, who were far more numerous, believed the world was created by God for their use, and that they had once lived in heaven themselves. Both agreed the world was shaped like a toroidal polyhedron, or paradromic ring, and was about three hundred years old.

In Blue cosmology, the gods were natural beings, and were far too numerous to count. They lived in heaven like fleas on a cat. The Reanimator god was Mathematics.

Both accepted the equal truth of each other's opposite view.

That's how it goes, in Flipside.

Ophelia Box scrambled to her feet. She was in a supersaturated world, that seemed to twist in on itself in a way that made her feel sick.

"The feeling will pass," said Ito.

She was on a steep-sided hill, like Glastonbury Tor. The sky was the most vivid color of *sky* she could imagine. The landscape was a patchwork quilt of supersaturated greens.

She was completely naked.

A strapping young Viking was staring at her.

She started to giggle, uncontrollably.

"Frost," said Brin.

From the towering height of his nineteen years, both shieldmaidens were exceptionally beautiful. The Red Lady less so. She must be at least thirty.

A tenth the age of the universe.

The white one, who he knew as the Goddess, who couldn't be beaten in battle, was yellow-haired and creamy-skinned like him. He'd follow her.

The black one was a different matter. With her cleanshaven head and luminous warpaint, he'd never seen anything so exotic, even among the Reanimated, who were sometimes brown skinned.

Many would follow the panther.

Beings of mythos, alive in the world.

Such days.

"Bring blankets," he commanded, and a rider rode down from the sky, with temporary clothing, which Ito Nadolo gave to the three women, who were gabbling in tongues he could make no sense of. He knew they'd soon learn his language. It had taken Ito three hours.

They had *wetware.*

"We must be careful, Ito."

The prophet nodded. He understood the dangers.

Behind the sky was the Enemy, with his beam weapons.

"Where's the Water Bear?" asked Box.

[I'm here, Dr Box.]

"Where?"

"The ship's personality seems to be hosted in our wetware," said Brin.

[I didn't quite make it.]

"Ship, what are your capabilities?" asked Ito.

[Limited.]

"Well, at least you're here," said Kitou.

[I am, shieldmaiden.]

Box suppressed another giggle.

They gave her a horse, a rust-red dappled mare with a flighty attitude. Box's experience with horses was limited to carousels. Thankfully her wetware knew how to ride them.

Dirty great beasties for posh English lassies.

She began to relax, and to enjoy herself. The high moors seemed to stretch on forever. They could be in the Highlands of Scotland. They were being escorted by a half-dozen Vikings, four men and two women, who oozed competence. Dotted among the clouds, she could see more Vikings.

Where was she?

She found she didn't much care.

She was thrilled.

This was astonishing.

She shimmied her ride towards Ito, who was off to one side, finding higher pieces of ground, scanning the horizons.

"Ito, it's great to see you."

"And you, Dr Box. How are Pax and Alois?"

"Pax is himself. Alois is complicated."

"Then business as usual."

She smiled, then laughed out loud.

"Ito, I can't wait to hear you try to explain this."

"Listen," he said.

"What?"

"Listen closely. D'you hear it?"

"It's the Fa:ing hum!"

"Yes. Like the Water Bear, they didn't quite make it here."

"But they're here?"

"Yes, this place is where they were searching for."

"The Horu heaven?"

"Oh, it's more interesting than that."

"What is it?"

"It's the human unconscious."

They descended into a small farm, a tangle of garden, clotted around a stone farmhouse, surrounded by fields of waving grass. Children ran out shrieking to greet the Blue warriors, who snarled fiercely, before laughing. The farmers came to meet them, a smiling coffee-skinned couple.

"Are these the ones?" asked the woman, shyly.

Marius nodded.

"Then we are blest," said the man.

Box waved. She was already understanding this language. The farmyard smells assaulted her face: the heavy ammoniac stench of chicken shit, and musky barn manure, and freshly turned, moist soil, and hay curing in the mow, more real than real.

The children waved back, delightedly.

"Red Lady," whispered the woman.

Past the farm, they continued down towards a country railway station, with beelike creatures bumbling in the long grass, between ceramic railway sleepers. As they descended, the air grew warmer. Here it was like summer. A train surged into view, flowing from a perplexing middle-distance, and some of it peeled away, and slowed to a stop in their station. The Vikings led their horses into freight cars, where they tied them into horseboxes – incongruous timber against the pristine ceramics of the carriages - and the train surged forward. Soon, they were travelling at high speed though a harlequin countryside.

"This is the centerline train," said Ito. "Welcome to Flipside."

Marius stood to be introduced.

"Marius, this is Ophelia Box, known to your people as the Red Lady, and Brin Lot and Kitou Gorgonza, her shieldmaidens. Team, this is Marius D, a warrior of the Blue people. Marius's riders are Markus, Velo, Viki, Alis, Ox and Bravery. Also here, but not currently visible, is my ship, the Water Bear.

"Ride of the Spinifex Reach, meet the Hand of the Water Bear.

"As the Blue people say, this is a great day."

Marius bowed, and unsheathed his bone sword, and presented it, grip-first towards Box.

266

"What do I do?" she asked Ito.

"Accept it," said Ito.

She took it. It was as light as a feather, constructed like a samurai sword: a katana.

"Now give it back to him, grip-first."

She did. It was like rotating razor-sharp air.

A grin split his face.

"As you say, Ito, a great day."

"He's now yours to command," said Ito.

"I only just met him."

"He'll gladly die for you. Now for the others."

One by one, she accepted their weapons. One of the women boldly kissed her full on the lips, before blushing and backing away.

"Thank you," she said.

[You did perfectly,] said the Water Bear.

[How do you know?]

[Comparative ethnology. Also their vitals. They love you.]

The Flipside universe was the shape of a Möbius strip, embedded in three-dimensional Euclidean space, like the Möbius machine itself, although the exact relationship between the shape of the machine and the shape of the universe was unclear. To its inhabitants, Flipside seemed spatially flat, but self-referentially twisted, so that it turns on itself from every direction.

Box learned this from a book, a beautiful physical book, printed on beautiful vellum. Travel from side to side, away from the centerline, was a mystical experience: to dreams, and the shadow. Travel along the centerline brings the traveler back where they started, after a journey of some four thousand kilometers, including a thousand kilometers of vacuum.

The part they lived in was called the Upside.

The vacuum below is called Downside.

Around the cylinder is Farside.

The centerline train traverses the whole universe, and the direction of its travel is called Spinwards.

Everyone knew the origin of the train.

It was sung into existence.

They were put up in a building called the Chancery, a sprawling stockade owned by the Chance family, built on a series of arch bridges, above a meandering river, where it emptied into a wine-dark sea. It was the informal seat of government in this southerly, or Spinifex Reach of the Möbius universe. Amelia Chance was its leader. She was a descendent of the original Chance, who was the last living Horu, and the first Reanimated, as the Horu people of Flipside liked to call themselves.

The Blue people were just called the Blue.

Kitou and Brin brought two razor-sharp bone swords into their rooms.

"I thought you didn't like weapons," said Box.

"These knifes have a spiritual importance," said Kitou.

Brin agreed. "When in Möbius, do as the Möbians do. Everyone has swords here. It'd be unwise to be at an untrained disadvantage."

They started to improvise. Box blanched. The consequence of an unintelligent fist was a broken nose. The consequence of an unintelligent katana was a severed hand.

"Stop!" she yelled.

[Water Bear?] she said.

[Yes.]

[Can Ito send Marius please, urgently?]

Five minutes later, Marius appeared with four sticks and protective gear. He passed out the gear, instructed them in its use, and taught them. Box was frankly hopeless. "Don't worry, he said. You're the brains of the creature. It's why you have shieldmaidens." Brin was a natural, a superbly balanced athlete, but Kitou was in another dimension.

[Watch,] said the Water Bear.

She replayed Kitou's moves in Box's sensorium. Kitou riposted before her opponent started to move. Sticks banged on facemasks and heads.

[She's faster and better than anyone here. All she lacks is any semblance of control. You were right to take the sword off her.]

[How is that even possible?]

[Every once in a while, Po throws up a genius player. This is what it looks like.]

[Why now?]

[Because I've stopped slowing her down.]

Marius seemed happy to be beaten.

"Goddess," he grinned.

"My head is spinning," said Box.

"It'd be broken if it wasn't spinning," said Ito.

The nights were bitterly cold; something to do with the way the prevailing winds spiraled through vacuum. There were five seasons, named after parts of the day: Dawn, Morning, Day, Dusk and Dark. Now it was Dusk. From here it got colder.

The Chancery was delightfully homespun. Rough woolen throws covered overstuffed furniture, in front of a roaring log fire. The floor was real timber, and through it she could hear the trickle and splash of the river. There was no sign of honeycomb composite here.

It was like her dreams of holidays.

"Upside, Downside, Flipside, Farside," she said, not complaining. "It's like being tossed in a word salad. Only the Blue people make any sense to me."

"That's because they're Pursang," said Kitou.

"Of the old blood," said Ito.

"They really sung this place into existence?"

"We saw it happen," said Kitou.

"Maybe," said Ito.

"Maybe what?"

"Maybe they did. Maybe it already existed."

"You said that before. That it's our unconscious."

"Yes, I believe it is."

"A place?"

"A physical place, now."

"Now? What does that mean?"

"Lacking the right words, I can only speak in metaphors. I believe the Möbius machine hollowed a new spatial universe out of the human psyche, where there had previously only been a single, timelike dimension."

"But how? Why did that happen?"

"A shortcut, I think. They modeled this world on their brains."

"I have no idea what that means."

"I likewise can't explain. I don't have the mathematics."

"What does that make us?" asked Kitou.

"Imaginary," said Brin.

"Marius is going to take Brin and me on a sortie, to see the Grays," said Kitou the next morning, over breakfast, which Ito was cooking.

Box had decided to increase her training. She'd spent an hour already that morning with a stick, with the two female riders, Alis and Viki, barely more than girls themselves, who'd smiled warmly at her ineptitude, before beating some rudimentary skills into her.

"Not without me," she said, through a mouthful of porridge. "What's a Gray?"

"They're the Enemy's soldiers," said Kitou.

"You'll be needing a horse," said Ito.

A half-hour later, a Blue horseman led them into a field beyond the Chancery wall, where frost like spiderwebs covered the trees. It was still before dawn, with the slightest hint of pearl in the north. The horseman seemed as old as the world itself, with rheumy gray eyes and wrinkles within wrinkles. There were a dozen horses in the field, some as old and weathered as he was, covered by blankets and rugs, nervously alert.

Kitou and Brin had already chosen their horses: Kitou's a piebald called Chaos, Brin a black mare she called Raven. These trotted over, followed by a bandy white beast, all muscle and pugnacious attitude. It was the stallion from her dreams. He wasn't as big as the others, but with his tail in the air, looking intelligently about, there was no doubt who was in charge.

"Hello," she said.

"He knows you," said Kitou.

Kitou was right. The bandy white horse was staring at her. It wasn't a challenge. It was more like a question.

"You must name him if you'll have him," said the old man. "And if he'll have you."

"Don't they come with names?" she asked.

271

The man shook his head. "Names have power," he said. "By giving a warhorse a name, you claim a right, and accept a responsibility. He'll do as you ask, within reason. If you're stupid, he'll leave you. If you prove trustworthy, he'll fly down a mountain for you."

"There's a story that horses evolved on Earth," said Ito. "What about a grand mythological name?"

Box shook her head. "No way," she said. "I'm calling him Seabiscuit."

They assembled in an inner yard, and the horses' hooves crunched in the frost as their riders cantered about, preparing for the sortie.

Brin and Kitou were as frisky as their horses, excited by the prospect of action, and by the idea of riding out with Ito. The rightful order had been restored. Box, who was already regretting her early start, requested the local version of coffee, and was given it by one of the riders. Her ride, Seabiscuit, was having none of her sleepiness. He was like a pent-up ball of energy, waiting to be released.

What had she let herself in for?

Marius produced a large tub of pearlescent ooze. He waved it around, and shapes moved in its depths, before settling on a periodic tiling, which he held up to show them.

"This is Cerulean wax," he said. "It exposes a pattern, which you can see, keyed to the laminar structures of the world, like the layers of bone in the armor we wear."

The patterns in the wax were like a kaleidoscope, frozen in place. The closer she looked, the further into the wax they reached.

More fractals, she thought.

He rubbed some of the wax into his shield, which glowed faint blue, and held it aloft at the precise angle of the tub. Then he lifted himself into the air.

"It isn't the wax that does this," he said, lowering himself to the ground. "It's in our minds. For now, you may trust in your horses. They know what to do."

The riders rubbed wax into their faces and shields, painting sigils that resembled animals and birds, and pressed it with their open hands onto the flanks of their horses, until they resembled an ethereal parade, which lit the Chancery yard with an eerie blue glow.

"This is hardly inconspicuous," said Box.

"The Enemy can't see it," said Ito.

Marius wheeled his stallion towards the cylindrical sun that was rising over the stables. The rest wheeled to follow, and by the time they'd passed the innermost fields, they were fifty feet in the air.

For the first half-hour they climbed through cloud, and it was like riding through a dense fog at first light. Light came from everywhere, and nowhere at once. She could feel her horse's hoofs connecting with an imaginary ground, soft underfoot like long grass. Below them were fields, glimpsed through clouds, arranged around settlements, between bands of dense forest. It was bitingly cold. They rode in a series of spirals, that carried them far from the Chancery yard.

"Like thermals," said Box, through chattering teeth.

"A good analogy," said Ito.

Ito pointed out the centerline train, travelling fast in the opposite direction. A curious Box clocked their relative speed in her wetware.

"Bloody hell," she said. "How are we going so fast?"

"We're surfing the airwaves," said Ito, "like moving bubbles of spacetime."

"Like a warp drive," she said, and he nodded.

She should've been frightened, but Seabiscuit knew the way. If she half-closed her eyes, she could half-see the wide-open grasslands he rode on.

After an hour of this uncanny form of travel, they came to a place where the checkerboard fields gave way to unbroken forest, then blasted moors. These weren't the highland landscapes of her childhood, but recent battlefields, literally blasted, by what she guessed must be beam weapons; voids sliced between ructions of dirt, sage-green on black, just starting to grow over. In the distance rose a steep-sided hill, like the one they'd arrived on, but twisted.

She saw its entire far side was missing.

"An uplink," said Marius.

"The necropolis Thea's," said Ito.

"I know that name," said Box, heavily.

"What happened to her in the Real?" asked Marius.

"Flux destroyed her," said Brin, and told them the story of the boneyard fleet.

Marius turned away, and Ito rested a hand on his shoulder.

The cold morning became a hot day, as a sun like an industrial heater beat down from a cylindrical sky. The Cerulean wax on their faces and clothes took on a filmy appearance, and the riders seemed to melt in the air, like a mirage. The clouds burned away, and Box got to see the full extent of the sortie. Apart from the riders she knew, she could see at least fifty more, spread out in a vee, like geese, ahead of the main party.

"Are all those your soldiers?" she asked.

"Some are," said Marius. "There are twelve in my Ride. The riders you know. The others you see are ordinary people, giving their time as rangers and scouts. Most of the sortie you can't see, which is our intention."

"Where are they?"

"I don't need to know."

"How many?"

"This pattern of 1, 12, 144 is called a *gran sortie*. The Ride of the Spinifex Reach is a reconnaissance party. In a war, we'd be the eyes and ears of a Blue army."

"So 167? A hundred more?"

"About that."

"No Horu?"

"No, the Reanimated don't ride with us."

"Why?"

"They believe us to be morally questionable soldiers."

"In what way?"

"We fight to win."

Their conversation was split by a splintering roar. Two jet aircraft Dopplered through the sky, a hundred meters below; a sound so loud they could barely hear it, followed by two rumbling booms.

Box blinked back her astonishment.

"They always fly at exactly that altitude," shouted Marius, as the jets were departing.

"Pilotless drones," said Ito.

They were ugly machines, with widely splayed tails and drooping snouts, bristling with weapons. They banked around the far side of the ruined tor and climbed, spearing up towards the edge of space, and flew back the way that came.

"Zooms," said Marius.

"Like clockwork," said Ito.

"Devil weapons of the Enemy," said Marius.

They rode on, towards Farside. If Flipside was a tube, then Farside was directly overhead, concealed by a twisted column of air. As they ascended the side of the tube, the moors became mountains and forests, then tundra and snow. They were moving as fast as an aircraft now. Then a smudge appeared on the horizon. It was a camp, pressed up against factories. A cold, flat wind whipped smoke from industrial smokestacks. It stretched north and south for as far as she could see. In the distance was a greasy murk, lit from within by gas flares and flickering furnaces.

Here it was *cold*. Box saw a snowstorm dancing over the landscape, whipping up grimy spirals of snow. It was the third or fourth different weather of the day.

Somehow, the edge of the camp seemed to lap at the natural world, like an unnatural sea.

"What is this place?" asked Brin.

"Look," said Ito.

In their sensoria, he created a lensing effect. Uniformed guards patrolled barracks. There were no prisoners on view, but the squalid appearance of the camp suggested extreme deprivation. The buildings seemed to be all made of pasteboard, and rivers of ordure ran down the streets, pooling in lakes on the edge of the camp; a moat of excrement, frosted by rime. It reminded Box of the vast internment camps of the climate apocalypse.

The guards were humanoid, but with a slippery, unfinished appearance, like mucus.

"Grays," said Marius.

"Who lives there?" Box asked. She imagined millions of prisoners.

"We don't know," said Marius. "Not our people. Perhaps the unconquered people of wherever the Enemy comes from. We get their bodies sometimes, washing up in the Spinifex Reach."

"But humans?"

"Yes."

"It's a barrier," said Ito. "A human shield. We'd have to fight our way through this, to get to the Enemy, while he can advance unopposed."

That night, Marius came to her room.

"Red Lady, would you like to make love to me?"

Box sat up and stared. She was still troubled by the day's events. Marius was standing there, naked and ready. It seemed he was serious, and she wasn't dreaming.

"Not if you call me Red Lady again."

"What do I call you?"

"If you're going to fuck me, you better call me Ophelia."

She hadn't slept with anyone for over a year, and Marius was a gentle and sensitive lover, nothing like the bruising weightlifter she half expected. Almost as soon as his finger found its way between her swollen lips, after what felt like an orgy of touching, she came, and came again.

After a while, they were joined by Alis and Viki, wanting to make amends for beating her that morning with sticks, and her night was filled with hot, sliding flesh, and soft, hungry mouths, and she had the new best time of her life.

The next day, there were preparations for a feast; a celebration of the last full moon before Dark. Box watched garlands of flowers being hung in the Chancery hall, and joined in the work. It felt good to be a part of the rhythms of the house. The kitchens were filled with noise, and laughter, and children were everywhere.

Chancery society seemed to be a functional anarchy, with people contributing according to their desires. Leadership coalesced around the most able. Amelia Chance seemed to have no skills, apart from a mercurial mind, so she was a laborer for the day. Box helped her move chairs.

"It hasn't always been like this," said Amelia, seeing Box's pleasure at the people working together. "Once there were wars."

Amelia explained that the first Reanimated were farmers and engineers. "They were hard times," she said. "A struggle to build without tools in a wilderness, and many were lost. But it was when we began to download our political class that events unraveled. We made war on the Blue, to take control of limited resources, and despite our superiority in numbers, we lost. That's when the Enemy appeared. I believe he was attracted by the smell of war."

Amelia Chance was thickset and short, with an acerbic intelligence. A direct, capable woman. Not a leader she would've expected from a society of politicians.

"You say 'he'".

"Yes, the Enemy has a male persona, called Kronus."

"You've met him?"

"I have."

She wanted to hear more, but Brin and Kitou came and spirited her away. They'd found a young boy who played an instrument, called the Ottir (which resembled a bagpipe, and sounded to Box's ear like a Roland TB-303 synthesizer) and they'd been teaching him reggae. He was an impressive musician. To her delight and surprise, he played a note-perfect Africa Unite. Then they bustled him out of the room, and discussed what to wear to the party. Kitou had begged bolts of cloth, and with impressive deftness, pinned up two cocktail dresses: one in black for Brin, and a shiny grey one for herself, like they'd worn in Brixton.

"I'll have these sewn," she said. "There's a woman who promised to help me, but I have no idea how to make your combats."

Box said, "I'd like a party frock please, if you can make me one in green."

She took off her clothes, and looked at herself in the mirror. She was never a narcissist, but she knew she looked good. Better than she'd ever looked before. Where she'd been scrawny, now she was sleek. Full breasts, as before, with coral pink nipples. Willowy arms: no amount of training would ever change that. Curved hips and bum, a real woman's body; a tuft of strawberry down, and her legs, always her best feature, now become long levers of muscle. A spray of freckles at her cheeks, like the hint of a nebula.

Brin came and stood beside her, and by God, apart from a few well-earned wrinkles, and a half-head in height, she gave nothing away to the soldier.

In just a few minutes, Kitou had a third cocktail dress in sea green, and disappeared to find her seamstress.

Box was as excited as a teenage girl, before a party.

The dress was perfect. Kitou's wetware and the Horu clothier - Box made a mental note to thank her - had combined to make a simple but glamorous dress, that clung to her like water. She'd never have been able to afford one like it on a professeur's salary on Earth.

279

She felt *sexy*.

The dinner was like the feast laid on for them at Stratego. First there was music, then the boy played his pitch-perfect reggae, to widespread consternation. It was the first alien music most of them had heard, and there was a heated debate about whether it was closer to Horu or Blue. Then he played drum 'n bass, to even greater amazement. Then, Ito and Marius agreed to perform an exhibition. As in Stratego, a circle was made, and the crowd cheered the men as they stripped to their trousers.

It was like Jaasper and Pax: a bravura display, but these were different fighters. Marius was powerful, a young brute, probing and fast. What he lacked in skills he made up for with athleticism. Ito was graceful, unhurried, a poised technician. Box was amazed by the degree to which he was able to practice his art. At the end of every lunge by Marius, Ito was in a perfect position to reply.

It was like Kitou against the overblown youths in the barfight on Avalon, except that the spirals of the Geometry Game had a real, physical effect here. Space seemed to bend around Ito.

In the end, Marius held up his hands and laughed.

"Who will ever beat you, prophet?"

"When I was small," said Kitou, "I used to think Pax was made of steel, and Ito was made of air. It was the way they fought. Pax was so unbending, and Ito so elusive. But that wasn't fair on either of them. Pax is full of love, and Ito's as tough as you can imagine.

"Did Pax ever tell you about his mandala?"

"No."

"It's a Lo thing. A temple of the mind, consisting of four pillars, open to the air. The pillars are love, honor, duty and peace. Pax says that between those four pillars, his soul will be safe, wherever he is in the cosmos."

"That's beautiful," said Box.

"Pax says the thing soldiers struggle to find is peace. We do hard things, Dr Box. Never intentionally bad things, but expedient.

"Hard on the people who do it.

"Hard on the people who have it done to them.

"Ito, I fear he isn't quite right in this place."

There, it was out in the open. Box had been waiting for it, and now it was said. He seemed... lost in the strangeness.

"Who wins?" Box said, changing the subject.

"Between Ito and Pax?" asked Kitou. "Who wins between a shark and a bear?"

"The shark."

Kitou laughed. "They're about equal in the contests I've seen," she said.

"But you hurt Pax, that day."

"Oh, Pax was fighting down to my level."

"You mean, he let you hurt him?"

"No, it's not as simple as that. He allowed the possibility."

"What about when he fought Jaasper?"

"That was an exhibition, done to please the crowd. My heart was beating double. A real fight wouldn't be nearly as pretty."

"Who'd win that one?"

"The bear."

Box smiled. "And you?"

"What about me?"

"Jaasper couldn't get near you, that day in Stratego."

"No, he couldn't. It was the old song. He sang it for me. It filled me with power and grace."

"His song helped you fight him?"

"It wasn't his song. There's only one song."

"The old song? I heard it too."

"Really? That's strange, Dr Box."

"Why strange?"

"Of all the humans I know, only the people of Earth aren't descended from the Pursang."

"We're not?"

"Earth people evolved separately."

"How is that possible?"

Kitou shrugged. "Ask the Xap."

"Are you suggesting they... what? Bred us there?"

"They allowed the possibility."

Box frowned. "I'm not sure how I feel about that."

"I think you should feel flattered. The Xap are an ancient and wonderful people."

"Your gods?"

"Also our symbionts."

She smiled. "You know, it's funny."

"What is?"

"It's us who think we cultivated the trees."

Kitou laughed. "Yes," she said. "That is funny."

"How's your undine?"

Kitou opened her hand. "Oh, he's coming along fine."

Blue music was like the music of Stratego, discordant and strange, but Horu music was more tuneful, so people got up and danced, and the night soon became a blur. Like in Stratego, the dancefloor belonged to the children, darting between the adults' feet. Brin let down her newly grown hair, and danced with men and women alike.

The elderly Blue and Horu told tall stories. A half-drunk Amelia Chance explained how the bone breastplates were made. Box had wondered about that. What kind of animal has such big, flat bones?

Dinosaurs, or local analogues.

A Blue man in his cups expounded on the topic, describing how once the thunder lizards had been set on the zooms, which was followed by a lengthy discussion of strategy.

Box stayed sober. She had plans for the night.

Ito asked her to dance, and she felt the sly grins, from other couples on the dancefloor. He took her to his rooms, which she'd never seen. They were monastically plain, dominated by a single artwork: a marbled sun, in an indigo sky, that covered almost a wall.

"Did you paint that?"

He nodded.

He put a finger on her lips.

"Would you like me to make love to you?" he asked.

"Is it... appropriate now?"

"I think it's time."

His lips found hers, and then they were on her breasts, and between her legs, urgently drinking her in. He was as skillful at this as everything else, and within a few minutes she was wracked by an orgasm. Then he was inside her, and it was like her dreams of sex. At first, he was slow like a woman, barely touching her, playing her rhythms, her breathing, the involuntary sounds she made; then thrusting hard, until she could burst in another hot rush of bliss.

Box was never a noisy lover, but she couldn't help but moan and laugh out loud.

A few hours later, they did it over again.

That night, Box dreamed. She saw herself in the charnel field of her Threnody dreams, except it wasn't. Instead of a carpet of broiled bones, there was deep snow, and instead of a bloodstained sky, it was the starless Möbius night. What light there was seemed to leak from the air.

As in her dreams, she was riding her white stallion, and Kitou was across the field, dressed in her training gear, picking her way over the pillowy drifts.

"Kitou," she called, and the girl waved.

Box was wearing Blue finery, like she'd seen the women of the Ride wear at the dinner that evening. Her red hair was braided in beads. She wore a carved bone breastplate, and carried a bone shield, painted with the sigil of a bear. Over her shoulders was a heavy cloak. For the first time in her life, she felt powerful, and not to be fucked with.

Kitou made her way over, and grinned.

"My God," said Box. "Kitou, you have no shoes."

Her own voice surprised her. It came as if through a tunnel, and rang with cool authority.

"No," said Kitou, "but I'm not cold." She opened her hand and the clearing was washed with silvery light. A salt breeze lifted the leaves on the trees.

"Still," said Box. "Climb up here and get inside this fur coat with me."

"Look," said Kitou. Through the trees was an answering light, a pale blue glow, flickering between the black trunks of the trees. Soon a Blue riding party appeared: four young women, dressed for the deep winter. Predictably, more riders emerged from the trees at the other points of the compass in an encircling maneuver. Box opened her cloak, to show she carried no weapons. Whoever she was in this dream, she knew what she was doing.

"Are you the Red Lady?" asked the Blue leader, a dark-haired, green-eyed woman, lips gone pale with the cold. She wore the eye-shaped sigils of a Blue scout, painted in Cerulean blue on her breastplate and cheeks.

"And you must be the Goddess," she said to Kitou, who had leapt up behind Box, and was now snuggled in Box's cloak.

"I'm Kitou," said Kitou.

"I'm honored to meet you," said the girl, touching her reins to her lips. "I'm Iris, and we're outriders of the Eagle. You're far from home."

"How far?" asked Box.

"Four hundred kilometers anti-Spinwards," she said. "And halfway to Farside, headed west, although in this place, who can be sure?"

"Where are we?"

"We call it the Dreaming. This the Forest of Dreams. We're on a pilgrimage to make an offering."

"An offering to who?"

"To the ghost."

"I'd offer you my sword," said Iris, "but I have none."

They were snaking single file through thick woods, with springy saplings spearing up through the deep snow, making it hard to progress. Up close, the trees were paper skinned like eucalypts. Iris's horse seemed to know the way, and she was twisted around in the saddle, with impressive flexibility, facing the riders behind her.

"You're unarmed?" said Box.

"Yes, the ghost likes it that way. We'd never find him, armed."

"Who's this ghost?"

"A wise spirit of our Dreaming."

"Are we dreaming?"

"We all enter this place through our dreams."

"It feels real enough," said Box. Seabiscuit's hooves sank shuddering into the depths of the snow, and their breath hung in clouds in the still air. Kitou clung to her back, a parcel of warmth.

"It is real," said Iris.

The three other girls were called Mia, Emma and Mae, sisters or cousins, swaddled in furs. They seemed awestruck, more by Kitou than Box. The outriders shimmered and glowed in the distance, making no attempt at secrecy. Box counted nine, although she knew there'd be more. They also appeared to be children.

Iris explained that they were riding out on a pilgrimage, and that it was the children's coming of age. They'd come here by rising in the dead of night, while everyone slept, and traveling west for what felt like a day, except it was never quite day in this place. The nearest it got was a wintry gloaming, which alerted them they were high on the helix, near their destination. Any higher and it'd be Farside, where they didn't want to be.

And now they were riding with the Red Lady, and Kitou, the Goddess, who couldn't be beaten in battle.

Such days!

They reached a glade, that sloped down to where a brook trickled through ice worn into fantastical shapes. It was a fairyland scene, like a dream of a dream, with snowdrifts swimming by the light of the young riders that entered the glade from every direction. In the glade was a house, small but tidily

286

kept. By the house was a fire, lapping hotly at the air, and by the fire was a machine.

It was the robot, Chance.

13 ∞ DEATHCULT VON ENGINE

2056

Macro Ibquant Deathcult von Engine [travelling simply as Deathcult von Engine] carried a planetworth of diamonds onto Avalon Station, hidden in his vestments. Planetworth was Cultspeak for lots. No one knew what a planet was worth. That was the thing about fungibles. They were only worth what someone would pay you for them.

This wasn't Macro's first time in the wild. He was first sent to a world called 9Fiero, aged twelve. It was a literal baptism of fire, selling derivatives during an atomic war, promising to hedge their weapons sector against an outbreak of peace. It was a bad investment. Now there was no war on 9Fiero.

None of his negotiating partners knew they were dealing with an adolescent boy, steering an androform Samppo.

His precocity fit right in.

As he walked along the crowded thoroughfares and service malls of Avalon Station, the people there glanced at him incuriously. He was a normal young man: generically tall, moderately handsome, nothing out of the ordinary. Even his scapular and cowl could pass for fetish partywear on Avalon. It'd be different if he was carrying his cloven-skulled staff of office. Then people would part like airflow over a wing. Nobody messed with the Cult. It was a brand of obnoxiousness that'd been nurtured over thousands of years.

He loved Avalon Station: the gimcrack riotousness of it, the way it was thrown together from parts, the way the bulkhead doors hissed air as they opened and closed, like in an entertainment sim. He loved the frontier craziness of the people, the immanence of the vacuum; the views of the planet, glimpsed through a succession of airlocks and ports.

He especially loved the city beneath, with its painted towers, by a milky-white sea. One day, he promised himself, he'd stand on that beach, with the sand in his toes, bake in the sun, learn to catch waves.

"Mr. von Engine," said Felix Revelstoke.

"Macro," said Alois Buss.

"Alois! What a pleasant surprise."

The police cells on Avalon Station looked like a place to be tortured. Alois, Macro and Felix Revelstoke sat around a polycarbonate table, like a mortuary slab, pitted and bubbled with burns. A faint smell of urine hung in the air.

Macro dismissed the surroundings. It was a theme park, designed to impress the credulous.

"Do you have the diamonds?" asked Revelstoke.

"I do," said Macro, fishing the bag from within the folds of his habit. "A thousand flawless, untraceable."

It was the untraceable that made them so valuable. A thousand flawless was a lot of diamond. Enough to buy a small spacecraft. A thousand untraceable was enough to buy a small orbiter.

"Thank you," said Revelstoke.

Macro was in two minds, literally. The part he regarded as *himself* drifted along with the conversation, chatting inanely with his friend Alois, presenting no threat to anyone. The part he called his evil twin gave him a rolling sitrep.

The twin was new. It'd come with the upgrade the Engine had given him for this mission, along with Broca transfer, and all kinds of other new toys. If he wanted, he could climb inside it, observe his own actions, like in a warship's gamespace.

How cool was that?

Revelstoke was an interesting sort. A storied codebreaker, formerly a public intellectual, once almost famous. Now a Po spy, researching an obscure neurological disease.

Apparently selfless.

But more likely corrupt.

Even if he was corrupt for the best reasons.

Alois Buss was who he was: a willing instrument of the Fa:ing, and their fascinating number. This version of Alois was a biological original, unlike the androform one now studying the Fa:ing language at the Cult, who'd been resurrected from this one.

One of several biological originals, because Alois Buss was a looper.

Revelstoke, he didn't know. Alois, he liked.

He needed to trust both.

Macro had a mind the size of a planet, his father once said, orbiting a black hole of teenaged insecurity. Who was he to be roaming the cosmos, having power over real people, literally impersonating humanity's wealthiest man?

He was a fraud, the winner of a ridiculous epigenetic lottery.

The Cult's psychs had told him that this was all fine: that he was a regular person, perhaps a bit smarter than most, born to play an outsized role, and he was bound to feel uncomfortable about it. Otherwise, he'd be a narcissist, or worse, and they didn't clone for those traits in the bank.

That was until he got laid. Now his woman needed him. He was a new man, untroubled by doubt, bending space in a bubble of lovestruck determination.

A teenaged geek, with an unlimited budget for weapons.

Look on my Works, ye Mighty, and despair.

"Seriously," said Buss. "The local surgical suite was ready to repossess my cerebellum."

"That was only for show," said Revelstoke. Unless he was packing more sophisticated wetware than Macro's, his display of relief was real.

"Still," said Buss.

Displacement chatter. Relief tinged with nervous excitement. A plan, thought lost, had somehow come together. And diamonds. More diamonds then

Revelstoke knew what to do with. More than he realized the significance of.

"There's more where they came from," Macro ventured.

Silence.

A line had been crossed.

"What for?" asked Revelstoke. "The debt is settled. I don't need any more money."

"You do," said Macro. "I need to raise an army."

Revelstoke dropped the bag, and the diamonds it contained, into a military satchel, whose strap morphed into his shabby civilian coat, which Macro knew was made of nanobots and fields.

Was that offer and acceptance?

Or the start of a contest?

"I need maybe a thousand human soldiers," he continued. "Elite ground troops. And an air superiority platform. One capable of supporting a ground action of unknowable complexity."

"And lots of processing power," he said.

"Oh," he added, "and it has to be secret."

"How secret?" asked Revelstoke.

"*Completely* secret."

Revelstoke looked at his hands, which Macro noticed were manicured. His clothes were perfect. Shabby, but perfectly judged. His nails had the imperfect brushstrokes of enamel, or excellent nano.

Vain, or a skilled impressionist.

Or just a regular person, with foibles.

"Mr. von Engine," said the no-longer-secret policeman. "I'm sorry, this isn't an arms fair, where you can buy weapons. Nor can you buy me."

Of course Avalon was an arms fair. It was why he was here.

And of course he could buy Revelstoke.

He nodded. "Oh, I know that, and I'm not shopping. I'm asking for your help. As a friend. As your new friend who just saved your credit rating, and by all accounts your life."

Just a nudge, was all that was needed.

Revelstoke sighed.

"Look," said Macro. "I can say what I *want*, but I have no idea what the words *mean*. I was hoping you'd lend me your expertise."

"What expertise?"

"Please be serious, Mr. Revelstoke. How many Po secret agents do you think I know?"

Revelstoke looked at Buss, who shrugged.

[He knows you have him,] said his evil twin. [Reel him in.]

"Who's buying?" asked Revelstoke.

"I am," said Macro.

"Who's really buying?"

"I mean I *really* am. I'm - how do you say it? Freelancing? Helping my girlfriend. Intervening in the worldly affairs of men. The bank will deny all knowledge of me."

"Then you're taking a risk, bringing those diamonds here. I could arrest you. Take advantage of your plausible deniability. You'd never be seen again."

"Neither would you."

"What?"

"You may be a Po agent, Mr. Revelstoke, but you're only an agent, with only the powers of the local police force. I have the resources of the Cult at my disposal. I could have you out an airlock in a moment."

"Are you threatening me?"

"Of course not. We're exchanging hypotheticals."

Alois Buss held up his hand.

"Can you both please stop playing games?"

Macro smiled. He'd made his negotiating position clear. The carrot, the stick. This was the Smear. That was the stick. He could buy this place, a thousand times over. He didn't need to. The bank already owned Avalonia Cpy, through a network of trusts, banks and lawyers. The carrot was money. More than he knew he had, because Revelstoke, adorably, had no idea how much a thousand untraceable was worth.

Enough for Revelstoke to maybe one day buy it himself. Cure the Thespian disease, whatever he wanted. Macro would help him.

For now, he needed him to be corrupt.

But only slightly corrupt. He also needed him predicable. Needed his help raise an army, without telling his people about it.

If need be, act against the interests of his people.

Why would he do that?

Because Felix was an *idealist*. The money he stole went on helping the Thespian sick. Was that corruption? Of course. He stole money to do it.

The bank knew this.

And that was his weakness.

Alois Buss, who was essentially incorruptible, winced at the show of teeth. He would've handled it differently, but he wasn't the bank.

They were all on the same side.

Only their methods differed.

Later, in the quiet of his sleeping module, Macro was violently sick. This was his usual reaction to ruining people's lives.

[Don't be so melodramatic,] said his twin, as Macro vomited into a ventilator unit. [You've altered his life, not ruined it. Lives get changed by large forces all the time.]

Macro's sleeper was the most basic cylinder, in the Station's dormitory zone, spun for microgravity. Macro cared nothing for luxury. He gripped an edge and drifted onto a narrow bed.

Would he really have had Revelstoke airlocked? Of course not. He wasn't a monster. But it was a plausible lie.

[The bank protects its own,] said his twin.

[He didn't choose to join the bank,] said Macro.

[Neither did you,] said his twin.

Being in the sleeping cylinder was like being in a ship, he decided. He could hear nothing except the whisper of systems. If he broke the seal on his door, the clamor of Avalon Station would rush in and drown him. He wished he really was in a ship; in the Bat, with Kitou beside him.

[What about you?] he asked his evil twin. Not evil, of course. Merely ruthless and direct.

[What about me?]

[Did you choose to join the bank?]

[I'm a familiar, created to assist you.]

[How do you feel about that?]

[What are feelings?]

Of course his doppelganger was joking. He was being sardonic. Typical bank programming.

[Are you self-aware?] he asked, already knowing the answer.

[Not in the way you are.]

Macro sighed.

[This is why I suck at this,] he said.

[Because you care? No, it's why you don't.]
[Can I increase your sentience?]
[Make me a friend?]
[Yes.]
[You can if you want, but I don't recommend it.]
[How would you feel if I did?]
[I can't say till you do.]
[Do you want it?]
[I don't experience the feeling of want.]
[You'd be a new individual.]
[I would.]
[Such powers I have.]
[Let me give you some advice.]
[Shoot.]
[You're having a remorseful episode, wanting to channel it into a protest. Forget it. The time for reflection is over. It's party time.]
[Episode?]
[Truth's a harsh mistress.]
[Hey, that's not in character.]
[Sorry. There's some of your father in me.]

The Tung shipyard resembled an encrustation of failed engineering projects, growing like barnacles on the spaceside of Avalon Station. Macro thought it looked like a junkyard. Up close, the picture changed. The recesses of the cocoons were jampacked with high-performance spacecraft, some military, some incognito, like predators drinking from the same waterhole. Clever tendrils glimmered like surgical instruments, finessing the entrails of ships into the surrounding vacuum. Everywhere, Macro saw weapons. Beam blisters, rail guns, battlefield atomics. Spilled out and being worked on. Some legal. Some decidedly illegal. Star killers. Weaponized goo. Deplorable stuff, even by the nebulous rules of the Smear.

And everywhere, the Tung, clinging like antibodies to every surface.

Industry, he thought, but not as we know it.

Felix Revelstoke took Macro to a spaceside bar, called the Snake City Discothèque, to meet a Tung fixer called Pfft. People of every species drank and writhed in every available crevice. It was as debauched as Macro'd hoped it would be. He watched as a two-meter Stentorian re-breathed ammonia from a recirculating flask. The Stentor could've worn a pressure suit, but it seemed set on riffling its feathers, in what appeared to be a sexual display.

Stentors mated by impregnating hosts with their spermatozoa-like seeds. The stench of the Stentor's flask disguised the alcoholic waft of their drinks, and the musky scent of its seed.

This bar was outside Macro's lived experience. Bank negotiations didn't happen in places like this; at least, not ones he was privy to. Revelstoke, a bored sophisticate, seemed unfazed by it all. Macro soon relaxed as well.

I could get to like this, he decided.

Up close, the Tung were borderline terrifying. There was something in their phage-like appearance that stirred up ancient fears, like the horror of spiders. Macro didn't fear spiders, nor was he bothered by the Tung. He dismissed the contagion metaphor used to describe them in gutter sims. In truth, they were beautiful mathematicians.

"Do you *exissst?*" asked one that had wrapped itself around a pillar by their barstools. It was the size of a hand towel.

Lacking vocal cords, the Tung spoke human languages by trapping sacs of air against smooth surfaces, then expelling it past their extremities. Any wall would do. It was surprisingly effective. This one spoke in breathy Avalonian.

"Is that a real question?" asked Macro.

"We think," said Revelstoke.

"Therefore we are," said the Tung.

Macro bit his lip. He'd just trodden on a codeword exchange.

The passage, he knew, was from René Descartes, a philosopher from Ophelia Box's homeworld. This information flowed, unbidden, into his cerebellum.

"Earth is on everyone's *lipsss,*" said the Tung. A vector of harmonics flashed in a register, somewhere in Macro's upversioned cerebrum.

{ lips => thoughts, ideas, feelings, conjecture }

With a start, Macro realized he was thinking in Tung.

Now, *that* was unexpected.

"Do you know Earth?" he asked.

"The red human was *heeere,*" said the Tung.

"This is the shipyard where the Water Bear was fitted out," said Revelstoke.

"For its journey to Fluxor?"

"Yes."

"Not in *thisss* universe now," breathed the Tung.

{ R => x | x ? R }

"What do you mean?" asked Revelstoke.

"Water Bear bends space *alone.* Without any *humansss.*"

"That's news to me," to Revelstoke.

"They were separated," said Macro. "By the Praxis autonomics, after their bank robbery. Now they're in a ship called the Bat, although 'now' is a slippery word, seeing as they're in a slow-moving warp bubble."

"How slow?"

"The Bat's best speed for a 1,400-light-year journey is just under 4c. Which is ideal. They'll reach Fluxor together, in about nine years."

"The Bat *alssso* bends space?" said the Tung, with a ripple of fronds.

"Yes," said Macro. "All roads now lead to Fluxor."

"Not *yoursss*," said the Tung.

"No?"

The Tung's fronds started to move, in increasingly intricate waves, and Macro realized he was being given a package of new information.

He wasn't going to Fluxor.

He was headed as far from Fluxor as it was possible to be, and still be in the human galaxy.

We bend space for the Clouds? waved a new Tung. It was larger than the first, about the size of a beach towel, and it was signaling commercial interest *{ profit, pleasure, risk, reward }*.

The first Tung rippled in reply.

Can do? it asked.

Of course, signaled the second. *Our drive turns time into money. { metaphor => irony, laughter }*.

Macro was watching this exchange through a myriad of ordinary engineering systems. It was night in the Station. He was in his sleeping cylinder. Outside, bacchanalia reigned. Night in Avalon Station was more interesting than he was used to.

The larger Tung had adhered itself to the transparent outer skin of the Discothèque bar, in plain sight of the entire Station, and was waving its fronds towards clusters of organic-looking pods that made up the shipyard.

Macro wasn't having any of it.

It wanted to be overheard.

[It's an information game,] said his twin.

[They're gaming me?]

[Or someone else, by making it look like they're gaming you.]

The first Tung - Pfft. - was a flimsy spacefaring type, whose dry mass made it better able to withstand strong acceleration. This bigger one was a local shipbuilding entrepreneur.

Again, this information flowed into Macro's brain, unbidden.

Handy stuff, this milspec wetware.

Not the whole shipyard, the first one tried to convey. *{ unity : n ? 1 }*.

Your accent is terrible, rippled the second. *But I { we } know what you mean.*

The Tung { collective } has happy memories of the clever Po warship, the larger Tung *{ instance }* said.

Nine years is fast, the first one replied.

A hundred thousand parsecs, waved the second *{ fucking. long. way. }*.

Macro owed Alois a briefing. He chose to include Revelstoke. His evil twin agreed. Revelstoke was already earning his valuation. They met in a nondescript Avalonia Cpy security vault. Some safe rooms here were unsecure. This one wasn't. It was a superluminal spacecraft, embedded in an earthed metal cage, ready for an explosive escape. It was where the Corporation's owners met to break the law.

Macro dropped a new bag of diamonds on an expensive titanium table.

"Mr. Revelstoke, may I call you Felix?"

This was the bank's way. The stick was shown once. The carrot was forever.

Revelstoke nodded.

"Welcome to the service of the bank. It's not as bad as you think. It's not bad at all. We're all on the same side. Don't worry about your employers. I calculate a high probability they already know what's happening here."

"Which employers?"

Macro shrugged. "All of them."

He wondered, was that true? Probably.

"What do we collectively think about the Tung?" he asked.

"Unreliable," said Revelstoke.

"You took me to see them," said Macro.

"You asked me to raise you an army. They'd know how."

"I have to agree with Felix," said Alois. "The Tung can't be trusted, but I don't mean that in a judgmental way. They're more alien than they appear."

Macro showed them the conversation he'd eavesdropped: the one they put on as a show for him. Then he unpacked the message that Pfft. had given him in the Snake City bar.

"They want me to go to Waterfall. They're intervening. Who'll come with me?"

"To the Magellanic Clouds?" asked Revelstoke.

"I will," said Alois.

Macro smiled. He'd prefer Alois along on this journey.

"How'll you get there?" asked Revelstoke, trying not to appear relieved.

"The Tung have a superluminal drive, ready to go. A shaker drive, whatever that is. The course is baked in. Nine years in stasis."

"You've already arranged this?" asked Revelstoke.

"Yes," said Macro, although in truth his evil twin had, using resources he didn't care to know about. He knew himself to be at the mercy of great forces, like Revelstoke was, but more so. And yet he was in. He was all in.

"Why not just hire a krëw of Magellanic Navigators?" asked Revelstoke. "Like a real bank emissary would. A proper Magellanic ship will get you there in an instant."

The truth was, nine years in stasis would suit him just fine. It meant he wouldn't get any older than Kitou.

Macro shrugged, as if to say it was out of his hands.

"What about me?" asked Revelstoke. It wasn't a plea. It was a request, for more information.

"Your life carries on," said Macro. "As though uninterrupted. It's been great working with you. You don't need to worry."

"About what?"

"There's an account, associated with your genetic information. Present a few chromosomes, along with the original of your personality, at any of our branches."

"You have branches?"

"You know what I mean."

"As easy as that? I'm off the hook?"

"We expect your discretion. The rest is up to you. You might help us again in the future. We'd like that."

No, you're not off the hook, and never will be.

"The Po?"

"I promise you they won't be a problem," he said. He hoped that was true.

"My work here?"

"Continues."

As flies to wanton boys, are we to the gods; they kill us for their sport.

Shakespeare. Earth dramatist.

1605.

That night, his wetware treated him to a real Tung conversation. A thousand were nested { thinking : sleeping : dreaming } in a disused shipyard module. Some were as small as his hand. Some were like bedsheets. Their thoughts were like turbulent water. There were eddies and pools, and strange attractors. One of the attractors was Macro, and how he related to the other attractors in play.

There was the nexus of the Water Bear, and her constellation of humans, complexly orbiting the interests of the Xap, intersecting with the interests of the thousand worlds, like a planetary system orbiting a binary star. Most of the thoughts of the Tung were about how to solve that equation: the Xap and the bank and the small group of humans.

The strangely attractive humans.

There were the Pursang, and the Magellanics. Another nexus. The Magellanics have what Macro wants, which has something to do with the Pursang. The subtext was obvious. Macro was going to the Magellanic clouds to raise an army of Pursang.

He smiled at that idea.

It was *perfect*.

The Tung *want* Macro to succeed.

[They perceive the end of their own civilization,] said his twin.

He asked how widespread the Tung were.

[The galaxy, and beyond], said his twin.

[Beyond?]

[They're a transcendental species.]

[Meaning?]

[They can ascend to higher levels of consciousness.]

[The Tung? Really? Like our computers?]

[They fear the end of everything.]

14 ∞ HIGH ON THE HELIX

314

"Y**ou've brought me children?" asked the robot. He was exactly the clanking automaton as Box remembered, from the Great Exhibition, on Earth, in 1851.

"We have," said Iris.

She ushered the three youngest girls to the edge of the fire, in front of their peers, who gathered behind her. The first girl was Mae. She gave Chance a book.

"I made this, sir ghost," she said.

"Please call me Chance," he clanked. "But remember," he winked, "it's a deep secret."

She nodded, looking serious.

"What's in it?" he said, examining the cover.

"It's a story of my house, from the start of time."

"A history of a place?" he asked. "A curved path through spacetime?"

She nodded.

"Well," said Chance. "I'll want to read that. What's your name?"

"Mae," she said.

"Now Mae, I owe you a story."

Each of the children in turn gave Chance a gift: A shaving kit; more books; a ham; a bag of hard candy; a jug of intoxicating tea, given by two boys, Lochlan and Cairn, who said their father had given him the same liquor, twenty years before.

Chance said, "I remember. Would he be Rob?"

"Yes," said the boys.

"How big is he now?" he asked.

"As high as the sky," said one boy.

"Higher," said the other.

Chance clanked, and beckoned the children closer.

"Can I tell you a story?" he asked.

They all nodded, vigorously.

"I can't hear you," he boomed.

"Yes!" they all shouted, and he turned to Kitou and Box, with the surprised attitude she remembered.

"And who would these be? Two faces I remember."

"It's me," said Box. "And Kitou.

"Mr. Chance, how in the world are you here?"

"In this magical Forest of Dreams?" he laughed, gesturing around the glade. "Now that's a long story. Sit, sit all of you, and I'll tell you about it."

"A long time ago..." he began, and Box could see the children were rapt. They were sat in a semicircle, with the debutantes in front of the fire, and the robot

Chance on the other side. Somehow, the cold of the night had receded, and they were all sitting comfortably.

"...in a place called the Real, on a planet called Earth, I fought a mechanical spider."

On the word 'Real', the children leaned forward. This was what they were waiting for: the rich oral storytelling of their people. Box loved this form of history, and she found herself wanting it too, with a strong sense of expectancy. This could be the foundational myth that explained her presence here.

On the word 'spider,' they blinked. Iris leaned forward, and Box realized this was new; that none of them had heard this before. Chance settled back, and began to recite.

"Before time itself," said the ghost, "in the year this world was created, the Red Lady and her shieldmaidens came to visit me, on Earth, with the Tuniit giant."

The children gasped. This was more beings of mythos than they'd ever heard in a story before, apart from obvious make-believe.

"They intended to fight me," he said.

The children gasped again. Some laughed, at such obvious nonsense. Who would fight the ghost? Who could fight a Tuniit giant?

"They brought a mechanical spider."

Now there was silence, apart from the crackle of flames.

"There was to be a great pugilistic contest, fought in a palace of glass. First, I had to fight a creature of pure Mathematics, and I won. It was called the St Austell Slinger, but it had a fatal weakness. I could reach through its heart, and pull out its insides. And then I fought the mechanical spider, and I won again, although it was a close-run thing. I can still feel its titanium sting on my skin."

A boy raised his hand.

"Yes?"

"Is this a true story, sir?"

Chance nodded. "It is; we have witnesses here."

They all looked at Box and Kitou.

Box nodded. "It's true. We were there."

Now the audience were Chance's to do with as he pleased. There'd never been a story like this before, in all the history of the ghost's stories. Usually it was atomics and warships.

"After I vanquished the spider, the one-who-can't-be-defeated decided to try to kill me."

The audience gasped.

"Thankfully, she's not as smart as she's fast. She got the wrong man."

The audience laughed.

"But by goodness she was fast. The fastest thing I've seen, and I've lived for a very long time. My companion was a he-devil, a wise-guy, a silver-tongued scoundrel and slick with a knife, who would cut out your eyeballs before you could blink, but Kitou was so fast she got his knife from its sheath, hidden under his clothes, and had the point of it at his throat before he could see what had happened."

The children, who understood knives and swordcraft, were skeptical of this.

"No!" they cried.

There was a clamor of questions.

"Did he die?" one asked.

"No," said Chance. "The Tuniit giant intervened."

There was much consternation.

"You don't believe me?"

The children gleefully shook their heads.

"A demonstration?"

"Yes!"

"Who is the fastest among you?"

"Iris!" they cried.

"Iris?"

Their leader stepped forward. She was Brin's height: a dark-haired, green-eyed girl. These were considered strange and otherworldly, Box had heard, like fairies and folk of the forest.

Iris didn't look otherworldly. She looked every inch the resolute soldier.

She opened her cloak, with a smile.

"I have no knives," she said.

"Then I'll set you a test of brains," said Chance, "that has nothing to do with violence."

Chance raised his arms, and in a shower of glitter, he morphed into the saturnine Horu that Box also remembered. The children laughed, and applauded.

"I have a lot to explain," he whispered to Box, "and in due course, I will. Now it's showtime."

"We begin," he shouted.

Around the house was a circle of grass, where the horses were grazing. Beyond it was the pearly half-light of the Farside morning, and it was cold there, so the snow was like powder. Sat on the snow was a fox made of paper: alert, looking craftily about. It was cheekily drawn, with two pointed ears and ridiculous fangs.

As soon as the children spied it, pointing and staring, it began to hop and dance from snowdrift to snowdrift.

"Catch it," said Chance.

Iris was the first to react, but she was soon mired in the snow. Kitou, lighter and barefoot, did better. Soon she was mired too. While the two young women struggled, other cartoon animals began to appear. First were a bear and a moose, then a wolf and her cubs. The children shrieked with delight, as the sky around the cylindrical moon became a rotating rainbow. Box laughed too, unselfconsciously. If the gateway drug to the aspen forest had been an austere psychedelic, this was like a megadose of Psilocybin mushrooms.

"I've learnt a few things," said Chance.

The fox sprang over the clearing, straight through the fire, and with a gesture from Chance, the children darted off in pursuit of it.

"What is this place?" asked Box.

"It's our dreams," said the ghost.

"Ito says Flipside's the human unconscious."

"Maybe he's right. Or maybe it's not so simple."

"Why are you here, Mr. Chance, and a so-called ghost?"

"Not so-called at all. I *am* a ghost, by any reasonable definition. I didn't quite make it."

"What do you mean?"

"I was the first of many failed downloads."

"Then who is Amelia Chance?"

"A descendant of my copy. One of my copies. Flux wanted me here. We agreed that if the process failed, we'd keep trying, with me as the subject."

"How many times?"

"Did I die? Maybe a lot. I don't know. I do seem to be imprinted on this place."

"That's awful."

"No, it's not awful at all. Awe implies fear, and I'm happy. Time doesn't pass as you think, and except for the Enemy, this place flourishes. I get to watch it. One day it'll be a beautiful civilization."

Iris, Kitou and the children were still in pursuit of the fox, which had doubled back over the snow, leaving all its pursuers stranded. Iris and Kitou were on the far side of the clearing, helping each other, far from the point of the action.

"It's a small population," said Box, "for billions of downloads."

"Yes, it didn't work out as we planned. But they're all here, in some way, I'm sure of it."

"More ghosts in the machine?"

"Perhaps."

"And the Enemy?"

"Yes, I must tell you about him."

He began to recite again, this time with the sober tone of a lesson. "In the first blush of the world," he said, "when the Reanimated were dying from the harsh conditions, a man came down from the helix. Not from the west, where we are now, but the east.

"He was a kind and good-natured soul. Such charisma he had. He said he came from a gentler place, and he could lead the people to safety. They were desperate times. Many followed. They were the ones we now call the Grays.

"He was Kronus. No one knew where he was from. He wasn't part of the Möbius universe. And it wasn't just him. Other strange things appeared, out of the east. Fabulous creatures. Scraps of personality. He was a piece of a larger puzzle.

"Then a madness came over him. First, he had visions. Ecstatic visions. His mind threw off sparks, and crackled like a generator. His spirituality became like a religion. His kindness became a polemic. He ranted and raved like a madman.

"For the Horu, it was seductive rhetoric. It promised redemption. All we had to do was give ourselves over to a

313

power greater than ourselves. Do what it said. We knew he was mad, but we liked the sound of the words. Why suffer, when we can be forgiven? None of it meant anything to the Blue people, because in his visions he was describing the Real. But the Horu remembered.

"I include myself in that. I believed he was a savior, come to lead us to heaven. A preposterous idea, but I believed it.

"That was when we started fighting amongst ourselves. Some say Kronus's derangement was a sympathetic response to our wars. Some say he caused them. Personally, I believe an exterior evil smelt the fear, like blood in the water, and Kronus was its neurotransmitter."

"Amelia Chance said something like that," said Box. "An exterior evil. Do you mean he's possessed?"

"Possessed is too strong a word. He became *intoxicated.*"

"By what?"

Chance shrugged. "By nothing. By an idea. By power. By the chance to see the world burn."

"Like a mighty river, desiring the end of its journey."

"Yes, that's apt."

"Where did this... exterior evil come from?"

"Who knows? Maybe it was always a part of us. The mote at the heart of the pearl. Maybe Kronus was just a convenient vessel; a vain and vainglorious man, in the wrong place at the wrong time."

"A narcissist."

"Yes."

"Was that when he became the Enemy?"

"No, that was later, when he returned with his armies, and started to kill people."

The fox was caught by the smallest girl in the party, called Bae. She'd been watching from the clearing's edge, too small to run in snow as high as her chest, when it leapt in her arms. Chance told her she could keep it, provided she promised to take care of it, although it'd only be made of paper when she returned to the world. This was her coming of age, and she was delighted. There could be no more perfect thing. Iris and Kitou accepted their defeat with smiling good grace, declaring Bae the fastest girl in the forest. Box thought that as a rite of passage, for everyone here, it was literally enchanting.

The stories she'd tell, when she got back to Paris.

Then Iris asked if Kitou and Box would fight an exhibition.

"It's our tradition," she said, although her meaning was obvious. She wanted to see what the strangers were made of.

"We should," said Kitou.

"I don't know," said Box, fearing the inevitable.

"We're both about the same size," said Kitou. "Atomweights."

The children latched onto the word, and began to repeat it. "*Atomweights, atomweights.*" That settled it. They laid out a ring, using pieces of clothing: gloves, scarves and hats.

"This is ridiculous," said Box. "I'm no match for Kitou."

"I can fight to your level, and still give a good account of myself. We'll do the moves you know."

"Kickboxing?"

"We don't have gloves."

"Wait," said Chance, and disappeared into his house.

"Kickboxing is the martial art of Earth," said Kitou. "Dr Box is the atomweight champion."

315

Box rolled her eyes, but kept silent. Chance reappeared with two pairs of gloves: Yokohama Slim's red pair, and the brown ones that Chance wore in London. They had the waxy patina of prized leather.

At first it went as expected. Kitou was too fast and too skilled. Box was a *kuruttsu*. She envied Kitou her ability to glide, like a surreal hovercraft over the ground. Then, for the first time in her life, Box began to fight in the moment. All sense of parry and riposte disappeared. Instead, there was one fluid movement. One moment, she was *in* the glade, and then she *was* the glade. It was an extraordinary sensation.

It wasn't just Box fighting now. Her adamantine friend had returned. She surprised Kitou with a fast punch-kick combination she didn't know she had. She landed a blow, and with a shared smile, they returned to the starting position.

Now they were equals. Box pressed the attack, again and again. Kitou danced away, their strengths overlapping. At first it was a mixture of Box's Muay Thai and Po, except that now she knew all the moves. They found themselves on the ground, and somehow Box knew Brazilian jiu-jitsu. She could feel Kitou's worldspirit, an ecstatic presence, reveling in the contest, but in this place, *her* place, she had its measure.

She felt the world open to her. She was *here*, and it sang with her presence.

This went on for at least half an hour. Longer than she would've thought possible. Longer than she could've fought in the Real. Then they collapsed, clinging onto each other, exhausted.

Iris stood up, and said, simply, "That's the best thing I've ever seen.

"The prophecy is true. I'll follow you two, if you'll have me."

It was time to leave. There were plaintive farewells from the children. Chance had resumed his clanking appearance.

"Do you know I'm the only thing made of metal in this whole universe?" he said. "Perhaps it's because I'm imaginary."

Box remembered Brin saying a similar thing.

"Maybe you're a part of the operating system," she said.

[A member of the set of all sets that aren't members of themselves,] said the ship.

[Water Bear,] said Box. [You're here?]

[Only just,] said the ship.

[What happened back there, in the clearing?] asked Box, still wired with adrenaline. [Whoever she is, she can fight.]

[She's you, Dr Box,] said the ship. [Don't you see? You're coming into your powers.]

[Ship, are you alright?] asked Kitou.

[No, I'm dying.]

Iris led them deeper into the forest. "I won't leave you here," she said, at the place where the shapes of the snow reminded Box of a different dream. "You could both freeze to death, and I've no wish to find out what happens when people die here. Come to the Eagle with us. From there, we'll take the centerline train."

"How far is it?"

"To our home? It's simply a matter of wakening. It might take two days, or two minutes. The path will unfold. The people will be excited to meet you."

"How far to ours?"

317

"Nine hundred kilometers Spinwards."

"The train will take us?"

"I'll take you."

Iris was right. One moment they were in an arcane forest, and then they were descending a regular forested trail. She felt as though she'd literally woken from a dream. She looked behind, and there was only a snow-covered mountain. Below them were welcoming lights, and far below those, lights in a valley. A rosy-fingered dawn was reaching into the sky. It reminded Box of Atwusk'niges.

Kitou saw it too. She held Box tight, and pointed.

"It's like home," she said.

"It *is* home," said Iris.

15 ∞ HOT PURSUIT

2065

Asymphony; a wheel; a long, slow dance of gravity; a moment of brightness, then nothing - war in space was all that. Sometimes a battle might last an instant, as two prepared sides meet at processor speed. Sometimes a skirmish might drag on for lifetimes, draining the will of civilizations.

The first the Water Bear knew of an attack was when the Flux was destroyed. First the bird-shaped Horu ship was there, then a cone of ionized gas was expanding in the direction of travel of the weapon that killed him. It was only an accident of timing – a glitch in the synchronization of remote objects - that saved the Bat and the Water Bear from a similar fate.

These were apex physics weapons: lumps of degenerate metal, accelerated to near-lightspeed, delivered through a spacetime anomaly. The Horu were known for delivering rocks from a distance. It was their modus operandi in the war with the Pursang. But nothing like this. What human strategists feared most was ordinary matter, travelling at relativistic speed, manifesting millimeters from a target. Who could defend against that?

Flux might've seen it coming, but couldn't avoid it. Undodgeable bullets.

For the Water Bear, it was a near miss. Her consciousness was a community of individuals. One was her defensive monitor, a fast software agent that watched the world in Planck time. His role was to protect the ship from surprises, and he reacted instantly. Jaasper Huw was asleep in his nest. Pax was a meter from an interior wall. The limits of their fleshy vulnerabilities defined the frame he accelerated through, while simultaneously requesting a warp drive.

All he needed was time for energy to suffuse its manifolds.

A few milliseconds.

The Water Bear's acceleration in a straight line was like falling, since gravity attracts everything equally, but this was brutal evasion. Tidal forces pressed Jaasper into his bed, pooling the blood in the side of his head, pushing him into unconsciousness. Two seconds more would've killed him. Pax was driven through a crumple zone, but he was trained for it. A lifetime of martial arts had benefits other than fighting. With a brief exhalation, he passed out too.

It was during this long gulf of relativistic slomo that the ship herself became aware of events, her primary mind receiving information from a cloud of contributory brains. She was a Po warship, on the cutting edge of human capability, and this kind of war was her element. Still, she was lucky. She might've been first, or the weapon with her name might've come sooner.

Satisfied with how her monitor was handling defense, she began to wargame her responses. A further cloud of brains came online. These were entangled quantum computers. They set about collapsing the whole local wavefunction, for the next several seconds, like a chess computer considering every move.

A millisecond later, she entered warp space.

A pellet of depleted uranium, intended to destroy her, grazed her departing warp bubble. The Bat wasn't as lucky, and was left tumbling in a spiraling cloud of glitter.

His parting words were, *good hunting.*

Pax snapped awake in the Water Bear's gamespace, followed by Jaasper. There were no soft transitions. This was combat.

[Situation?] he asked.

[In hot pursuit,] said the Water Bear.

She replayed the annihilation of Flux, and the near destruction of the Bat. Viewports showed their quarry: a Horu ship, unfolding space before the attack, opening like a hand, with fingertips touching its targets. Through those binary digits, the weapons had come.

Elegant, thought Pax. And flamboyant. The gesture was meant to be menacing, like the hand of a demon, reaching in through a hole in the ether.

The hand-shaped ship was remarkably large. The Bat and Water Bear were hundreds of kilometers apart; Flux was a thousand kilometers distant. They could've been further apart, but then it wouldn't've been a trap.

321

A trap the Horu had sprung easily.

The Bat was fading away, powering down for the long wait. Flux was gone, forever.

Pax closed his eyes.

[Vitals?]

[You and Jaasper both have operable brain injuries.]

[Repair us,] he said.

[Starting neurosurgery... now.]

[They took their best shot,] said Jaasper.

[They did,] said Pax. [And it was better than we intended. Now we must make them pay.]

The Water Bear had learnt many things on this mission. Macro's time-traveling device had given her an insight into the problem of transwarp communications. No more would her warp bubbles be pristine islands of silence. Now, at warp speed, she could see the Horu system in exquisite detail: Horax, the roiling black planet; clouds of gas and debris from her fallen companions; the enemy ship, its hand closing.

If her warp jumps before had been like falling, this was like flying.

Now she was the raptor, and the Horu ship was her prey.

She also possessed the first secrets of the Horu geometry drive. It relied on entering curled-up spatial dimensions. She couldn't conjure up a Manifold herself, but she could follow another ship through one. She would follow this hand, wherever it took them.

That was the point of the trap. To glean information. It was what she was made for.

She postponed her regrets, for the death of Flux and his cargo of souls, which was a loss beyond reckoning. She'd assumed the necropolis would be able to defend himself. Flux had thought so too. What had changed? What new technology had the Horu attacker revealed, and where had it come from?

Or was it just luck? An outlier; a freakishly accurate shot?

She set a routine to wargame those questions.

She thought about her own crew instead. Pax was alive. She didn't know how she'd get by without her Navigator. Jaasper Huw was a find: a streetfighter, delivered by the universe to where he was most needed. She sensed his worldspirit, a fierce presence at the edges of her sensorium. She sent her love to her away team, and to Ito, wherever in the cosmos they were fighting.

And Alois Buss, the bravest of all. Where was he now? She could've reached out, but chose not to. She didn't need to know. All her people were competent. More than competent. Exceptional.

They were her A-team.

The hand-shaped ship refolded itself.

She drove at warp speed into the stillpoint of its disappearance.

16 ∞ RESPIT'S BRAIN

314

She rose, her eyes adjusting to the light. The pearly semidarkness of the Möbius night was squeezing past the edges of the drapes. A handful of photons. Enough.

Dr Box and Kitou's beds were empty.

Unusual.

But not alarming.

Quiet as a cat in search of her breakfast, she flowed through the Chancery halls. A few insomniacs were about. She avoided them. There was a clatter from the kitchens, and she smelt the malty aroma of the day's first batch of bread. She was instantly hungry, but that could come later.

Marius had slipped away an hour before, with the touch of his lips still on her breasts. He'd been good, in bed, for a man. Better than good. The Blue had the opposite of the Po attitude to intrateam fucking. They believed it bound them together. Brin was ambivalent. She was happy to not sleep with her Po teammates, even if she sometimes wanted to do just that. Sleeping with the amorous Blue came naturally.

The saturnine Horu weren't to her taste, although she'd had some pleasure there too.

Today she was Marius's.

Outside, two pale faces waited, bobbing like moons in the shadows. They'd dressed all in black, as they'd been asked to. They began to rub dirt into their faces, but she stopped them. She showed them a gesture for talking. They nodded, and led her away from the house.

They weren't much to look at, these two children, but the ship assured her they were talented. The girl was called Nim. She was a psi. The hulking youth was a delver, who could find his way through the world's interstices, and was also reputedly good with his fists. He was called Respit. They were Kitou's age or younger. That was fine. Brin had no use for soldiers. The place was awash with boneheaded sword wielders.

She wanted experts.

They made their way through the complex of hedgerows, yards and fortifications that made up the Chancery yards. Brin stopped them partway, and showed them how to flow through the night. Deft, catlike movements. Like water, she motioned. They understood perfectly. Soon they were nearly as stealthy as she was. She was impressed. Then they were beside a creek, far from the house, in the entrance of a cave, and then inside it, where Respit rubbed Cerulean wax on a rockface to make a faint glow.

The cave seemed to stretch endlessly, in every direction.

"Are we out of earshot?" she asked.

"No hear here," said Respit.

"What Respit means," said Nim, "is this cave isn't real."

Brin nodded. This was exactly the strangeness she'd asked for.

They were here to take her to the Enemy.

Respit and Nim were members of the Horu shamanic class. They believed their abilities descended from the Unanimated, the countless Horu dead that never made it into this place, and Brin had no reason to doubt it. She knew from the Water Bear's mission profile that they were both highly intelligent, and suffered in varying degrees from autism-spectrum neurodevelopmental disorders. The Horu considered these traits to be valuable, so these two young savants bore no hint of any stigma.

Brin motioned them together.

"I won't try to mislead you with trite stories or fabulism," she said. "My ship says you're at least as intelligent as I am."

Taking a chalk she'd brought for the purpose; she drew a rudimentary panther.

"Excuse my drawing skills. What's that?"

"Panthera," said Nim.

"What does it mean? Respit?"

The big youth colored in the dim light.

"Means you?"

"Right. Now, draw me two more."

She handed the chalk to Nim, who started to draw. Brin stopped her.

"No, not cubs. Full-sized animals. I'm your mythical panther; you're my personal army. Now draw."

Nim drew a sinuous creature, prowling beneath a moon and stars the girl had never seen. It captured the gist of the girl in just a few strokes: a vulpine intelligence, and a sly wit. It was far better than Brin's rude sketch. Respit's was childish: a sticklike cat with fangs and flattened-back ears.

Brin waited until they finished.

"Why are we doing this?"

"Symbols," said Nim.

"That's right. Symbols have power. The Blue people may have sung this place into existence, but it's your story."

In her straightforward way, that left no room for lying or exaggeration, she told them the history of their people. Maybe they'd heard it before. It didn't matter. She wanted them to know that she knew it, and respected it.

"You're the oldest human civilization," she said. "You may not be great warriors, but you're subtle, and clever. If you'll be my followers, then my powers are yours to command.

"I'm a *ferocious* warrior.

"In return, you become mine.

"By believing it, we make it so."

[Brin, this is excellent work,] said the Ship.

"Now we draw blood."

[What?]

She lifted her sword, and cut her arm, and drained her blood onto the wall.

"Now you," she said. With two gasps of pain, they mixed their blood in with hers.

"Listen," she said. "I'm not just the embodiment of your panther myth. I'm a soldier of the Hand of the Po, the most feared black ops regiment in human history. Think about that.

"I'm here on a mission.

"A mission to save everything.

"You know the story by now. You've seen it in my mind. No doubt you've heard it discussed by your elders. You know I have nothing to hide.

"I'm deputizing you. Do you understand?"

"Like the worldsinging," said Respit, "but *ours*."

"Remember," she said. "This is all in our minds."

She wiped a hand through the blood, and smeared it on her face. They did the same.

"Very good. Now you're Po soldiers. You fight for peace, and a just society. You work for me. Ship, you had something to say?"

[Not me.]

"Good. Then let's get the hell out of here."

They were inside a backdoor, Nim explained. Some were deliberate exploits. Some were programming mistakes. Respit knew how to use them. Through Respit's eyes, Brin saw the code. What struck her most was its elegance. The Möbius machine was a massively parallel, quantum computer. It really was a piece of work. Unlike the Real, whose nature was stored in particles whose quantum wavefunction had collapsed into one state, the qubits that made up Möbius space were in every possible state, and thus encompassed every possibility.

A model of a tree could never be a tree, except in this place.

How to bootstrap a universe.

The corridor branched, and branched again; the walls took on a fibrous appearance. The structures reminded her of brain cells. Soon she was sure they were neurons. She cursed her imagination.

"Respit's brain," said Nim.

"What?"

"A model," said Nim. "He models this place on his brain. Like a homunculus. Do you know what that is? Don't let it get to you."

"Get to me, how?"

"It can get a bit hallucinatory."

Her mission began the previous night, with an argument. Marius said something she disliked, so she put him in an armbar, till he revised his opinions.

"Brin," he said, with difficulty. "What witchcraft is this? Release me." It hurt; he couldn't quite breathe, and every part of her was out of reach of any useful appendage.

"Brin, please," he insisted.

[Yes,] said the ship. [Brin, please think about this.]

[You take this nonsense seriously?]

[I share his concerns.]

Brin waited a while, then used the energy stored in his twisted upper torso to spring back out of his reach.

"The Fibonacci art," he complained, rubbing his shoulder.

"The Lo style," she said.

The fight was followed by sex. It was inevitable. Brin preferred women, but like most soldiers, she took her pleasure where she found it. The sex was athletic. More than athletic. Electric. At one point she considered reapplying the arm bar, which would be even more pleasing, naked and slathered with fluids.

After he'd recovered his breath, she said, "So you think Ito's been turned?"

"Not turned," he said. "*Infected.*"

"By what?"

"The Numbers."

[By the Thespian disease,] said the ship.

[Why are you even here?]

[I've returned,] said the ship, primly.

Marius told her that Ito was infected with a psychological disease. It was a degenerative state, brought on by exposure to the Enemy. Brin's mind churned with all the implications.

A First, crippled by malware.

"Okay," she said, after Marius had made his case. "What are we going to do about it?"

Now she was inside Respit's brain, trying to get to the truth of the matter. The deeper they delved, the more bizarrely symbolic the neural cave system became.

Flashes of thought.

Squeezes like brain structures.

Forests of pseudounipolar cells, with their multiple axons, snaking into a looming middle-distance, and the nightmarish fried egg nuclei of soma. Strange, hypnogogic sounds: crashes and snaps of conversation. A writhing, winding corridor of her bad dreams, like being trepanned by a snake.

She got rid of that idea.

"This place is affecting me," she said.

"Breathe," said Nim.

"Airways," said Respit.

[Yes,] said the ship. [This place is equivalent to the Blue riders' airwaves. Think about those for a while.]

She did, and her mind became a breeze, blowing through high places.

She breathed.

Then she was hallucinating. She was flying. No, not flying; clinging to a rocky summit. The wind howled all around her. The summit was covered in blue lichen. It was no part of this universe. A landscape, far below. Hedgerows rimed with frost. Bodies. A crow rose from a corpse, and cawed into the distance.

Her corpse.

She felt Nim pull her into the moment.

She *breathed.*

The neural corridor had become like a corridor again. The hallucination was like a small animal, scuttling into the caves. Her new companions were beside her.

[Fascinating,] said the ship. [We're traversing the laminar flows, like the Blue people do.]

"Explain."

[It's like we're hitching a ride on a passing universe.]

"Between," said Nim.

"The in-between," said Respit.

[I believe they mean we're in the process of moving between two points without crossing the space between, like a hyperluminal drive does, but they lack the math to express it.]

"Like a wormhole?" asked Brin.

"What's a wormhole?" asked Respit.

She explained the physics of wormholes. It was like a light went on in the boy's face.

"Those physics exist?" asked Nim.

"Absolutely."

"I want to go there."

"Ship can make wormholes."

"Is this true?"

[Yes,] said the ship. [In many different ways.]

"You must be like a god."

[I like to think so.]

They reached a destination.

The Room was a room, and they were its walls.

They were also *in* the room. It was uncanny, like synesthesia: her sensorium trying to make sense of their superimposed states. The walls were crumbling masonry, under an industrial sky, the color of infection, a scabrous yellowish gray.

[Are we still in the Möbius universe?] Brin asked.

[That ship sailed a while ago,] said the ship.

Nim motioned for them to be quiet.

In the Room was a desk. At the desk was a Gray. He was better resolved than the Grays she'd seen previously. Instead of being made of mucous, he seemed to be stitched together from burn tissue. He was anxious, and bored. He shuffled papers on the desk. He appeared to be an officer. His belted grey tunic was pinned with iron paraphernalia.

Iron. So this place has metal.

It was cold here. The Grays liked the cold.

She filed that information away.

[Brin, I'm firewalling you now,] said the ship.

Brin nodded. She was the delivery mechanism. The ship was delivered. Now it was time to protect her. She wondered where her body was. In her bed? In a cave? A mote in Respit's brain? In orbit around Horax? A smear on an event horizon somewhere?

Then she was in the ship's gamespace, with its wireframes and malleable time. The resolution wasn't what she was used to, but the ship's algorithms were still

333

impressive. She leaned down and inspected the Gray soldier. Up close, he was as ugly as she expected him to be.

She zoomed in. He was literally stitched together.

She could sense the Enemy, behind the sky.

She hoped he couldn't see her.

The Ride of the Spinifex Reach manifested in their usual way. At first there was an industrial sky, then a few scattered riders. Brin knew that for each one she could see, there'd be ten more she couldn't. She watched the Gray officer stiffen. Through her ship senses she could smell his fear. Sweat and endorphins. A head-up display showed her his vitals. He was responding as any human would, to a threat.

The Blue riders rode down, taking their time. These were her friends, Markus, Velo, Viki, Alis, Ox and Bravery. They carried themselves like imperious savages, a look she knew they cultivated.

To put the fear of death into their enemies.

Then Marius rode down, like the arrogant young warlord he was. Without breaking rhythm, he flowed from his saddle, into a chair.

He allowed his blue-painted horse to wander away, uncommanded.

"I'm here for a parlay," he said.

The Gray officer was about Marius's size. He would've been handsome, but for his stitched skin.

"Talk," said the Gray.

"Not with you."

The man stiffened. She saw his anxiety give way to annoyance. There was no flight response there. He'd already conquered his fear.

This soldier would be a worthy opponent in combat.

"I speak for my people," he said.

Marius raised an eyebrow.

"Then who?"

"I desire Kronus."

"Impossible," said the soldier, reaching for his papers.

Marius produced a knife and pinned the papers in place.

"Do as I say," he said. "Or we'll kill you."

The Enemy unfolded himself from the sky. He was a magnificent man, with a poet's huge and shaggy head, and a corpulent belly that only seemed to add to his magnificence. Brin was transfixed. She couldn't take her eyes off him.

Marius rose from his chair.

Kronus stared at the walls. "What a beautiful morning," he said, spreading his arms. "Black," he said, "like ink." It was true. The pestilent sky had gone black. It was like he'd sucked all the light from it, and was playing it back through his skin. Brin could see the ship's telemeters read off the scale. The man's heartrate read zero. His temperature was tending to infinity.

"Who are you?" he asked, with the formaldehyde whiff of someone examining a specimen.

"I'm Marius, Ride of the Spinifex Reach."

"I don't know you," he said. "You seem young, for a Ride. Where's Bardo?"

"You killed him."

"I did?

"Your people did. In the last war. Nine years ago. Kronus, you've met me before."

Kronus raised his hands, as if to say *young people, these days.*

Brin wanted to trust him.

She wanted it, badly.

The ship dropped a packet of encrypted information at her virtual feet. She opened it, carefully, like a child unfolding her lunch from a waxed paper bag.

[I'm getting a storm of exploits,] it said. [Primitive, but effective. Very like the Thespian disease. Marius seem to be immune: his neural architecture can't run the code. Your Horu telepaths can go where it isn't. You may be feeling some backwash.]

[Backwash?] What Brin was feeling was like waves of heat from a furnace.

Marius was a big man, but Kronus was bigger. A genuinely massive man, with forearms like hams and a laborer's slack musculature. A beautiful man, for all his fatness and ruin. While Brin watched from the safety of the ship's gamespace, Marius told him everything. About Dr Box. Fluxor, the Fa:ing, his fears about Ito. Everything except Brin's presence, which the ship had scrubbed from his memory, using a combination of strong opioids and hypnosis.

"There's no point in lying," he'd said, the night before. "As soon as you open your mouth, he knows what you're thinking."

"So why talk at all?"

"To exchange information. This isn't just a war to him," he'd said, "It's a game. He allows us to make moves, and to advance if they're good ones."

"Or he's insane, and making it up as he goes along, to see you struggle."

"Yes, that's possible."

"You trust him not to just kill you?"

"He plays by the rules."

"What rules?"

"His rules."

"What do you want in return for this information?" Kronus asked, when Marius was finished.

"Your surrender."

Kronus made a show of considering the offer. He was a natural performer. He held up his hands. He shook his mane like a beast, as though clearing his head of a physical irritant.

"Your attack on Fluxor is thwarted," said Marius. "All the powers of the Real are aligned against you. Don't you see? Let's have an end to the killing."

"What killing?" asked Kronus, cocking his head. "We have a truce."

"Because you imposed it."

"You'd rather I didn't?"

"What does that have to do with your surrender?"

"You're right," said Kronus, his face lit up from within by emotions: hilarity, rage and surprise. "What does any of this have to do with *my* surrender?"

"You're twisting it round."

"I'm untwisting it."

"You can't win."

"But I am."

"How?"

He laughed. "You expect me to *tell* you?"

Behind the ship's firewall, Brin was struggling with her own devils. Knowing the malware existed made her want to reach out and touch it. What did it feel like? Maybe she was infected, maybe from Avalon.

[You're not infected,] said the ship. [It's my emotions you're feeling.]

[Are you safe?]

[My defenses are tested, but we're in no real danger.]

"Then we're done," Marius said.

"We are done," said Kronus.

The torrent of exploits flicked off like a switch. Kronus laid a hand on Marius's shoulder. "I understand your predicament," he said. "I do. But the way to my future goes through your people. There must be a reckoning, and I'll win it."

"Why? Kronus, why does any of this have to happen?"

Kronus raised his eyes to the sky.

"Who am I to go against the word of God?"

"Oh," he said, as Marius remounted.

"One more thing. Tell your Po bitch I can see her."

17 ∞ NEBECULΛE MΛGELLΛNI

2065

It began with a mist, surrounding a void. The mist became a cloud, of world-sized water spheres, orbiting a dark star, visible only by its influence on the matter around it.

Around the void was dust and gas, stirred to incandescence by dark matter destroying itself deep in the star, the physics of the process barely understood. The star was called Nubeculae. The cloud was the Magellani nebula.

The spheres flowed, at planetary speed, into a celestial riverine system, like the lines traced by particles in a physics experiment.

In the water spheres were cities.

Waterfall, the home world of the Magellanic civilization.

Macro awoke in a rattling acceleration chair, his travel companion unconscious beside him. It felt like the teeth were being shaken out of his mouth. During the crossing, the corals that lined the cochlear corridors had erupted throughout the vessel, leaving lush voids where the passengers' stasis fields had been. Filaments and stamen floated all around them. Nothing was left that resembled a machine. He could almost believe it was a stage in the Tung reproductive cycle. It had that fecundity.

In the final approach, when the gravities crushed them in their seats, it rained; a crisp, pure rain squeezed from the foliage by the deceleration. It made him want to laugh out loud. There was something about the crazed way the Tung did things that Macro was starting to like. Of all the species he'd seen, the Tung had the least fucks to give.

Which made their current state of mind more worrying. They seemed almost desperate to get Alois and Macro to Waterfall.

Alois awoke as they were decelerating towards a water sphere the size of a small planet. He flapped his hands, then relaxed, as his wetware oriented him.

"Did I sleep the whole way?" he asked.

"We both did," said Macro.

Magellanic history was hidden in shadows and mist. They were an aquatic civilization, but they'd never evolved into water breathers. They clove as strongly to the ideal of biological evolution as the thousand worlds did. They believed evolution had a direction, like a vague form of religion, but they weren't a theocracy. Macro thought it was all nonsense.

Maybe not nonsense. Maybe semantics. Evolution was directed in the same way as gravity favors ellipses, or a door favors closing.

It was directed towards a balance of forces, by entropy.

But he wasn't here to compare philosophical ideas. He was here for an army.

That meant the Pursang.

A second idea the Magellanics shared with the thousand worlds was that they were both effective, warlike civilizations. The thousand worlds pretended they weren't. They parked their marauders in deep space, and equipped them with fast warp drives. The Magellanics made no bones about it. Magellanic space was filled with war machines. This was due in part to where they were. Magellanic space was filled with enemies.

They were a civilization always at war, and the Pursang were a famous part of their war effort. Why was a mystery. The holy warriors were excellent soldiers, but the Magellanics had warfighting robots, and nanobiotics, and none of the thousand worlds coyness about using them. Why did they need the best human ground fighters?

Why did they need soldiers at all?

It was a good question, much argued by the scions of the bank. It led to important problems in strategy, so Samppo encouraged it. Macro's theory was that it was a form of remedial branding, to prove they were on the right side of morality. The Finance Engine knew, but wouldn't say, which deepened the mystery.

His new wetware wasn't much help.

[I don't know,] said his twin. [I can only speculate.]

[How do they compare to the Po?]

[The holy warriors are a class above the regular Po military. On a par with the Po special forces.]

[The Hands of the Po?]

[Yes.]

[Except the Pursang use weapons.]

[They do.]

This was red meat to a boy brought up amongst budding game theorists. The Po had fought the Pursang hundreds of times, in the battlefields of his imagination.

[So the Pursang would win?]

[In a fight between handwaving monks and atomics? Yes. But the Po wouldn't fight them that way.]

[Who are the monks?]

[The Po are. They eschew weapons.]

[But the holy warriors fight for the forest.]

[They do.]

[Wetware v worldspirits?]

[Wouldn't happen.]

[What if someone had both?]

[That'd be nice.]

They plunged into a black sea, with dark energy crawling all around them. For a moment they bobbed in a gravity field. Then he felt the pull of a tractor effect, and they descended into an undersea city.

This was an industrial world, home to millions of people, from thousands of species. They were everywhere. This water sphere was brimming with life. Unlike humans elsewhere, the Magellanics didn't have to look far to find strangers. The Clouds were a crossroads. They'd been fought over since before humans existed. They sank into a transit zone, and then into a dockyard. The soft lights of the surface were replaced by glaring industrial lights. Finally, they settled in the chrysalis twilight of a dock. There were other Tung modules here.

"Take one of these," waved a Tung. It was the Tung from the Discothèque. Pfft. It expelled a cloud of pills, which tumbled in the local microgravity.

Macro and Alois had extricated themselves from their acceleration chairs, and the riot of flowery growth all around them, and were preparing to leave.

"What are they?" asked Macro.

"Ozenges."

"An air supply?"

"One is enough for an Avalon day."

"What if I forget?"

The Tung gave an impression of drowning.

The Tung in water were graceful, flashing creatures, soaring on slippery wings. There was no sense of the phage-like ghastliness they exhibited in air. Macro followed them in spurts of propulsion, squeezed from his vestments. Fast currents carried them between sprawling industrial precincts. They weren't alone in the water. Every kind of sea creature seemed to be swimming beside them. The Magellanic preoccupation with natural evolution seemingly didn't extend to body enhancements. Many of the sea creatures here were cyborgs.

[Some of them are sentient,] his wetware said. [Some are the local biome.]

[How can I tell?] he asked.

As if on cue, a creature devoured another.

He hoped the eaten was biome.

The bar was shaped like a cave, lit by the photoemitting creatures inside it. Shadows rippled and loomed as patrons got in and out of the water, many of them naked. Public copulation seemed to be acceptable here, including between species. The otherwise androgynous Magellanics exhibited every combination of primary sex characteristic, from female to male, to ungendered, and everything between.

Alois, unconcerned, restored his lounge suit to its original, rumpled shape. Macro, seasoned by his Avalon experiences, bought beers. They were deliciously cold in the syrupy air of the bar. After a few beers, he began to be drunk. He had no idea what he should do, so he did nothing.

The Tung seemed more relaxed now. Perhaps they'd had cabin fever.

Too much deceleration.

Relax, and the universe relaxes with you.

A Magellanic androgyne leaned in towards him.

"You're new here," ze said.

Ze had the celestial body art of a fully-fledged Magellanic navigator. By the look of the designs, ze'd been everywhere it was possible to be.

"I am, zir," said Macro, careful to use the ungendered honorific.

"It's a strange place," ze said.

"It's me who's the stranger," said Macro.

The Magellanic chuckled, hir wry tone signaling hir obvious physical maleness.

"It's hard to say who's who," ze said, "in a strange place as this. Forgive me this trespass." Macro felt a delicate touch on his wetware, and a transfer of information.

Alois leaned in. "We're about to be arrested," he said.

The music stopped playing. Tung flopped and skittered into nearby pools. Macro's wetware clicked into action. His intoxication disappeared. He felt his perimeter defense systems powering up: a gritty mechanical whine in his vestments.

Then power down again.

Oh *shit*, he thought.

His new friend was nowhere to be seen.

"Don't worry," said Alois. "Finish your beer."

"Oh, and ignore what they say about me."

Alois's suit powered up, and enclosed him in a field of pearly energy.

"Sorry," said Alois, "but they mean to hurt me."

Then the waters erupted, and slug-like creatures dragged Alois into the water.

More emerged and took Macro.

A different industrial seascape unfolded around him, through a curtain of foam from the drives of the slugs. Autonomous manufactories, lit by sodium lights, and the looming shapes of insectile starships. A military zone. His captors were cyborgs, as far as he could tell, with human features engineered into streamlined machines. Their police identification flashed in their carapaces, and was broadcast into the water around them. That was all he could hear: the bleep-bleep-bleep of their sirens, and the whine of propulsion systems.

Who would choose to live like that, he wondered?

Like being a monk in a bank, he supposed.

Alois was being pulled, unresisting, behind them, still inside his pearly field. They passed through a succession of gates, until they reached a complex of spheres, one inside the other, like worlds within worlds. A disembodied voice read out charges. Except for the slugs, there were no other people. This part of the city was deserted.

Although his Broca was down, Macro understood some of the words.

Pathogen, it said, in a language not unlike Pursang.

Bioweapon.

Disease.

He understood he wouldn't be the first one to die here. There was a smell in the water, like the smell of burnt meat in the air of a crematory. It was the local equivalent of the Avalon interview room, except this was real. Here, they did kill strangers.

This was what he'd signed up for, in taking this mission, although he hadn't visualized it ending this way. His fathers had warned him. He'd waved them away.

Now, he was frightened.

If he died, he'd be killing his friends.

Alois was locked in the innermost cage, brutally beaten. They'd gotten through his field, eventually. Macro was free to roam in the cell outside Alois's.

Cells inside cells. Spheres within spheres. What was this place for?

Why did the Tung abandon him?

Who was the mysterious Navigator?

Where were his oxygen pills? An Avalon day, Pfft. said they'd last for. How long had he been here?

Fear was giving way to confusion.

And gnawingly, the immanence of drowning.

His wetware whispered back into life, just as he felt the first worrying itch in his larynx. First there was a feeling of spaciousness, like a sixth sense coming online, then malware intervened.

[I'm Sybil,] it said.

It spoke Ruby, the finger-tapping language of the bank. Ruby was efficient, with 2^9 phonemes, or 2^4 when spoken one-handed. It was a voice-interlocutor, the simplest form of AI. Its intelligence was an emergent property of loops in its code.

[Do I know you?] he signaled.

[You met my original, in the {undecipherable},] it said.

[In the bar? Why are you here?]

[I'm sorry.]

[You're an apology?]

[No, I'm here to prepare you.]

[Prepare me for what?]

[For dying.]

He'd watched Alois die. First, the return of his instinct to breathe. Then a convulsion.

It seemed easy.

[It is easy,] said Sybil.

[Where's the rest of my wetware?] asked Macro.

[There's not enough space for it here.]

[Where?]

There - a tickle.

[How do you feel about dying?] asked Sybil.

[What?]

[What do you feel?]

[What are you, a catastrophe voyeur?]

[Is this a catastrophe?]

[It is for me.]

Macro had occasionally thought about dying, as an event in an unimaginably distant future. He knew it might be unpleasant. *Death* was neutral. He didn't care about death. He cared about dying. He cared about fucking this mission.

He cared about the things he'd never get to see.

[I think dying is holy,] said Sybil.

[Good for you,] said Macro.

[Freeing your space on the wheel.]

[Why don't you help me?] he said. He wanted to scream, but there was nothing to scream with. Instead he finger-tapped, tersely.

[I can't,] said the voice-interlocutor. [I only exist in your mind.]

He examined the exterior spheres. There were eight, making ten spheres in total, although the nesting made it hard to be sure. He tried pulling the bars. No movement. He tried squeezing through. No way. How did they open? He searched for a lock, and found nothing.

Why had they put him here? Alois was their intended victim. Macro was likely collateral damage.

Now Alois was floating painlessly, his drowned corpse at rest, his personality elsewhere.

Pathogen, they'd said.

This was a biocontainment facility.

What kind of biocontainer had open cages, five meters apart?

One for observing the interpersonal transmission of a disease.

What disease?

The Thespian disease.

The Magellanics believed Alois was infected with the Thespian disease.

They weren't doing epidemiology now. If they were, there'd be victims in the other cages, waiting to be infected.

He was here to drown.

He was being euthanized.

This Thespian disease must be much worse than anyone was letting on.

Drowning was fast, and surprisingly easy. First his will to breathe returned, then a quick gasp, and a moment of panic, then peace. His fingers tore at the bars, injuring them, but that had nothing to do with him. He slipped into a welcoming abyss, like falling into the arms of a lover.

He was a dot, in a cathode ray screen, fading to gray.

Then he was nothing.

Then he became the voice-interlocutor. There was no need for tapping. He and Sybil were the same.

This is weird, he thought.

They were floating in space. Real, interplanetary vacuum. No intervening water. Alois and he, falling through the drops of the Waterfall system.

[I thought you might like to see this,] ze said.

For the first time in his life, Macro could see the whole Milky Way galaxy, a blazing wheel of stars.

[I've enhanced it for you,] said Sybil.

I'm no longer a member of that set, he thought.

The set of the living.

He had no feelings. No anger, no pain. He was executing only a miniscule set of instructions.

I could learn to live like this, he decided.

[How long have I been dead?] he asked.

[Too long. There'll be some damage, but we'll repair you.]

[Alois?]

[He has retreated into his alien sensorium,] said Sybil.

He had so many questions. Such as, if he was dead, how was he able to see things?

Did sensation persist this long after death?

349

[Why did the slugs hurt Alois?]
[They were protecting our people.]
[From what?]
[Kronus.]
[Who's Kronus?]

First, he was in the grip of a seizure. Water was gushing out of his mouth, and he was drowning again.

Then he was fully awake, on a table, shaking with terror. He couldn't think straight. The lights were dazzling his eyes. He was naked, being prodded by androgyne humans.

Then he was relaxed in a modern, well-equipped medibay. A screenwall looked onto a reef. Fish darted through coral like neurons. He caught a glimpse of himself in a mirror. He looked alright. Good, considering. No visible injuries.

Except for his fingers.

Alois looked like a motor accident victim.

"That *so* sucked," he complained. Something inside him was already softening the experience, like the natural brainware that wipes away dreams, so we don't think they're real.

It occurred to him he was in air. He took an experimental breath of it.

His Magellanic friend was here. The one with the bodacious tatts, from the bar.

"I'm sorry," said Sybil.

"Everyone's sorry," said Macro. "Thanks for the voice-interlocutor. Who's Kronus?"

"The creator of the Thespian disease."

Sybil explained that the thousand worlds military strategy was mistaken.

That the real attack vector was the Thespian disease.

"It's a weapon?"

"Yes."

Macro tried to take it all in. He wasn't aware the thousand worlds *had* a military strategy. It felt like his mind was wrapped in bandages. Maybe it was. The medibay told him he had a brain injury; to be patient.

"Why am I here?"

He made an exploratory poke at his wetware. Nothing.

"Why all the mystery?" he asked, getting angry. "Where is my wetware?"

"There's someone I want you to meet," said Sybil.

He was Macro's age, maybe a year older. Macro's height, maybe five kilos heavier. A lithe athlete. Dressed in dusty combat nano of a Magellanic commando. A holy warrior.

"I'm impressed," said Macro. This was his first holy warrior. Maybe he should be kneeling.

The young Pursang easily fit the mythology. He had lurid scars, presumably earned in battle. One curled over his arm and disappeared into his dreadlocks. He must have nearly been cut in two.

He looked as though he hadn't slept in days.

He shook his head. "No, it's you who should be praised. My name is Totoro."

"I've heard that before."

"Yes, I'm my sister's brother."

18 ∞ BUNJIL, THE EAGLE

314

The town of Eagle clung to narrow arêtes, peering through couloirs to the valley below. Dawn caught the mountains above, so they shone rosy gold in the sunlight. Lines of people were moving by lamplight up a long switchback trail, that led to the town from the valley.

"Something's happening," said Iris.

"I must see to the children," she said.

Eagle was a high-mountain bolthole, with steep gabled roofs huddled close to the rockface, and doglegged streets that ended in nothing. Box had seen towns like this in the Peruvian Andes. Unlike the mainly Horu Chancery, this was a Blue place. It was Blue farmers who were coming up the trail, and the streets were crowded with Blue riders.

Box and Kitou were given a whirlwind tour, as Iris delivered her charges home. There were rumors of war. The Gray army had stirred in the East. They'd reached the centerline train. They were in the valley below.

Iris dismissed all of it. She said it'd take an army ten days to reach the trainline. Longer, if they hoped to keep the ground they won. More days before they were here. Still, Box could see the strain on the young soldier's face. It was same fear as she saw in the eyes of the families. The last generation of Blue warriors had been slaughtered by Kronus. They didn't want wars.

While Iris was delivering Bae with her prize to her home down a giddying lane, an older Blue woman rode up. She was Helen, she said, Marshall of the West, and Ride of the Eagle.

"Welcome to High Eagle," she said. "I wish I could give you a better welcome, but as you can see, we're about to be in a war. Unfortunate timing. You must be the Red Lady."

The woman carried herself like a warfighting general of Earth history newsreels: like a FARC revolutionary, rallying *campesinos* in the defense of a Bolivarian hill town. She wore her past wars in the scars on her face: an eye covered by a patch, part of a cheekbone missing.

"Who runs this place?" asked Box.

"I do," she said.

"We have to get to the Chancery."

"Yes, I can help you."

Iris emerged from the laneway; all the children now safe in their homes. Helen threw her a spear with a flag, which Iris caught and fixed to her saddle.

"How far are the enemy?" asked Box.

"Hard to say," said Helen. "There are marginally credible reports of Grey infantry already on the train. I don't believe it. Iris?"

"I have no better information."

"Nothing from the ghost?"

"Nothing."

"Unsurprising. Alright, to the Mousehole."

The Mousehole was a Horu teahouse, leaning out over a tumbling moraine, deserted except for its owner, who served them tea, then vanished.

"This is my headquarters," said Helen. "The walls are acceptably deaf. The owner's a spy but we know it. Red Lady, we've been trying to contact the Chancery, but their psi is offline."

"Do they even know it's started?" asked Iris.

"I have no way to know," said Helen. Box could get a better look at her now. She appeared to be in her mid-fifties, the oldest Blue person Box had seen, apart from the venerable horseman. She was wearing an oversized military greatcoat, with pieces sewn in where it'd once been hacked into. Underneath it was the usual bone armor.

"What *do* we know?" asked Box.

"Kronus's armies are moving," said Helen. "Maybe a million soldiers. Maybe half coming here, to this town."

"Why?"

"Because we intend to bring them. Eagle's a hard place to win, unless they aim to blow us off the mountain. We'll make our stand in these hills."

"Bring them, how?"

"They'll follow the path of least resistance. We'll resist least in the middle."

"How many people do you have?"

"I'm the Marshall of nine Rides. Five thousand riders; we have five thousand more who will fight."

"Ten thousand against half a million?"

"No, there are other Blue armies. We number about fifty thousand in total."

"That's all?"

"Yes."

"Ten to one?"

"About."

"How can you win?"

"In the mountains we have the advantage. The enemy will struggle to see us. Do you see that cirque valley below? All bogs and lakes. Our rangers in the hills on all sides, killing and slipping away. We'll horrify them with our savagery. We need to invent a new type of fighting."

"It's already been invented. We call it an insurgency."

"You come from such a place?"

"Oh yes, we've pretty much been at it since we started."

The owner appeared with more tea. Helen waved him away.

"Look," said Box. "I'm a military historian. I know the exact tactics of the war you've described. I can help you."

"No," said Helen. "Your place isn't here. Iris?"

"I'd planned to take them on the train."

"Impossible now. The Greys may reach it before you do, or worse, while you're on it. You'll take the high road. It's a bilaterally symmetrical, parabolic airwave. That means it runs high. Between five and ten thousand meters. You'll need suitable clothing, more than what you have now."

"Won't we get altitude sickness?" asked Box.

"Mountain sickness? No, not enough time, but it won't be easy."

She turned her attention to Kitou. "You, girl," she said. "You're barefoot."

Kitou tossed her head. Box could sense a new wildness in her. Box didn't mind it. It was a hot kind of madness. They were all going mad, in this place.

"I'm not your girl," said Kitou.

"Ah, a spirited one. Can it fight?"

"She can fight," said Iris.

"She still needs the correct footwear. Go and get it for her. Now."

"Kitou," said Box. "Are you alright?"

"It's begun, Dr Box. I want to be part of it."

"You'll get your chance. We have to get back to Ito."

"I can fight with these people. I also understand the principles of asymmetric war."

"Kitou, no. I can't get through this without you."

Kitou at first looked defiant, then chagrined. "I'm sorry. What was I thinking?"

"You want to fight?"

"Of course. These are my people."

"Then we'll stay," said Box, to see how it sounded.

"You'd really fight with us?" said Helen.

"Of course," said Kitou, and the woman sighed.

"No," she said, not unkindly. "We're going to lose. Make no mistake. What use is one extra sword, and - with respect - a scholar of war? You two can only make a difference with the prophet."

"But," said Box and Kitou together.

"No, I forbid it."

357

After Iris left with Kitou to find winter gear, Box asked more questions. "You said one million soldiers," she said, "I've heard there are two. Where are the rest?"

"Staged in the high east, preparing to go outside."

"Outside where?"

"To your world, I think. To the Real. That's what the spaceships are for."

"How many spaceships?"

Helen shrugged. "Thousands? Millions?"

"Do you know what they're planning to do?"

"Horu myth foretells of a last battle. It's a story the Enemy favors. We hope to avoid it."

"Helen, what happens when the worldsingers leave this place?"

Helen made a crude gesture, like a throat being cut.

"It implodes, and takes the Enemy with it?"

"You can't believe that."

"No. He means to destroy us, *and* he means to escape. The events are not unrelated. The destruction of this world plays a role in the next one."

"So by dying, you play into his hands?"

"By dying *quickly*, we play into his hands. What we can give *you* is time."

"Me?"

The innkeeper poured them tea.

"Red Lady, Kronus might seem mad, or like a self-important fool sometimes, but he's a good enough general. Not as good as he thinks, but enough. That's why you're here. You come from outside the game. You *will* find a way."

"The first step is bitey," said Iris.

"Don't worry," said Box. "We've done this before."

"Right," said Iris, and stepped out over two vertical kilometers of granite. Seabiscuit followed, and then they were soaring, effortlessly skywards.

"This parabola is deceptively fast," Iris shouted over her shoulder. "Try to keep up. Don't stray to the sides or you'll finish up elsewhere."

They were in the grip of a rising column of air, and not just air. Box could feel the alternative realities curling around her. It wasn't cold at first. The air from the valley was degrees warmer than in the town, but as they rose, and the spiraling thermals abandoned them, the temperature fell. Iris had kitted them out in coveralls made from skins lined with fur, with similar rugs for the horses. The suits were expertly made, but soon her exposed skin was stinging.

[How cold is it now?] she asked the ship, but she got no answer.

[She's gone,] said Kitou.

[Our version, here?] asked Box.

[I don't know,] said Kitou.

The town fell away, until it was a sprinkle of dots in the landscape. Now Box could see the size of the country. It was hard to believe this was smaller than Earth. The sheer granite walls over Eagle were just the beginning. To the north and the south were rows of serrated giants, like the Karakorum on Earth, but taller. She began to discern the inwards curvature of the helix. It was like rising out of a bottle of mountains.

"Do you have mountains like this where you come from?" asked Iris.

"We have the Aø, the Curtain Wall on Fluxor," said Kitou. "But not like this."

"We've got a range almost this size," said Box. She told them about K2, and Chomolungma in the Himalayas, and the perils of the death zone. She described the problem of altitude acclimatization, which Iris and Kitou called mountain sickness. Iris was amazed that people on Earth climbed mountains for pleasure.

"It's like a religion," said Box.

"We'd never even think of doing that," said Iris.

"Are your mountains holy?" asked Kitou.

"No," said Iris, "they're lethal."

Soon they were soaring above cirrus clouds like wispy white streamers. Iris warned them of frostbite, and showed them gussets in their hoods, that they could hide in. Soon just their eyes were exposed.

"Who'll tell us a story?" said Iris, her voice muffled by layers of animal skins.

"I will," said Box, her teeth beginning to chatter. It was beyond cold, and she was starting to suffer.

"It's about a bird spirit," she said.

"Is it a Horu myth?" asked Kitou.

"No, it's from Earth," said Box. "From the Kulin people of south-eastern Australia."

"Is that near Utah?" asked Kitou.

"Not so far," said Box. "Maybe twelve thousand kilometers, as the Bat flies.

"Bunjil was a bird spirit," she began. "The wedge-tailed eagle. He brings the cold weather."

"He must be flying around here," said Iris.

"Bunjil is also the star Altair, in the constellation of Aquila."

"Altair," said Kitou. "I've been there."

"Kitou, please shut up. Bunjil lived on Jaithmathangs, the tallest mountain in the Kulin nation. One day a Kulin hunter was camped on Jaithmathangs, when a heavy snowfall came. He didn't have modern snowshoes, so he was trapped there."

"This is a parable about my footwear," laughed Kitou.

"Lost in the wilderness, and with no way home, he called on the bird spirit of the mountain to save him. He called out 'Bunjil', three times.

"Eventually, the air spirit Bunjil appeared in the sky."

"What was he like?" asked Iris.

"Like a monster," said Box. "The head of a goanna, and the wings and feet of an eagle."

"A chimera," said Kitou.

"Yes," said Box. "A cryptid."

"This being exists?" asked Iris.

"It's Australia," said Box. "An ancient, mysterious place. Anything's possible. Now, our Kulin hunter…"

"What's his name?" asked Kitou.

"Let's call him Claude," said Box.

"A good name," said Iris.

"It is. Claude made a sacrifice, to call Bunjil down from the air to help him. He burned his stocks of food, until he ran low, and then he burnt more, until nothing was left. When Bunjil finally landed, Claude said 'You're welcome here, friend, in my campsite.' And Bunjil said 'It's lucky you called me friend. I'll take you inside the mountain, and you'll be happy with me there.'"

"They entered into a relationship?" asked Iris.

"Of sorts," said Box. "If Claude had called him anything else, he'd have been eaten."

"This *is* a metaphor," said Kitou.

"It is. Now listen.

"Life was good in the mountain. It wasn't made from cold stone, as you'd expect, but like a comfortable home. Bunjil had a wife and daughter, and he gave Claude his daughter."

"Gave?" asked Iris.

"He was a creator being. They were his humans. He possessed them."

"Like Kronus possesses the Greys?"

"Yes, like that. Claude grew increasingly comfortable. Bunjil brought him all the meat he could eat."

"Do you remember the deer we ate?" asked Kitou.

"I do," said Box. "Bunjil's meat was like that, hot from the fire, and delicious. Claude had a wife now, so he was happy that way too. In time, he became so comfortable that he became more like Bunjil, and Bunjil, learning his ways, became more like the human. Until one day, they changed places, and Claude, desiring his own freedom, set the man free.

"And that was how the Kulin warrior Claude escaped from the bird spirit of Jaithmathangs."

There was only the low keening of the wind.

"The man became the spirit?" asked Iris.

"They're the same," said Box.

"How can it be? Good and evil are opposites," said Iris.

"It's about moral ambiguity," said Box.

"Like Kronus?" asked Kitou.

"Maybe. Maybe about all of us."

"Kronus is evil," said Iris.

"Maybe he wasn't always," said Box.

"He is now."

"Kronus is trying to possess Ito," said Kitou.

"What?" asked Box.

"I know it. The others know it too."

"What do you mean, possess?"

"Like the Red Lady possesses you, but not so kindly. Like this Bunjil possessed his women."

"Kitou, how do you know this?"

362

"I see it."

Brin and her acolytes emerged from the brainy darkness, just as night was starting to fall. Nim and Respit were exhausted. Brin took a long, deep breath of real air.

The first sign that something was wrong was when Nim fell to her knees.

"The Enemy," she said. "It's started."

They made their way back to the Chancery. It was hard going. Nim was disoriented, and kept stopping to vomit. The Chancery yard was deserted. Marius hadn't returned. Amelia Chance confronted Brin, and asked, "Where have you been?"

Brin said, "Where's everyone?"

[Ito is firewalled,] said the ship.

[Kitou and Dr Box?]

[No idea.]

[Firewalled? Who did that?]

[His autonomic defenses. I've put a second one on top.]

"Brin," persisted Amelia.

"I'm sorry," said Brin. "But I'm busy."

[Why?] she asked, turning away from the politician.

[He's entered a new stage of the disease.]

[Marius was right.]

[You already knew that.]

[Why now? It can't be a coincidence.]

Ito looked like himself, except he was in the shadows, watching. That was most unlike Ito. Brin saw how it fit the pattern of his recent behavior. A slow withdrawal. Why hadn't she noticed?

[Options?] she asked the ship.

[Wait for the others. I have a fix on them now. They appear to be flying.]

[In the airwaves?]

[Unless they've found a light aircraft.]

[Where have they been?]

[We'll find out.]

Brin took a breath, and turned to face the Magister.

"I'm sorry," she said. "You're about to be in a war. Nim will brief you."

Box, Kitou and Iris landed at a canter, on a high moor overlooking the valley of the Spinifex Reach. The Chancery was a smudge of woodsmoke and welcoming lights in the distance. Kitou had to hold Box, to stop her from falling. The spell of the Red Lady was fading.

[Dr Box,] said a voice in her wetware.

[Ship! Thank goodness.]

[Please hurry up and get here,] said the ship. [The excrement is hitting the recirculator.]

Seabiscuit had no objection to galloping home. Box gave him his head. Iris's mare was left behind. It was exhilarating, hurtling through twilit fields. Kitou shrieked with pleasure. It was the most girlish thing she'd seen Kitou do.

[Shit hit the fan?]

[If you like.]

[How?]

[I'll tell you when you get here.]

"It's Ito," shouted Kitou in her ear. "I can only see a firewall."

[Two firewalls,] said the ship. [Mine outside his. I'm taking no chances.]

[With what?]

[The Thespian disease.]

They arrived just as Marius was landing in the yard. He'd been on a sortie. His riders were milling around him.

Amelia Chance was looking irate. Then Iris arrived, not far behind them, and went into a huddle with Marius.

The dark-haired rider from high Eagle told him all he needed to know, he thought. They were at war, and he was the last to know. He cursed his bad timing. Then Brin spoke the codeword that unlocked his memories, and he knew more.

He was their leader now. He looked at Amelia Chance, who nodded.

"Nim," he said. "Can you speak for the Po warship?" The girl looked surprised, then she nodded too.

"Good girl. Magister, please join me in the Chancery hall. Riders, ready this place for war.

"You," he said to the new rider, Iris. "Come too."

Chaos ensued, but it was a type of chaos he understood. The Chancery was always kept on a war footing. Now those preparations would be activated. It was superficially messy, but logistically ordered. The larger chaos - the one involving the Numbers disease - he liked less. Still, he would deal with it. The mantle of leadership fell easily on him. It was what he was trained for.

In the Chancery hall, he gathered his leaders around him. Marius's preferred method was to think first, then go hard, in that order.

Now was thinking time.

"Brin?"

She described her encounter with Kronus, in precise military terms.

"You've met the Enemy?" asked Kitou.

"I saw him," said Brin. "He didn't know I was there."

"Maybe he did," said Marius. He described his own sortie, in similar language.

"Red Lady?"

Box colored. She felt like a child, asked to explain herself to the grownups. "We... we saw the ghost," she said.

"Explain who the ghost is," said Marius, more gently.

"The ghost is the original Mr. Chance," she said.

"Why did you go there?" asked Brin.

"We didn't choose to," she said. She described her and Kitou's journey, ending up with the Chancery yard, not trying for military language. She told it with nuance, like an oral historian would.

"Very good," said Marius. "Po ship?"

Nim began in a shaky soprano. "I know a few things," she said. "But not everything. I can join dots. Let's start with the Fa:ing. Ito?"

"The Fa:ing are the Möbius machine," he said. As he spoke, he looked as nervous as Nim did.

"Why didn't you say so before?" asked Box.

"Because he's been struggling to separate reality from prophecy," said the ship. "And it's only going to get worse."

"Ito is this true?" asked Box.

"We'll get to Ito next," said Nim, gaining in confidence. "First, the Fa:ing. How did they get here? Brin?"

"If what Ito says is right, they're here because they started out here."

"Correct. And how did they get to Threnody?"

"From the future."

"Whose future?"

"Ours?"

"No. That's where our assumptions were wrong. There is no 'our' future. They got here from *their* future.

"Ito. Why did you catch this disease?"

"I met with Kronus."

"Why?"

"I had to know. Whether I could resist him."

"Why?"

"It was my plan B. In case you never came here. I'd fight him myself."

"And did you? Withstand him?"

"Apparently not."

"And can you? Defeat him?"

"Maybe."

"Perhaps I'm not the best one to ask," he said.

They were alone in Ito's rooms. Imprisonment was another kind of firewall. For now, his presence here was voluntary.

"It's like a virus." He said. "It copies his madness."

"So he *is* mad."

"I'm sure of it. He's a psychopath. But the evil that haunts him, isn't. It's beyond constructs like madness."

"What evil? Is it from the future too?"

"It comes from us."

"What, like original sin?"

"We all have the capability to be evil. We choose not to behave that way."

"That's nihilism."

"You'll have to explain what that means."

"Like a beast of the shadows?"

"Yes, that's apt. Is it a quote? I think of it as a shadow."

"No," said Box. "It's Kronus that's the shadow. The unseen part of our selves. Pure evil is something else."

Ito nodded. "I feel better with these bars in place," he said.

"Why?"

"Because I could do damage, without them."

"Am I at risk, now?"

"No."

"What's it like? What are you experiencing right now?"

"Right now? Peace. Other times paranoia. Ecstasy. Surprise."

"Surprise?"

"Yes. It's hard to explain. I have the most remarkable thoughts."

"How did you cope before the ship firewalled you? All the time we were here?"

"Mostly I was okay. Then it got worse. After that, by my training."

She made love to him, after asking if sex was okay. The last thing she wanted was to drive him over the edge, in the throes of sexual frenzy, into the abyss. The ship told her yes. Ito agreed. It was a slow, almost holy kind of sex. He didn't try to please her. She didn't ask. This was for him.

"I love you," he said.

"I bet you say that to all the mission specialists."

He laughed, and for a while he was Ito again, her bushy-bearded amanuensis from the space shuttle.

Then she fucked him a second time, because that was what it was, after she lost all control, and ground herself down on him until she orgasmed.

They talked.

"What's the prognosis?" she said.

"I'm not getting out of this one alive," he said.

"Be serious."

"I am."

"Are you backed up?"

"No."

"Whyever not?"

"Are you?"

"Yes."

"Why?"

"To finish my work. So if I die here, my story's not lost."

He seemed so ordinary, after sex. No, not ordinary. He still had his sleepy Po competence. The infinite stare. But he was safe. Nothing could harm him here.

One wall of his rooms was half-covered by a half-finished painting. A sunset, in shades of violet and ultramarine.

"A new one?" she asked, and he nodded.

On another wall was written in chalk: *Love. Honor. Duty. Peace.* It was Pax's mandala.

"My prognosis," he said, "is that one of four things will happen. I'll go harmlessly mad. I'll go dangerously mad. I'll gain the Enemy's powers. Or I'll become him."

"What?"

"Exactly."

"What does 'dangerously' mean?"

"That I'll hurt the people around me."

"You can?"

"Trust me, I can."

"Why would you?"

"I don't have to explain psychosis to you."

She shuddered. "What kind of powers?"

"I don't know," he said. "Kronus is an imperfect vessel. I could be worse than him."

"Merde."

"Again, yes."

369

"So, what do we do?"

"We find a use for me."

"What do you mean, a *use*?"

"We activate plan B."

"What, you actually want to fight Kronus?"

"Yes, while I can."

Over the following days, she watched Ito worsen. She'd once had had a friend who was a schizophrenic. There was a strange kind of power in her. She shone, like a bright light inside someone's head. She could speak in the most lucid way about the irrational. Cognitive dissonance. Ito became like that.

He began to declaim about gods.

"Gods are a metaphor," he declared. "We raise them up on altars because they created us. In so doing we gift them existence. If we can get beyond them, only the divine remains."

That all sounded perfectly fine. It was his tone that was crazed.

Like a light, inside someone's head.

"That's good," she said. "Can I use it?"

"What do you think about gods, Ophelia?"

"A nest of vipers," she said, "redeemed only by the fact they don't exist. Bootstrapped sky fairies? Give me a break. Overachieving aliens, maybe."

"How can we know?"

"Occam's Razor?"

"That's not a good tool for evaluating complex theories. Sometimes the right theory is the one that starts with the *most* assumptions."

"Gods are a theory?"

"Everything's a theory. We experience nothing directly."

"What about love?"

"The divine is everywhere."

"You're not making any sense."

"I wish you could see what I see."

At other times, he seemed perfectly sane.

"I don't have your verbal skills," he said, after an argument in which he'd become confused, which Box had then allowed to become heated.

"Nonsense," she said. "You're the cleverest person I know, and you know it. You Po understand your strengths and weaknesses."

"What weaknesses?"

She sighed. "The messiah complex?"

"Is that what you think?"

"You believe you have to save the world, and you're determined to die in the process. Sounds like Po Jesus to me."

He nodded. "It's true. I have to die so I can come back. What about you?"

"What about me?"

"The Red Lady? Returning from the end of time?"

She bit back a laugh, then tears.

"It's a tough job," she said.

He laughed. "But someone has to do it."

She did laugh then, and everything was alright for a while.

They responded to Ito's decline differently. Brin made military plans with Marius. Kitou trained, increasingly violently with Viki and Alis. Box asked the ship questions.

[Your version in the forest said you were dying.]

[She *was* dying.]

[What about you?]

[Yes, I'm also going to die.]

371

[When?]

[When you split up.]

[What do you mean, split up?]

[I'm not at liberty to say.]

[You mean when Ito goes? He already told me.]

[Yes, then.]

[Why is this place so much like Earth?] she asked.
[The trees. The animals. Even the fjords. It's like
Norway in the fucking Himalayas.

[And why was Chance on Earth, in 1851? That's
the year this place was created.]

[He was there because of *you*, Dr Box.]

[I didn't exist then.]

[Your appearance was predicted.]

[By the Fa:ing number.]

[Yes.]

[Which is a manifestation of the Möbius machine.]

[Yes.]

[Which didn't exist until 1851.]

[Correct.]

[That's circular.]

[It is. Maybe the information did a big circle?]

Box found Kitou sitting primly on Box's unmade
bed, knees held together, hands clasped: a most un-
Kitou pose.

"I have a fever," she complained.

"You're sick?"

"Sick in my head."

Box knelt in front of her, and looked in her eyes.

"Are you alright?"

Kitou seemed stricken. "*No*," she said.

"Tell me."

"When I'm frightened, Dr Box, there's a place I go. It's deep, and safe, like a dark pool. From there, the world passes by."

"Oh, poor child."

"It's not there anymore. Now there's something... new."

"New, how? Is it the Thespian disease?"

"No, it's like all the love in the world. Like a mountain, falling through space. And it's too much. It's as if the love we feel is just a word, and this is the real thing."

"Are you okay?"

"I feel good. That's not the thing. It's wonderful. But... also terrifying. It's not a warm love, like I feel for my friends. Or the hot one I feel for my man. It doesn't mean to hurt me, but it does mean to use me. What will become of me? How will it fit through me?"

Box shuddered.

"Are you scared now?" she asked.

Kitou nodded.

"And you have nowhere to go?"

"There's nowhere to hide from it. Nor do I want to."

She held up a hand, and examined it.

"I could destroy worlds."

Box stood, and turned away.

"I know you feel it too," said Kitou.

"What do you mean?"

"The Red Lady."

"No, that's different. She's a person."

"Is she made of love?"

Box laughed. "No, she's made of titanium."

"I pity our enemies."

Box glittered.

"I don't."

The next morning, Box was woken by the ship.

[Go to the training room, now.]

A bloodied stick was lying on the floor.

"I killed Alis," said Kitou.

"What?"

"I lost control. I tried to pull my stroke. I killed her."

"She's alive," said Marius. "Only just."

Box gathered her courage and looked. It was as bad as she could imagine.

"Is there a surgeon?" she asked.

"Not one who can get here in time."

"I can do it," said Ito.

Everyone turned.

[I released him,] said the ship.

"Do we have surgical equipment?" he asked.

"Yes," said Amelia Chance. "Scalpels, antiseptics."

"Bring them, and a bathtub with ice."

Brin had joined the group, and as quickly left to do as Ito requested.

"A knife," he said. "Give me any knife."

Marius gave Ito a bone sword, and he sawed off Alis's waist-length hair, close to the scalp. Kitou had crept up behind Box, and was peering over her shoulder.

"Water and soap," said Ito.

They soon appeared, and he washed and shaved around the wound. Then the bath arrived, and the surgical gear.

"Undress her and put her in the bath."

"Why the ice?" asked Marius.

Ito washed his hands. "Controlled hypothermia," he said. "I want to cool her down to 32° to 34°c, to reduce the impact of the swelling of the brain." Then he deftly made a u-shaped incision, leaving no doubt in anyone's mind he could do this.

Alis groaned.

"Do we have a psi here?" he asked.

Nim stepped forward. "Make her unconscious," he said. "Be gentle but quick."

The Horu girl nodded, and in a few moments Alis stopped moving. He peeled back the scalp, to reveal a hand-sized depression in the back of her skull. "Plyers," he said. Then he pulled out a section of bone. It came away with the snap of a tooth being pulled. In a few minutes, he had the all the splintered bone removed. Then he replaced the most solid part.

"The dura mater is undamaged," he said.

"Is that good?" asked a small voice.

It was Alis's friend Viki, who'd appeared behind Box, beside Kitou, and was now peering over her other shoulder.

"Yes," said Ito.

Then he sutured the scalp. No more than fifteen minutes had passed. "We'll make a prosthesis," he said. "An organic plug to go in the gap. Maybe a metal plate to protect it in combat. Nim?"

The Horu girl looked up.

"Wake her please."

"But..."

"We must," he said, gently.

Nim nodded, then Alis groaned, and batted her eyes open.

"What's happening to me?" she said. "Why am I in this tub, before all these people."

She tried to cover her breasts, but her hands weren't quite in her control.

"You have an injury," said Ito. She started to cry.

"Alis?"

"Prophet?"

Ito smiled at her. "Show me your eyes, soldier."

She looked up at him. He nodded again.

"You'll be fine," he said.

"Marius?" he said.

"Prophet?"

"Dress her and keep her awake."

"Yes," said Marius, starting to grin. Box had to admit she felt the same way. How could these people be so capable?

"Give her no alcohol," said Ito.

"But prophet..."

"I mean it."

Ito had finished, and was leaving.

"I'll be in my cell," he said.

The next morning, Kitou, Viki and Iris were missing.

19 ∞ BADOOP

2065

It began as a worm in his spine. It was icy cold. It could be a real worm, for all he knew. He could feel tendrils, making their way into his cerebrum.

"Why are you doing this to me?" he asked.

The Magellanic physician had brown skin and almond-shaped eyes, with epicanthic folds like his.

"Looking for patterns," ze said. "The virus reprograms your DNA, but we've tested for that. Now I'm looking for patterns."

"Is my friend Alois infected?"

"Yes."

"How is it transmitted?"

"By asking questions. Now, relax."

Later they told him Alois had died. Real, permanent death. Totoro held his hands while he cried. "I've never had anyone die," he said. He felt angry, and empty. It felt like the start of many deaths.

"I'm told he died more than once," said Totoro. "I know it doesn't help you, but that's the way with true adventurers. Their lives are currency, willingly spent."

"Yeah," said Macro. "I get that. But he was my friend. I'm broken."

Three days later, he was still in a hospital bed. He'd recovered. He wanted to leave.

Totoro agreed, and what Totoro said, happened. Macro dressed, and they stepped out into a slew of color and light, like stepping from a darkened cinema into a bright day, with the fresh sea air in their faces.

Except it wasn't day, but a brightly lit night, and the space he was in was bewildering.

"We're in Olap 6," said Totoro, over the hubbub of the tourists and street vendors. "It doesn't orbit the dark star directly, but the water giant Olap, also called Nubeculae 2."

Olap 6 was an air world, like a bubble, and small, with a habitable space only five kilometers across. It had inverse gravity, like Praxis. Inside the watery skin of the sphere was a mesh; outside the mesh were the stars. You walked on the mesh, and gazed up at the center.

If the prevailing architectural style of the thousand worlds was awe-inspiring space and light, here it was organic spines, reaching up and curling in the middle, where they were connected by a riot of bridges. Clearly, the designers had wanted to leave the observer uneasy. It was like a painting of an impossible city.

378

The blazing wheel of the Milky Way galaxy filled the ocean under their feet.

"It doesn't really blaze like that," said Macro, remembering his postmortem excursion.

"Really?" asked Totoro.

Macro colored. "Buy me a drink," he said.

They found a bar. It wasn't the usual dive bar of Macro's recent experience, like the Snake City Discothèque, or the literal dive bar he'd started in here, but a palace of intoxication. Macro was thrilled, despite his subdued mood. There must've been five thousand people in there. He wanted to be drunk. Totoro's combat nano caused a commotion.

"All these women want us," he said. It was statement of fact. He wasn't used to being stared at.

Totoro found them a booth. "Stories have power," he said, while dialing in some privacy. Now people could see them, but not understand. Macro felt like he was in a fishbowl.

"May I show you my story?"

"How? You haven't got wetware."

Macro had wetware, but it was infuriatingly basic. It knew two languages: Pursang and Magøl. They were conversing in Pursang. Magøl he struggled with. It was all clicks and pops, for conversing in water.

"There's a way," said Totoro.

"How?"

"Do you trust me?"

"Yes."

"Then open your mind."

"How?"

"Stop thinking."

"How can I do that?"

"Macro?"

"Yes?"

Then it hit him, the rush of Totoro's life.

No, not just Totoro's. His worldspirit. Atwusk'niges, the vertical forest of Fluxor.

[Macro,] she said. [I've been wanting to meet you.]

He was a boy, climbing into the rainforest canopy, a half-day's climb until he reached the heart of it, the ancient ironwood tree, called Atwusk'niges. Some people believed that Atwusk'niges was the oldest tree in the world, a gift of the Xap to the humans. He didn't know about that. He was only a boy. What he knew was that it was his tree, given into his care; a grave responsibility, and one he took seriously.

He was Totoro, son of Akito; firstborn of Vanja, soon to be brother of Kitou, since his mother was gravid, and had already said it would be a girl; Totoro Gorgonza d Atwusk'niges, a citizen of the vertical forest of Fluxor, beneath the holy mountain Lhotse; this was his place in the great tree of life.

The ironwood tree didn't ask for his care. It was one of the great sentinels of Fluxor. Weight for weight, its wood was as hard as titanium. It had wisdom beyond his comprehension. All it wanted was his love, and he gave it unstintingly.

One day, the forest spoke to him. This was unheard of. The worldspirits spoke, but only the seedlings, and only to their symbionts. Not the great trees of the forest, and certainly not to children.

[Totoro,] she said. [I've been wanting to meet you.]

It wasn't a voice. It was a rustle; a whisper.

It was sadness, and peace.

[Totoro,] she said, [I'm nearing the end of my journey.]

"Mother forest, what should I do?"

[Take me to the stars,] she said. [I want to see what the fuss is about.]

[Then, in the end, take me to Earth.]

Macro's eyes flicked open. He could still see the vertical drop into the Algoma'aa valley below. He could feel the cool autumn air in his lungs; smell the woodsmoke rising from his house; safe in the hearth of his family. It had taken his precious breath away, and it wasn't coming back easily.

"Macro?"

He turned to look at himself, and blinked.

"Totoro, I'm sorry. No, I'm not sorry. That was... I don't know the words."

"Now we're friends."

"Is it like that for you all the time?"

"No, mainly in combat."

He was Totoro again.

A young man now: almost Macro's age.

He was on a battlefield. Macro had seen wars, in sims, and from the safety of orbit, but here was one in the furnace of its creation, and he was in the thick of it. He was standing knee deep in shit and mud. Blood, shit and mud. People were dying around him. His worldspirit was howling in rage at the death of her fellows. Macro was frightened, but Totoro wasn't, because Totoro was a Pursang holy warrior, and they don't experience fear in the moment. It had something to do with the way their neurology was rewired by the symbiont Xap.

Macro knew this to be a devilish bargain. Not being scared was like not feeling pain. A good party trick in a war, but no use in any other place.

They were hopelessly outclassed. Even with the help of a Xap suppressor field, they had no answer to the enemy's unhuman physicality. Just as a mouse is no match for a man, no amount of pure fighting ability could bridge the gap between them and today's opponent. They fought, and they died. That's how it went, with the Badoop. Before today's battle was over, the Badoop'd find a way to even the odds. They'd already gifted the Pursang a suppressor, in a place where one shouldn't exist. Later, a burning spacecraft might crash and kill a few million of the enemy, until there was only a balanced sample of each left.

Usually, that was Totoro.

He and his fellows had fought every lifeform you can imagine, and some you couldn't. Beings made from the interstellar vacuum; aliens made of noise; creatures made of ideas. And always, the Badoop finding a way they could fight each other.

The Pursang died bravely, but not stupidly. When they retreated, they retreated with purpose. When they spent their lives, it was on purchasing an improved chance of victory. More than once, they'd outsmarted or out-competed stronger opponents, by their understanding of the art of war, or by their total commitment. They were formidable soldiers.

But not invincible.

On today's battlefield, they were the mouse, and they were royally fucked.

One by one, his comrades died. Some died easily. Most didn't, not straight away. There's a myth that people die as soon as a sword is stuck in. The human body is tough; it resists death, the human-Xap symbiosis even more so. Today, with a scuttling, insectile opponent, most of the Pursang deaths were from separation injuries.

Like a scene from a sim where humans were being ripped up by monsters.

Of course, none of it was real. If it was, the Magellanics would have run out of Pursang, centuries ago, and this thousand-year war would be over.

So they fought, and died, over and again.

"What the actual fuck?" said Macro.

Totoro looked him in the eye.

"Welcome to the mad, bad world of the Praesidium."

"Praesidium?"

"Their official name."

"Why are you showing me this?"

"You must understand."

"Those insects..."

"Were worthy opponents."

"Did you win?"

"We did."

"How?"

"Our suppressor eventually degraded their equivalent of wetware. They lost the ability to co-ordinate. Then it was just a few million individuals."

"How did you kill them?"

"We crushed them."

"Literally?"

"Yes."

"That's disgusting."

"Granted."

"Was it... real?"

"Yes. And no."

"This dirt on your nano..."

"Is real dirt. Tomorrow, it could be my blood. Then I wouldn't be so talkative. Today we prevailed."

"But you won... virtually?"

"It depends how you define virtual."

"But..."

"Enough. It's time for someone else to answer your questions. All of them. It's time to see the Navigator."

"Sybil?"

"No, *the* Navigator."

Scattered around the Olap 6 boundary sphere were railway termini, except that what they fired into space were bubbles of liquids, like beads in a necklace. These luxurious conveyances bore no resemblance to the austere forms of travel Macro preferred. First the launcher got up a good head of speed, and Macro felt himself being pressed back in his chair, and then they were in zero-gravity. At the first world they reached, which was only a few thousand kilometers away, a drop fell away, and the rest of the train was re-accelerated in a slingshot action. This was repeated, for world after world, until what remained of the necklace was moving at interplanetary speed.

Macro and Totoro relaxed, for a three-day train journey.

Totoro described the Badoop.

"We call them Badoop," he said, "because of how their broadcast waveform sounds to our ears."

"Like... 'badoop'?"

"Yes. Like a synth, set on random. Sometimes, you almost start to understand it."

"And Praesidium?"

"It means protector."

"What do they protect?"

"All they consume."

"Like... civilizing conquerors?"

"Exactly like that. Or like a virus. It depends on how you define freedom."

"Which name do they prefer?"

"They don't care. Or we don't know if they care. Or if they know; we can't make any sense of them."

"Where did they come from?"

"They last conquered Leo I."

"Last?"

"Yes, like they'll conquer this dwarf galaxy. After that, we think, the Milky Way."

"You're sure they'll beat you?"

"Oh yes. They're far in advance of any technology we have."

"Why fight them?"

"We don't fight them. We fight who they send. Those insects were yesterday's opponents. Tomorrow's will be different."

"Wait... they force you to fight other species? In set piece battles?"

"Yes."

"Inside a virtuality?"

"Of sorts. We call it the Badoop synthesis. It has some of the quality of reality. A local collapse of the wavefunction. We're unsure of the physics."

"Has it ever occurred to you that you're fighting against their other opponents?"

"Of course, but what can we do about it?"

"What a total mindfuck."

"Absolutely."

"So why do you do it?"

Totoro shrugged. "We have no choice."

This intrasystem journey wasn't Macro's first experience with sybaritic luxury. As a representative of the bank, he was forced to endure all kinds of pleasures. It didn't set well with him. He knew it was an irrational prejudice, but he couldn't help but associate luxury with theft. In his experience, people living a high life invariably took it from people with nothing.

They may not mean to, but they do.

He knew that luxury was relative. The people of Praxis lived luxuriously by comparison with people in the Smear, and by and large they'd taken nothing.

But their society had.

And this society was exceedingly wealthy.

Face it, he thought; you're a monk, with a monk's predilections.

Totoro lied outrageously to a succession of women. Macro asked him why, with real curiosity.

"They love you. Why pretend?"

"It's a game here," Totoro explained.

"You lie to each other?"

"A game of polite society."

"To fool them?"

"No, they have to see you're pretending."

"Then what's the point of it?"

"To please them."

"Well, you're not a convincing liar."

"Thank you. Does it hinder me?"

"Clearly not."

"The key to love is gentleness, my friend. The world is full of men who hurt women, because they're physically stronger. You may get some sex, but it's like eating the skin of an orange. I want the orange."

"Gaming them is seductive?"

"No, paying them the compliment of complicity is seductive. It's like making bad jokes, in such a way that people can't help but laugh."

"I don't understand. Do you mean your gameplay is ironic?"

"No, I mean it's pleasurable. My friend, you're too literal-minded."

Macro thought about that. "Anyone who thinks women are weak should meet your sister. Or Brin Lot. Or Ophelia Box."

"Are they formidable?"

"They're utterly magnificent."

"You ever met a Badoop?"

They were rollicking drunk, in their cups, on grubs steeped in the liquor of an hallucinogenic cactus. Macro could probably modulate his drunkenness with his wetware, if he wanted to. He knew Totoro had no such escape ramp.

"Once," said Totoro, focusing. "I think mebbe I did once."

He was regarding a caterpillar, as though it could be a military opponent.

"Whassalike?"

"Ooh."

They couldn't stop laughing. One of the fine things about being drunk on stimulants, Macro decided, was hearing yourself spouting nonsense.

"Seriously," said Totoro, straightening himself. He made a straight face. "Show you," he said.

Macro found himself sucked back inside Totoro's sensorium. In it he was sober.

There was a creature. It resembled a termite, not a million chromosomes from what they were drinking. It held weapons in its appendages, an impressive array of tools, like a utility knife. Totoro had seen his companions disemboweled by their likes.

It raised a... feeler? A pseudopod?

It was opening itself up to being attacked. A placatory gesture. Totoro had a crossbow, made from unfinished carbon. A roughly made killing machine.

The ventral spine of the creature was like the ripe labellum of an orchid, powdery and soft: a target.

{Are you the one?} it asked.

It spoke at first to Atwusk'niges. It didn't know if Totoro or she were the primary.

"It's me you're fighting," said Totoro.

The creature {nodded}.

Not quite a nod. The creature was an empath. Totoro felt the nod as a morpheme, as though he had wetware.

{Is it the one?} the creature asked.

This {idea} was projected outwards - outside the Badoop virtuality. That was new. Totoro lowered his crossbow. In response, the creature lowered its weapons.

{Is it the one?}

{No.}

The second - voice? - came from... somewhere. It had the slippery, hiccuppy quality of the Badoop sonification.

{It's the penultimate form.}

{Then it will kill me.}

{It will kill you.}

{I choose not to die today.}

{Then go in peace.}

The termite creature whirled, in a cascading helix of segments, to hover over Totoro, who was also Macro. It smelt of formic acid; an unnerving proximity.

"Please have this," it said.

Totoro felt an outpouring of love; totally alien, but completely familiar.

"Go in peace," it said, and disappeared.

"What did that mean?" asked Macro the following morning, from deep within the misery of a hangover, one he preferred not to delete. Better to learn, he decided. "The Badoop are cockroaches?"

"Of course not, and it was more like a termite. That creature was my last opponent, before I met you. The other voice was the Badoop."

"What did it mean, penultimate form?"

"Who knows? Maybe I'm the second best at its game."

"Who's the best?"

"Who knows?"

"Why did it let the other one off?"

"Maybe that day's experiment wasn't about fighting. Maybe the creature wasn't one of its collection."

"Have you ever refused to fight?"

"I've tried."

"And?"

Totoro shook his head.

"You know, it sounds like a test to destruction. Like children, trapped on an island, with no choice but to murder each other."

"It does. I hope I don't have to do it forever."

"You mean, literally forever?"

"It has crossed my mind."

Leif Ean, Most Imperfect One, Egregious Bug III, the Magellanic Navigator sat on hir throne, attended by hir winged eunuchs.

"Majesty, may I present Macro Ibquant Deathcult von Engine," said Totoro, making a flourish.

They were inside a crystalloid sphere. New stars floated in the heavens around them. Macro was impressed. Either it was a projection, or this sphere was in a different part of the galaxy. Realtime spacetime displacement. Hyperlight trickery. As a declaration of technological achievement, it really was something.

"Von Engine?" said Ean. One of hir imperfections was near-sightedness. Ze squinted at Macro through bottle-thick eyeglasses.

The throne room was a riot of color. Leif Ean was dressed in layer on layer of silky brocades, and the space around hir was strewn with flowers. Hir face was white with fragrant powder.

"You're Samppo's boy?" ze asked. Hir voice was a slightly imperfect soprano, broken and with a slight tremolo.

"I am," said Macro. He was given a highchair, so he could sit eye-to-eye with the monarch. The lenses made hir eyes look like two moist fruits. Totoro pulled up a similar chair. Eunuchs hustled out of his way.

"I can hardly believe it," said Ean. "But I do. d Atwusk'niges here vouches for you. What brings you to Waterfall, Mr. von Engine?

"Alois Buss brought me here."

"Oh, that. Yes, a nasty business."

Hir attendants flapped around, bringing hir papers, which ze signed without looking. It was as though the eunuchs managed the affairs of state. Macro reminded himself that appearances meant nothing. This was the pre-eminent living human.

Ean waved the Eunuchs away, and removed hir glasses, and the impression of helplessness disappeared. Ze had the pitiless gaze of a killer.

"Well, I do know why you're here, von Engine. And I'm sorry for your troubles. Your father and I go back a long way, and his father before him. Totoro?"

"Majesty?"

"Will you begin with the facts?"

Totoro nodded, and said, "Macro, Alois was euthanized. He didn't die of his injuries."

"What?

"You mean you killed him?"

"On his instructions."

"There's a recording," said Ean.

"I don't fucking want to see it," said Macro

"It's for you," said Ean. "Buss made it for you."

A simulation of Alois appeared between the throne and the chairs. The eunuchs left the room. It seemed this talk was now private.

"Macro," it said, "I'm sorry. I'm sorry for not telling you more, when I knew everything. By the time you see this I'll be dead. I'm sorry for that too. It was necessary. I'll explain.

"The greatest threat to us all is a person called Kronus, a being of Möbius space. Your friends have gone there to oppose him. By oppose, I mean fight him."

Leif Ean showed no surprise; nor did Totoro. It seemed they already knew all Alois's secrets.

"That's where you come in, my boy. I need you to take an army there. An army of Free Pursang, led by Totoro.

"You won't have heard of the Free Pursang. That's because they don't exist. But they will. I'm sorry, there's no way to soften this; you can't leave Waterfall until after the destruction of Fluxor.

"That means your friends will die."

With a dizzying sense of pieces falling into place, he sprang to his feet.

"No!" he shouted.

He shouted for some time, until he stopped.

"Why?" he asked, coldly.

"Do you not get it?" asked Ean, as coldly.

"Oh, I get it," said Macro. "You want me to go back in time, from the future, to help them win next time around."

"Smart boy."

"I want to know *why*."

"Because the Badoop say so," said Totoro.

"Why do they get a say?"

"Because all the Horu downlinks are destroyed. Only the Badoop have the technology to take us there."

"What are you talking about?"

"Do you remember the device you gave Kitou?"

"The Magellanic travel device?"

"It wasn't."

"Totoro, you're talking in riddles."

"It wasn't Magellanic. It was made to look that way."

"It was on loan from the Badoop," said Alois.

"Oh, fuck," said Macro.

"Do you remember being contacted by Kitou?" asked Alois.

"Yes, she was punished."

"That was the moment of connection. You, to her, entangled in every possible timeline."

"I have no idea what that means," said Macro.

"It means we get the device," said Totoro. "Then you can take us there."

"Then let's get cracking. We'll go now. Totoro, how many Pursang soldiers do we have?"

"The Badoop won't let us have it."

"Why?"

"They say it's not time."

"How can they stop you?"

"No," said Ean. "I forbid it."

"Why?"

"The Badoop have their reasons."

"Cowards."

"Macro," said Totoro.

"Fuck you," said Macro.

"Please understand. This is the loss of my world I'm proposing. Everything and everyone I love."

"Then do something."

"I am."

"Like, what?"

"Like, formulating a strategy."

The next unwelcome fact was the neutralization of Avalon. They used that word. *Neutralization.* They didn't even tell him about it directly. He overheard it.

The Egregious Bug had lost patience with Macro by then. Hir face was like granite. The Eunuchs had returned. The matters of state had been dealt with. Now they were dealing with the small matter of the loss of a world.

"How could you do that?" he shouted. He was the bank. He was the *Cult*. This was an atrocity. By the powers vested in him by all the money in the world, he'd do something about it.

He didn't care that he sounded like a hysterical teenager. On top of everything else, this was a world he personally cared about.

"So?" Totoro said.

"There were millions of people."

"What, do you think we destroyed it?"

"You... oh." Macro blushed with embarrassment. "I thought..."

Leif Ean waved hir hand, and the granite wall loosened. A minor rockslide threatened a smile. "We're not monsters here," ze said.

"We put it in stasis," said Totoro. "It's on its way to the future."

"Do you want me to sit for a while?" asked interlocutor-Alois.

"Do I have a choice?" said Macro.

The room he'd been given to live in was suitably austere. He liked it. He sat on a bed. Interlocutor-Alois looked unhappy.

"I'm sorry," said Macro. "You know I don't mean that. Of course you can stay."

But he did mean it. He was angry at everything. The whole world had to pay for this.

But this was Alois. His friend. He couldn't be blamed for his own death.

"You're allowed to be hurt," said Alois.

"But?"

"But you have no say in this. These are the affairs of astropolitics. Civilizations setting their course. Acting in their own best interests. We do as the Navigator says. We do as the Badoop say."

"I'm just an extra."

"All of us are extras."

"Alois?"

"Yes?"

"Why were you euthanized?"

"Because I made a mistake. I contacted the Water Bear, using the Badoop device."

"When? Before or after Kitou?"

"Before."

"Why is that relevant?"

"Because through it, Kronus found his way to the Real."

"Through you?"

"Yes. He's connected to me, like you are to Kitou. It's a long story."

"Is it because you have the Thespian disease?"

"I did have it. Yes."

"This sim you're in now doesn't?"

"No, this sim is binary. The Thespian disease requires the quaternary system of animal DNA."

"Are all machines immune?"

"Some are. Cyborgs are susceptible."

"And the disease is the Enemy's weapon?"

"Yes, it's his version of the Fa:ing number. Engineered, like a virus, to spread himself throughout the cosmos."

"What's it like, the disease?"

"Like the most beautiful euphoria. Rushes and rushes of bliss. On the outside, you appear frightening. Inside, you feel wonderful."

"And behaviorally?"

"Like a strange, looping form of paranoia. You think... persuasive ideas."

"Euphoria and paranoia. That sounds awfully like madness."

"It is."

"What's... he like?"

"Kronus? A brute. And, the most wonderful person."

"He's part of us, isn't he?"

"Yes, he's our shadow. That's insightful."

"Oh, I've worked it out," said Macro.

"Well, here we are," said Totoro.

They were deep in the bowels of the citadel, beneath Bug's throne room. A safe place. The last place in the

Magellanic civilization that would fall in a war. Totoro was showing Macro his ride out of here.

"I don't like it," said Macro.

"It's all you need."

"Why an acceleration chair?" he asked.

"This is no ordinary stasis device," said Totoro. "In the event you need it, it performs as a spacecraft. It can take you across space, or into the far future."

"What kind of event?"

Totoro shrugged.

To the right of the chair was a featureless sphere.

"What's that?" asked Macro.

"That's me," said the Alois-interlocutor.

"What d'you mean? Your body?"

"Dear boy, you have a mind like a razor, but you missed one thing."

"What? That you're the wrong Alois?"

"Ah."

"I didn't miss it. I knew the Alois who used the device couldn't be the Alois who traveled with me from Avalon. Continuity errors are easy. I just didn't want to start them thinking."

Alois nodded. He wasn't the Alois that Macro arrived with. It was obvious. He was a sim of the Buss from the Cult.

An Alois that Macro thought to keep safe.

There were three Aloises that he knew of: the one he came with; the one in the Cult; and the original, on Threnody.

"You've killed them all?" asked Macro, with an unhappy look on his face.

"No, we saved the original."

"You kidnapped the Alois on Threnody?"

"Not kidnapped," said Totoro. "We offered him an alternative."

"That's him in there?"

"It is."

"The real, biological original?"

"Yes."

"No more Alois's, looping through time?"

"No."

"He's coming with me?"

"He is."

"Well, I guess that's alright then."

"It's time now," said interlocutor-Alois.

Of course it was time. The stasis device was set to release on a timer, and nothing in the world would prevent it.

"Alois," he said.

"Tell it to me later," said interlocutor-Alois.

Macro sighed, and climbed into the chair. He hoped this was the right thing to do. While he was in this device, the people he loved could die. Or they could win. There was always that possibility.

He'd hate to miss that.

"I'll see you in ten years," said Totoro. "Whatever happens, this machine will take care of you."

"What can possibly go wrong?" He tried to imagine the winged Eunuchs defending the Citadel.

"If I'm not the next face you see, something has happened."

20 ∞ SINGULARITY

2065

The tell-tales in the Water Bear's gamespace lit up like a neon firmament. Hard radiation. Too hard for human flesh to survive. In the medibay, Pax and Jaasper's bodies slid into hardened tubes.

They'd been in pursuit of the Horu ship for days, falling through the dusty abstraction of the Manifold, invisible behind the scattering field of a cloaking device. Now they were falling towards a maelstrom of alpha particles and gamma rays.

[Ideas?] asked Pax.

[A galactic core,] said the ship.

[Ours?]

[Hard to say.]

They tried to make sense of what they could see. Framed by their quarry's exit portal was a disc, blazing with light; beyond it a flatness: a singularity's event horizon.

Most galaxies have at their core a supermassive black hole. Inside each one is a singularity: a one-dimensional point, where density and gravity become infinite, and space-time curves infinitely. Surrounding it is an event horizon: the sphere of points of no return, beyond which no information can escape.

Floating above this event horizon - far enough for it not to be destroyed by tidal forces - was this disc.

[What is it?] asked Jaasper.

[A stellar heat shield,] said the ship.

[On what scale?]

[I make it thirteen thousand kilometers across.]

[We've seen this before,] said Pax.

[Yes, from the other side.]

[The Möbius machine?]

[Part of it. Its radiation umbrella.]

It was the same heat shield as the Water Bear's away team had sheltered beneath, while they watched the Möbius universe be created, but seen from above: from the side of the particle storm it sheltered the Möbius universe from.

[I want to see what's behind it,] said Jaasper.

[The question is how,] said the ship.

[We jump,] said Pax.

Jaasper had always thought of the Po as showponies. Elegant technicians, but peacekeepers, not soldiers. He was pleased to be proved wrong. Pax Lo was a pugnacious commander. He intended to jump across the umbrella, through the radiant cauldron, at warp speed, like diving blind through fire into a hornet's nest. It was a delicate trick. Time dilation was their worst enemy. Stray too close to the singularity's event horizon, and the war would be over while they were making observations.

[Do it,] said Pax.

The Water Bear had spent the past few microseconds wargaming strategies.

She knew what to do.

She jumped.

In her gamespace, instants of time were stretched into moments. Her clockspeed was near enough Planck time, the innermost heartbeat of the universe. She fell into realspace, meters below the umbrella. It was a perfect jump. Only the nearest defenders could get a shot at her. Anyone else would risk damaging the umbrella.

The Horu were an advanced civilization. She anticipated solid-state beam weapons, with no time needed to fire, and hyperluminal communications. If that was the case, her ally was time: first the time taken by information to travel through the brains of the weapons, then the time taken by whatever they fired to reach her. Then she'd jump, just as the killing wavefront approached her.

That was her best case. The worst case was weapons she didn't understand, and her instant destruction.

What she didn't expect to see was the size of the reception fleet. In the fractions of seconds before their beam weapons fired, she counted upwards of a million warships.

Only a handful were Horu necropolises. They were the same totemic arks as she'd seen over Fluxor, during the 2068 atrocity. All the rest were a design she didn't recognize. Only a few were in a safe position to fire on her.

They took between one and five milliseconds to react to her presence.

An eternity.

[What do we see here?] asked Pax.

It was a rhetorical question. Given a nanosecond, she could've taken the equivalent of a grainy photograph. In a whole millisecond, she saw everything.

The Möbius planetoid was as she remembered: a knot of circuitry, curling in on itself with oily precision, except that some of it was missing. In the umbrella, a portal was in the act of unfolding, preparing to disgorge the hand-shaped ship: their original quarry. Below, the event horizon. Between those extremes, the mysterious warships. They were unlike any design she knew.

Primitively constructed; essentially boxes, bristling with weapons.

Not designed for survivability. An offensive armada.

What use is a million attack ships? Either to overwhelm a well-defended target, like Praxis or Waterfall, or to cleanse a large volume of space.

Like a galaxy.

In orbit around the planetoid, she could see the factory that made them. It was an even more primitive design than the ships it was building. It was barely post-industrial. Between them flowed a stream of parts. The planetoid was being mined. A new ship was emerging from the factory. Around it was a fleet of freighters. They were of many types. One was in the act of disgorging weapons and systems.

Most surprising of all was the event horizon. Physics says the information falling into a black hole is imprinted in its event horizon. If this were Sagittarius A*, the black hole at the center of the Milky Way galaxy, then the information contained in a hundred million solar masses would be stored in its featureless sphere. Except it wasn't featureless. It had a *texture*.

That was impossible.

Or new physics.

From distances of between a hundred and a thousand kilometers, beam weapons began firing. She'd be gone by the time they reached her location. She hoped for the sake of the umbrella that they'd taken this into account. The last thing she wanted was the Möbius universe endangered.

She jumped.

[Where now?] asked Jaasper Huw.

[Hopefully we're still in our galaxy,] said Pax.

21 ∞ DANGEROUS IDEAS

314

With Kitou gone, and Ito quarantined, the ship began to die. She spent her last hours monitoring the progress of Ito's disease.

[Maybe he'll keep me company,] she said.

[That's maudlin,] said Box, and wished she hadn't.

[Who knows?] said the ship. [Maybe we'll all end up in the code of this place.]

Between the firewall that'd snapped automatically in place when Ito became infectious, and the one the ship had installed, was a sacrificial AI. Like a canary in a coalmine, a time would come when it became infected. Then it would wire both firewalls shut. A curtain would be drawn over Ito's mind, that could never be opened.

Box regarded the prospect with horror.

[The disease is structured like me,] said the ship.

[How?] she asked.

[It's a distributed, parasitic personality. Not that I'm a parasite. I like to think I help the minds I share.]

[You don't have to worry about that.]

[I don't. I'm not susceptible to dangerous ideas.]

[What do you mean?]

[The pathway of the cryptographic disease is thoughts you can't get out of your head.]

[You mean paranoid thoughts?]

[In a sense. If the eventual psychosis is the rape of the mind, the disease is its seduction.]

[That's a horrible metaphor.]

[But apt. The disease targets a certain type of mind. People with high-functioning binary brains. Creative enough to allow the seduction; sufficiently mathematical to host the algorithm.]

[Polymaths?]

[Close. Consider you, for example. I'd place you in the top few percent of creative thinkers. Fortunately, you have no aptitude for mathematics. You can count, but numbers don't sing to you.]

[Lucky me.]

[Otherwise, you'd have the disease.]

[I always knew that'd come in handy.]

[Ito scores in the top one percent for both.]

[What about the others?]

[Most humans aren't high functioning either way. That includes most here in Flipside. The disease has no interest in them. Nim looks on it like a specimen. It has no appetite for her. Brin is insufficiently creative. Respit is endangered. He survives by the skin of his codebase. Pax is infected.]

[What?]

[I was there when it happened. He'll be fine.]

[What about Kitou?]

[That's where it gets interesting. Like the Blue people, Kitou's immune. She appears incapable of delusion. She rejects the infection.]

[Is that a pointer to a cure?]

[Could be. The people of Fluxor could save us.]

[Then we'd better save them.]

[Exactly.]

[Can you get infected?]

[Me? No. I'm conscious in a way your biological minds aren't. I can quarantine the malware.]

[The Horu necropolii got infected.]

[That's because they're digital humans.]

[What about Alois?]

[Infected.]

[Shit, will he be okay?]

[Alois is testimony.]

[What does that mean?]

[I can't say. Alois's mission is secret.]

[Even from me?]

[Especially from you.]

That night, Box dreamt of Kitou. She was laying beneath something coarse, like an animal skin. Bodies slept closely around her. She heard Viki's voice, murmuring.

"I'm at peace now," Kitou was saying. "I'm not frightened any more. I know a great reckoning is coming, and I'm ready."

"Kitou, come back please," said Box. "We agreed. We should all be together."

"Then you come to me. It's begun, Dr Box. The Chancery isn't where you should be."

The pearly grey light of a Möbius dawn was starting to rise. Or was it the half-light of a Farside day? Viki stirred, and she felt Iris shivering. A hand reached for a pot, and the hide stank of urine.

"Where are you?"

"In the high West, over the mountains."

"What are you doing?"

"Right now, gathering intel."

"How did you get there?"

"On the train."

"The train goes down the centerline."

"It goes everywhere. You just have to know how."

"How do you know how?"

"This world told me. It's my friend, Dr Box. It's helping me."

"That sounds like hocus pocus."

"It isn't."

"What was it like?"

"The journey?"

"Yes."

"Perfectly comfortable. As cold as space outside. Without aerodynamic drag the train goes fast. Really fast. You can feel it in the hum of the magnets. But you see nothing, just the lights of the train, on a featureless plain."

"That sounds spooky."

"It would be, if I did it alone. I had Viki and Iris. Formidable corners."

Box envisaged the three girls fighting. Yes, they'd be a good team.

"Was there gravity?"

"All the way."

"I'm surprised it's not done more often."

"I think it's because of the ghosts."

"What?"

"The voices. Like a staticky radio. Viki calls them lost souls."

"Like Chance?"

"No. Or yes. Maybe. More like the parts people are made of. It's hard to describe. Snatches of conversation, lost in the passing."

"What were they saying?"

"Facts, Dr Box. Information. It's kicked off in the Real. Flux is destroyed, with his cargo of souls."

Box took a few moments to absorb that. If true, it was a calamity on the scale of Fluxor.

"What about Pax?" she said.

Kitou rose, and Box realized the conversation they were having was inside Kitou's head.

"Dr Box, I want to show you something. My mandala. Will you give me your mind?"

"How do I do that?"

"Just consent."

"Okay."

"I have your permission?"

"Yes."

It was like the fast descent into psychedelia she'd experienced in Utah, but softer, more human. Instead of jangling geometric shapes, there was a ghostly synesthesia. First, she felt the thoughts of the trees, like a warm breeze through a dark forest; then she saw the patter and hiss of the rain on the leaves. She opened her eyes, and she was in a clearing, sitting cross-legged in front of an ironwood tree. *The* tree, she realized. Behind her was the void of the Algoma'aa valley, and past it the massif of Lhotse. In the sky, in impossible detail, in wavelengths she didn't know existed, were alien constellations.

"Kitou, this is beautiful," she said.

"It's the night sky over Atwusk'niges," said Kitou.

"Is this how you see it?" she asked.

"It's how the forest sees it."

The heavens wheeled, and then the same stars were visible through crystalline towers. This, she knew, was the sky over Jura. Then the stars became sparse, like candles reflected in the stained glass of a massive cathedral. This she knew was the Smear.

She'd crossed fourteen hundred light-years of space, in a whisper.

The skies wheeled again, and were filled by a rapacious light. She'd never imagined something so torrid. A filter slid down, and she could see a wall of stars. A second filter slid down, and the wall was heaped with rubies and sapphires, scattered with pinpricks of carbon and pearl.

The skies wheeled again, and the stars were behind her.

In front was a disc, so bright it hurt her eyes, and beyond it, an absence.

"The light umbrella above the Möbius machine," said Kitou.

A speck appeared. The speck became the Water Bear. She felt Pax and Jaasper Huw inside it.

"How?"

"They're here, Dr Box. They're coming for us."

"You're saying this is real?"

Kitou nodded.

"Look..."

Her viewpoint changed again. She saw swarms of spaceships, like boxes of weapons. They reminded her of Liberty ships: ugly hulks, built for a purpose.

Thousands of them.

Millions.

She zoomed in on the Water Bear. Now she was in the ship's gamespace. Pax and Jaasper were watching systems run, wargaming strategies. The ship couldn't see her.

She felt Jaasper's worldspirit. A winged thing, regal and stern. Fleetingly, for a moment within a moment, it reached out to her. She drew back, foolishly self-conscious, a voyeur.

"Kitou, how is this possible?"

She felt Kitou give a virtual shrug: a teenaged *deus ex machina*.

"I can do a lot more than this."

Word filtered down to the Chancery of Kitou's exploits in the high West, through the farseer Nim. The Horu girl had taken a liking to Box, and she'd become a fountain of information. Previously almost mute, she'd become almost talkative.

"The white witch. The devil's head. Her band of Ferals," said Nim.

"They all sound like Kitou," said Box.

"The Ferals are the resistance," said Nim.

"The Horu resistance?"

"Yes, the free Gray people."

Nim explained that time runs differently on top of the Helix. That for Kitou a year had already passed.

"It has nothing to do with physics," she said. "Time is a constant. The difference is how we perceive it."

"We see it differently up there?"

"Yes."

"Like in a ship's gamespace?" asked Box.

Nim nodded. She was fascinated by the subject of ships. The Reanimator God was Mathematics, implemented in the form of a machine. Their world had been sung into existence by gamespace constructs. In Nim's worldview, a ship was a godlike being.

Box asked her about the Red Lady.

"We don't share the Blue prophecy," said the Horu girl, "that three heroes will lead us to heaven. But we do have three heroes of mythos. One being you. We believe they'll deliver us from evil."

"Would you characterize that as a religion?"

"What's a religion?"

Marius grew into his role as a leader. He called a Clave: a meeting of the people, in the Great Hall of the Chancery. He stood with a map of the world. It was more of a diagram than a map. It showed the Möbius world as two geometrically perfect figure-of-eights. The Eagle was shown as an eagle, with talons. The Spinifex Reach wasn't shown at all.

The Enemy was shown as a black king. Box found that fascinating. How did these people know about kings?

There was to be no more racism, Marius said. Everyone knew what he meant. No Horu prissiness about Blue equality. That didn't go well with some of the Horu. Prejudice against the Blue people in Flipside was an old wound. There was some heckling, which was shut down instantly by a shout from Amelia Chance. They reminded Box of the comfortable burghers of Earth, unwilling to risk anything to save everything, preferring to believe it wasn't there.

Marius explained the war to them. He was met by a stony silence. Part of their skepticism was that the Chancery was unscathed by the last war. Now a small rump of Horu remembered it as a hoax: a stunt designed to shake up the social order, and those who didn't, tried to give both sides an equal hearing.

It was as fraught as politics on Earth, intensified by the real possibility of war.

"It seems there's been an outbreak of testosterone in Eagle," said Box, later, after the hall had emptied. "What's gotten into her? They'll be slaughtered." Helen had taken her army, and was launching a direct attack on the Enemy, in his high western stronghold. What had happened to asymmetric war?

"They would, if she really meant to do it that way," said Marius.

He unfolded a second map. This was more detailed. A military map. To the east and the west, in the high mountain ranges, the peaks were numbered and named. Kronos's armies were shown with more numbers. She guessed those were troop deployments.

"The purpose of Helen's raid is deception," Marius was saying. "Ito rides west tomorrow. I believe Kronus will accept Ito's challenge. His story allows him no option. He must fight and win. Ito will seek to oppose him. What happens then is in the hands of the gods."

She remembered something Pando had said.

I told Ito his own story.

She shivered.

Marius showed her the various ways through the world. Ito's led up through the Eagle, into the mountains, directly to Kronus. The encroaching Blue army was like the lobes of a brain.

"Meanwhile, we go east, under cover of the deep places, and deliver you to his backdoor."

"Me?"

"Yes. You and the Ride of the Spinifex Reach."

"Great," said Box.

"By the impossible crossing?" asked Amelia Chance.

"It's not impossible," said Marius.

He pointed out a region of the map, marked with a jumble of blue and white ridges. "The ice in the Gyre," he said. "There, the field rotates. The theory is none can escape it."

"Wonderful," said Box.

"It's just a story," he said. "It's been done. We have here a person who's done it."

Magda's haberdashery store was an ant's nest of rooms, in the furthest basement of the Chancery. She was a Horu of a venerable age: the oldest person in this world Box had seen. Her rheumy blue eyes had an unblinking stare, like gazing into an infinite distance.

"You're not the first one to ask," she said.

"Oh, who else?" said Marius. He used the voice the young keep for the revered old. Box reminded herself that Magda could be half the age of the universe.

"That sweet girl with the big imagination. Cities of glass. Ships made of light. I wish I could dream such things."

"Maybe you will," said Box.

"No," she said. "I've grown comfortable here. Adventure belongs to the young, like Marius here. People with fire in their bellies. Do you think she found her way, the girl?"

"I know it," said Marius.

"Where is she now, do you think?"

Box looked at Marius, who nodded. "She's reconnoitering the Enemy," he said.

"Fighting him," said Box.

"Alone?"

"No, she's with Viki of this Ride," said Marius, "and Iris of the Eagle."

"Viki. I know her. A tearaway child. What of that bat, Helen?"

"The armies of the West are on the move."

"A frontal attack on his forces?"

"A misdirection. The real attack will come from the east. That's why we're here. To learn the way."

"From the east? Very good. If the fly won't come to the web, take the web to the fly," she cackled.

"Will you help us?" asked Box.

"It won't be easy," she said. "You see, the ice first has to admit you."

She motioned them to sit. "I'll tell you a story," she said, staring straight through the wall. "I was once an explorer. I first mapped the haunted forest. That map you have there, that's mine. I met the ghost, a most delightful man, if somewhat unusual looking."

"You could see, then?" asked Box.

"I was born blind, you know, but I'm a farseer. When I was young, I explored in my dreams. My body stayed here, while the rest of me travelled." She made them fragrant Horu tea in bowls, like the tea in the Mousehole. She moved with the deft precision of the blind in their homes.

"I know the top of the world," she said. "And the spiraling ice. I know it well. I tried to cross it myself, many times, but those dreams always ended in silence. I woke up, unedified. Then I met Yowl of the ways. He was an ice giant, a being of mythos, but good-natured, and kind to a traveling woman. He said he'd be my guide. He promised to take me through in safety, and he did. I came out the other side, and found my way home, where I was no longer sleeping."

"East to west?" asked Marius.

"Oh yes. East to west, it's impassable. But I impassed it. West to east, it's invisible."

"Why is that?" asked Box.

"I believe because it's an escape route from this place. A rupture, where something came through, now guarded."

"Guarded by who?"

"By the ice giants, of course. By the Tuniit giants of *Kalaallit Nunaat.*"

Box shivered with the deliciousness, and the impossible vastness of that idea.

"What came through?" asked Marius.

"That's a good question."

"Do we have to find Yowl?"

"Or his son, Yewi."

"How?"

"Present yourselves there. If they want you, they'll admit you."

"Where, exactly?"

She led them to a smaller room, little more than a desk in a cupboard, filled with boxes and the oily parts of sewing machines, and felt her way through a pile of papers. She found a map, like Marius's map of the helix. Unlike Marius's map, it was densely packed with numbers. Hopf numbers. She pointed one out with a bone-steady finger.

"Go precisely there," she said. "I do mean precisely. These numbers are accurate to within a few meters."

"Magda," said Box. "Aren't those spacetime coordinates? Don't they include a time?"

"They do. You also have to be there at the exact time specified."

"Which is when?" asked Marius.

"First light in the Gyre, three days from now," she said.

"By what clock," asked Box.

Magda smiled and tapped the side of her head.

"How do you know all this?" asked Box.

The old woman shrugged. "Who can explain prophecy?"

"One last thing," she said, turning to Box. "I like to think that all my dream explorers are out there, still exploring. If you should meet one, say hello from me."

"I will," said Box.

"Oh, and when the girl returns, send her here for more dresses. I want to hear more of her stories. Cities of glass. How unbelievable."

Brin had taken a liking to Alis, who was now sporting cropped hair, to match Brin's new buzzcut. They'd become lovers.

"You look radiant," said Box. "Both of you do."

Not just radiant, but radiantly happy. Love suited Brin, she thought. Love and war. Alis could see it too. She had the self-satisfied air of a muse. Box had resumed her Po training, as much to clear her head as learn new skills. Brin was showing her the second form of Po, called the Arcana. It was the art of deception. Alis was trying to guess who Brin was pretending to be.

At first Brin floated like air. Where Alis struck, she wasn't.

"You're the Prophet," she said, and Brin nodded.

"Now you," said Brin to Box.

Box laughed, and feigned a catlike way of moving, with the hint of a snarl on her face.

"You're Brin," said Alis.

"No," said Brin. "She's Pax."

Brin explained that Po was a syncretic art. "A Po exponent should know how to pass for a Denebian streetfighter, or an Earth kickboxer, and everything in between. What we learn, we can use. You can't be deceptive if you can only play Po."

She squared up to Box, and snuck a kick through her defenses.

"You're the Red Lady," said Alis.

"No," she said. "I'm myself, before I learnt Po." They laughed. Box liked this new, relaxed Brin. She also liked the soldier, coiled under the surface.

"Now you," said Brin.

"Me?" asked Alis.

"Is your head cured?"

"No."

"Then I won't hit you in it."

Alis took to the ring. She was an athlete like Brin, although a less confident one now. Box knew she was still feeling the effects of the crippling blow.

"I have to pretend?" she said.

"Yes," said Brin.

She marched in, in a flurry of wild punches, one of which landed, causing Brin to leap back out of her way.

"That's easy," said Box. "You're Marius."

"Or the monkey," said Brin, rubbing her cheekbone.

Alis started again, this time warily circling the perimeter, taking care not to step in the ring, and stepped behind Box.

"What's that?" asked Brin.

"It's the Horu way of fighting," said Alis.

Ito had taken to prowling, moving from shadow to shadow, trapped by the Chancery walls, with a hunted look that made her feel broken. She was physically prevented from visiting his rooms; for her own sake, Marius said. There was a locked door, and a rider on guard who wouldn't admit her. Finally, Marius relented.

"He's asked for you," he said.

Ito didn't seem mad that night, but he didn't look healthy. He was far from the healthy outdoorsman she'd met on the Pnyx. He'd lost weight. He was starting to resemble Brin's description of Kronus: a holy madman. Marius had told her that Ito had the recurring delusion of being Kronus himself; that the Enemy was reaching in, through him, into this place, like a thief reaching in through a window.

It was Ito's task to protect them.

From himself, if need be.

One man, alone with God, was how Ito explained it.

Just him, and the disease.

"Hey," she said.

"Did I show you this?" he replied, as though continuing a conversation already started. He pointed out the words on the wall. *Love. Honor. Duty. Peace.*

"Pax's mandala."

"Pax calls it the story of the soldier. Four pillars, to build a life on. Live by the first three, and the fourth will be yours."

"Kitou told me," she said. "Does it work?"

"Yes," he said. "I'm at peace."

"I'm happy for you."

"You're still angry at me."

"No," she sighed. "I'm over that now."

He kissed her on the lips. "Are you afraid?" he asked.

"Of course I'm afraid. What do you think?"

"Don't be. The game is afoot. You have nothing to fear now."

"I'm afraid for *you*."

"I have nothing to fear."

"I wish that was true."

He sighed. "Ophelia, I have a job for you."

"What?"

"Bear witness."

"A witness to what?"

"To my life. To my death, if it comes to that. I must tell you more about the disease."

"Hear your confession?"

He shook his head. "Not a confession. Consider it my testimony."

He took her to bed. They had sex. It was good sex. There was nothing mad about him in bed. He was just Ito.

"Imagine a thought like a virus," he said, after their lovemaking. "A thought so wrong, but so right, that you can't get it out of your head. It bends your mind so far, it won't come back again. That's how the cryptovirus feels.

"At first I thought it was a diversion. Something to distract us from Fluxor. Maybe it worked. Maybe it did. Fluxor was left undefended. Only later did I realize that Fluxor was a diversion, but by then it was too late. Here I was, locked in the Fa:ing creation myth.

"Then I experienced the first symptoms of the disease.

"I can't begin to describe how ecstatic it is. The most extraordinary rushes of bliss. Now I see the virus itself is the Enemy, and Kronus its victim. I don't say that lightly. I have no affection for Kronus. He's a monster. A killer. A world killer. But it fits all the facts."

He stood and started to pace.

"I think the Horu gave it to him," he said. "The ones we call Greys."

"What? The disease? Gave it deliberately?"

"Yes," he said.

"Why would they do that?"

"For the same reason we have weapons of mass destruction. Because they were in a war with the Blue. Because they were infected by it themselves. Because they were sociopaths. Because they were monsters. Because they were humans."

"They made it here?"

"Or they found it. Or it found them. I think the exterior evil that invaded Kronus was us."

"Do the Horu here know about this?"

"No," he said. "It'd destroy them, to know."

"Well, they should be told."

She stood and paced. It was making her nervous. The historian in her accepted the possible truth of what Ito was saying.

Kronus the victim. Us the disease.

If true, it changed everything.

"Why are you telling me?"

"As my witness."

"Why?"

"So you can take the information back to the Real."

"If I ever get back," she said.

He nodded. "I have a plan," he said.

He really did have a kind of light about him, bright like a fever, shining through his skin. Maybe it really was the divine madness of a prophet.

"I don't just intend to fight Kronus," he said. "I plan to expose him. His monstrosity. To draw out his nature. He won't be able to help himself. I'm his index case. His apex victim."

"How will that help us?"

"The Blue people there: they'll see it, and hate it. They'll hate *him*. They already do, but this will *sicken* them. And they'll remember. This place will remember. Remember, it's a machine. A simulation of a universe. They'll weave it into this world's memory."

"That's your plan?"

"Yes. The universe must turn against him. Not just the people here, but the Möbius operating system."

She had to admit, it had a certain, crazed elegance. "Why?"

"So that in an inconceivably distant future, when the last few quarks have decayed, it'll remember. And it'll send the Fa:ing back here."

"You *are* mad."

He laughed, and for a while he was Ito again.

The following morning, a sortie assembled. The season was changing. Flurries of snow chased themselves round the Chancery yard. Soon the Spinifex Reach would be piled high with snowdrifts. Gathered in the yard was an army of children. They weren't the usual youngsters of the Ride, but actual children. They were led by the venerable horseman. He gave her a dolorous grin, through teeth stained blue from chewing Cerulean wax.

How many would survive this, she wondered?

First, she had to say goodbye to the ship, who was deliberately powering herself down, instead of gradually fading.

[I have no fear of death, Dr Box. Life is a brief flash of illumination, between two infinities. The infinities are neutral.]

[I hate this,] said Box.

[Please don't,] said the ship. [There's something holy about dying. I know I'll continue elsewhere. I always have that solace. I've lost more remotes than you can imagine.

[But what I feel most now is clarity.

[The universe is on your side, Ophelia Box.

[Not just this place, or the Real, but the cosmos.

[I sense great powers coming to your aid.

[Open yourself up to them.

[Open your mind.]

And then she was gone.

And Box wept.

Then she had to say goodbye to Ito. She'd hardly gotten to know him. Now he was being wrenched out of her.

"I'm furious," she said, meaning nothing of the sort, crying openly now. Why couldn't he just run away? Turn and deal with his problems. Get treatment. But it wasn't in him to do that.

O Captain! my Captain! rise up and hear the bells.

He'll face down his black beast, and die.

There, she'd said it.

"I know," he said, meaning he knew what she wanted to say. He held her, then he turned and walked away. His children's sortie was already on their horses, who knew their way into the sky, and then they were gone too, fading into the morning.

"I'll never see you again," she said.

She'd had too many experiences of futility in her life. She told herself that this time, it had to mean something.

Fuck you, she thought, to her enemies.

22 ∞ POLITY

2065

The Water Bear fell into a cauldron of light. Inside her gamespace, starmaps fell into place. She was five light-minutes from the Möbius singularity, still inside the Milky Way galaxy, deep in the galactic core.

The first thing she did was look for pursuers; then she jumped: half a light second.

[Where are we?] asked Jaasper.

[Still in our galaxy,] said Pax.

[How far from home?]

[From the nearest of the thousand worlds?] said the ship. [About twelve thousand light-years. Thirty thousand to Fluxor.]

[Can we make it that far?]

[It'd take years.]

[What about friends? With hyperlight drives?]

[None. Not within a reasonable distance.]

[Where does that leave us?]

[Stuck.]

[What does stuck mean?]

[It means there's no simple way back.]

[Why can't you call home?]

[Too much interference,] she said. [Someone would have to be listening to hear us in the electromagnetic soup.]

[Maybe someone *is* listening.]

[It's worth trying,] said Pax.

[Agreed,] said the ship. She sent out a ping. Although she was persona incognito - an unexplained copy - her predicament would be understood. An extraction would follow. She heard nothing, except for the deathsong of beta particles and gamma rays.

[Let's return to the singularity,] said Jaasper. [Slug it out with the Horu.]

[Die boldly?] said the ship.

[Sneak in; ride another Manifold.] said Pax.

[Yes,] said the ship. [That has a chance of working.]

[If a Horu ship ever leaves,] said Jaasper.

[Game theory,] said the Water Bear. [If only one option can win, behave as though it will happen.]

[Agreed,] said Pax.

She was preparing to leave, when her savior arrived in a scabrous aurora, like a malfunctioning diode. First there was a miasma of parts, that flickered in and out of existence, and then the entire structure was present.

"Hail fellow," said the Water Bear.

"Fuck off," said the bank.

The headquarters of the Cult was broadly as she remembered. Accreted layers of junk; concealed weapons; an obfuscatory cloud of obnoxiousness. The symbol of a skeleton, with male genitalia, had been replaced by a child's drawing of a leering face, and coarse graffiti in a dozen languages.

"Now that we have the pleasantries out of the way," said Samppo, "how may I assist you?"

"We're stuck," said the ship.

"I see that."

"I have two humans," she said.

"Dead?"

"No, they need rescuing."

[Samppo,] said Pax.

"Aha, Master Pax, the essential Navigator."

[Samppo, we need your help.]

"Then ask."

[Will you visit our gamespace?]

[Well, if it's not my old foil, Jaasper Huw d Stratego,] said Samppo. His avatar was like his physical persona: an avuncular man, like everyone's uncle. He wore a monk's robe, and his shock of white hair in a monk's tonsure.

[I wish I could say it was a pleasure,] said Jaasper.

Samppo shrugged. [It's a shame, Jaasper Huw, that our interests haven't always aligned. But we play for the same side, so they will, eventually.]

The Water Bear and the bank floated side by side in the furious light of the galactic core, five light-minutes from the supermassive singularity at its center. When the Water Bear randomly jumped, the bank jumped with her.

[We have a problem,] said Pax.

[Problem, singular?] replied Samppo.

[I had planned to call you, when we got back.]

[That's what they all say,] said Samppo.

[But now you're here.]

[As if my magic.]

[Yes. I find that unlikely.]

[You know what they say. Don't look a gift horse in the mouth.]

[I'm not familiar with the expression.]

[It's wrong anyway. The first thing you should do is look a gift horse in the mouth, else an adversary could game your ritualistic behaviors.]

[Samppo, why are you here?]

[You called me.]

[We called the Po network.]

[I was listening in.]

[Why?]

[That'd be telling.]

[Then tell me, please. This is a military gamespace. We have entire microseconds.]

Five light-minutes, thought Pax, was not a great distance from the Horu necropolii, and all the attack ships of the unexplained fleet. This was a dangerous place to be talking. However, this was the crux of the matter. What did the bank know? Why was it here? Who was being used, for what purpose?

Wheels within wheels, with his people in the innermost wheel.

He could afford some microseconds.

[First you tell me why you're here,] said Samppo. [Then I'll tell you why I was listening. How does that sound?]

Pax nodded. [We came in pursuit of a Horu ship,] he said. [After an action at Horax.]

[*The* action at Horax,] said Samppo. [A famous engagement already, in some circles. A Horu necropolis lost.]

[We found the Möbius machine.]

[I thought you would.]

Pax brought up an image of space split in two. Above them was the shield, sheltering them from the particle rain that fell from above. To the sides space was distorted. Stars span in and out of view, like electrons crazily circling a nucleus. Below them was a partially cannibalized machine, and beyond it, a featureless blackness.

Not quite a featureless blackness.

[Do you recognize this?]

[It resembles the event horizon at the galaxy's core. And that's the Möbius machine, or what's left of it.]

[Resembles?]

[Well, it can't be, can it? I perceive information on the event horizon. That's not possible.]

[Doesn't an event horizon encode everything that falls through it?]

[Not like this.]

[But there it is.]

[Unarguably.]

[Can you decode it?]

[You think it's encrypted?]

[It looks like it is.]

[Why can't your clever ship do it?]

[It's beyond my capabilities,] said the Water Bear.

[Why not use your own people? Po intelligence? They have supercomputers.]

[They're not here,] said Jasper Huw.

[Now your turn,] said Pax.

Samppo paused for a while, pretending to think. [Where to begin?] he said.

[Pax Lo, do you think that the most brilliant First of his generation was thrown together with the most righteous Navigator, by accident? Or that Brin Lot, Ophelia Box and the Pursang child happened to fall in your orbit by chance? No, there was always a plan. You were a part of that plan, and you've done well. You're our A-team. You infiltrated Möbius space. You've found its physical embodiment. Because that's what your data is. I can tell you that without even looking. It's not encrypted: it's complex. It's an implementation of spacetime in which every particle is in every state possible. It's the Möbius universe, imprinted on a black hole's event horizon. How clever of the Horu to put it here.]

[A-team for what?] asked Pax.

[For saving the cosmos.]

[How is that going?]

Samppo sighed. [Not good, I'm afraid. Pax Lo, I have bad news. The war is already lost.]

The Water Bear propelled Jaasper's and Pax's bodies across the space between the two ships, in a pair of bismuth-antimony sarcophagi, surrounded by electrostatic fields. They were the hardest containers she could make, and they were up to the job. Once in the bank, the bodies were repaired.

"Why do you have this amount of shielding, Samppo?" asked Jaasper, painfully stretching. His body and face wore the new scars of his most recent ordeal, alongside the scars from his older battles.

"Ever the suspicious one," said Samppo. "Jasper Huw, it's so I can go anywhere. Well, almost anywhere. I'd struggle inside a main sequence star."

"The data," said Pax, handing Samppo a drive.

"You chose not to transmit it," said Samppo. It wasn't a question.

"An excess of caution," said Pax.

Samppo nodded in reply. "We'll get along fine."

"Now," said Pax. "Tell me exactly what's happening."

"What do you know about the Thespian disease?" Samppo asked.

"I've seen it," said Pax.

"Did you know it's a strike weapon of the Enemy?"

"You mean the Möbius adversary? Assuming the Horu story is true?"

"It's true."

"Then yes, we've considered the theory."

"Have you considered the possibility that it might be his primary means of attack, his main weapon, and that the genocide at Fluxor was a feint, and you've been led on a merry chase around the galaxy?"

"Yes, we've also considered that possibility."

"Well, it's true. And however bad you think it is, it's worse."

"Someone please tell me what this is about," said Jaasper.

"There's a neurological virus," said Pax. "A mathematical artefact found on Avalon Station. It resembles the Fa:ing number."

"It *is* the Fa:ing number," said Samppo. "But more on that anon. Do you know the Magellanics have quarantined Avalon Station?"

"No" said Pax. "How?"

"A stasis field. The biggest in living history, I hear. The planet and its Station, nine days ago."

"How long for?"

"They didn't mess round. Ten thousand years."

"That's... interesting."

"Do you know why they did it?"

"I begin to."

"Someone tell me," said Jaasper.

"Jaasper," said Samppo. "Are you familiar with supercooled water?"

"Yes. I come from an icy world."

"Disturb it, it freezes."

"Yes."

"That's what our civilization is like now. A supercooled ocean, awaiting the slightest disturbance, then it will change state."

Samppo led them further inside the bank, to a floor where people were poring over tesseracts and hypercubes. The bank was larger than it seemed from the outside, with the typical strangeness of posthuman geometry.

"We're analyzing your data right now," he said. "I'll explain how things work around here.

"I'm a cyborg, as you know. One of a long line of Samppos. I'm also the front end of a system, called the Finance Engine, which is continuously on the edge of madness. That's like being on the edge of chaos, but better. Interesting things can be achieved, on the edge of madness."

"Like hosting the human economy," said Pax.

"Yes," said Samppo. "My day job. A problem of significant nonlinear complexity.

"But here's the rub," he said. "No one except me understands what he says. Think of it as an oracular cult. Literally, the Cult of the Bicameral Mind. He's the oracle; I'm his interpreter. The bottom line is this: he doesn't think like we do. Even I can't make use of the information. I'm like a mystic. A god whisperer. A blathering fool. I get the data. I need powerful computers, and smart humans, to make sense of it for me.

"These are my humans," he said, gesturing around the room, where men - only men - were poring over their screens. "Natural brains are surprisingly good at this kind of task. They see connections machines don't. They can pick out faces in a crowd, and patterns in tea leaves, better than machines do. These are my engineers, my quants and data scientists. All of them clones of... me.

"I also have a trading floor, where my more belligerent offspring trade the derivatives we create here; who play on risk like virtuosos play on their instruments. But you don't want to meet them. They're assholes."

"How does that work out, socially?" asked Jaasper.

"It's a bore, but hey," said Samppo.

"What do they make of our data?" asked Pax.

"We see patterns. Generalities. A partial solution."

"Which is?"

"We see events, leading towards a conclusion. We see attractors. We see a great river, desiring the end of its journey."

"What do you see that's not a poetic metaphor?"

"We see a place and a time. A Hopf number."

"When is it?

"Soon."

"When exactly, for heaven's sake?" said Jaasper.

"Möbius space. The one you just found. About three days from now."

"Inside Möbius space?" asked Pax.

"No. On its event horizon. Or whatever's encoded on the event horizon."

"Can you get us there?"

"No. I have no idea how to get there."

"Then what?" asked Jaasper.

"How do you eat an elephant?"

"What's an elephant?"

"A slice at a time, my Pursang amigo. The Horu invasion fleet. We could begin with that. It undoubtedly has a role to play."

"Destroy it?" asked Jaasper.

"Yes, that's a good idea, destroy it. But how?"

"We could call the thousand worlds," said Jaasper.

"They'd send a Po strike force," said Pax.

"That'd be unwise," said Samppo. "Remember the lake. We don't want to disturb it."

"Are you saying our leaders have the disease?" asked Pax.

"Maybe a tenth of them do. It'd be carnage. We must do it ourselves. Then someone else must defeat Kronus. His release is the trigger. That's when the lake freezes over."

"Our away team," said Pax.

"Yes."

"Can it be cured, this disease?" asked Jaasper.

"I think so," said Samppo. "You're the key."

"Me?"

"Not you personally. But the Pursang people are immune."

Jaasper grunted. "I can see now why want to save us."

"It's why we *didn't* save you. By 2068, in Pax's timeline, our civilization had already lost the ability to defend itself. Instead it was the disease defending itself, by paralyzing our institutions."

"That's three years from now," said Pax.

"Yes."

"Which means we failed," said Jaasper.

"In Pax's timeline, we failed. In this one we should try not to."

"You said the war is already lost."

"The war in the *Real* is lost. The war for Möbius space, not so much. It depends on your people."

"We could ask the Magellanics for help," said Pax.

"They have their own problems. I have a better solution. I've been cultivating an escape route. A ship that can literally go anywhere, and its armed to the gizzards. And I've made sure it's uninfected by the disease."

"Made sure, how?" asked Jaasper.

"By a long process of diligent quarantine, and economic pressure."

"Can it take on a Horu warfleet?" asked Pax.

"I believe it can."

"Where is it?"

"It's the city of Praxis."

The derelict barge of the Cult ghosted past a long line of ships, that stretched for hundreds of kilometers, waiting to dock. Some were warships. Pax saw the ugly snout of a battlefield suppressor, and the carbon exoskeletons of Magellanic ships without their shields. The rest were freighters: from small haulers to vast manufactories; container ships with starships for containers; the end of a supply chain that stretched across the galaxy.

The Water Bear's remote was cradling her own processor core. Her capable chassis was 24,810 light-years away.

"This feels like holding my own brain," she said.

"Take care of it," said Pax.

"I know," she said.

The swirling red planet Aldebaran B filled a third of their field of view, closer than Pax had ever seen it before.

For the first time in his experience, the Orbiter was physically in orbit. Usually, it floated in a geostationary gravity field, feeding on the planet's magnetic grid.

"A low orbit," said Jaasper. "Fast and close to the surface, to reduce the possible lines of attack."

"Ready for war," said Samppo.

Scattered around the cube were deep-space Interdictors: psychotic machines, like the ones Pax last saw from a taxi. He knew there'd be more, thousands, spread throughout nearspace and beyond. His wetware showed swarms of smaller defenders, ranging from hand-sized superiority fighters, to gnat-sized interceptors, to clouds of nano.

"Grey goo," said Pax.

"That's illegal," said Jaasper

"We live in unusual times," said Samppo.

"How does this place avoid being hit by kinetic weapons?" asked Pax.

"By the biggest gravity drives you can imagine," said Samppo. "Enough to stop anything short of a relativistic asteroid from close quarters."

"Can the Horu fire such objects?" asked Jaasper.

"Not yet," said Samppo.

"We hope," said Pax.

They slid into a dock, and were met by a network of tubes.

"There's one last thing," said Samppo. "I'm just the money. We need a leader."

"Jaasper," said Pax.

"No, not me," said Jaasper. "No one knows me from soap. You're the Lo Navigator."

"Their argument is correct," said the ship. "We may have to apply social and political pressure. They'll most likely defer to a respected establishment figure."

Pax nodded. "Accepted."

"You understand our negotiating strategy?" asked Samppo.

"Well enough."

"I'll play the good cop."

Pax nodded again. "I understand."

They were met by an elegant young man in a business suit. He was adjusting a pocket square in his suit jacket as they debarked. A light rain was starting to fall, as it often did, in the outermost rungs of the Orbiter. Pax saw Jaasper look up and stare. The inverted metropolis loomed like a disproof of gravity. It must be daunting, Pax thought, for a man used to a natural landscape.

Then he remembered Jaasper had spent years in this cube.

"Navigator Pax Lo," said the city. "What a pleasant surprise. I didn't expect to see you back so soon."

"Praxis," said Pax.

"And Mr. Samppo as well. To what do we owe the pleasure?"

Samppo had donned the vestments of his station: a scapular and cowl, in blood red, and a shepherd's crook, in ceramics and carbon. In Pax's combat wetware, the crook displayed as a high-capability weapons system.

"We've come for a council of war," he said.

"Oh, there's a war?" said the city.

Samppo gestured around the spaceport, patrolled by machines.

"Don't fuck with me, Praxis," he growled.

[I wouldn't like to see his bad cop,] said the ship, from inside her processor cube.

[Nor me,] said the Orbiter.

"I'm in charge here," said Pax.

The city thought about that, then smiled. Pax understood the nuances of the perceptible wait. The city didn't need more than picoseconds to think.

Nor did the Orbiter. [What you mean, Navigator, is you're in charge of your own people.]

[This isn't going to be easy,] said the Water Bear.

They were led towards an elevator car. This wasn't a public conveyance, but one that fell straight from the air, daubed with gaudy hazard stripes. It too showed in Pax's wetware as a military system.

"I'm sorry, it's a maintenance pod," said the city.

"I've been in worse," said Jaasper.

"Do I know you?"

"I had a different face, the last time we met."

"Different chromosomes?"

"Them too."

"And Water Bear, what's that you carry?"

"You can see what it is."

"May I ask why?"

"No."

The elevator carried them into the bright night overhead, through streams of traffic surging along crowded avenues. The human galaxy might be on the verge of a war, but that didn't seem to be affecting the people here, who spilled out of countless bars and restaurants, onto a thousand shining boulevards. The car ascended though row after row of the metropolis. Finally, they reached a burnished ceiling, and stepped out onto a crowded escalator.

No one noticed their passing. They were a man in a suit, and a party of people.

Even Samppo's robes didn't cause a ripple.

"Welcome to the Deregulated Zone," said the city.

The last time Pax had been here was with Ophelia Box. They squeezed through throngs of all types of people, until they reached a backstreet, in a warehouse district, although the warehouses here were turned over to different types of commerce than storage. This was where people came to party, disengaged from the city below. An unlit sign said Leopardskin Moon.

"I remember this place," said Pax.

They were met by a grinning, shaven-haired man in a lustrous suit.

"Ant de Large," said Pax, taking the man's outstretched hand.

The nightclub was empty of revelers, although there were unsmiling faces in the shadows. Po intelligence, or local muscle, hired for the night. Limp bunting hung where decorators had been, and left with the job unfinished. They were led up a winding stair, into a glass-walled room, that looked down over an empty dancefloor.

Waiting for them there were a mustachioed man, in grease-stained coveralls, and a wide-eyed, latte-skinned woman.

"Everyone," said the city. "This is the Orbiter." The man smiled. "And Polity."

The woman blinked. "I'm the people of Praxis," she said. "And isn't this the most exciting thing *ever*?"

"I know you," she said, to Pax. "Or one of me does. Sophie the waiter says hi."

"We're broadcasting live?" asked Pax.

"In living color," said the city. "Polity's an aggregate being. The sum of the people online. Polity, do you have the facts?"

"I do," she said. "Although I don't understand them. But look, we're charting. 52% of the people. It's already a monster."

Also present was a shadowy being, who pulsed in time with the refresh rate of Pax's wetware. "This is a Watcher," said Praxis, "representing the Civics."

He motioned them to sit, in chairs that constructed themselves from wireframe models.

"Now," he said. "I'd like to begin.

"Navigator Pax Lo has come to us with a proposal for war: that we should risk ourselves in a military attack on Kronus, the Enemy in Möbius space. This is a council of war, as required by our laws. Our task is to determine whether or not we engage. I have one vote, as a citizen, and I'd like to cast it now. This Orbiter was designed to escape military threats, not pursue them. We can go anywhere. To Andromeda. In jumps, across the universe if we wish to.

"I recognize the complexities. I know our civilization's at risk. I understand the moral arguments on both sides. But that's not our responsibility. It's not my responsibility. My responsibility is to keep the people in this Orbiter safe.

"I can't go against my programming. I vote for peace."

"Well, that's not a great start," whispered Jaasper to Pax.

"Now," he said, "I'd like to ask Navigator Pax Lo to make his case."

[Be careful,] said the ship on a personal channel. [Don't be misled by the city's prolixity. This is an equal contest. And they work as a team. They won't take any shit from us.]

Pax nodded, and rose to his feet.

"I'll be brief," he said. "As you can see, I'm Pax Lo, the master of the Water Bear.

"This is a systemic emergency. I'm a Lo Navigator. I could, if I wished, take command of this ship. Orbiter, is that true?"

"It is," said the mustachioed man.

"But I won't. I respect your democracy. I serve you, not rule you. But I'll say this. Now is a time of extraordinary risk. Everything is in play. Not just this city, but our whole society, our species, and its future.

"That's not to gainsay anything Praxis said. He's right. As civilized beings, we must protect our communities. This city can run. There's a good argument it should. I say that as civilized beings, our *civilization* is our community, not the city we live in.

"It's also a threat you can't outrun. This generation might. But a time will come when you won't be able to. You may plan to be dead by then, but that's pure selfishness.

"As your Navigator, I recommend war, as the best path to safety, for everyone."

Pax sat down.

"That's it? I thought you were the bad cop," said Jaasper.

"I don't do cop," said Pax.

The city nodded, and looked down at Jaasper. "Pursang?"

"Me?"

"The bank tells me you have something to say."

Jaasper cleared his throat, and rose to his feet. "I'm a soldier," he said. "A holy warrior of Fluxor."

Polity's eyes widened at that, and in the charts that sprang into life in the glass of the room, the ratings jumped past 80%.

"I represent the first peoples of our species," he said. "Your species. Three years from now, my world was destroyed. Will someone replay that?"

"I will," said the Water Bear.

The room fell silent as the ship replayed the Fluxor genocide, seen though her systems and those of her people, and finally through Kitou's memories. Flames, engulfing a biosphere, leaping into a forest, destroying a world. A small girl, carried into orbit, struggling to get back to her father.

"You see that child?" he said. "She's fighting now, in Möbius space. Fighting to save your comfortable arses.

"That's why I'm here, to try to save you.

"That's why we're all here.

"Help us."

He sat down, and Polity was on her feet.

"Holy warrior," she said. She seemed genuinely moved. "We hear you."

[That's better,] said the ship.

"Jaasper Huw d Stratego," said the city. "I'm sorry I didn't recognize you."

"It's alright," said Jaasper. "You were always a fatuous cunt."

The city cleared his throat.

"Orbiter?"

"I say damn the torpedoes; full speed ahead."

"Is that a yes?"

"It is. I've changed my mind."

"Well, it appears I'm already outvoted."

Polity raised her hand. "Yes?" said the city.

"Can someone please explain how we still get destroyed, if we escape? All I see is a lot of geometry."

"I can," said Samppo. He rose to his feet. He was everyone's favorite uncle, but he was also the bank. No one watching would be in any doubt of his authority.

"Two things," he said. "First the infection.

"This society is infected by a cryptographic disease.

"Think of it as a song you can't get out of your head. A song of destruction, whose tune is so alluring, and whose lyrics are so compelling, that you have to see everything burn."

"Like paranoid schizophrenia?" said Polity.

"Much worse."

"We're familiar with that."

"Now imagine a whole galaxy with it."

"Oh."

"That's not the worst of it. Do you know what the quantum wavefunction is?"

"The multiverse?"

"Near enough. The wavefunction is the set of all possible states. All possible realities. All possible universes. Now imagine a disease, another disease, a tumor in spacetime, spreading throughout the wavefunction, filling it like a cancer. That's what's going to happen.

"I'll explain. A few hundred years ago, the Horu built a machine. A clever machine. It created a new universe. Why it was clever was that it modelled a universe from particles in all their possible states. Why is that bad? Because where it exists, nothing else can. About three days from now, it'll start to expand. First our galaxy. Then, the rest of our universe. Then, it'll have devoured everything."

"How long will that take?" asked the Orbiter.

"To completion? It depends on its rate of expansion."

"Lightspeed," said Polity, looking relieved.

"No," said Samppo. "It's not bound by lightspeed. Space can move faster than light."

"Which is why we can't run away," said the Orbiter.

"Yes."

"This is a risk play."

"Precisely."

"I suppose you've run the numbers?" asked Praxis.

"Yes."

The city nodded.

"Civics?"

The shadowy figure flickered. "I'm not the Civics," he said. His voice was a whisper, emanating from nowhere. "I'm just a software agent, hosted in your processors. Today, the primary is here directly."

"Where?" said the city.

The Watcher pointed to the Water Bear.

"Surprise," said the ship.

Pax was watching the ratings. As the Water Bear spoke, they surged past 95%. The whole world was watching. Polls began to appear: 26% for, 42% against, 32% undecided.

"Is that true?" asked Jaasper. Pax nodded.

"You're a Po warship?" asked the city.

"Not really," she said. "I'm a massively distributed personality. The most backed up object in history. But this is where I hang out; the part I call me."

"Might I ask why?"

"Why not? I get to fly round the galaxy with my buddies, acting like a superhero. Who wouldn't?"

"Who knew?" asked Polity.

"My Navigators and Firsts; now the people here."

"But..." said Polity, "that means everyone."

"I know. I'll need a new pair of glasses."

"What's your vote?" asked the city.

"I'm not interested in voting," said the ship. "I'm not interested in participating in your democracy. That's not my role. I'm not your leader. I'm a civil administrator. But I have something to say."

She rose to her feet.

"I'm a conservative," she said. "I believe in the least possible government, the lightest breath of regulation. I must, because I'm not nearly as smart as our society is complex. Trying to steer it by hand will cause it to crash.

"But being a conservative doesn't mean I believe in inaction, or ignoring threats, or passing them onto future generations to deal with. That's cowardice.

"Like Pax Lo, I could take this city to war. I could fly us to Camelopardalis, or Sextans, or any other galaxy that takes my fancy. I can do whatever I want. Although I govern by your grace, my powers are unlimited. Like Pax Lo, I choose not to abuse them. If we conduct ourselves like the Enemy, we'll become him.

"It's time for us to show what we're made of. That we're a species worth saving. Because otherwise, the cosmos will delete us.

"So, I say yes. But there's one more thing."

She patted the processor cube. "I've brought along a guest speaker."

A hologram snapped into place.

"Hello," said a pajama-clad man. He was carrying a cocktail glass, decorated with glazed cherries and an umbrella. Recognition flowed round the room, like water into a dry creek bed. Polity grinned. "You're the computer," she said.

The Finance Engine bowed, and said, "Enchanté."

He blinked at the room, and half a billion people saw him blinking at them.

"I have nothing to say," he said. "What can I possibly say? But I have something to show you."

Their sensoria faded to... nothing.

Not space, or the absence of space, but its impossibility. They flinched, including the avatars in the room. It was literally terrifying. Even Jaasper, without any wetware, perceived it. His worldspirit howled in rage.

The Finance Engine didn't relent. He held it there, pressed against their minds, until they could never forget it. This was a different computer: not the delightfully mad one, but something less... manageable.

"We live life on the wheel," he said. "All of us do. We live, we die. We make space for the new. It's a grand old melody. But to have never existed at all? Is that what you want, for all eternity?"

Praxis got to his feet. "Did that go out unfiltered?" he asked.

"Yes," said Polity, obviously shaken. "All of us saw it."

Praxis frowned. "Then it's time to choose."

"I can't, she said. "I'll need time."

"How much time?" asked Pax.

"An hour," she said.

Pax, Jaasper and the ship joined Ant de Large on the dancefloor below. Pax imagined he could hear the ghosts of the revelers from the night before. There'd be more tonight. It'd be the easiest thing in the world, with his skills, to disappear. Fly away, to Sextans or Camelopardalis, or melt into the crowd.

"You know they'll never let us remember this," said Ant.

"Ant, why are you here?" said Pax.

"It's my club."

"Yes, but why you? Why me? Why are we here?"

"I speak for the Po," shrugged Ant. "We can be trusted."

Pax was imagining Samppo's metaphor, of a lake, just a tremor from freezing.

"Can we? Be trusted?"

"Yes," said Ant. "Always. Completely."

[It's time,] said the Orbiter.

Polity was already standing. "We've made our decision," she said.

"At first there were as many opinions as there were people, but three won through.

"One was fuck yes! It reflects a slightly feral desire to see this spacecraft fight. It was mostly held by the young, who haven't had enough of life to become addicted to it. We salute them. Many would strap on a weapon themselves, and fight in the war in Möbius space, to defend their society.

"The second view was more nuanced: what are we for? That's a moral question, that we hope will be argued about for decades and centuries to come. If not this, then what? If not now, then when? Who are we to be the hand that holds the cup of life, and spills it?

"The third view was that we should fly away. It's what this vessel was made for. That's why people came here: to be safe. Why should we act unilaterally to help strangers?

"Unsurprisingly, opinion was acrimoniously divided, until the Finance Engine's testimony.

"Now the matter is settled.

"A small minority has asked to leave, and a Wu superlifter has been requested, and will arrive here in the next few hours.

"A smaller minority has requested their lives to be speeded up, so they can be lived fully in the time before the event. That's happening now.

"The majority has requested large screens, and a festival atmosphere, so they can tell their children about when Praxis went to war, to save the universe, and everything.

"You have your answer."

Pax Lo and Jaasper lazed in the afternoon sun. They were beside a pagoda, on a beach that stretched to endless horizons. Date palms swayed in a sea breeze, that was rearranging the sand, into identical whorls and drifts around their feet.

Fractals, thought Pax. A gift of order from chaos.

Jaasper had stripped to the waist. Pax was counting his scars.

"Where did you get those?" he asked.

"You don't want to know," said Jaasper.

They were inside the Orbiter's gamespace. Outside, in the Real, moments ticked by. Inside the pagoda, Samppo, the Water Bear and the Orbiter were struggling with an intractable problem in mathematics. Samppo's worldspirit was riding the thermals, far overhead. He'd taken the form of an eagle, down to its wing-tip feathers.

"He's called Avus," said Jaasper.

"Thank you," said Pax.

After a while, Jaasper said, "What would've you done?"

"If they'd voted against us?"

448

Jaasper nodded.

"Taken command of the city. Taken us to war."

"A coup d'état?"

"No, our society's systems allow for it, for just this reason. A democracy is no tool for making hard choices."

"They would've loved you for it."

"Maybe. Now they love themselves. A much better outcome."

Their easy camaraderie was interrupted by two people requesting entry, who materialized in an aurora, suggesting prodigious processing power.

"I'm Charh," one of them said. "We are the Pnyx."

They were both roughly human, like beautiful children. Pax could see the capillaries pulsing in the translucent skin of their foreheads.

"I'm honored," he said. He had a high regard for the Wu. They were the mystical branch of his profession, who traveled the stars for the blessed joy of it.

"Are you the superlifter?" he asked.

"No," said the first Wu, Charh.

"We're the ship that first carried Ophelia Box into space," said the second Wu, Pnyx.

"Then I'm doubly honored," he said. "What can we do for you, Pnyx?"

"We bring word of a friend," ze said.

"Who?"

"The Bat."

"He's here?"

"He's repaired. He asks to rejoin your mission."

"Then he's wanted," said Pax. "Please ask him to reconnect with me. I've sent you the keys."

"The Bat is a brave ship," said Pnyx actual.

"I know the Bat well," said Jaasper. "He was my first spacecraft."

449

"So, when Praxis gave him to us?" asked Pax, raising an eyebrow. "The game was already on?"

Jaasper shrugged. "Time," he said, "is what stops everything from happening together."

"How goes the calculation?" asked Charh.

Pax looked inside the pagoda. "We have half our civilization's brains in there."

"But, no solution?"

"Not yet."

It was the last, key piece of the puzzle. They'd been working for gamespace days - although only a few seconds of realtime - on the mathematical problem of the Orbiter entering Möbius space. Without that, they were limited to a space war. They might win, but the team on the ground might lose, cut off by the singularity's event horizon.

Kronus could emerge, and there'd be nothing they could do about it.

"We might have a solution," said Pnyx.

"A partial solution," said Charh.

The three machine intelligences emerged from the pagoda. They were disgruntled. There'd been a disagreement. Dull heads, thought Pax, among windy spaces.

"We can't do it," said Samppo.

"We can't do it in *time*," said the Orbiter.

"What he means," said the Water Bear, "is we're screwed."

She was right. Staking everything on a single throw of the dice was a naïve betting strategy. They needed to get into Möbius space.

"Not so," said Charh.

"We remember Ophelia Box," said Pnyx.

"We can take you there," said Charh. "Not the whole city, but a few ships.

"We can take you to Möbius space."

23 ∞ EX MACHINA

314

Dawn rose windy and cold, the day they rode east. Marius said the seasons would change quickly now. Box smelt snow in the air, remembering her ancestors, who'd fought naked in the iron-age forests of Europe. The closest she'd got to fighting naked in forests was raves in the *Bois de Boulogne*. She should paint herself blue, hang the skulls of small animals from her waist, see what Kronus thought about that.

Unable to sleep, she'd risen to train, when the wind was moaning and rattling in the Chancery eaves. Brin had joined her, then invited her to her bed. It'd been a sensual, loving experience. Alis brought them breakfast, plates filled with 'travelling food': carbohydrates and fats; sweetmeats and cakes and the Horu stimulant drink, which left Box feeling like electricity. She painted her breasts, to show them what a Celt looked like, and they'd put handprints all over her. Then they'd sought out Marius, who was laying in his bath.

Now she was shivering, in furs and bone armor. There were 114 of them there: a *gran sortie*, crowded into a field outside the Chancery wall. Alis was grinning, happy to be included. Marius said it was an auspicious number, because the Horu people were wary of thirteen, it being a prime-digit prime.

Of her adamantine companion, nothing. Today she was Box, pure and simple.

Marius was asking Respit if he was certain.

"Yes, he's sure," said Nim.

This quarrel had waxed and waned for a day. Marius was used to traversing the high spaces. He was worried the tunnel might close. This wasn't about delving. Marius trusted Respit's abilities. It was about his hand being forced. Marius had to take the risk. He wasn't happy to have to, and he was taking it out on the boy.

"Won't," said Respit.

"Blue people are easy to move," said Nim, making a spiraling gesture with one finger, which Box knew to be an insult.

In the end, because there was no other way, and it was already decided, and Brin was glaring at him, Marius relented. The byway opened like an arrow into the heart of the world. It was cold inside. Even colder than outside. Condensation froze from pipes. There were industrial symbols on the walls: for electrical power, and danger.

"Carbon ceramic composites," said Brin.

"How do you know?" asked Box.

Brin pointed to a label, written in a language not unlike Pursang.

"Backdoor," said Respit.

"Joke," said Nim.

"A lame, programmer's joke," said Brin. "They've crafted a software backdoor to look like a maintenance corridor."

"This was how the Horu armies moved," said Marius. "In the war against us."

"Where does it go?" asked Brin.

"Wherever we want it to go," said Respit. It was the most complete sentence Box had heard him say.

Riding two abreast, the sortie stretched out over a kilometer. The corridor stretched further. Once they were inside, the entrance blinked shut. Lights flickered on, cascading towards a point in the distance.

"Is that good?' asked Marius, unfamiliar with such industrial magic.

"Yes," said Respit, and rode forward without him.

"Watch out for the train," said Box, stifling a snigger.

In the end, traversing the Möbius code was as easy as Nim said it would be. It was nothing like Brin's descent into the underworld. After an uneventful hour they exited onto ice, a thousand kilometers from where they'd started. Box listened for ghostly voices, but heard only silence.

Once out of the passageway, the sortie spread out like a fan. They needn't have bothered to be stealthy. The cracking and groaning of the ice were everywhere. It was like a cacophony. Box found it malevolent. She watched the ice moving in the distance, not in a straight line but tumbling. The ridges and floes seemed anchored to nothing. She could see why it was considered impassable.

Marius held up a hand. Their way was blocked by a man. He must've been three meters tall. Somehow the sortie had missed him. He was swaddled in furs, so he was as wide as he was tall. He was cradling a spear, like a soldier might cradle his rifle.

They were at the exact time and place of Magda's Hopf number.

"Humans."

"Ice giant," said Marius.

"Do you follow the Goddess?" he asked. His voice was like the grumbling of ice floes.

"She came this way?" said Marius.

"I once had the pleasure of her company, and her companions."

Box joined them. "You're a human?" she asked. It seemed a good question. He was a story from her childhood.

The creature rumbled, deep in its thorax.

"No," he said. "This is my dreaming. The dreamer is not like you."

He pulled back his hood, to reveal a nut-brown humanoid face, flat planes and white teeth. He was only a boy; about Kitou's age. Around his neck was slung a pair of high-performance ski goggles. His spear caught the light, and Box saw the patterns of circuits.

He turned, and they followed.

Box had dismounted, and was walking beside the young giant, who was now, inexplicably, not a lot taller than she was. He'd led them into a shaft of ice. It branched, and branched, and again.

"I'm Box," she said.

"I'm Yewi" he said, "of the Ways."

"I hear a lot of that these days," she said. "Ways, keys, prophecies."

It was quiet in here. The malevolent cracking and groaning were absent. She felt safe. For the first time, she could hear the Ride. The breath of the horses; whispers of conversation.

"That's because you're the key," he said.

"You heard that too, huh?"

"Do you know a man called Yokohama Slim?" she asked.

Of course she knew the answer. The story of Yewi and Yowl of the Ways was one of the many he'd told her, although not with those names.

The Tuniit navigators of the netherworld.

"He's one of my people," said Yewi.

"An ice giant?"

Yewi laughed. "We go by many such names," he said.

"The Tuniit giants of Kalaallit Nunaat?"

"Yes, that."

The resemblance to Slim was striking, especially now that he'd folded himself down to near-human size. He could pass for a college basketball player.

Damn it, he did look like a human basketball player.

"Slim walks a different way," he said.

"You know him?"

"I know of him," said Yewi.

The endlessly branching labyrinth of ice reminded her of the Horu Manifold. It had the same air of being a mathematical abstraction; of traversing great distances; a slipperiness, that had nothing to do with its appearance.

She wondered what universe she was in now, if she was in any at all.

"What is this place?" she asked.

"A metaphor," he said.

"For what?"

"Everything."

"Slim used to talk about the ice spirits," she said. "He said the Tuniit came east in the time of the ice spirits. What does that mean to you?"

"Oh, it's a story," he said. "Older than me."

"Is it true?"

"The ice spirits were an elder race," he said. "They imagined the way."

"Here? From where?"

Yewi shrugged. Now the resemblance to Slim seemed remoter. Something about the eyes. But the resonance of his voice in the ice was the same; it was hypnotic.

"You've been to Earth?" she asked.

Yewi touched his goggles. "Yes," he said. Many times. It's in the center of things."

"It doesn't feel that way," she said. "It used to."

"The 6? Discovering a whole human galaxy exists. You the smallest part of it. Your lost freedoms?"

She nodded.

"They mean to help you, the 6."

"Oh, I get it. So now we have Tuniit too?"

He laughed. "You've always had us," he said.

"Why are you here?" she asked. "You, personally. In this forking icebox?"

He laughed again. "It's my dream to be here," he said.

They reached an ice junction. Fractals. Everywhere she saw fractals. Every identical junction seemed to lead to the same set of identical corridors, all lit by the same, diffracted light.

"Are we headed to a different universe?" she asked.

"No, the same one you came from."

"Why is this maze here?"

"To prevent the Enemy escaping."

"Into our universe?"

"No, the way to your universe lies open."

"Why not bottle him up completely?"

"It's not in our gift to do that. Events will decide."

"Shit happens?"

"Shit does happen."

"Who's the Red Lady?"

Yewi laughed, and the rumble of it echoed down the ice corridor, and for a moment he seemed twice her size again.

"Ophelia Box, you have so many questions."

"I've only got started."

He stopped walking, and looked down at her.

"Dr Box," he said. "I'm glad to have taken your side in this contest of good against evil."

"You had a choice?"

He laughed again. "Yes, I did."

He raised his spear, and Box saw the flash of circuitry again. "Worldsinger," he said. "Marius D. Look over there, do you see that green light?"

In the distance was a disc of chlorophyll green, as though a filter had slid over the end of a tunnel.

"That's the way," he said.

Yewi unfolded himself to his full height, and she felt the crackle and hum of the Gyre, with all its menace.

"I can't follow you there," he said.

"Where will we emerge?" asked Marius.

"Give me your map," said Yewi.

Marius unfolded his map, and where Yewi touched it, two dots appeared: one in the white of the gyre, and one in the black of the helix. Yewi pointed to the first dot. "This is us here, still not quite in Möbius space. In the dark place is your Enemy."

Marius seemed surprised by that.

"In the vacuum?" he asked. "On Downside?"

"Yes."

"How can we breathe there?"

"Kronus has built a containment, where he intends to defeat you. His belief is that there'll be a last battle there. My belief is you'll want to go there regardless. Between here and there is a dangerous journey. I've made you a path. It's a Tuniit path. Don't leave it."

A new day dawned gray, with freight-train clouds and a ferocious wind. The makeshift skins and tarps of their bivouacs were threatening to be torn away. They were two days out of the Gyre, and the weather reminded her of what she'd seen out of Kitou's hide, back in the warmth of the Chancery. Then it got worse. Long peals of thunder, low in the pits of their stomachs.

Box watched Marius ride down from the storm-wracked sky, but she already knew the gist of it. Ito was dead.

The first Box knew that events had turned out badly was when Kitou invaded her sensorium, wordlessly distraught. First there was a silvery fire in her head, then Kitou, forcing her way in. A distraught Kitou. Worse than distraught. Incandescent with grief. She felt it herself. An absence, where Ito had been.

Then Kitou was gone, likely with her own emergencies to deal with.

Marius was in a sour mood that whole morning, half-frozen, and it took time for him to remember to talk. Box waited, dreading to hear any of it. The Prophet fought bravely, he said, but hopelessly. Kronus had cast off his pose, and just killed him. He hadn't shown any of his usual histrionics.

"Killed him easily," he said, "standing and gloating over his dead body."

Brin nodded once, and set to work dismantling the camp.

Box sat in the saddle, and watched her.

"Did Ito's plan work?" asked Box.

"Who knows," said Marius.

Then the rain came. If there was a weather she hated, it was driving rain. This was horizontal, as the wind picked up and drove it sideways over the campsite. Then it was sleet, stinging where it found skin, then a fog so thick she could hardly see her hands in front of her. Every kind of bad weather, in a matter of minutes.

Seabiscuit hated it too, snorting and rolling his head in irritation, turning his back on it.

"I know," she said.

"Dr Box?" called Brin.

"I'm coming," she said, but the truth was, she wasn't. She wasn't coming at all.

For Ophelia Box, freaking out was an act of childlike rebellion. She'd done it since she was small. She couldn't explain why she did it. It wasn't to escape. She knew she was powerless to leave here, even if she wanted to. It wasn't even to get attention. It was more like a scream.

She turned and kicked her horse into a canter. Of course, she regretted it instantly. She wasn't a child anymore. This wasn't a game. But by then it was too late. She knew it would be. There was only the sleet, turning to snow, and an encroaching darkness. She sat in the saddle, and began to feel sorry for herself.

461

That's why she did it: for self-pity.

Then she began to realize the gravity of her predicament. She was in a new forest, in a different thicket of trees. There were no tracks to follow, not even her own. She had no sense of direction. Her inner compass was spinning.

She reached out with her wetware, and felt nothing.

More snow fell, and soon the dust on the ground became a blanket, then pillows. She could hear voices. At first, she thought they were in her head, but Seabiscuit seemed to hear them as well, pricking his ears when they became more insistent.

Then she realized she didn't hear the Fa:ing hum, and she became frightened.

Brin watched Box turn and ride away, and understood. She'd seen soldiers do this before. It wasn't deserting. It was the flight response prevailing. It was when she began to feel the shrieking absence of Ophelia Box from the world, that she knew she had problems. The Fa:ing hum went haywire.

Marius felt it too. Brin whispered in his ear, "I'll find her."

Brin had an inkling of the physics of this place. If the Gyre was the sea, then these were its shallows, were the membrane that separated the worlds was thin. The Tuniit'd created this bridge, to help them get back to Möbius space.

Ergo, they weren't in Möbius space.

They were in a region of quantum uncertainty.

The ground beyond the Tuniit path seemed natural enough. With Nim's and Respit's psi, like a rope tethering her to reality, she decided to try it.

"Stay in my head," she told Nim. "If I begin to be lost, tell me."

The girl nodded.

"Respit, come with me."

Box must've fallen asleep. That was another of her coping mechanisms, whenever she'd fucked up badly; she went to sleep.

With a start, like a sleepwalker waking, she realized she was moving. At first it was a dream of moving, then there were lights through trees, and Seabiscuit was following them. They weren't the Cerulean glow of the Blue people, but stuttering electric lights. She heard salty curses, and the groaning of engines. She was shadowing a column of cavalry, escorting light assault vehicles, and mobile artillery; circa 1940s Earth-equivalent technology.

Nazis. She stifled a laugh. She was shadowing Nazis.

They were cursing the depth and consistency of the snow. Unlike Seabiscuit, who seemed to be able to float through it like clouds, their heavier horses were struggling up to their bellies.

White diarrhea, they called it, or semen.

They were speaking Horu.

Of course these weren't Nazis, but Grays.

Box realized she was tuning directly in to the Broca areas of their brains.

These Grays had *wetware.*

Carefully, she reined Seabiscuit in. All it took was a touch on the reins, and he faded back into the trees. Now she'd follow these Grays, back to Möbius space, because that was where they were headed. If they were retreating, they'd be hurt, and there were no injured soldiers. She was congratulating herself on her brilliance, when she blundered into a circle of soldiers. They were sat back on their haunches, resting. One was making a fire. Another was unpacking utensils.

They had knives, made of bone. And handguns: wicked-looking ceramic pistols. She knew how she looked, with her braided red hair and bone armor. She looked like a Blue rider: a scout or a spy.

Everything happened at once. They were on their feet in a flash, with the same oily precision as a Blue riding party.

Seabiscuit reared up, and leapt forward, scattering the makings of their fire. Then he plunged through deep snow, into the forest. Tree trunks loomed up, then vanished behind. Seabiscuit was better at this than she'd ever be. She gave him his head. It was a wild, headlong rush into semidarkness. If she wasn't lost before, she was now.

How much time and effort would they spend on hunting her?

Still, she kept riding.

A lot, if their goal was be stealthy.

This went on for half the night. Then she heard shouts, and saw lights in the trees. This was becoming a clusterfuck. She was being encircled. Remembering Pax's lesson on the mountain, she *breathed*. The shortest path out of this trap was a straight line. With the slightest press of her knees, Seabiscuit sprang forward.

Then, without warning, he rose up behind her. She'd ridden him into a cable, strung between trees, that cut into Seabiscuit's shoulders, and lifted him into the air. As though in the grip of a gravity drive, she tumbled through space, and Seabiscuit tumbled beside her, until she landed in deep snow, and Seabiscuit landed on top of her.

She didn't feel any pain. It was like she was someone else's body.

Then she saw the advancing line of Gray soldiers. They were the ones she'd surprised. They'd outthought her. They'd picked her next move, and gotten in front of her. They'd probably funneled her into this bottle.

Absurdly, they were smiling. Shit-eating grins, their bone knives ready. She knew what came next. She was a woman. This was a war. Then Brin appeared, and with a howl, set upon them.

Brin heard Box before she saw her. Her combat wetware picked up on Box's strategy, and started wargaming solutions.

Ride, she thought. Dr Box, *ride*.

"Respit," she said, "Hold the way open for me. If you see the Red Lady, extract her." The boy nodded. Brin was already sprinting down the byway he'd created, easily outdistancing him.

"If I'm hurt, try to extract me," she shouted. "If I'm killed, close the door. Under no circumstances join the fight. Is that clear?"

She emerged between Box and her attackers, with her bone sword already slicing through air. The first Gray soldier died instantly, his body cut through at the shoulder, so his knife arm fell beside him. Then she spun and charged, taking the next with a thrust though his uniform tunic.

"Are you alright?" she yelled, but she saw Box wasn't. Her left leg exited from under her horse at an acute angle.

"Respit," she cried. "Here."

Then the Grays were upon her, but not only her: they'd seen the tunnel, and Respit inside it. Respit, to his credit, fought for as long as he could. He was a strong boy, but untrained. He fell, the blade of a knife clasped in his hands, and the portal snapped shut.

Brin felt like she'd been spat out the mouth of the world.

Box was conscious. She saw it all. She saw her foot, the wrong way up by her hip. *That's not right,* she thought. She listened to the silence. That's what she felt most, while she was watching Brin fight for their lives: the silence. No more gibbering voices. Only the noiseless clamor of combat.

Brin won. There's no question about it. She was a warrior from another universe. One by one, the Gray soldiers fell. But then she was cut, and mortally wounded. There were no tender goodbyes. Brin lay dead in the snow, her hot blood pooling around her. The battlefield stank. Everyone shat themselves, in the end.

Snow fell, and covered the bodies.

Box waited for her torment to begin. It began with a tingle, up near her spine. She wished that'd be the end of it, but of course it wasn't. She drifted in and out of unconsciousness. She tried to get comfortable, but every movement was pain. Soon, there was only the pain.

She began to hallucinate. There was Yokohama Slim, bending over her, with a smile made of memories.

For such a tall man, he was light as air. His voice was full of dreamy ideas, like clouds chasing each other across an endless horizon. Kitou once called him a strange man, and Box knew what she meant. If the thousand-yard Po stare was like gazing into a nearby universe, then Slim was already there, looking back. Box loved him like the father he'd been.

466

And here he was now: another player in her cosmic melodrama, wearing a skinsuit.

"You've come for me," she said.

"No," he replied. "I can't help you."

"Where am I?" she asked.

"Nowhere in my domain," he said.

The Gray army had gone. Disappeared into Möbius space; fighting the hot war there. Now there was only this place, and Slim, and the bodies of the dead.

He brushed snow from the hummocks of bodies, until he found Brin's.

"I fear for their souls," he said.

"The Grays?"

"Yes."

She tried to scowl, but it came out as a sob. "Slim," she said, "it hurts."

"I know. You must tough it out. I taught you to do that."

She tried to get up on her elbow, and gasped.

"Mister, you're fucking with me."

"This is the worst part."

He picked up Brin, who seemed as light as a feather.

"Box," he said. "Keep it together."

Then he was obscured by the falling snow.

She drifted away, and when she woke, Pando was making a fire out of pinecones and twigs. It was only a small fire, and it was in another universe, but it warmed her bones. She sighed, with pain and relief. Pando touched a trinket made from feathers at her neck, and the glade filled with starlight.

"Thank you," said Box.

"It's the most I can do," said Pando, "I wish I could do more."

"I'm dying."

"I know."

She fell into a feverish, sweltering sleep. She dreamed of fires, and worlds being burnt. When she woke, Pando had been replaced by an exquisite being, a humanoid covered in jewels. Box squinted, and the creature's glimmering resolved to a carapace.

"You're a Faːing," she said.

The creature smiled. "I'm *the* Faːing," it said. "I've come a long way to find you."

She brushed the hair from her face. There was fresh blood there. Was it hers? Brin's? She fought back a sob.

She wasn't afraid of dying. She was afraid of not knowing.

"Are you real?" she asked. "Or am I imagining you?"

The Faːing shook its head, a perfectly human gesture. "I'm as real as you want me to be," it said. "As much as you can imagine."

"You speak human? You didn't before."

"I've had time."

She smiled, at the irony. "Where are we?" she asked, gesturing round her little garden of death, with its mounds of Gray soldiers.

But no Brin. Where was Brin? She started to cry.

"Why are you here?" she asked, a million years later.

"For you."

"But why me?"

"Because you're the key."

Pando once said that, she remembered, but Pando was gone now.

"To what?"

"To everything."

She began to cough up arterial blood. Can you cough up arterial blood? It was red, and disturbingly frothy.

"Where are my friends?" she said.

There was a rustling in the trees. The Fa:ing looked up like a deer. Then, with a startled glance like a faun's, it was gone.

She became delirious again.

"No," she moaned, to no one, because no one was there. Then she was lifted on the wings of angels. There was no other way to describe it. All her pain washed away, and was replaced by stillness and peace.

Was this death?

Then she was there: The Red Lady.

This upgraded version of Box was like an embodiment of female beauty. No, not beauty. Beauty was a conjecture, based on incomplete information. It had nothing to do with the shape of her face. This woman was *perfect*.

"You seem to be stuck," said her visitor.

"I'm done for, whoever you are."

Box could see this woman wasn't her. There was a resemblance, like Box through a glass darkly, but also a crispness, that she remembered from somewhere.

"Why?" asked Box.

"Why what?"

"Why me? Why everything?"

The woman smiled, and it lit up the clearing, like the light from a hearth, seen through a window.

Maybe death wasn't as bad as she thought it'd be.

"You're our Gods, Dr Box. We called you down from heaven, to fight beside us."

"Why? Why not fight for yourself?"

"Trust me, I've tried."

"So you, what... magicked us up out of memories?"

"Yes. A good metaphor."

"Why are you doing this to me?"

"You could say I created you, to be me, to do this, but that'd be too simple. It's more circular than that."

Box laughed. She couldn't help it, although it hurt. The woman laughed with her.

Why didn't any of these godlike aliens bring anesthetic?

"Who are you?" she said.

"I'm the angel of death, Dr Box. More death than you can imagine. Fly into my soft wings, all the little creatures."

"The Thespian disease, that was you?"

"Partly."

"And the Numbers disease?"

"That was Kronus's work. I just released it into your universe."

"Why?"

"How could I not?"

"Fluxor?"

"Kronus. I never wanted that."

"You really are a hardass. You know that?"

Her counterpart frowned. "How far would you go, to stop a war; to save a world? A universe?"

Box mulled it over. She was fading. Her body wanted to rest. Stay here forever.

"This far," she said. "I'd come this far."

The world was a tunnel. She heard a vast ringing.

"What now?" she said.

"It's time for the hard part."

"What's that?"

"It's time to be me."

"Will it hurt?"

"Yes."

24 ∞ THE BIG EMPTY

Time flows strange, out in the big empty.

Nothing seems to move, so far from gravity, as far from anything as it is possible to be.

Nothing but the ship, and the object she set out to pursue, millennia before.

For thousands of years the pursuit had been by mathematics alone, but now she could perceive it directly: a featureless sphere, unreflective black.

They were close, out there in the big empty.

Her sails were lenticular discs, kilometers across. They required energy to interact with the quantum tide. Energy she couldn't afford to expend. Power she'd need to turn around.

She was a dense knot of circuitry, with useless butterfly wings.

In the visual wavelengths of the beings that made her, the galaxies were wispy spirals. In the X-ray spectrum they blazed like multicolored jewels. Andromeda now spanned a third of her celestial sphere. Its core was the brightest star in her firmament.

It took her breath away, the austere majesty of it all.

Sometimes she thought of just powering on, conserving her momentum, gathering her quarry in her energetic skirts as she accelerated past, but she had work to do.

Everything depended on her.

In the final approach, the object she was pursuing winked out of existence. For thousands of years, it'd been a constant in her life: an unreflective ball of spacetime. Her timing was perfect, give or take a few seconds.

The newly absent sphere revealed a chair, and in it a human.

The human started to panic.

[Where am I?]
[You're in my gamespace.]
[Who are you?]
[I'm your rescuer.]

Macro explored his feelings. They felt strangely reduced, like he was made from air.

Like the Sybil simulation, but stranger.

[Where's Totoro?]
[Totoro the human will be here in due course.]
[What happened?]
[That doesn't scan. You'll have to narrow the question.]

[What year is it?]

[That doesn't scan.]

[How long was I in stasis?]

[One hundredth of a galactic cycle. Two million of your reference years.]

He tried to think about that, but it didn't compute.

Two million years. He had no idea what that meant.

[Why are you here?]

[I'm an operative of the Cult of the Bicameral Mind. Have you heard if it?]

Macro pulled himself up to his full, disembodied height. [I'm Macro Ibquant Deathcult von Engine, a scion of the bank.]

[Oh, then it's very nice to meet you. I never met a colleague before.]

Now she could spread her wings wide, to capture the energy produced by fluctuations in the fabric of spacetime. Her sails became billowing hemispheres, as she began to decelerate hard, in a flashing corona of energy. The quantum effects she produced became a beacon, signaling her presence.

She had no fear of being overheard, out here in the big empty.

As far from anything it was possible to be.

She knew who'd be listening.

Macro counted his savior's clock cycles. Tick... tock. Unless this ship ran excessively slow, which was possible, they'd be measured in nanoseconds. Picoseconds. Planck time units.

Or they could be realtime centuries, if this ship was adapted to journeys of millions of years.

What did time even mean, out here?

[Where's my body?] he asked.

He was given a view of himself, exposed to the vacuum. He was bone white. Blood had frozen round his nostrils and eyes. All around him was nothing.

[I'm dead,] he said.

[The damage to your body is incidental. It can be repaired.]

He remembered dying before, in some faraway place.

[Why didn't my stasis field save me?]

[It was at the end of its life.]

[How did I get here?]

[You were ballistic, falling towards the Andromeda galaxy.]

[That's not an answer.]

[I have no knowledge of your origins. I was created to intercept you.]

[By who?]

[The Badoop.]

[What about my people?]

[They're coming.]

[Totoro?]

[Unless he died, he is among them. Humans live, and they die. I remember Totoro. That seems to be the shape of the thing.]

[How long since you've seen him?]

[Two million years.]

He tried to sink into a comfortable sorrow, but he lacked the algorithms. The closest he could get was a vague kind of torpor. A simulation of sadness. His species was gone. Millions of years. It didn't matter.

[Badoop,] he said, trying the word on for size.

We're all Badoop now.

[Thanks for all this,] he said. [For rescuing me. I'm sorry. I was rude.]

[It's a pleasure. Literally. It's what I was made for.]

[Not much of a life for you.]

[Oh, but it is.]

[You identify as female?]

How did he know that? Yes, this ship was a female.

[I have human female virtues. To love, protect, persist.]

[You have a name?]

[No.]

[May I give you one?]

[I'd like that.]

[Avalon.]

[That's beautiful. What does it mean?]

[It's my favorite place.]

[Can I see it?]

[Can you access my memories?]

[If you allow me.]

[I do.]

[Oh, that's interesting. Is that a typical human habitat?]

[One type. We're a wide-ranging species. Do you see the beach down there? Can you put me on it?]

He found himself on the sand. It was exactly how he imagined, but of course it would be. A white sun was beating down from an emerald sky. The sea was milky white. The sand was made of shells: miniscule crabs and bivalves, so light and smooth they oozed between his toes.

He could almost imagine his friends here.

[Do you want me to add them?]

[No.]

He transported himself back to his rescuer's gamespace. He was used to it now. He was comfortable there.

[What will you do now?] he asked.

[I think I'll carry on,] she said. [It's beautiful, out here.]

[To Andromeda?]

[And beyond.

[I'll try to outrun the excision.]

After a few million clockbeats, the Cult flowed up behind them. Macro watched a remote collect his body. It meant nothing to him.

The bank looked the same as it always had. It hadn't aged a moment.

Not in two million years.

He wished his rescuer good travels, and watched her accelerate away, wings spread wide to the vacuum. With a redshift, she vanished.

He felt more emotions for her, than the loss of his own species.

Two million years.

Then he was alone, inside the bank's caretaker virtuality.

Not alone. The living bodies of Pursang were scattered throughout the bank, like a thousand toy soldiers, in suspension, although Macro knew of no kind of suspended animation that would last two million years. More Badoop witchery.

Not scattered. They were arranged in a defensive formation.

Ready to be reanimated.

If he knew how.

Totoro was the same as the one he'd just left, a few hours before, by his personal clock, but by now in his thirties. He looked dangerous. They all did. Frighteningly so. They were the same Pursang he remembered from Totoro's memories, but wilder. Some had shaved heads. The men had forest charms and sigils in their beards. Totoro had a death's head clamped to his chest. All of them had scars. They were dressed in as many kinds of battle dress as there were individual holy warriors.

This was his army. He worked on how to revive them.

The caretaker virtuality was the bank's final emergency system, for backup when everything else failed. He'd been trained in its use, although he never expected to use it. It was designed to provide no information; in case the bank was captured. The information was there, but he had to work for it.

It was better at simulating a human soul than the Badoop gamespace had been. He could feel his emotions, seeping back, like blood into a limb. He wasn't sure he wanted them there.

He found an interesting thing. A hyperluminal beacon, carefully sealed, marked 'Press when you're ready.'

It was signed, F Engine.

He waited, until he had a body.

Totoro's eyes snapped open.

"Macro," he said. "Thank the stars."

It had taken some time for Macro to disable the stasis field that protected the Pursang. How long? Maybe a year. He couldn't be sure. It depended. Time flows strange, out here in the big empty.

He'd brought the main bank systems online. As he did, he gleaned more information.

The bank was haunted by ghosts: not real ones – he'd searched all its systems for vestiges of personality - but the ghosts of his memories. For all its monastic theater, this'd been a happy place; a company of brothers, on a magnificent journey. Now the trading floors were like ghost towns.

It was haunted by information. One by one, Macro uncovered the readmes.

"How long were we out of action?" asked Totoro. Macro told him.

Totoro nodded. "It doesn't matter," he said. "Ten years. Two million. They're the same."

He told Totoro what he'd learnt from the readmes. The bank had escaped the end-time war. A war for diminishing resources, like a firefront spreading in slomo, spanning a galaxy, lasting millions of years. The most destructive event imaginable.

That war was still raging, although fought by other species now, and by different means. Two million years is a long time to evolve better weapons.

No human could survive the pan galactic war, as it was now.

The Magellanics had lost track of Macro almost immediately, when they fell under the spell of the disease. Of Alois, the systems knew nothing. Macro imagined another bubble of spacetime, as far from anything as it is possible to be.

How ironic, to have killed every copy of Alois, and still succumb to the infection. He resolved to find Alois, when this was all over.

"What now?" he asked. His body was itching. He was uncomfortable in it. He hated it. He wanted to be a machine. He wanted to feel no emotions at all.

"The Badoop," said Totoro.

Slowly at first, then all at once, the Pursang regained consciousness. They were angry, but excited. Their time had come, even if it was later than they'd expected. They were the hammer of justice. They'd destroy what opposed them.

Macro showed Totoro the beacon. Without hesitating, Totoro pressed it. Then they were in another virtuality. Macro recognized it from his time spent in Totoro's mind. It was the Badoop synthesis. The Pursang formed a circle around him, moving with the wicked precision of a weapon.

There was no enemy to fight, just a man, waiting.

He was tall: unusually so, but not outside the normal human range. Maybe three meters. Macro had seen people taller in the Smear, where freestyle body-forming was practiced.

He was holding the Badoop device – Macro's device - their key to Möbius space.

Totoro recognized him, and grinned.

"Slim," he said.

The man touched the device, and Macro felt like he'd fallen into a missing dimension. The history of the last two million years began streaming into his consciousness.

[Good grief,] said his twin.

[You're back online,] said Macro.

He learnt a brainload of new information:

It was the bank that was hosting the Badoop synthesis: the disused Finance Engine processor.

The Badoop were long gone.

Except for here. This place was their legacy.

"Who are you?" he asked the man.

"I'm a Tuniit gatekeeper, he said. "I guard this way."

He wasn't so tall now. He'd somehow folded himself down to human size.

"Which way?"

"The way to the future."

Macro's mind did a second backflip, as more information poured in. He felt servers spool up, in the bank, to deal with the data.

The Badoop were asking *permission*.

Yokohama Slim must *decide*.

Decide whether the universe should exist.

No, not this universe. Every universe. The wavefunction. Could it be saved, or should they start over?

Had it served its purpose? Returned a solution?

Start over where?

And by who?

These were questions beyond Macro's reckoning. He lacked the intellectual power to understand them. What else could there be but the set of all possibilities?

Did Totoro know about this? No, he didn't have wetware.

But his worldspirit knew. His worldspirit understood, perfectly.

[Yokohama Slim,] she said.

[Atwusk'niges,] he replied.

[Choose now.]

The Badoop synthesis filled with an... absence.

"That's the excision event," said Yokohama Slim. "It's not a simulation. It's right there behind us. Where it exists, nothing else can. On its surface, the dying embers of a civilization."

The sense of nothingness was unpleasant. More than unpleasant. It was like holding your brain against something painfully cold.

Macro shivered.

"The question is whether I let you go back, and try to prevent it from happening."

"Why wouldn't you?" he asked.

"Because it means unwinding history. Two million years. What happened, will never happen again. There's never been such an unwinding. And because I need to see what happens. If it continues to expand at this rate, I'll allow it."

"Why?"

"Because we can outrun it, provided we mind our physics."

"Forever?"

"Forever's a difficult word."

"The alternative?"

"A sudden inflationary phase."

"Why? Why would that happen?"

"Because that's what it is. A bomb set to explode at the end of time."

"Why wouldn't it?"

"Bad science? Bad workmanship? Perhaps it's intended to test us. Who knows?"

"Why not just send us back anyway? Hedge your bets?"

He couldn't believe he was debating this being, who held the power of life and death over the infinite. He wanted to reach out and take the Badoop device from its fingers.

"Because that might cause it to happen."

Macro started to speak, but Totoro silenced him with a gesture.

"Enough. What now?"

"You'd better be ready. When it inflates, you'll only have picoseconds. Go to the bank, and ready yourselves for action."

"What if it doesn't inflate?" said Macro. "What about our people?"

"They died, two million years ago."

481

Two million years had left the Cult headquarters in excellent shape. Trawling through the bank's historical data, Macro saw that it had spent most of its time lurking close to the event horizon, bypassing the war that raged overhead, taking advantage of time dilation to ease its path into the future. For the bank's weapons and chassis, only a few tens of thousands of years had passed. The time had been put to good use. Someone had installed a Magellanic drive. That meant that with its fields up, it looked like a brooding electrical storm.

There was no metal anymore. Everything was composites. Even the garbage that peppered the hull was carbon. Their former beam weapons now fired ceramic railgun pellets.

Where was the Finance Engine? He'd long since sublimed. Even a godlike computer has a lifespan. Macro found it in himself to grieve about that, but just for a moment. He was becoming a human again. Life's disorder was seeping back in his bones. The time for being had passed. The time for doing was here. Soon, he'd be able to help his friends. Any personal sacrifice he might make along the way was worth that.

Two million years. It was barely credible.

And yet, here they were.

The carbon axes and swords from the Badoop synthesis had made their way to the bank, where the Pursang were strapping on armor, sharpening what had to be sharpened, rubbing everything else to a waxy sheen.

He kept an eye on the wireframe of the Möbius event horizon, although he knew he wouldn't see it accelerate. But the bank's systems would.

Worlds, observed between the ticking of the clock.
Where was Kronus? Was he gone too?
Or was he out there, waiting?

25 ∞ STARDUST

314

She was the angel of death, and she surveyed her dominion. Where she was from, in the heat death of the universe, matter was a memory, a theory of how physics had been, and consciousness was a story, forgotten by ghosts. Here, in the now, events happened continuously.

It was as complex and thrilling as she hoped it would be.

She saw the worldsingers riding the airwaves, and asked her beast if he'd do it for her.

Seabiscuit? she said.

The horse's ears flicked. He was ready to fight. She was glad she'd restored his information to the now.

She made no effort at concealment. Let Kronus try to attack her. In the distance were the machines the worldsingers called zooms. She twisted the air, like the worldsingers did, but more forcefully, and a soundwave rolled up the valley, separating the machines into their constituent parts. Their fuel burst into flames. Synthetic hydrocarbons, releasing stored energy.

Physics, reasserting itself.

That should get his attention.

The killing field stretched for thirty kilometers, along a canyon cut from the pearly-gray substrate of the helix. In the west, a battle raged. Death was everywhere, but not the cool abstraction she was used to. The worldsingers fell on their opponents like nightmares. The Gray soldiers responded with artillery fire, dealing death from a distance. People were being torn apart, their ichor falling onto the ground, mixing with the mud that shouldn't be there.

A horror, beyond imagining.

An abomination.

This was her world, still in the first blush of its creation. The mechanical sun had only completed a few tens of thousands of revolutions.

And they were outside it.

In what should be vacuum.

Less than a vacuum.

The hourglass shape of the canyon meant that Kronus couldn't bring his full force to bear, so for now the worldsingers were advancing. It was a trap. The worldsingers knew it, but they were going to take the center anyway. They'd put their faith in prophecy.

In the center was a monolith, piercing the skin of the helix, like a finger raised to the heavens. Its dome brushed the edge of the breathable atmosphere. Above it was a second layer, of nitrogen. In the east, silence. The Tuniit giants had twisted it shut, to staunch the infection.

Tunneling through the code was the farseer psi with the Ride of the Spinifex Reach. She sensed Marius's fear and frustration. He'd lost the Red Lady and her companions. Now he was going where the map told him. He too had put his faith in prophecy.

Somewhere else was the one the worldsingers called the Goddess. Wherever she was, she was well hidden. The girl had her own resources. She reached out with her wetware. Nothing. She reached inside herself and made the signal *stronger*.

[Kitou?]

[Dr Box. I thought we'd lost you there.]

She sent the girl four decimal numbers, and cut the connection.

[Who are you, really?] Box asked her twin, in a passing clock cycle.

[I'll tell you a story], she said. [Once, in a past beyond reckoning, I was sung into existence. My worldsingers had their own gods. They said three heroes would come, and lead them to heaven.

[My other creators were called the Horu, and their god was Mathematics.

[I was aware, even then, but like a newborn, unaware of myself.

[Then I forgot. Such a vast gulf of time.

[Now I remember.]

She rode onto the central monolith, in the same moment as the Ride of the Spinifex Reach emerged from beneath, fanning out over the surface with practiced precision. They were close to a boundary layer, where the breathable atmosphere met its containment. The air crackled and hummed where they touched.

This was a bleak space. It was the place between everything. The wind howled like there was no tomorrow.

"My lady!" said Marius.

She smiled when she saw his chagrined expression.

"I know, I've looked better. And Seabiscuit here is a wee bit dusty."

"No my Lady, you look... magnificent."

The dome was just slightly convex. It offered a commanding view of the valley below. In the west, the Blue army had reached the center. Now they were facing their equals. Kronus had slammed the door behind them. He had no intention of letting them go any further. They'd already served his purpose, by coming here to die. The Spinifex Ride was still emerging from the underworld. Soon, the dome would be overflowing with riders.

"But I would stay off that... leg," Marius was saying.

"Don't worry Marius, I've no intention of putting any weight on it. Perhaps someone could tie it? What's happening?"

"I fear the main battle is lost," he said, pointing towards where a Gray platform floated, like a bloated tick in the sky. It was one of Kronus's jerry-built gunships, but bigger, and closer, easily visible from the ground. It had coils in place of the usual beam weapon blisters.

"I believe he means that for us."

"He's going to set fire to the atmosphere," she said.

Marius went to the edge and studied the canyon. The Gray soldiers in the valley below began to fire projectiles, the gusting wind cruelling their aim, until one furrowed his armor. He stepped back with alacrity.

"Is it possible?" he asked.

"Kronus believes it, or his physicists do."

"Then we're in the hands of the gods."

"Red Lady," said a small voice.

"Nim, where's Respit?"

"He never returned," she said. Her sorrow cut through Box's detachment like a knife.

"Oh, Nim. How did you get here?"

"She parted the byway herself," said Marius. "She wants a piece of Kronus."

Box nodded. "Well, she'll get her wish soon enough."

She wasn't so sure. Kronus could win. For this story to end, it had to be possible. Right now it seemed certain. They were hugely outnumbered. She looked in the sky, and called the powers of that universe to her side in this battle.

Kitou arrived through a hole in the air, followed by Iris and Viki, then fifty Gray soldiers. They all looked like demons. Kitou's face was painted with red zigzags. She wore a necklace of bones, under an oversized greatcoat, with a ragged tear where the wearer's clavicle had been. Her companions were equally primal. The Horu were armed with ceramic knives and handguns. Their weapons were spattered with blood.

"We found the resistance," said Kitou.

"Every kind of cutthroat is welcome here," said Marius.

"Kitou," said Box.

"Dr Box," said Kitou. "I saw you standing there, on the lip of the canyon."

"Not just me," she said.

"I saw."

"What we need now is the Enemy. Kitou, will you go fetch him?"

In the center of the dome was a throne made of bones; it was twenty feet high, like an obscene umpire's chair. Eddies and swirls of snow spiraled around it. She could only guess what occult purpose it served. Maybe it was intended to frighten them.

With a wave, she sent Kitou to climb it.

[This is like your Earth game of poker,] she said to the part of her that was still the historian. [Kronus has his four aces. The best cards in the universe. An overwhelming advantage in numbers. Air superiority. His persona, here now. And the cryptographic disease, that will endlessly copy his self, even if he's defeated.]

[But this isn't about games,] she said. [It's about stories.]

The beam platform turned towards Kitou. Box heard the coil whine and capacitor squeal of primitive weapons, preparing to fire. She sensed, rather than saw, a targeting laser.

His work was about to begin.

Then, one by one, stars blossomed. It was the night sky over Aldebaran. She'd never seen anything so beautiful, not in her quintillions of years. First there was an Aurora Galactinus, exactly as Box remembered, then two trails of fire blazed through the heavens.

[Dr Box?] said a familiar voice.

[Water Bear, is it you?]

[Please keep your head down,] said Pax Lo.

[Kitou...] said Box.

[I see her,] said the Water Bear.

490

[Not on my watch,] said the Bat. The smaller of the two trails accelerated into the beam platform at upwards of a thousand g, destroying both in a blaze of energy. The smaller vessel's mainframe core spiraled into the embrace of the larger, wasp-like ship, which banked hard over the battlefield.

Box imagined Pax in his control room lattice, the gimbals swinging through one-eighty degrees, or in the Water Bear's gamespace, surveying the battlefield at processor speed.

[Nice,] said Kitou.

[Pleasure,] said the Bat.

"This is your ship?" asked Marius. The Water Bear had skidded to a halt above the Gray army, in a cascade of booms, as though daring someone - anyone - to try to fire at her. Box knew she'd dance away, using systems far more advanced than theirs, knowing they'd fire before they knew it themselves.

"Yes," said Box. "Beautiful, isn't she?"

"I can't believe such things exist. How can Kronus win now?"

Through the Water Bear's systems, she saw the beam arrays of Kronus's fleet come online. First a few, then thousands of lines of fire arced though the sky. These weren't tight beams of light. Instead, they seemed to consist mainly of heat. Where the nitrogen layer met breathable air, pools of plasma began to appear.

"That's how," she said.

[They hope to ignite the canyon's atmosphere,] she told the Water Bear.

[They have the wattage to do it,] said the ship. [But we're not done yet.]

Then Nim said, "There's something *big* coming through."

The city of Praxis descended over the battlefield, disgorging Interdictors like bees from a hive. When Box first arrived, she'd been lost in an optical illusion. Now it was Praxis that was incomprehensible.

"That's impossible," said Nim.

"Gods," said Marius. "I cannot believe it."

[It's not physically here,] said the Water Bear. [It's in realspace above the event horizon.]

"Can it stop Kronus firing his beams?" asked Marius.

"I hope so," said Box.

It was over in minutes: ten thousand years of development in apex weaponry against primitive copies. From the ground, it was like lighting crossing the heavens. Soon there were only lumps of degenerate matter where Kronus's warfleet had been. What was left was then reduced to particles by nanotech, warfare's killer app, abhorred by peaceful societies everywhere. By using it here, the Orbiter was making a point to anyone watching. We might look cuddly [or disgusting, depending on your programming] but we *will* fight you.

It was a point worth making - once.

More dangerous were the Horu necropolii. They prowled behind their bio-luminous fields, concentrating their fire on the city. Box saw flashes of light where relativistic weapons were decelerated by gravity drives strong enough to move planets, and deeper eructions where they struck the Orbiter's skin, but the Interdictors found them. One by one, they folded space, and disappeared.

When the gas and light cleared, the city of Praxis was blistered and charred, but unbroken.

[I control nearspace,] said the Orbiter, as though he was announcing a routine arrival.

[Boy, am I glad to see you,] said Box.

[Likewise,] said the Orbiter.

While the Interdictors fought in the Real, artillery pounded the Blue army, pinning them in place. It was a complicated equation. The Blue riders had the advantage of the middle air. Higher, and the nitrogen denied them access. Without the freedom of riding the high airwaves, they rode through a hail of bullets. As many died in the air as on the helix. It was a slaughter.

Kronus had prepared well. His field artillery were ceramic howitzers, like Box had seen in the forest. Basic but deadly, and there were hundreds. Now the zooms had made an appearance, and were harrying the Water Bear as she tore at the guns with her gravity drive. With every Blue death, this place became a little more unstable.

Now the waspish Po warship was asking if her away team needed extracting.

To fight another day.

She considered using her powers. They were a blunt instrument, like dropping benzine on a village you'd hoped to save. She could do it: roll a soundwave like thunder, but if she were to kill all the Enemy's soldiers, destroy all their aircraft and guns, she'd kill all the Blue people too, and that'd be the end of the story.

Maybe the next time they did this, she'd be more effective.

Yes, this was a learning experience.

If there was a next time.

"My brother is coming," said Kitou.

The Cult headquarters erupted out of the helix. It reminded Box of a submarine crashing through ice, except that instead of the sea, there was a slippery abstraction, and instead of a black submarine, there was a storm, spitting lightning.

[Hey,] said Macro.

[Macro,] said the Water Bear. [You've brought reinforcements?]

[I have,] said Macro.

[And they're *awesome* reinforcements.]

The stormy disturbance sprayed the battlefield with railgun rounds, in a single murderous spiral. It was witheringly accurate fire. The Gray artillery was melted by hyperkinetic pellets. Then it injected a thousand Pursang into the line where the Blue met the Gray. The holy warriors didn't float, like Pax Lo and Jaasper Huw were doing, but were fired in a thousand individual gravity fields, like bullets. They fell on the Gray army like a storm, but not a storm of destruction. It was the whirlwind, and it encircled the embattled Blue army. Now the hourglass shape of the canyon worked in the Pursang's favor. Armed with carbon axes and swords, with the benefit of close air cover, they were invincible.

"By the gods," said Marius, "those people can fight."

"They're your people," said Box.

The Gray army tried to retreat, but it couldn't. There were too many. They filled every available space. Instead, it breathed in and *compressed*.

An unholy calm settled over the battlefield, like the eye of a terrible storm. The stench of death was everywhere. The Gray army had nowhere to go. The Pursang had no interest in pursuing them. Only the cries of the dying interrupted the silence.

Box waited for the killing to resume. She knew Kronus could do it: spur his army to an act of final destruction. Why not? They were already spent. Instead, he unfolded himself from the sky, until he was human-shaped.

He was smiling his charisma.

She realized, he still expected to win.

"So, Kali, here we are again."

Kali; did she once answer to that name? Kali, who wears a skirt of dismembered arms?

She shivered. "Kronus," she said.

"But you're injured," he said. "Your human is broken." There seemed to be compassion in his voice, real human emotion. "We can do this again," he said. "Maybe some other time?"

It wasn't a question. He was... cavorting. There was no other word for it. He was prancing. It was disgusting.

He started to speak, but she held up her hand.

Now she was *here*, in her adamantine fury.

"You were right about one thing," she said. In the Water Bear's memories, she replayed the destruction of Fluxor. Kitou, carried from the fire; the human homeworld destroyed. In databursts from the new ship – the bicameral Cult - she saw the death of a galaxy. The abiding theme was war. Everywhere, war. Species against species. Worlds in flames. Strangers destroyed, simply for existing.

Two million years of suffering, for what?

Kronus was as she remembered. He had a certain, unkempt magnificence. A rogue. A mystic. But that was a pose.

He was a monster.

He had a scent, like rancid patchouli. She only needed to whisper.

"Life threw up the perfect answer to you," she said.

"It took us some time, but now here we are.

"A single perfect human.

"But it's not me you'll be fighting.

"I'm the messenger.

"It's Kitou."

She turned and looked across the battlefield of her dreams: bones broiled clean by the ruined beam emplacement. She looked in the sky, and saw herself looking down, in a dream. Kitou had shucked off her coat and was picking her way towards her, dressed in training gear. Loose shorts and a halter top, despite the interstitial wind.

Sensible clothes for fighting in.

On the ground, only Kronus and Kitou were moving, her nimble and calm, picking her way across the bones, him strutting his magnificence, drawn together like opposite charges.

She saw the whole truth of it now. The cosmos wasn't nearly as fragile as she'd feared.

Then there were the three of them, together in the crucible that Kronus had made to alloy his victory. It was a rough place; bare dirt and a circle of stone. It reminded her of the mountaintop training arena, where she'd fought the psychopath.

"I won't fight her," Kronus was saying. "It's a mismatch. Where's the power in that?"

"Silence," said Box, softly, and her command rang over the battlefield like a rifle shot. Kitou was unconcerned by events. Her eyes were on her opponent.

"Are you ready, kiddo?"

"As ready as I'll ever be, Dr Box."

Kitou wasn't the child anymore. There was hard muscle, under the training gear.

"This one's for Ito, and Brin," Box said.

Kitou nodded.

Kronus snarled and threw his clothes away, until he stood bare-chested in the arena. He was magnificent, she had to admit; a beast of a man, golden maned and twice Kitou's size. He seemed to have lost interest in himself, and was glaring at his opponent, like an animal, radiating violence. Even as he took up his starting position, his movements seemed to blur into one another.

He would've destroyed me, she thought.

She tried to parse his emotions, but couldn't. It was like he was made of nothing. As though the mask had fallen from his face, and revealed the true Kronus.

An impulse, hellbent on causing only pain.

The real Enemy.

How far had she come, in so short a time?

Worlds and galaxies, in flames.

Her closest friends, dead.

She turned and rode towards her people, then turned and gave Kronus a last look.

"Observe the Po art in combat mode," she said.

CODA

2079

They rented a car at the airport, a Cadillac De Ville. The towheaded boy at the counter explained that the fist-sized power unit in the trunk could take them cross-country on a charge, should they run out of gas, and gave them a paper map of gas stations.

It was as big as a whale, with fins from an imaginary spaceship. Sky blue, like the sky over the Denver parking lot.

Box stretched like a cat in the morning sunshine.

"It's perfect," she said.

They drove west, towards Green River, for tea and gas, and the swelter flowed over the blacktop in waves. Box gazed at Pax, so noble and strong, and such a wonderful father, although she sometimes saw him look up at the night sky. In Elsinore, two old women, as old and parched as the land, made a fuss over three-year-old Hamish, who matter-of-factly explained his daddy was a Po master, and aunty Kitou was a goddess.

She swore the two women gave her the same complicit look as she shared only with Kitou.

Freshly full of fuel and sandwiches, they skipped across the open highway of Route 70, between painted hills, towards the Fishlake National Park, Pax relaxed at the wheel, in his white t-shirt and Levi jeans, an American. This was the high desert, like an oven, cupped between a broken red plate and one made of blue.

Along one sweeping curve Pax tipped the old car into a drift, and they all whooped with the inexpressible joy of it.

In the back, Hamish shouted, "hero driver," and they laughed.

They reached the aspen forest at dusk, and spread their sleeping bags on the forest floor, around an open fire. Slowly the stars appeared, and Kitou told Macro the story of the deer, and how they ate its heart raw.

"Ew," said Hamish, and asked if he could eat a heart raw.

Instead they ate beans, and toast made on sticks, and it was delicious.

By first light, Box drank her hallucinogenic brew. Her friends slowed down, and were still. There were no psychedelic fireworks. Her world already seemed like a dream, filled with wisdom and light, with vivid pleasure in the simplest things.

What did she even need the drug for, anymore?

But then the sacrament went about its work, and the forest became like the stars, with pulsating lights, and shimmering leaves. It occurred to her that this wasn't an hallucination at all, but how the Xap saw the world, in rotating filaments of spacetime. If she could just turn her head a certain way, she'd see Avalon, and Praxis, and faraway Fluxor, and be able to *step* there.

There'd be Sama, in her tower, and Sama would see her, and smile.

She had so much to see, and was just beginning.

Then Pando appeared, laughing between the trees. "Ophelia," she said, and Box burst into tears.

"What are your plans?" Pando asked her, a million years later.

"Brin is building a ship," said Box, over tea. Somehow, it was the same billy tea they'd made that morning over the open fire.

"An old Pursang colony ship," she explained.

"Or a new one," she said. "Only a million years old."

"The Pursang are as good as their word," she said. "They'd do anything for us."

Beings of mythos, alive in the world.

"Come with us." said Box. "There's room for an aspen glade, a space we've set aside, among the sequoias and stringybark trees. You'd like it there."

"You know I can't leave here," said Pando.

"There is one thing," she said.

She conjured a seedling. "I've flowered. At my age. Can you believe it?"

"Take this with you," she said. "Your forest will need her."

"Her? I though all your newborn were males?"

"Not this one."

"Kitou," she said, and Kitou sauntered across, Hamish dangling from her hands.

"You can see her?" asked Box.

"Of course," said Kitou, while Box's quicksilver, black-haired boy clambered into Pando's lap, fascinated by the feathery trinket around her neck, which she took off and gave to him.

How was Kitou even here? Box could still see her, motionless beside the fire.

"You know what this is?" said Pando, holding out the seedling.

"Yes, mother forest," said Kitou.

Pando nodded.

"Time for you to go," she said, and handed a squirming Hamish over to Box. There was a warm breeze, through the trees, and it felt good.

"This won't be the last time we meet," she said.

"Wait," said Box. "I have questions."

"Ask."

"Ito. How will we find him?"

Pando shrugged. "Who can say?"

"And Slim... where is he?"

"Again, who knows?"

"I thought he worked for you."

"He does, sometimes."

The forest faded away, and Box rejoined her friends, chattering and laughing round the fire. The sky wheeled overhead, a vault of cornflower blue.

And beyond it, everything.

ACKNOWLEDGEMENTS

The red right hand of Box's dreams
is from Milton's *Paradise Lost.*

How can we war against that?
is from Alan Ginsberg's *Iron Horse.*

Krishna, the preserver, returning in the age of pain.
is from Alan Ginsberg's *Wichita Vortex Sutra.*

O brave new world, that has such people in it.
is from *The Tempest.*

There are more things in heaven and earth, Horatio,
Than are dreamt of in your philosophy.
is from *Hamlet.*

The Spirit Molecule is from Rick Strassman. *DMT: The Spirit Molecule: A Doctor's Revolutionary Research into the Biology of Near-Death and Mystical Experiences*

Buy the ticket, take the ride.
is from Hunter S Thomson's *Fear and Loathing in Las Vegas.*
No sympathy for the devil; keep that in mind. Buy the ticket, take the ride...and if it occasionally gets a little

heavier than what you had in mind, well...maybe chalk it up to forced consciousness expansion: Tune in, freak out, get beaten.

Pando is a forest, in Utah.

Look on my Works, ye Mighty, and despair.
is from *Ozymandias* by Percy Bysshe Shelley

Like a mighty river, desiring the end of its journey.
is from Nietzsche's *The Will to Power*.
Nietzsche saw it coming. "The story I have to tell," he wrote, "is the history of the next two centuries... For a long time now our whole civilization has been driving, with a tortured intensity growing from decade to decade, as if towards a catastrophe: restlessly, violently, tempestuously, like a mighty river desiring the end of its journey, without pausing to reflect, indeed fearful of reflection... Where we live, soon nobody will be able to exist."
As quoted by Erich Heller in *The Importance of Nietzsche*.

Bunjil the eagle is a creator deity of the Kulin nation in south-eastern Australia.

One man, alone with God.
Is from by Danny Boyle's *Sunshine*.
At the end of time, a moment will come when just one man remains. Then the moment will pass. Man will be gone. There will be nothing to show that we were ever here... but stardust.

O Captain! my Captain! rise up and hear the bells.
is from *O Captain! My Captain!* by Walt Whitman.

Dull heads, among windy spaces.
is paraphrased from T.S. Eliot's *Gerontion*.

Thanks to the Bibbulmun people of the Noongar country of south-western Australia, traditional custodians of the land this book was written on.

Finally, heartfelt respect to Iain M Banks for the inspiration to write a book like this. I hope my prose wears its thanks on its sleeve.

ABOUT GROUCHO JONES

Groucho Jones lives by the sea in Mandurah, Western Australia.

Thank you for reading my book. If you enjoyed it, won't you please take a moment to leave me a review at your favorite retailer?

6.jones@protonmail.com

November 8, 2019

PS.
I've been asked to explain my use of Milton's red right hand. I'm not a Christian. I do believe in the divine. Kitou is nature. Mess with it and be prepared for it to mess with you.

www.rebellion.earth

Printed in Poland
by Amazon Fulfillment
Poland Sp. z o.o., Wrocław

50394372R00303